A journalist and documentary film maker, Reggie Nadelson is a New Yorker who also makes her home in London. She is the author of several novels featuring the detective Artie Cohen ('the detective every woman would like to find in her bed' — *Guardian*).

RED HOOK

It's a summer Sunday in downtown New York City and Artie Cohen is getting married . . . A message from his old friend Sid McKay asks Artie to come out to Red Hook in Brooklyn. It's his wedding day, but Artie goes — and finds a dead man spread-eagled in the water off the old docks. When Sid shows up he's scared and edgy; Artie suspects he's holding something back . . . It's not his case, but it drags him in, threatening his friends and a former lover. In the tense pre-election atmosphere, Artie becomes involved in uncovering the betrayals that have led to death on the Red Hook waterfront . . .

Books by Reggie Nadelson
Published by The House of Ulverscroft:

HOT POPPIES
SOMEBODY ELSE
DISTURBED EARTH

REGGIE NADELSON

◆

RED HOOK

Complete and Unabridged

CHARNWOOD
Leicester

First published in Great Britain in 2005 by
William Heinemann
London

First Charnwood Edition
published 2006
by arrangement with
William Heinemann
a division of
The Random House Group Limited
London

British Library CIP Data

Nadelson, Reggie
  Red hook.—Large print ed.—
  Charnwood library series
  1. Cohen, Artie (Fictitious character)—Fiction
  2. Private investigators—New York (State)—
  New York—Fiction 3. Murder—Investigation—Fiction
  4. Detective and mystery stories 5. Large type books
  I. Title
  813.5′4 [F]

  ISBN 1–84617–235–7

Published by
F. A. Thorpe (Publishing)
Anstey, Leicestershire

Set by Words & Graphics Ltd.
Anstey, Leicestershire
Printed and bound in Great Britain by
T. J. International Ltd., Padstow, Cornwall

This book is printed on acid-free paper

To Richard David Story

Part One

1

'Blue skies, smiling at me, nothing but blue skies do I see.'

I was still half asleep early Sunday morning when I heard someone down in the street whistling 'Blue Skies' and it was the kind of tune that ran through your head all day. I had heard it on and off for months now, most of the summer, the guy whistling so clear and pure.

I swung my legs over the edge of the bed and got up and, still naked, picked up some cigarettes, went to the window and pushed it open wider, then leaned out.

The light was just coming up in the sky, smudgy, pink, metallic. Below me, on the sidewalk, I saw him. He had on a neon orange work vest, blue pants and shirt and a baseball cap. Head down, he was shoveling garbage, pushing it along the curb with a broom into a gray plastic garbage can on wheels. He went on whistling 'Blue Skies' and I watched him and listened, lit a cigarette and sat on the window sill of my place on Walker Street. It was late summer and hot out. I was happy.

I was getting married and I was as content as I'd ever been since I got to New York more than twenty-five years ago. The music was a good omen, so piercing and sweet, especially coming from the garbage guy; he probably worked for one of the community groups that hired the

3

homeless to clean up what the city didn't.

That was it: the sun coming up over the East River to my left; a hot bright day; the pavement swept clean, and the guy in the orange vest, whistling. I love the Stan Getz recording of 'Blue Skies' but this sound, the whistling so pure it was more like singing, somewhere between Mel Tormé and a hymn.

My cellphone went off. I listened to the message. Sid McKay had called me again. He had called the night before, had asked me to come out to Red Hook, said he was worried about something. I didn't go, was caught up in my own plans, then felt bad. Now there was the urgent message. I looked at my watch. It was only seven. I could make it out to Brooklyn and back in plenty of time for the wedding. Sid had helped me out on a case that mattered to me a lot. He took a big risk to help me and he never asked for anything back. Sid was a friend, and I owed him.

I took a shower, put on some jeans and a T-shirt, went out to my car and headed for Brooklyn. The city was quiet so I took the Brooklyn Bridge instead of the Battery Tunnel, which was faster but cost eight bucks coming and going.

From the bridge, I cut across to the Expressway and down to Red Hook on the river. It took me fifteen minutes. Van Brunt, the main street, was deserted. Along with the squat two-story houses were a bagel store, a few delis, a barbershop, a liquor store, a place that did

4

metalwork, a church and not much else. I drove down to the water.

The old docklands were silent Sunday morning, ancient as the city, full of its romance with the water, beautiful, serene in the early light glinting off the river.

★ ★ ★

The dead man in the inlet a few feet away from me, what I could see of him, was trapped under the rotting dock. Spreadeagled, legs drifting in the water, I heard someone say he looked like a Christ figure.

The old receiving dock in Red Hook ran alongside an inlet that fed out into the river. On one side of the inlet was an abandoned plant where sugar had been stored. On the other side was a long brick warehouse.

People stood in a row at the edge of the water, muttering to each other, staring in the same direction like people on the street looking at fancy TV sets in a store window. A pair of detectives were there along with a guy in uniform, a diver, his wetsuit glistening and black, and a department photographer. A bearded man in overalls and work boots with a dog on a leash stood a little apart from the others, probably just a passerby out walking his mutt.

I looked at the corpse again. I had been on my way to the brick warehouse where Sid had an office when I saw the flashing lights on a car near the inlet.

'How long has he been in the water?' I said to

5

one of the detectives, her hands jammed in the pockets of a red cotton jacket.

She wore jeans and sneakers and she was chewing gum. I let her know I was a detective in the city, but not much more. I didn't want to spell it out, or say where I worked. I'd been doing a lot of stuff on child crime, lousy stuff, people who abused kids and I didn't talk about it if I didn't have to.

'A while,' she said. 'They're saying maybe since last night some time, maybe, hard to tell until they get him out of there.'

While I was out drinking, I thought, while Sid was calling me and leaving messages.

'Any idea who he is?'

She shook her head. 'Not yet. They been down in the water for an hour, trying to get him loose without chopping anything off.' She took off the thin red jacket and tied the sleeves around her waist. 'Jesus, sometimes I hate this fucking job, you know? I hope they're not going to cut him,' she added, gesturing to two men in yellow slickers who appeared from behind a truck holding bolt cutters and a saw, and a bag of other tools. They headed for the dock where they crouched down and examined the body, what they could see of it.

The detective removed the gum from her mouth. 'Fucking nicotine gum, tastes like crap,' she added. 'You don't happen to have any cigarettes, do you?'

I handed her my pack; she took one and gave it back.

'Thanks,' she said. 'I don't know what the hell

I quit for anyhow. Thanks a lot.' She smiled and she was a pretty woman, not more than thirty-five, great smile, good figure.

'Sure,' I said. 'You'll be here for a while?'

'For you, anything.' She laughed, flirting, then walked towards the dock.

I didn't want to stick around much while they chopped the guy free. I started over to the warehouse on the other side of the inlet, a couple of hundred yards from the dead body.

The building was divided up into studios and workshops, and I went through the main entrance, up a couple of flights and found Sid's place. I banged on the door. There was no answer. I went back down.

A new cement pier, maybe half a mile long, ran along the front of the warehouse out into the basin. Phone in my hand I walked out on to the pier. I was uneasy now; I was edgy; where the hell was Sid at this hour? I looked at my watch. Eight a.m. Where did he go this early on Sunday morning? He had said he was here, at the office he kept in Red Hook.

I looked out at the water; the Statue of Liberty in front of me, lit up by the morning light, was a greenish color, maybe from the old copper facing.

Red Hook was a weird fat lip of land cut off from the rest of the city by a couple of highways that had been jammed through Brooklyn. It was a square mile of what had been the biggest shipyards on earth, isolated, surrounded on three sides by water, but fifteen minutes from downtown Manhattan.

7

In the other direction, away from the city, was the long Brooklyn coast, the piers and warehouses and marinas that ran all the way to the Atlantic Ocean and the beaches that were the seacoast of New York. Out in the water, a yellow water taxi sped by.

Sid had been half crazy when he called me the day before. I opened my cellphone and played back the message I got this morning. On Saturday he had called me two, three times. Please come, Artie, he had said. Please can you come on out? I'd be grateful, he had said. Drop by, he said, as if it was a social invitation, then more urgent: Can you hurry? Hurry!

Where are you? I'd said. A Mexican place, he said. Over on Columbia, corner of Van Brunt, you can't miss it. I can't come, I said. I can't, Sid. I'm getting married tomorrow. I'll call someone for you. He kept calling anyway, rambling, talking about the restaurant where he was, talking about some homeless guy he was scared of. I'm afraid, he had said. I'm scared.

★ ★ ★

All that Saturday afternoon, Sid McKay sat out on the roof deck of the Mexican restaurant on Columbia Street, sipping beer as he watched the river turn to liquid tin. He had the iPod his son sent him and for a while he listened to some music, a little Mahler, some Schubert and Gershwin. Above the river, the city was stacked up on itself, like Mayan ruins.

Sid had dropped in to the bar downstairs for a

beer, then come up to the deck for lunch. He sat on after everyone was gone, drinking cold beer, reading, a stack of books and newspapers and folders in front of him on the table.

No one bothers him up here. Shutting his eyes for a minute, soaking in the last of the sun, he feels at home. Sid's a regular. He knows the guy who built the place. Sid knows the bartender, the waiters. It's his neighborhood. In some strange way, he feels altogether more at ease with himself these days, in a way he never has, not in his whole striving ambitious screwed-up life, though he's aware how febrile he is, how his mood can change like a fever rising, then cooling down.

Sid's wearing shorts, something he never does out of the house, but it's a hot day and he came out in khaki shorts and an old green tennis shirt. There's no one much to see him. Anyone still left in the city is heading out to the beach. You can hear the silence.

The end of summer. The city emptying out like a drain. The Republicans are coming into town for their convention. Life in the times of George W. Bush, Sid thinks. A lot of praying. Lot of propaganda in the news. The Republicans are coming. The invasion, he thinks.

He looks out at the water again. Like everyone else, Sid's eye is first caught by the vacancy in the sky. Can't help it. Like your tongue finding the missing tooth. Three years next week since the Twin Towers went down. Three years since everything changed.

He takes off his reading glasses, gets up and leans out over the railing, craning his neck to catch a glimpse of Liberty in the harbor; he's still plenty sentimental about the view he's been looking at his whole life. If you go downstairs and across the street and over to the edge of the water, you can look Liberty dead in the eye. Governor's Island, too, and the Buttermilk Channel in-between.

The history of this area of Brooklyn, of the old docklands, its images occupy Sid's mind like antique woodcuts: in them he sees the ships and warehouses, the sailors, the carts and horses, and the women who once walked the channel, muslin caps on, long dresses hitched up around their waists, carrying wooden pails of fresh milk; the channel so shallow that they could walk across it in the time it took for the milk to turn to buttermilk.

What was Brooklyn like, he always wonders, when Walt Whitman was the editor of the original *Brooklyn Eagle*? When this was a separate city, the third biggest in America, alive with people protesting slavery, abolitionists raising their fists and Whitman urging people to stand up for the 'stupid and crazy', to be invulnerable to fear. And there have always been black men in Brooklyn, men like him he thinks, too, half proud, half sardonic. Arms still on the railing of the deck, Sid polishes off his third beer.

There's even been talk of reviving the *Eagle*, the great newspaper. People talked about Pete Hamill, of course, also of Brooklyn, for editor. Once, Sid would have liked a shot at editing it himself.

Sid grew up in Brooklyn, has lived here all his

10

life, not near the docks, of course, which were forbidden. The waterfront was dangerous when he was a kid.

It excites him, though, the way this part of Brooklyn is coming back. Out of the wreckage, he thinks. It is thrilling, people coming in, everyone wanting a piece of the action. Developers prowl Red Hook's streets these days, wanting in, and some of them call Sid because he knows his way around; they wheedle and plead for information. The historian, the philosopher, the poet of Red Hook, Sid has seen himself described in a magazine article.

Laughing to himself, leaning against the railing for support, he gathers up his books: Pushkin short stories, biographies of Walt Whitman and Paul Robeson. Real poets. Collectively, they are Sid's bible. He puts the books in the worn green book bag and tries to reclaim the scrubbed boy who bought the bag decades before as a Harvard freshman. Sid puts in the folders that are full of his own notes.

Still standing, he looks down at the street and he sees him.

Sees him again. Sees the homeless man and feels panic. The sight rips into Sid's reverie. His mood changes. He grasps his cellphone

He calls Artie Cohen again to say where he is, what he sees. Artie doesn't answer.

He's already called Artie once, or maybe twice, that morning when he saw the homeless man near his building, the man watching his windows. In spite of the heat, a chill ripples along the skin of Sid's arms. The man has been

11

around before: a week earlier, he walked up to Sid, hand out, begging. Crossing the street, Sid pretended he was in a hurry, not giving the man a second look. I should have helped him. I should have given him a buck, he thinks now. He dials the phone again.

Artie answers. Artie? Can you come? Drop by? He makes it as casual as he can, but he's scared.

I can't come, Artie tells Sid. I'm getting married tomorrow. Sunday. I'm sorry, Sid, he says and reminds him he's invited to the party. Sunday night, he says. Tomorrow. Come on into the city.

Sid won't go to Artie's wedding, though, not a party with strangers. Once maybe, when he was a pretty famous guy, when he worked at the *Times*, when he showed up on TV, and knew people and went to parties every night, but not now.

They were pretty close, him and Artie, and he tries not to feel resentful at his not coming to Brooklyn. When Artie worked cases that interested Sid and he was covering the city, they had seen a lot of each other. They kept in touch. They helped each other out. But Sid can't face a crowd.

I used to love it, Sid thinks; I loved parties, I went to all of them, knew everyone, always up for a good time. I was a lot younger. I'm sixty-five years old and retired, and I don't like parties much.

Sid thinks: who else can I call? He doesn't trust any other cops the way he trusts Artie Cohen.

12

★ ★ ★

Over the river, the sun's getting ready to slam itself down into the water in an outrageous splashy New York sunset. Sid puts some money on the table, tries to laugh, tries to feel detached, ironic, but he looks down at the sidewalk again, searching for the homeless guy.

It's getting late. It's September, the melancholy time of year he hates because it starts getting dark early. Already, though Sid has barely noticed, people are settling in at the other tables around him on the deck, inspecting menus, ordering food and drinks.

Sid picks up the cane he's been using since he hurt his ankle playing tennis, an old walking stick made out of sassafras wood, he gathers up his book bag, then begins to limp towards the stairs, still regretting he lost his favorite stick long ago, the Jimmy Carter peanut-head stick he got when he covered Carter's presidency. He's too vain to use the aluminum cane the hospital gave him, and he knows it.

In the bar, Sid orders a last beer. He gets a pack of cigarettes, something he hasn't done for years and, bag over his shoulder, heads for the street.

Unwrapping the cellophane, feeling it crackle, smelling the tobacco, he lights up like a kid sneaking a smoke. It tastes great.

Looking up and down the street, Sid waits anxiously in the doorway of the restaurant, but the homeless guy has gone. The street lights are on. People drift into the restaurants along the block.

It's fine out, a balmy evening and Sid sets off to walk the mile or so back to his place, leaning hard on the cane, but enjoying the cigarette, the night air. He passes close to the Marine Terminal, and the vast desolate lots for impounded cars, all of it butting up against the water.

'I was a fool to be worried,' he says and realizes he's said it out loud. 'Old fool.' He tosses away the cigarette.

On Coffey Street he walks across the little park and out on to the new pier. Halfway, his ankle begins to throb and Sid stops short, sits down hard on a bench. It's a few minutes from his place. Somehow he loses track of time and nods off.

A few minutes later, Sid's eyes snap open. His nerve endings feel raw. Someone close by is watching him. He gets up, brisk now, walking as fast as he can towards his building, and then realizes he's heading right for it, whatever it is, because he can smell it. He smells the stink.

He smells the guy before he sees him, then he hears the voice, whining, asking for change. The man is in front of him, coming closer.

Change, the guy says softly, got any change? A dollar? Fifty cents? I'm hungry, man. Please.

It's the same man Sid has seen before. His own height and color. Medium brown, but ashen from booze and drugs. Inside the layers of rags and filth is a human being who looks like him. He can tell that the man knows it, too.

14

Eyes gluey with glaucoma, thickened by cataracts, the man peers into Sid's face. A kind of dim surprise registers. He reaches out a hand. Sid keeps moving.

See you around, the guy mumbles in a drugged daze, and looks at him again and Sid feels that in the man he can see his own death.

Stop, Sid says to himself. Cut the melodrama. Then he wishes, for the second time that night, he'd given the man some money.

Before he finally disappears, the man circles Sid one more time, leaving his stink, like an animal marking out territory.

2

'You have any idea what color he was, the dead guy?' I said to the detective in the red jacket who was still near the water when I got back from Sid's warehouse.

'Watch it,' she yelled and grabbed my sleeve. 'Jesus, you almost fell the fuck in,' she said.

I said again, 'You have any idea? His color, I mean. White? Black?'

'Black. I think someone said he was black. I heard them say. One of the guys got a look. Why?'

I felt cold. 'How long is this going to take?'

'Give it half an hour. You OK?'

I passed her my cigarettes again and for a few minutes we stood and smoked and I looked across the inlet at a ten-story metal cone where sugar cane had been stored when it came off the ships. I'd read somewhere that Ferdinand Marcos owned it once, him or his cousin, or some other Filipino con man.

The place was derelict. Fire had reduced the machinery, the chutes, gears, wheels and slides that had serviced the cone, to a mass of burnt twisted metal.

The detective looked at the inlet.

'Poor bastard was probably in the wrong place at the wrong time. There's not much crime around here anymore. I bet he was all boozed up and fell the fuck in.'

She said she'd lived around here her whole life and had seen plenty of crime, especially after the shipping moved out to the big container ports over in Bayonne.

'Jersey,' she added contemptuously.

She could remember when there were crack deals on every block, people squatting in abandoned buildings, using them for toilets, gunfire all night. When she was still a kid, the school principal had been gunned down in broad daylight.

'Used to be a bucket-of-blood kind of place,' she said. 'People dumped their shit by the water, they even tossed out their dead cats, garbage guys would come once a week and scoop it up.'

Times were better, she added, the waterfront getting developed, a supermarket coming in, even Ikea sniffing around.

'Red Hook is now officially cool.' She grinned. 'People fighting over real estate. Artists moving in. They're planting parks along here in front of the old warehouses. It's good,' she said. 'It's OK. My pop would have died laughing. He was a longshoreman, old school.' She crossed herself and threw her half-smoked cigarette into the water. 'You know something about the dead guy? You have an interest?'

I nodded.

A police photographer I hadn't seen before, in a vest with neon yellow stripes, darted in front of me, trying to get a good angle on the dead man in the water. It struck me: there was a lot of manpower.

17

'You always get so many people out here like this?' I said.

'I was thinking the same thing. Fucking beats me how there's so much attention,' she said. 'I mean the Republican convention coming to town, every fucking law enforcement person doing double, triple time getting ready for the politicians, and you get a bunch of people out by the docks in Red Hook crack of dawn Sunday? Someone with connections must have been interested.'

'Yeah.'

'Boy, I'm glad this summer is almost over, what did they call it, Summer of Risk?' She grinned sarcastically. 'Now all of us are supposed to cancel our vacations, and go guard rich Republicans and the rich assholes giving them a kazillion dollars. Not to mention the fucking protestors. You ever been around one of those political events?'

I shook my head.

'I was down in Houston once, first Bush, Bush the father, not Junior, not the shrub. I was a kid just starting college, and it was something. There was like nutjob Christians throwing plastic fetuses at people because they hate abortions and there was some really rich ladies, I never saw such big diamonds, and it was like hot, like a hundred and fifty degrees. Never mind, where was I?' she said. 'We got a system where only rich people get elected, and no one even cares, you know? I mean I'm for law and order, and I'm for capital fucking punishment, and I want to kill every terrorist bastard myself, with my bare hands if I had my way, I mean I think we should just like cull them, you know? Like animals. But it doesn't mean I like rich people stealing from me either, and I don't like seeing American soldiers abuse prisoners in Iraq, I mean what the hell are we, you know? They keep telling us, get over it, get over it, things are better, and then they crank up the fear, and I think: what the fuck are they doing?' She shrugged. 'I just wish they'd fucking let us alone, bastards in DC who don't give us a nickel for security.'

Everyone was pretty pissed off at the constant change of alert levels by Homeland Security. Red, Yellow, Orange. Everyone was fed up because New York got a lousy deal on federal dollars for security.

I said, 'Yeah, Feds.'

She laughed. 'Don't know shit from Shinola as my grandma used to say, right? They could come to New York once in a while, but they sit on their fat asses out there in DC and we never see anything. You read that last FBI bulletin with what they call indicators associated with suicide bomb attacks?'

Distracted, thinking about who I could call, and where the hell Sid was, I nodded. You could almost always get help from another cop in New York if you made conversation about how ludicrous the Feds were.

She said, 'I love the part about how you should look out for 'Sweating, mumbling prayers or unusually clammy and detached behavior.' Or wearing disguises. Or the chemical odor. Sounds like every asshole that rides the subway.

Chemical odor? My kid got plenty of chemical odor, you know? It's called weed, you know? I come home I smell chemical odor. Some War on Terror. Why don't they take a look around the ports, you know? You could bring a radioactive elephant in and no one would notice. You need anything I can help you with, apart from waiting until they get the dead guy up?' She put up her hands, palms out, and shrugged. 'Nothing's over, you know?' she said. 'Hello? You OK? You were on a different planet, man.'

'Yeah, I know. I'm sorry. How much longer until they get the body out of the water?'

'Like I said, give it half an hour maybe.' She put her hand on my arm. 'So if you wanted, one night I could take you to one of the Republican shindigs, you get tons of free drinks and food and stuff. Good stuff. I heard one place they were serving Chateau fucking Lafite and Kobe steaks, you know? I can always get assigned to this stuff, I'm a woman, I'm Hispanic, you know.' She smiled and put out her hand. Her nails were bright pink. 'Clara Fuentes,' she said.

'Yeah, thanks,' I said and introduced myself. 'Not this year, but thanks.'

'You're taken right? I'm not surprised. Sure,' she said, then got a card out of her pocket, scribbled her home number and her cell on it, handed it to me, and added, 'If ever.'

'Thanks.' I started to turn away.

'Hey.'

I turned around.

'Take it easy,' she said.

I walked along the inlet away from the corpse to where a few small boats were tied up. I didn't like boats much. All the times I had gone fishing, I loved it, but I was always scared, so I drank plenty of beer and concentrated on the fish. Also, I was a lousy swimmer. I almost drowned off Coney Island when a girl — a sad Russian girl trying to make a life and failing — walked into the waves and I couldn't save her.

Trouble was that I loved being near the water. I loved the city waterfront. It was one of the things that had seduced me about New York from the beginning. But boats scared me.

All the time I was waiting, I could see the guys down in the water now, trying to free the corpse, still setting up to chop off the dead guy's arms, but hesitant.

It came back to me, the little girl who was murdered out by Sheepshead Bay on a case I did. Everyone thought it was a copycat at first, a repeat of an old cold case where another little girl got cut into pieces by a monster who was still out there. I didn't want to think about it. It wasn't related.

For maybe the sixth time in half an hour, I tried Sid's phone and tried not to listen to the sound of the saw. Saw on flesh, on bone. A small whirring noise in the quiet morning when the only other sound was a lone tug that hooted out on the sun-drenched river.

'Artie? It's Artie, right?' It was Clara Fuentes, the detective, and she was yanking my arm. 'I'm

21

not supposed to say anything, but you obviously got an interest, and I heard someone who was down in the water say it definitely was a black guy, and also about sixty years old, maybe seventy, far as they can tell, I just heard, one of the guys went down under the pier and said best he could see was he'd been in the water, the black guy that is, a while, hours anyhow. Can't tell if he just sucked up water, or there was booze or drugs.'

'Jesus.'

'Yeah.'

I said, 'Anyone been around this morning? You notice anyone passing by? Locals?'

She shook her head. 'I've been here all the time; except for the guy with the dog, and a couple of other residents we all know, not a lot of people coming out, and if they did we kept them way back. Who did you have in mind?'

I thought about Sid. 'It doesn't matter. What else?'

'You look like shit. You need to sit down? You think you knew this guy?'

My hands were shaking. 'Yeah, something like that,' I said, sure now that it was Sid. He was dead. He had called me. I didn't go.

'It's the stink, you know?' she said. 'Even when you can't smell it you think you can, right?'

I nodded and dug out my cigarettes. The pack was empty.

★ ★ ★

22

I went to the deli over on Van Brunt Street where I bought a fresh pack, cracked it open, held one in my fingers while I ordered some coffee, then stood and drank it staring at bags of pork rinds and potato chips and boxes of cookies with labels in Spanish. I tried to keep calm, keep focused.

Over the counter were a couple of signs offering specials on 'Swis Chez samwiches' and 'Hot Kanish'. New York English had become a different language, and I laughed, thinking of the foodies who, driven by nostalgia, thronged East Houston Street on weekends for a real knish at Yonah Schimmel's. Me, I couldn't stand any kind of knish.

New York had the biggest immigrant population since the 1920s. Four out of ten people in the city born somewhere else. Like me. I swallowed some more coffee.

Standing in the store, wondering, like I always did, why they bothered putting ridges in the potato chips, I half listened to a conversation between the deli guy, a squat man with a pointy nose wearing a Mets shirt, and a customer, a woman with white hair and a shopping cart.

It surprised me that they were speaking Russian. Russians had moved out from Brighton Beach across Brooklyn, into the immense flat interior of Flatbush, like Muscovites moving out across the steppes. I didn't think they'd moved as far as Red Hook.

At the deli, the conversation in Russian was about how gas prices were killing everyone that summer, and even if you drove to Jersey they screwed you, and about how developers were

23

coming into Red Hook and there would be jobs for working people like them, finally, unless the artists fucked them over.

I finished the coffee and tossed the carton in a garbage can, and went back to the waterfront. I hoped like hell they were finished getting the dead guy out of the water. It was almost nine.

24

3

They were already loading a couple of rubbery black body bags by the time I got back to the inlet, zipping them up, piling them in an ambulance that had arrived. The corpse was gone. Disappeared into the bags. Body parts, maybe. I didn't know. One bag for each. More respectful, I heard someone say. Each what? Arm? The rest of him? His head?

I remembered suddenly how they bagged body parts in Israel. After every bomb blast, you saw them. The kind of blast that killed my father on a bus he took regularly to his chess games. Wrong bus. They got the wrong bus. It had been intended for a different bus on a different route. When I got there, there were limbs on the street, and the religious crews had moved in. They collected the pieces. They had special bags. Religious Jews gave body parts a burial: even if you got a limb amputated, even a little piece of finger, they gave it a funeral. Otherwise, someone told me, you'd make a lousy show in heaven or wherever the fuck people supposedly went. Which was nowhere. You didn't go any place. You were just dead.

In Brooklyn, in the heat, I thought I could smell the bags. It was boiling now. I was sweating.

'It was supposed to be me, I think,' a voice said and I turned around and saw Sid McKay standing at the edge of the dock, leaning on a cane with one hand, a shopping bag in the other. 'You look surprised, Art. Maybe you thought it was me,' he said.

'Jesus, Sid, Christ, I'm glad as hell to see you, but where were you? I've been calling you, I've been at your place, where the fuck were you?'

He held up the shopping bag. 'I went out to Brighton Beach to do some shopping,' he said. 'I like Russian bread. I'm always up early.'

I said, 'You know who he was?'

'I'm pretty sure.'

'You got a look?'

'Before they bagged him up, yes. So you felt sad when you thought I was gone? Sorry, I don't mean to be sarcastic, I just always wondered how people would feel when I was dead. Like the funeral scene in *Huck Finn*, you remember?' He looked at the cane in his hand. 'I did my ankle in playing tennis. I'm too bloody old, I guess. So you felt sad?'

'Sure,' I said, relieved and a little pissed off because now I didn't know if Sid was playing games, or he was relieved I was there, or what the hell was going on.

'Look, I am sorry. My cellphone is all messed up. I'm not really good with technology. Artie, I apologize,' he said. 'I got a little crazy yesterday, and I don't know, I didn't know whom to call or whom to trust. You wouldn't have a cigarette on you, would you? You notice that everyone's smoking again?'

Sid spoke impeccable old-fashioned English. Tall, thin, handsome, his gray hair cut close, he was around sixty-five now.

I offered him the pack of cigarettes. He handed me his bag, took the pack and lit a cigarette with an old Zippo lighter.

'Vietnam,' he said. Waving the lighter, he looked up at the sky.

'It's getting hot,' Sid said. 'Cold summer, hotter now. You notice the strange little rain showers popping up all the time, dry in Manhattan some days, wet in Jersey? Apocalyptic. Makes you wonder. It's not the heat, it's the humidity, my dad always said. He always said it. He was a very precise man the way he spoke, but he was given to clichés. His family owned newspapers all over New York and New Jersey, he was obsessed with the business, and it made him rich. I delivered papers from the time I was a tiny boy. There were always black people who read newspapers. Colored folk. Black people. Negroes. African-Americans. I'm sorry. I'm thinking aloud.'

I wanted to get back to the city. I looked at my watch.

'Sid, listen, I'm here because you called me yesterday. I should have come then, and I didn't, and I'm sorry, so I came out to see you and I got here and there was a guy trapped under a dock, dead, and you show up and say it was supposed to be you, so talk to me or let me go home. Who was he?'

'Forgive me. I'm rattled,' Sid said. 'I had seen him around, like I told you, he drank, people tried to help him out, but he always said, 'Just help me get a drink.' He told people he didn't

27

want to be reformed. He liked drinking. He had a room somewhere, I heard. I just want a buck for a shot, he said, and I didn't give it to him. Poor bastard came at me with his hand out and I refused him, I just went home and then someone pushed him. Someone who thought it was me. Someone whacked him with a piece of wood, he fell into the water. That's it.'

'He told you that? That he just liked drinking? You talked to him?'

Sid shook his head. 'Mostly I heard it from other people,' he said. 'This is a tight community out here, especially this side of Red Hook on the water, a lot of artists, crafts people, writers. We know each other. We know the locals. We go to community meetings, we talk about development, we pass the time of day. Urban Pioneers, we call ourselves, we call this our frontier village, forgive the expression and my irony. People who couldn't afford Manhattan, or got priced out of Williamsburg and DUMBO and the hipper parts of Brooklyn. People want a piece of the city before it's all gone, so they're finding their way to the fringes, the old industrial city.'

I cut him off gently as I could.

'What about you?' I said.

'I just like the water,' he said. 'Can you spare me half an hour more, Artie? I'd be grateful. I know I've messed you around, calling you. Forgive me.'

'You were scared of the homeless guy, is that it, Sid? And not because he was just a harmless drunk. You called me because you were scared of something else about him. You said someone

28

whacked him thinking it was you. I don't get it.'

'I'd seen him, you know, and I saw him the last couple of days and he felt threatening, he seemed to be on crack or something. Last night, when I called you the last time, that's when he really scared me. Not just because he looked crazy. I've known crazy people.'

'Then what?'

'When I saw him like that close-up, I felt I was looking at my own death.'

'Why?'

'He looked like me,' Sid said.

★　★　★

We went to Sid's place and he walked there slowly, leaning on his cane. He changed the subject. He asked if I remembered when we met, some party, he said, ten years back, maybe more.

'You asked me if I liked jazz,' he added.

'God.' I was embarrassed.

If you grew up in Moscow like I did, loving America, loving jazz, listening to Willis Conover's Jazz Hour on *Voice of America* under the covers — my father used to find me there and yell at me, but my mother like it that I was rebellious that way — because of the music, you had all kinds of fantasies about American black people.

Sid said, 'I thought it was charming, I had been in Moscow as a reporter, and I knew that there were two kinds of Russians as far as I was concerned: the racists who were more racist than anyone I had ever met, including when I was a

29

boy and went south to Virginia to stay with some cousins, I mean those Russians quite literally saw us as animals, a different species; and the other kind who thought we were wonderful, usually because of the music. You were the second kind. I was only insulted when you asked me if I knew Charlie Parker because you thought I was old enough. It was fine because I was obsessed with Russia, so there was a kind of quid pro quo, I wanted to talk about Pushkin and you wanted to ask me about music,' he said. 'You came to the party with a very nice woman with red hair. Someone I knew a little. Lily Hanes. That's it, wasn't that her name? Whatever happened to Lily?'

I didn't answer. I could see by the way he rambled that Sid was pretty shaken up. Near the entrance to the building, he put his hand out towards me as if to steady himself.

He looked old. Older than he was, and the flesh on his face was loose. His clothes, khaki shorts and a faded green polo shirt, were wrinkled as if he'd slept in them. I had known people like Sid whose sanity almost depended on the shell, on keeping it sharp. I looked at him again and saw a guy who was falling apart.

I held the door, and he leaned on me. The way he looked now, Sid seemed beaten. We climbed the stairs and he unlocked the door slowly, opening it as if it was too heavy for him. We went in. He put his cane down and then put his book bag on his desk.

I felt bad for him. I remembered how much I had always liked Sid. He was good company, smart, curious, ironic, a little mournful.

Inside the large loft space, an old poster for a Paul Robeson concert hung behind glass on one wall. Next to it was an oil painting, an authentic piece of Soviet Realism, with a triumphant Lenin pointing to the future and a crowd of workers looking up reverently as if at God.

Sid saw me looking and said, 'I used to collect that stuff,' then led me to the far end of the loft where the big industrial windows looked out on the river.

I glanced around. 'What is this place?'

'My office,' he said. 'I run a little publishing company. One-man press, things that interest me. Also, it's my bolt hole. My escape hatch. End of the world, you know? See people, not see them, whatever I feel like. Sit, please, Artie.'

'Escape what?'

He didn't answer, and I stayed where I was, leaning against the window.

'Let me get this straight. The dead man was a homeless guy everyone knew, and you think someone killed him instead of you,' I said. 'Is that it, Sid? Why the hell would anyone be after you? You were scared enough to call me, what two, three times yesterday at least? You thought whoever killed that poor bastard out there was coming for you, right, but you didn't call the cops, you called me the day before I'm getting married. Come on, Sid. We've known each other a long time.'

He walked over and stood next to me, face against the windowpane, closed his eyes, then opened them.

31

'The last stop in America,' he said, looking out at the water. 'Or the first. The edge of the world. You see all that? I look out, I see the old docks and shipyards, the warehouses and factories, the inlets and canals, a whole square mile, most of it empty now, a couple of miles from Manhattan. Red Hook's one of the last great places in the city. Some of these buildings are a hundred and fifty years old. Civil War times, some earlier,' he said, and stretched out his arms. 'The Brooklyn Shipyards. Biggest in the world, all the docks loaded with tea, cashews, mahogany, lumber, sugar, grain, all that grain coming from the Midwest, on ships through the Great Lakes to the Erie Canal to the Hudson River and down to New York. 1825, Artie. It was the opening of the canal that made this the greatest port on earth, the goods coming and going, the river running out to the Atlantic Ocean, connecting us to Europe.'

I tried to interrupt, but Sid was on a roll and I couldn't stop him.

'Warehouses bursting.' He gestured to a building close by. 'That one, over there, look, they had donkeys on the top floor that were whipped like crazy to work the pulley system that brought up huge bags of coffee that had been unloaded off the ships. I feel I can smell it when I'm out here, and I can hear them, the men who jammed these docks, men from Italy, Ireland, Syria, Sweden, Russia, working these ports. Can you imagine it, Artie? It was still here, some of it, when I was a boy. I used to sneak over here to look. It was forbidden, because I was a nice boy from a good family, and this was a tough neighborhood, there were rackets here, and gangsters, longshoremen who were really tough, but I loved it,' he said. 'I was a child spy.'

'What?'

He laughed. 'Not a real spy, Artie, but the kind you are when you're a child. Let me make us some coffee,' he said, but he didn't move. 'Look at it. Think about it. Some piece of real estate, right? A place on the water, your own boat tied up out front, great views of the city, ten minutes from Manhattan, a fast escape. Money. You could build your own little empire here. Lots of real estate. Lots of money.'

'Escape from what?'

'All that,' he said gesturing at the window and the faint outline of the lower Manhattan skyline.

'All what?'

'Fear.'

He moved away suddenly towards the small, makeshift kitchen at the far end of the loft, and began filling a coffee pot. I followed him.

'Do you speak Russian much these days, Artie?' Sid called out.

'When I have to. On the job.'

'I love your language,' he said. 'I always have. I loved it. I learned it when I first heard about Paul Robeson going there. Robeson was my idol. He was a superior human being, my dad said, he played sports, he sang, he was brilliant, he ran with artists and intellectuals, black people, white people. You ever hear of Carl Van Vechten?'

'Who?'

'It doesn't matter. He was close with Robeson.

33

Robeson went to Russia, he felt that the Slavs understood Negro spirituals in their inner being, it was about soul, and it was the Russian thing that stuck with me. So odd.' Sid's voice trailed off. 'I was always happy when you let me talk Russian with you.'

I didn't remember Sid talking Russian to me; I didn't remember it at all, and I wondered now if he was crazy; maybe the fear, whatever he was afraid of, had driven him nuts.

'Is this about something Russian, the dead man? Is that why you really called me?'

He set the coffee pot on the stove and turned on the burner.

'I hear things. People talk to me. I go over to Brighton Beach to buy the Russian newspapers and good bread, and sometimes caviar, and I have friends there, people in bookshops, people in cafes. Some friendly, some not so friendly. They see a black man, it's a crapshoot, you know?' He smiled. 'Excuse me, Artie, I'll just go change my clothes while the coffee boils.'

He left me then, and went through a door that I figured led to the bathroom.

I shifted my weight and the wide plank floor creaked. Two of the loft's walls were jammed with bookshelves. Books leaked from the shelves. Books stood in piles on the floor, and on a large pine table under the window. There was a computer on it. Sid's green book bag lay beside a mason jar stuffed with roses that had shed most of the petals on to the table and a neat pile of manila folders.

An old-fashioned wooden desk chair with

wheels was in front of the desk. In the corner was a round table covered with dozens of photographs, all in old silver frames. Opposite it was a worn leather couch covered with a faded blue and red kilim over it. On top were a blanket and pillow.

Sid returned in a pressed dark blue shirt, sleeves rolled up, crisp new chinos and Topsiders on his feet. He turned off the stove, poured some coffee into mugs and handed me one. He leaned against a small table where newspapers and magazines were arranged in rows.

'I'm a newspaper junkie,' he said. 'Always have been. I read three, four of them a day. I don't know who I am if I don't read them.' He smiled.

I looked around. 'No TV?'

'I hate the noise,' he said.

'So you live here?'

'No. This is commercial space, not residential, like I said, but I publish a few little things, arcane local history, monographs about Whitman, pieces about black newspapers. Things I love and no one else cares about.'

I drank the coffee and got out my cellphone. It was getting late.

'It makes me legit here, though not quite for living,' Sid said. 'I have an apartment in Brooklyn Heights, and a house in Sag Harbor. A man of property, Artie.' He looked at the ceiling. 'You hear the music? Cuban pottery guy. I like that, I like the sounds of other people in the building, you know?'

I knew.

'It keeps away the demons,' he added.

35

'What demons?'

'Loneliness,' he said.

'You stay here nights?'

'I don't really sleep. I sit on the sofa and look out at the water. I bought this place to work in and because I like the water and nobody knows I have it. Hide in plain sight,' he said. 'I can be here and no one cares, not the people who live at the front of Red Hook in the housing projects or the people who run little businesses, the pie-makers, the radical embroidery lady, the other one who makes kites out of silk, the glass-blowers, the painters, you know? No one minds what I do. It's the freest you can feel in New York City. Back of beyond. It will change. It's changing. We're getting a supermarket. Can I offer you something more than coffee? A beer? Is it too early?'

Behind the good manners he was strained, his face tight, the eyes distracted by some kind of inner terror. I looked at my watch. I had promised I'd be ready early; I promised.

None of it fit: Sid wandering the waterfront at night; his sleeping in the half-furnished loft; the crumpled clothes he had been wearing. It didn't fit with the soft formal speech, the good manners. He was scared. Something about the eyes. He had turned inward, for self-protection maybe, and part of him had disappeared from view.

'The dead guy, Sid. You think it could have been race? You think that? The dead guy? Let's talk about him, OK?'

'I don't know. Possibly. In the old days, sure.

But now? Why? Ninety percent of Red Hook is Hispanic or black.' He put his mug down and sat on the edge of the desk. 'I can't stop thinking that someone got tired of me nosing around, and came for me, and got the poor bastard who's now in pieces in a bunch of body bags, you know? I like talking to people, I like hearing the history of the docks, I like knowing what's going on. I'm in favor of development; I like the idea of the place coming to life. There are people who don't like it. There are people who fight over it. I thought about writing a book, I take notes. Perhaps someone thought I knew too much. Or not.'

'Do you?'

'What?'

'Know too much?'

He smiled slightly. 'It depends what you mean.'

'Maybe it was just an accident, Sid.' I waved towards the inlet where the corpse had been.

'You think? You think someone went to the trouble of killing an old drunk accidentally?'

'Then tell me what you really think if you want to, because I have to go.'

He hesitated, and I knew he was reorganizing reality. He went to the sink and washed out his mug and set it on the draining board, then turned back to me.

'You have another one of those cigarettes?' he said.

I tossed him the pack. He lit up and smoked silently.

I liked Sid, but it was getting late and he

wasn't talking. I couldn't wait. I was out of the door and halfway down the first flight of stairs when I heard the door open and Sid limping behind me.

★ ★ ★

'Can you just give me a lift?' Sid said, still following me into the street, admiring my car and putting his hand on the passenger door as I started to get in. I didn't reply. It was bullshit, Sid's attempt at a compliment. My old red Caddy was on its last legs; I need a new car, couldn't afford anything I could love, so I kept it. I still loved it, though it was nothing much to look at now. I was tired of Sid's game.

'Please,' he said. 'It won't take a minute. Just drop me up at Van Brunt Street, would you?' he said.

I drove.

'You think I should hole-up in my loft, Artie? You think it's safe now? It's hard to know whom to trust, isn't it? I didn't level with you. I'm sorry. I was shook up.'

He sat, and waited for my answer and looked out the window, then back at me, hesitant.

'You know when I stopped caring about the news, I quit working,' Sid said. 'They were glad to get rid of me. They wanted me out, to tell the truth, and I was happy to take early retirement and the money. No one wanted a grumpy old editor who cared if you faked pictures or made-up stories, and I realized I was sick of pretending I didn't notice, and then I stopped

38

caring. The manipulation of the news stopped mattering. I'm sorry, I don't suppose you know what the hell I'm talking about.'

I knew; I had grown up in a country where there was only manipulation, where propaganda was all the news there was.

I said, 'What do you mean safe now? There wasn't any crime against you.'

'Yes, I see what you mean. I understand. Thanks for humoring me. Thank you. There are times you just need someone to believe you, you know? Over there, you can drop me there, please. Nice little pub,' he said. 'Good food. Nice bar.'

I stopped, and he opened the car door, still hesitating.

I said, 'I have to go.'

'I understand,' he said, and he shook my hand and said, 'Call me one of these days, will you? Let me buy you a drink, or dinner, you and your wife, OK?' Sid got out of the car, then leaned down and peered in.

'What the hell did you mean safe?' I said.

'He said he'd be back, he said he would come back for me, or someone else would. Soon,' Sid said, pulling back and standing up straight.

Something occurred to me and I stuck my head out of the car window and called out as Sid started up the sidewalk. 'How did you know someone whacked the dead guy with a piece of wood?'

'I guess one of the detectives told me,' he answered, and I knew he was lying.

'Weird, a dead bum getting so much attention

on a Sunday morning like that, I mean when every cop in the city is doing double time on the convention. Sid?'

'Yes?'

'Was it you who called the cops? You dialed 911? You got through to someone about the dead man down under the dock?'

A plane flew low overhead and the noise seemed to distract Sid, or maybe he didn't hear me, but all he said was, 'Congratulations on getting married, Artie. Give my regards to Tolya Sverdloff. Tell him I'm sorry I won't make it to the party tonight. I just have to get out of here.'

'Out of where?'

'Red Hook,' he said.

4

'Artie? Congratulations, man!'

Sunday night and I was married; I was married, and guys I worked with and some I had worked with way back, twenty-five years ago, were pumping my hand and grabbing my shoulder and women were kissing me, and we were all beaming at each other. At Tolya Sverdloff's apartment, people crowded in, a band played, and they were good, and waiters swirled across the floor with trays of drinks. There was the smell of flowers everywhere from huge bunches of roses and lilies. I was married.

Late that afternoon, after I got back from seeing Sid in Brooklyn, after I put on my new suit, a judge with an actor's voice who came in special for us had married Maxine Crabbe and me in his chambers downtown; her two girls were witnesses. Now, a few hours later, we were at the party.

The band, a trio, bass, piano, drums, played 'Manhattan'.

'I'll take the Manhattan, Bronx and Staten Island, too . . . ' I found myself singing under my breath, caught up in the crowd, surrounded by it, celebrating.

Even from across the huge loft, Maxine seemed to shine in her new silk dress and I was starting over to her when Danny Guilfoyle, my first boss, and his wife Dinah appeared. I kissed

Dinah, and Danny hugged me so hard I figured he might lift me off the ground because, in spite of Dan being seventy-five now, he was still tough. Dinah, not much younger, seemed to have barely aged, and I asked her if she'd sing something. She had been pretty well known once, and she could scat great, and she grinned and said maybe, maybe I will, darling, for you, Artie. I got another glass of champagne.

Across the room I saw Mike Rizzi who owned the coffee shop opposite my building, and Sonny Lippert who I worked for a lot on special cases, and my half-sister, Genia, and her husband Johnny Farone. Lois and Louise, my ex-neighbors who had moved to Florida were there. Everyone had come.

People talked some about the Republicans and the convention; I heard someone say he'd been caught up in traffic earlier, the city jammed with delegates and demonstrators. Mostly people drank and laughed.

'Dance with me, OK, Artie? Will you?'

It was Maria, one of Maxine's kids. She wore a dress. Specially for you, Artie, she had said. Except for the hated school uniform, Maria only wore jeans that were so ripped they were like sacred rags. But she'd put on a red summer dress with flowers on it and thin straps and she wore red sandals. I got bouquets of roses for both girls to hold. They were twelve now, Maxine's twins. Millie was a real little nymphet, platinum hair, beautiful, knowing and vain. I could see her across the room, flirting with Tolya.

Maxine knew I liked Maria better and she told me I couldn't play favorites, but I figured it was OK because Millie got the attention. Maria was shy and smart, a daredevil. We listened to music together, I let her drive my car out of the beach and she got me to teach her some Russian words.

Later, I said. I'll dance with you later.

'Promise?'

'Promise,' I said, and then more people came up to me, and after a while I needed a cigarette.

Maria hovered near me while I stood in the doorway of the terrace that ran the whole way around Tolya's loft on top of a building in the Meat Packing District. I lit a cigarette.

'Artie?'

'What is it, sweetheart?'

'Nothing,' Maria said. 'Just I'm happy you're with Mom.'

'Me too.'

She stayed near me, not speaking. She made me feel connected. I liked kids. I wished I had had some. After the case with Billy Farone, my own nephew, it scared me, what they could do and how it got to you. I felt that way after Billy killed a man. A guy I worked with had said bitterly, 'All kids bring is shit.' He was wrong. In spite of Billy, I didn't believe kids brought you shit.

I reached for Maria's hand. It was warm, sweaty, and substantial. She held my hand tight and we went outside and looked out at the Hudson River together.

The buildings were backlit by the setting sun,

the sky silvery in the last late light.

New York was a city on water. The island city: New York. Forty percent of the city was water; it was a floating planet, an archipelago, islands, rivers, wetlands, swamps, ponds. Eight million people lived here, and the commuters and tourists all somehow moved back and forth over bridges, through tunnels, on boats. A lot of the city was built on landfill. Seawalls under the big buildings held the water back. One day the city would flood bad.

I loved it, loved the tribal way it operated with as many rituals and taboos as a chain of South Seas islands. You could be on Staten Island and have no idea what was going on in the East Village and not care. People near the Whitestone Bridge with its watery views were barely conscious of Chinese immigrants in Sunset Park in Brooklyn, ten miles away. On City Island in the Bronx people ate seafood looking out at Hart's Island where the poor dead were buried by the city in Potter's Field and where the dead guy in Red Hook would probably end up. I'd been out there once for a funeral of someone I felt responsible for and it was a bleak place where inmates from city jails did the burying and the wind blew off the river, like something from a nineteenth-century Russian novel.

In the outer boroughs people lived whole lives as New Yorkers. New York was made of the five boroughs, but Manhattan was different. Everyone referred to it as 'The City', a place apart.

'Artie, you OK?' It was Maria.

'I'm great,' I said, and she hugged me, and I

felt that heavy warmth you got from a kid who liked you, and then she skipped away towards a group of other girls, other people's children.

I turned my head and saw Maxine in the middle of the room, surrounded by people, and she waved and I waved back and then my phone rang.

It was a message from Sid. I leaned out over the terrace wall and looked south at the harbor towards the Statue of Liberty. Around the bend from where the statue stood were Red Hook and Sid. I didn't call him back.

I knew he had lied to me, I knew he was scared; he said that he felt threatened. I didn't know how real it was, but I had gone that morning, and I was here now and I didn't want to think about it or the corpse in the inlet, or the sound of the saw, or the stink, or Sid. I had talked to the detectives on the case. Enough, I thought, and I was putting my phone in my pocket when Maxine came up alongside me and put her arm around my waist.

The band was playing 'Someone to Watch Over Me'. I could feel my eyes fill up.

'You're singing out loud,' Maxine said.

'Which is not why you married me; my singing, I mean.'

She laughed. 'I love you a lot, but maybe not when you're singing. You look great, though, the new suit is really cool on you,' she said and kissed me. 'What's the matter, honey?'

'Nothing at all,' I said. 'To me, I always sound just like Mel Tormé when I sing,' I added, then I kissed her back. She smelled like almonds.

45

'The shampoo,' Max said, and took my hand and we went back inside where she gestured at the crowd. 'Did he tell you, your friend Tolya, did he tell you he was doing all this?'

'Are you OK with it?'

'Sure,' she said. 'Of course I'm OK. It's fabulous, but why would he, I mean there must be two hundred people, and half the champagne in New York, and God knows what else. I mean, just the flowers.'

'It's the way he is,' I said.

In the loft, half an acre of it, the central air conditioning purred, ceiling fans moved the filmy white curtains along the windows. Little trees with real lemons on them stood in terracotta pots, and everywhere there were huge clusters of white lilies and roses, white, pink, yellow, red, lavender, the kind that threw out a rich smell that mixed with the smell from the fruit on the long bar.

Four bartenders crushed fruit in blenders, fresh lime and pineapple for caipirinhas, peaches for Bellinis. The pineapple smelled exactly the way it had the time I went to Hawaii years earlier, up around the northern shore where there were pineapple plantations and the air actually smelled of the fruit, sweet, intoxicating; it made you drunk without the alcohol.

Waiters in black pants and white shirts and aprons circulated around the loft with platters of shrimp, oyster, lobster, and caviar set in glass bowls of cracked ice. There was more food on two tables opposite the bar. Around the edge of the room and out on the terrace were small tables draped with linen and set with more flowers, and already people were sitting down at them, eating, yakking, drinking.

In the middle of it all, circulating like the ringmaster of a circus, was Tolya Sverdloff. He had offered to give us the party and now I saw his head bobbing above the others, moving through the crowd, kissing the women, hugging men, holding up a glass, toasting, laughing. The music played louder. More corks popped. Half expected to see a girl swing down from the ceiling on a trapeze or a dancing bear appear.

Then out of nowhere an odd feeling, something dark, came over me like a cloud coming over the sun unexpectedly; things suddenly felt wrong, out of place, and I knew that the morning in Red Hook, and Sid's fear, had left me on edge.

A waiter passed with a tray and I reached for a glass of champagne and gulped it.

'You look like a dog when you shake yourself like that,' Max said and kissed me again.

'I do?'

'Yeah, didn't you know that?' she said. 'I asked you before, what's the matter? Tell. Come on.'

I kissed her. She tasted of pineapple. She wore a pale pink sleeveless silk dress and high-heeled silver sandals and her long legs and arms were tan, her arms so long they gave her the look of an overgrown girl or a rag doll. We had been together more than eighteen months solid, ever since I had worked Billy Farone's case on Sheepshead Bay. I had known her a lot longer; we had been casual friends for years.

Max had grown her brown hair to her shoulders and she had pinned it at the side with a little green orchid, and she was wearing her grandmother's pearls and the diamond ring I got for her on 47th Street from my old contact there; Hillel Abramsky had given me a good price, and now it was on her thin brown finger where she admired it constantly and held it up for me to see the rainbow it made in the light from a candle on a table near us. Max had elegant long fingers; I loved watching her fix dinner or do a jigsaw puzzle; I loved looking at her hands.

Hillel was at the party. I saw him in the crowd in a blue suit and I waved and he laughed because he had been trying to get me married for so many years. He said it was better for your health. He once told me he wished I would marry a Jewish woman, not for religion but for the sake of the tribe. I wasn't sure what he meant.

I had a ring, too, plain gold; Maxine had wanted me to have one. I have never worn a ring in my life and my hand seemed to belong to someone else, but that was part of it, being like other people, getting a life with Maxine Crabbe and Millie and Maria. Everyone I knew was relieved that I had grown up and settled down. After the case with Billy, and the kidnapping and the rest of it, I was finally OK. I wasn't at the edge of chaos anymore.

This is it, I kept thinking: this is how it should be. I left Max for a minute and went over to the band and talked to the pianist and found out he was a big Stan Getz fan. We discussed some of the obscure tracks, and then he told me his favorite was an old LP called *The Steamer* that I loved, too, and confided in me that he had once met Stan, and I was like a schoolkid, impressed. He asked me what songs I liked, and then as I went back to Maxie, he grinned and did a couple of bars of 'The Girl From Ipanema'.

Maxine was looking in the direction of her mother and her ex-mother-in-law — she had been married to a fire captain who was killed on 9/11 — and a group of girls she had grown up with in Brooklyn. She put her arms around me.

'I better go make nice,' she said. 'Artie, can I ask you something?'

'Anything.'

'Hey, don't look so gloomy, you look like a gloomy Russian,' she said. 'It's not so bad, getting married. Anyway, it's like we were already married, right?'

'Absolutely. I was just thinking about something,' I said, trying to shake the fear I'd heard in Sid's voice. 'And I'm not a gloomy Russian. I'm an American. I know all the words to the 'Star-Spangled Banner', I love the Yankees, Frank Sinatra, *The Sopranos*, Tony Bennett, Ella, Michelle Pfeiffer, bacon cheeseburgers, pizza, New York, you. Yeah, you can ask me anything you want, we can do anything you want.'

'Then can we look at some apartments tomorrow?'

'Sure. You think you found something?'

She lit up like a bulb, girlish and thrilled, and nodded. 'I think maybe,' she said. 'I think I did.'

We were still commuting. Max had stayed in Brooklyn at her place near Bay Ridge so the girls could finish middle school there. I was in my loft trying to figure out how to renovate it for the four of us. It worked OK. We had been together a pretty long time and we were used to it.

'Thank you,' she said. 'Thank you for everything.'

'I'm the one,' I said and kissed her but before she could start off towards her mother, Tolya appeared at her side, carrying an enormous bunch of pink roses two feet long, wrapped in crackling cellophane, dripping with white silk ribbons. He presented them to Maxine, a ritual offering, and then kissed her cheeks three times, Russian style. I could see Maxine, swamped by the flowers, loving it. I just grinned. It was such a Russian gesture.

Tolya threw his arms around me, and handed me a fat manila envelope. I thought I heard him hum 'If I Was A Rich Man'. He had started drinking early.

'A small party, you said. You promised. You lied to me.' I was laughing now, looking at the people still streaming in.

'Your wedding party, right? You cannot have wedding without party, or what is point?' asked Tolya, half in English, half in Russian, as he pulled a magnum of Krug from a passing waiter and poured some into my glass. I drank. He poured. Maxine looked at the champagne and Tolya took the flowers from her and set them on a chair and offered her a glass.

Anatoly Sverdloff had grown up, in Moscow,

50

like me, but we met in New York, what was it, ten years ago? In his white linen suit and green silk shirt, Tolya was six-six, three hundred pounds, big as a mountain, and as solid. His white Gucci loafers had been made of alligator or some other dead animal, eighteen-carat-gold buckles on them.

He saw Maxine gaze at the shoes, and a grin spread across the face that, square and dimpled, resembled an Easter Island statue. He pushed the shock of dark hair off his forehead. From his pocket he extracted a gold cigar case engraved with a cigar, a big ruby for the burning tip glittering; he snapped it open and took out a Cohiba and put it in his mouth, then lit it with a quarter pound of solid gold lighter. The smell was delicious.

In his element, Tolya talked to us, keeping an eye on the waiters and caterers, waving at guests, ringmaster, impresario, godfather. Half of me expected him to offer favors to his friends on the occasion of my wedding, but then I'd seen *The Godfather* too many times, usually over a lot of booze with Tolya.

'Tolya?'

'Yes, Artyom?' Tolya said, using my Russian nickname, practically the only person I still knew who did. I'd been in New York so long I wasn't sure how many people, friends, people I worked with on the job, even knew I was born in Russia. It was another life. It had faded. I was a New Yorker, an American.

'Who are all these people?' I said. 'I mean the ones I don't know?'

'Your friends, my friends, friends of people, people we should be friends with. I plan to be King of New York,' he said and burst out laughing. 'Maxine, darling, are you OK? Is there anything at all that you want? Tell me, just ask.' He suddenly slipped into perfect English.

Tolya Sverdloff had been a language student in Moscow in the late '70s; he spoke five languages, six if you counted Ukrainian. With me he switched between English and Russian without thinking. Sometimes, when he was drunk or pissed off, he talked the English of an immigrant Russian, dropping articles, mixing them up so he sounded like an uneducated hood. He also did it to mock me, too, because, as he had said more than once, 'You are so American Artyom, nothing Russian left in you, not one thing, nothing at all.'

He kissed me on both cheeks now. He was drunk. I was catching up.

I said to Tolya, 'Where's your girlfriend?'

He shrugged.

'You think I don't know why you bought this building?' I added and followed his gaze towards the small woman with a wedge of black hair over her forehead, a red mouth and a sullen expression. She was wearing dark Japanese clothes that looked wrinkled, and flat shoes that looked like they were made out of rubber. I couldn't remember her name.

In Russian, Tolya swore at me, but he watched the woman as she wandered through the crowd running her hands along the walls as if testing the structural value. She was an architect Tolya had fallen for a couple of years earlier; I didn't get it; normally, he liked models, he liked strippers, he liked babes, and he liked them young and gorgeous.

'She makes me smart,' he said and added that while he pursued her, the building was good for parties, and convenient to the river which he loved, and where, downtown near the Financial Center, he kept a large boat.

'Come,' he said. 'Come. Both of you.' He held out his hand to Maxine.

★ ★ ★

Near the window, Tolya gestured with both arms at the city. From up here, he said, he could keep an eye on the real estate, the new buildings going up, the glass towers in the West Village, the famous new structures by famous old architects that would change the city skyline. He pointed out buildings that he said he already owned, including a squat warehouse across the street, the letters on its side proclaiming it to be the purveyor of the finest meats in America.

'I am in love with old buildings,' Tolya added. 'I like to buy everything. You should buy something,' he said to me now.

'What with?'

'I help,' he said.

I said leave the money to me in your will. He laughed.

'You're older than me, you bastard,' he said. 'You'll die before me. You'll be fifty before me.'

'Yeah, by three measly years.'

'Four,' he said. 'And coming soon.'

Maxine watched Tolya. She had kissed him eagerly when he gave her the flowers, then drawn back, wary, worried she had been too effusive; like a little girl she was uncertain. Odd, because she was more of a grown-up then I ever was. She looked a lot younger, but she was thirty-eight, a single mother with two children who were almost teenagers; she was good at her job; she didn't take a lot of crap from people.

At her job in the forensics lab where she worked, she had seen more than anyone should ever have to on and after 9/11. She saw the bodies, but also the body parts. She had waited for pieces of her own husband, but nothing ever turned up.

Still, now, in front of Tolya she was shy, girlish, almost timid.

Max had always been unsure about him because she thought he felt that she didn't measure up to Lily Hanes. She felt Tolya had wanted me to marry Lily.

Lily was gone, though. Not part of my life anymore. Tolya leaned down and kissed Maxine again, and grinned, and moved back into the crowd.

'What did Tolya give you?' she said.

I looked at the envelope still in my hand. 'God knows,' I said.

'Open it.'

'Here?'

'Sure,' Maxine said. 'Don't you want to look?'

I said, 'I'm scared maybe he gave us money, I mean like those mafia weddings where they give

54

money for the little silk purse, and I wouldn't know what to do, keep it, give it back?'

Maxie said, 'You've had a lot of champagne, honey. Anyway they give the girl the money for the purse, she holds the silk purse. Also you've seen way too many movies. Open it.'

I opened it. There were two tickets to Paris, first class, a note from Tolya and keys to an apartment he had and a picture of it. I looked at the dates on the tickets, but they were open and good any time. Maxine took them from me and stared at them.

'My God,' she said. 'Is it OK to take it?'

'Do you want to?'

'Sure I do.' She sounded hesitant.

'What is it? Come on, tell me.'

'I've never been out of the country.'

'What do you mean?'

'I didn't tell you because it didn't come up and I didn't want you to think I was some kind of hick, and me and Mark, we talked about maybe going to Canada, or even Ireland some time, but it never happened.' Shyly, she added, 'I finally got a passport last spring, though.'

'Yeah? How come?'

'I got it when I thought maybe we, me and you, we'd go someplace together.'

'Where did you have in mind?' I said. 'Where would you like to go?'

'I don't know. Russia. Israel. Some place connected with you, or some place you lived, or something. Shit. Never mind.' She blushed.

'But Paris will be OK?'

'Shut up.' She kissed me. 'We could go if you

can get the time,' she said. 'We could do it. Couldn't we, Artie? Our next vacation. The girls could stay with my mom or something.'

'We'll go for sure,' I said, and added, 'I can see your mother is waving at you so crazy she looks like she missed her bus. On the other side of the room near the bar.'

Max said, 'Am I OK? I'm not wrinkled or anything?'

'I think you look gorgeous. I can't figure out why the hell you married me, but I'm not asking, and you look really great.'

'But not wrinkled.'

'Not wrinkled. I love the dress. The orchid didn't wilt, your hair is perfect, your mascara isn't running, even though you cried in front of the judge, and I love you.'

'I did not cry,' she said.

'OK, allergies.'

'So I better go inside and deal with my mom, and my nana who looks like she's going to fall down, I mean she's eighty-five and she's pretty good, but she likes a few drinks, you know. Honey?'

'What?'

'My mom's fine about us coming down to the shore, there's plenty of space. I'll take the kids tomorrow or the day after, OK, and then you can come and meet us Thursday, right? You'll come though, right, like we planned? I mean you'll come to Jersey, won't you? They want that, the girls. So do I. Artie?'

She went on making plans, arranging domestic details. I realized I had stopped listening.

'Look, I better get over to my family, before my mom and my nan and my ex-mother-in-law kill each other with kindness, like they say,' she said, and glanced out of the window. 'You know, my grandpa sold eggs down around here some place. He was an egg man, you know? I don't remember him real well at all, but I remember the eggs, so many of them in one place.'

I watched her go and realized I was still holding the envelope Tolya had given me. There was a box in it that contained a watch, thin as a dime, on a black strap, one like Tolya wore that I'd admired. I put it on.

I thought how lucky I was, lucky to make it to New York, lucky to get Maxine, lucky to have friends, as lucky as the guy with the winning lottery ticket. I could have been a cop in Moscow taking petty bribes to put food on the table, but I was here, in New York City. I went to thank Tolya for the watch.

'To you, Artyom,' he said and drank some of the champagne in his glass.

'I love the watch. Thank you. It's the most beautiful thing I've ever seen.'

'More beautiful than me?'

'Yes.'

He held out his arm. 'Same like mine. This makes us brothers.'

'We already are,' I said, and thought if you lived long enough, and like me you had no kids of your own, your parents dead or dying, like my mother who had Alzheimer's, what you had were friends.

'You're thinking of your mother?' Tolya asked

and I nodded. He knew. His own mother had died a few months earlier.

'I am planning to drink much much more,' he added. 'Please help me.'

'Yes,' I said and raised my glass.

We drank.

'I see you looking distracted at your own wedding, I know you're on a case. What? You need help?'

I thought about Sid McKay. It wasn't a case.

'I'm good,' I said.

★ ★ ★

Tolya went to greet some guy who had just arrived. I felt someone hovering. When I turned around, Sonny Lippert was standing near me, holding a square box.

I wanted to ask him about Sid. Sonny knew everyone in New York, but the box was an offering and I kept my mouth shut about Sid, at least for now.

I said, 'Thanks Sonny, that's really nice. You want me to get Maxine so we can open it together?'

He shook his head. 'No, man, it's for you. OK?'

Sonny Lippert, who I worked for a lot of the time, was small and tightly-wound, his hair still dark like a tight cap over his head; I figured he probably dyed it. Sonny was around sixty now. He'd been a cop, had risen up through the ranks, gone to law school, moved over to the federal prosecutor's office, worked as a US attorney. He

58

was driven. He was ambitious. I never knew exactly what he would do to win, to get what he wanted.

A while back he had started up a child abuse unit that almost killed him. The revelations of what people did to children were too much, and by the time he had a heart attack in May he was up to a bottle of Scotch a day.

A glass in one hand now, he stood awkwardly while I held the gift.

Sonny suddenly started coughing. He shoved his glass at me. I took it. He had worked at Ground Zero right after the attack, some of the time without a mask. I waited while he turned away, head down, and coughed the wracking sick cough.

People said, OK, enough with 9/11, enough. They said give it a break, stop talking about it, get over it. There's other stuff now, they said.

It wasn't over, though. In New York, it was part of the language. People looked up on a beautiful morning and said, 'It's a 9/11 day.' The Republicans were in town to exploit it, like all politicians. It was fixed. 9/11 was like a point on a compass where the needle got stuck; it vibrated constantly, but never moved.

'You OK?' I said.

'Yeah, sure. And stop looking at my drink.'

He was supposed to stay off the booze, but I wasn't his keeper. I gave him back his glass.

'You ever hear of a guy named Sidney McKay, Sonny?'

'Yeah, sure, everyone knew McKay, wasn't he the city editor at the *Times* once, something like

59

that? He worked for some of the other papers, TV, did books, a black guy, right? He still alive?'

'Yeah, why wouldn't he be?'

'I don't know why I said that, yeah, I don't know, man. Something. Some kind of trouble. So open the fucking box, man,' Sonny added. 'I need to sit down.'

We sat on a couple of chairs. Sipping the drink, Sonny waited while I unwrapped the gift. His eyes never left me as I opened the box, pulled out some tissue paper and then lifted out a Lucite cube.

'Fuck, Sonny, I mean, I don't know what to say.'

'It's OK. You don't need to get all fucking teary-eyed, man,' he said and drank a little of his Scotch. 'I wanted you to have it. You'll be around after I'm dead and I couldn't trust anyone else with it.'

I held up the Lucite cube and turned it around so I could see the baseball suspended inside. Signed by Jackie Robinson, it was a ball Robinson actually hit during the first season he played for the Brooklyn Dodgers, the first black man in major league baseball. He was Sonny Lippert's childhood idol. He had showed the ball to me a million times in his office, talking with a kind of religious fervor about the Brooklyn Dodgers and Robinson.

When Sonny split up with his wife Jennifer and moved into an apartment by himself, all he brought were his books and the baseball. Lately he'd been drifting backwards into his childhood more and more, talking about Brooklyn when he was a boy. I was pretty amazed that Sonny would give me the ball.

I said thank you and reached for his arm, and patted it because I didn't know what else to do, and he looked uncomfortable, but pleased.

'Yeah, OK, so I'm glad you like it,' he said and changed the subject. 'You believe people living in this fucking Meat District over here? I had an uncle named Stanley who was in tongues, you know that? He made tongues here, I ever tell you how they make a tongue, man? They used to take these shrivelled tongues and they pumped them up with water so they were four times the size of a normal animal tongue, and they sold them like that. I worked summers at the tongue plant. We used to pump them full of water, all the tongues. Listen, man, your lady's waving at you. I like her, Artie. Did I tell you? She's good, your Maxine. I need a drink.'

★   ★   ★

Old Maxine — Max had been named after her grandmother — was sitting on a chair, her face red, looking as thin and glazed as a piece of wax paper.

'She had a few too many,' Max whispered. 'I'm going to take her downstairs. We have a car waiting to take her home.'

'I'll go,' I said.

'Thanks, Artie.'

We rode the elevator silently, me propping up old Maxine, her concentrating on staying upright.

61

In the street, I found the car and driver, a shabby beige Towncar, and I helped her in and gave the driver some extra money. Then I tried Sid on my cellphone.

I stayed out on the street, watching people parade up and down the streets of the Meat District, preening, looking for action and waited for Sid to call me back. He wasn't a guy who panicked. He had covered war zones and race riots. He was plenty tough and I didn't get why he was so scared.

I tried calling a friend from a station house out in Brooklyn, but he was in midtown overseeing barricades going up around Madison Square Garden, then I got through to someone else; he put me on hold. I waited a couple more minutes, and then Maxine came out of the building. I closed up my phone.

'Hi.'

'I got worried about my grandma,' she said.

'She was fine. I put her in the car. I was just thinking. Come on, let's go back up.'

There was a crack of thunder, and a brief flash of lightning over towards New Jersey, but instinctively Maxine turned her head south. It was almost three years, but sudden noises in the city made her look south.

'It's just thunder,' I said. 'Maybe I should go AWOL, honey, and come out to the shore with you tomorrow. I could find someone to cover for me. I could try.'

'You can't do that. We'll be fine. You'll meet us, and anyway we could use the overtime. You'll come out in a few days like we planned,' she said. 'I know. I still get jumpy when I hear something. We all fake being OK, and then you hear something. I know girls I work with who drink now who never had a drink before 9/11. I think about stuff and I think, I can't do it again, Artie. That's what scares me, that I don't have anything left if it happens again, I figured that out during the blackout last summer, that I couldn't go through it again.'

★　★　★

August 14, the summer before, we were originally supposed to get married, me and Maxine. The day before we planned it, the city went dark. The lights went out.

Maxine was stuck at work downtown, the girls were with her mother in Jersey. My car was in the shop and I was on the subway, sweating.

That afternoon, getting ready to go home and get ready for our wedding the next morning, the electricity goes and I'm trapped. People around me get edgy first, then frightened; panic sets in. We wait in the dark and the heat. I start talking to the crowd, telling them it's OK. I talk to them through the dark crowded train. Afterwards, I help people out of the car and along the narrow path in the low black tunnel and up metal stairs on to the street. I do it because I'm a cop and I have to do it; they cling to me. I feel their sweaty hands.

It's dark by the time I start home on foot, no lights, the streets jammed with people, some of them, people who missed trains, lugging

63

suitcases. Everyone mills around, yelling into cellphones, gathering near yellow cabs that pull over to the curb.

Dozens of cabs everywhere, their radios turned up loud, have become mobile communications centers. Parked everywhere, the drivers lean out of their windows and pass news along to people who listen intently, convinced at first that it's terrorists. The next big attack, we all think; the one everybody's been waiting for. I look up. I look for a plane.

'Holy shit!'

I say it out loud: holy shit. It was the first thing we heard, the first piece of TV footage when the plane hit the Trade Center, before the ball of fire. Holy shit! This time it's only a blackout. A summer storm, power outage, a cascade. Whatever; just a fluke.

I get home that night thinking about my first blackout in the city. 1977 was my first year in New York. I'm uptown near Columbia, people crowding around the university, everywhere the sounds of breaking glass and screaming and sirens. Feral kids roam the streets, looting stores. I see a man hump a TV set out of a store window; another carries five radios.

I have applied to the Academy; I want to be a cop, I want New York. But that night I wonder, for the only time, if I should have gone somewhere safe and bland, Australia, Canada.

A girl walking by takes me by the hand and we go up on the roof of her building and there are maybe twenty other people, students mostly. I spend the night there on a blanket next to the girl whose name I never learn. When I wake up, I see the others, on blankets, plastic deck chairs, sleeping bags. Their faces are young and sweet in the early light. I look out over the city and watch the sun come up. I'm hooked.

5

All night long, through a kind of boozy haze, I kept thinking: who are all these people? The party swelled up with them, some I recognized, others seemed familiar as if from another life. By midnight, it was crowded and chaotic, and I loved it.

'You collect people, Artie,' Lily Hanes had once said to me. 'You are a wanton collector of friends. Women, but not just women. Promiscuous,' she said, laughing. 'It makes you feel secure, having so many friends and you do things for them, and you ask them for favors and there's always a trade off, isn't there, but you know that, don't you?' I remembered her saying it now, and then someone tugged at my sleeve; it was Millie Crabbe, and I turned to talk to her, and thought to myself: It's your wedding, let it all go!

'Artie! Artie, hi! Artemy.'

More people. People speaking English. Russian. People I knew from Brighton Beach, and their children, little kids, kids in their teens who trailed out on the terrace for cigarettes, Millie and Maria, following the bigger girls and looking awestruck by the attention they got. In a pack, they moved outdoors and their laughter seemed to linger in their wake.

The laughter grew. There was a rise in the voices, and the heat from the crowd and the

66

band playing something Brazilian. I was hazy with wine and trying not to think about Sid when I heard a familiar voice.

Ricky Tae.

It was Ricky, wearing a perfect black summer suit, incredibly handsome, smooth and lean, now in his late thirties. He lived upstairs from me. His parents had owned the building, they had helped me buy my loft. We had been close, Ricky and I, but we had somehow drifted apart. He was always on and off planes, always doing business in Asia. I hugged him. I missed him.

'You got married,' he said. 'You really did it.' He handed me a package wrapped in red paper. 'From the parents,' he added. 'My pop was too sick to come and my mother won't leave him. My mother was miserable, though, not being here.'

'I know. I talked to her. Listen, I didn't ask anyone to the ceremony, you know, no one, it's how Maxine wanted it.'

'Darling, I know that,' he said. 'Lot of people here,' he added, scanning the room.

'Yeah, it's great.'

Rick hesitated.

'By the way, is Sid McKay coming?' he finally asked.

I was startled. 'Why?'

'I'm just asking. You're friends with Sid, aren't you? Pretty good friends. I thought he'd come to your wedding. I just thought you'd have asked him. Or maybe your Russian pal, Sverdloff, doesn't like aging faggots.'

'What's with you? Sure I asked Sid. He said he

67

didn't feel like coming into the city. Of course I asked him. I didn't even know Sid was a friend of yours anyhow,' I said.

'I'm sorry. I'm a little bit drunk.'

'So you know Sid?'

'You introduced us.'

'What? When? I don't remember that.'

'Forget it,' Rick said.

I leaned closer to him.

'Listen to me. I saw Sid this morning. He called me, he was worried, there was a guy who died off Red Hook, you know anything about it?'

'No,' Rick said, making to move away. 'How would I know? I need a drink. Talk to my sister, she came all the way from Hong Kong just for you.'

★ ★ ★

'Darling, Artie. Congratulations!'

Her face near mine, her hand on my arm, the heavy sexy smell of Joy that she had always worn clung to Dawn Tae.

'Dawn.'

'Hello, Artie.'

We kissed and then she drew back slightly and I saw how much she had aged. The incredible girl I'd once known was now a middle-aged woman. She glanced around and a waiter appeared with her drink. Dawn was still imperious, a commanding presence. People noticed when she wanted something. She kissed me again.

68

I smiled at her. 'Hello, Dawn, I can't believe you made it!'

'I came back for this,' she added, keeping hold of my hand. 'And the parents. And I thought Rick needed cheering up. There he is,' she said, gesturing towards the bar where Ricky was standing.

'Is Ricky happy?' Dawn said. 'He doesn't talk to me about his life anymore. I feel he's so solitary, so obsessed with work. Is he seeing anyone? Does he have anyone? Is there a guy in his life at all?'

'He doesn't talk to me much, either,' I said. 'How are you?'

'I'm fine,' she said. 'I'm, well, I am what you see,' she added, her tone wry now.

When she married a rich guy who turned out to be an asshole who abused her, Dawn had been an exquisite ambitious girl, a brilliant trader on Wall Street. The creep she had married dealt in illegal immigrants and baby sales, and drugs on a global scale, including Hot Poppy, the worst junk that ever got into the system; Dawn got hooked on it. It was years before anyone picked him up and even then he got off on appeal. I never really felt easy about him being out on the streets.

I had been crazy about Dawn right from the beginning when I first moved into my loft and sometimes we sat out on the fire escape and fooled around. By the time we had a desperate fling in Hong Kong she was strung out on drugs. She got clean, settled over there, quit her job as a high-powered trader, and bought a house up on a hill looking out over the water where she raised her adopted kids.

Dawn was probably in her forties but she looked older now: she was stocky and her face was thicker than I remembered and there was gray in her hair. She wore a plain gray silk suit, very severe, very expensive, and flat shoes and big diamonds in her ears. Only her eyes looked like the girl I knew. But I could still smell the Joy she had always worn, that drove me crazy the first time I smelled it at her own wedding. Long long time.

She said, 'I'm just like some old Chinese lady now, don't you think? I look at myself in the mirror, I see my Auntie Petal.'

'You had an aunt named Petal?'

'Yeah, they ran out of flowers. It was a fashion, you know, Chinese girls, little flowers, flower drum song, fuck that shit,' Dawn added. 'They were already into weather and stuff when I came along. Dawn. I'm lucky it wasn't dusk, you know? Or evening. I could have been called Evening. I've had too much champagne.'

She saw me looking at her, and she said, 'It's OK, I have a mirror, you know? And I don't care anymore. I really don't care. I don't have to worry about getting old. It's a relief.'

'You look great. You always look great.'

'Give me a cigarette, Artie, honey, You're such a liar, and so am I. Actually, it depends. Some days I'm glad it's over, sex, men, business. I take care of the kids, I hardly ever go shopping, I read a lot, I listen to music. I've fallen in love with opera, weird considering what a rock chick I

70

always wanted to be. So I'm OK. It's just when I see old friends, when I see you, I hate the way I look, but what the hell, let's get drunk.' She looked around. 'Where's a waiter? You know, my Auntie Petal always said everything starts and ends at weddings, maybe it got to Ricky, you getting married, maybe he feels left out, maybe he feels he'll never find anyone, and he never will, you know, because he can't let anyone get close, no man, no woman,' she said. 'I should talk. Go celebrate.'

'Let's have lunch soon. Just us,' I said.

'Yes. Of course.'

'Dawn?'

'Yes?'

'Did you ever know a guy named Sid McKay? Back when? Someone we all knew, maybe, something like that?'

She glanced at her brother. 'Yeah, I remember him. He was twice Ricky's age. What about him?' Her tone was sour.

'Were they close?'

Dawn shrugged, and said, 'I don't really know. Why?'

'Never mind,' I said, and kissed her and then she stood back from me, straightening her jacket, and looking at someone behind me.

'Look who's here.'

★ ★ ★

'Jack?'

I was pretty surprised that Jack Santiago had come to the party and I didn't know who had

71

invited him, but I was glad to see him. The place was still crowded, but people had settled into groups, at tables, eating, on the terraces, smoking, flirting, the little kids cross-legged on the floor, a few already asleep.

'Hey, man, congratulations,' he said, shaking my hand with both of his, pumping my arm.

'Thanks for coming, Jack.'

He was medium height and wiry. He had probably been a skinny ugly kid, but he had turned his looks into a style. He looked like he went to the gym. He wore a soul patch on his chin, the black eyes glittered out of the narrow face. He had a good haircut; expensive, I thought. He wore a hip pinstriped suit, a dark blue shirt, no tie.

Jack could really write. He was a reporter who had won a Pulitzer for his work in Moscow during the collapse of Communism. He knew everyone in the city and when I was single I used to run into him in bars sometimes. He liked knowing cops. He reminisced about Sonny Grasso. He liked retailing other stuff he knew, movie gossip, mafia lore, choice pieces of city life that he fed to his audience at a bar or restaurant — where John Gotti's parents lived off Houston Street, who had done liquor deals with Frank Costello in the old days, which store on Grand Street Tom Cruise bought a suit at when he was filming in New York, which Klimov made money on gas scams in Brighton Beach. Jack knew where to drink, he knew the bartenders, the club owners, the guys at the door. He always had great-looking women.

He leaned in towards you when he talked and energy flowed out of Jack. He shook my hand some more and gave me a guy hug, and he listened to what I was saying even though it was probably just social stuff, how are you, where you going on vacation, joking about the city, the politicians.

Jack kept those hot coals he had for eyes right on me; it was the thing they talked about when anyone mentioned him, the way he gave eye-lock, the way he made you feel you were the most important person on earth; Clinton had it, people said, Jackie Kennedy, too. I once heard somebody say, 'Men want to be Jack, and women want to fuck him.'

He scanned the room for people he knew.

'You need a drink?' I said.

He held up the empty glass in his hand. 'I will, thanks. Good party, Art, really nice.'

I suddenly saw that Jack was loaded.

'So congratulations again,' he said, 'And hey, sorry I got here so late. Took me a while.'

I remembered that Jack had lived somewhere downtown, not far from me.

'You still in SoHo?'

'SoHo's so over,' he said. 'I'm out in Brooklyn now by the water. But where's the bride? I always liked Lily, man, always thought she was a seriously great woman, brains, looks.'

'Lily?'

'Didn't you marry Lily Hanes?'

'I married Maxine.'

'Holy Christ, am I an asshole or what, I only got a message by phone about the party today. I

73

never thought. Shit, I am sorry. Who's Maxine?'
'It's OK.'

'Yeah, well, good luck, either way, of course,' he said and then I saw he had spotted someone in the crowd and I knew he had been looking for a particular person all along. Jack moved off into the crowd and out on to the terrace. People stopped him, shook his hand, enlarged by meeting Jack Santiago.

I was heading for the bar nearest the terrace door a minute or two later when I heard someone yelling, 'Jack, stop it. Jack!' Over the music and the noise of voices, I heard someone else yell: 'Jack, get the fuck down.'

Outside, a group of people had gathered and they were staring up at Jack who was perched on the narrow stone wall that ran the whole length of the terrace. It was a six-story drop to the street. You fell, you'd break your bones and probably your neck. But Jack was up there, grinning, strolling along the wall that wasn't more than a foot wide, a bottle of champagne in one hand, a glass in the other. He waved at the crowd. He was showing off, letting everyone see how cool he was. He didn't look down.

'Get the fuck off there,' someone said again, and I didn't say anything, just stood and watched him suck up the attention like a magnet.

★ ★ ★

The girl on the terrace was six feet tall, maybe more, as tall as me, and stunning.

'I'm Valentina,' she said and kissed me on the cheek.

I'd only met Tolya's daughter a few times when she was much younger and living near Miami with her twin sister and her mother who was Tolya's ex. She was nineteen now and incredibly lovely. She wore a plain short black dress, and backless heels that snapped when she walked.

'I'm really happy to meet you again, Artie,' she said. 'I'm happy for your getting married,' she added, running her hand through her platinum crew cut.

One of Val's fingers was missing. It had happened when she was a little girl still in Moscow. She had been kidnapped and held for ransom. Tolya had wanted her to have it fixed. He had offered her plastic surgery. She refused and told him it was a badge for her. You looked at her, and your eyes went to the missing finger, but it was the imperfection that made the rest of her more dazzling.

Val's face, the cheekbones, the blue eyes, the wide mouth, was Russian; her accent was purest American, bland, featureless, suburban. She had lived in Florida since her early teens. I stood on the terrace, halfway between Val and Jack Santiago and I realized now that he was performing for her.

Glancing up at him, she was apparently unconcerned that he was still walking along the wall, drinking alternately out of the bottle and his glass. She ignored him and took my hand, and kissed my cheeks again.

'I know we sort of met when I was a kid, Artie,

75

but now I'm living here in New York, and I love it,' Val said. 'I mean all the bars and stuff over here in the Meat District and meeting you,' she added in a rush of teenage enthusiasm. 'I mean my pop talks about you all the time, of course, and so I just wanted to get to know you, you know? I've like had a crush on you from a distance.' She smiled, and I fell for her, of course, because who wouldn't, and then realized she could be my kid. She was Tolya's kid. I felt old.

'I'm glad you're here, Val, I really am,' I said when the crowd on the terrace suddenly went silent. I looked up.

On the wall, Jack stumbled. Everyone gasped except for Val who didn't flinch. Then, grinning, Jack jumped down and made a beeline for us; for her.

'You're an idiot,' she said.

It wasn't an accident that they were both here; she had invited him, or he had known she was coming. She towered over Jack and he was twenty years older, but it was electric. I had never seen that kind of electricity between two people. He took her hand and you expected to see visible sparks, and they went inside to dance, wrapped around each other.

'You know this asshole Santiago?' Tolya's voice was full of booze and anger.

'He's OK. He's a journalist. He's good.'

'What at? This prick is good at *what* exactly?'

'He's a good writer,' I said.

'You invited him?'

I shook my head. 'Maybe he came with someone,' I said. 'Maybe with Val. Valentina's been going out with him?'

'She doesn't tell me. She's nineteen, she had a place at Harvard, but she wants to be a model. She goes out to clubs all night until next morning, all night, Artyom, with men.'

'That's what she should be doing. She's a girl.'

'I don't like him,' he said coldly. 'I don't want. You understand? This doesn't work for me.'

'Let it go,' I said. 'You could dance with me if you want.'

It made him smile, and then I said, as casually as I could, 'So have you heard from her?'

'Who?' he said.

'You know who.' I tapped a waiter on the shoulder and asked him to get me a drink. 'Scotch,' I said.

'She's in New York,' he said. 'You knew she came back, I told you.'

'I didn't know she stayed. You said she came back, but that was a year ago, more than a year. Is she here? For good?'

He was silent.

It was the elephant in the room, the eight hundred pound gorilla, but I had refused to see it, or notice, and now I had crashed into it. Jack Santiago thought that I'd married Lily.

I had tried not to think about her. She had gone away. After 9/11, she left me and New York and got married and went to London. For a while, I felt like I couldn't breathe, like someone stepped on my oxygen.

It was almost three years since Lily, sick of what she saw as relentless patriotism that both bored and scared her to death, found someone to marry and take her away. And I felt dead. For a year, I felt dead. But that was all over, and even thinking about Lily felt like a betrayal. She was out of my life.

I saw that Tolya was only half listening to me, focused on Jack and Val.

'Let it go, OK? Let them be.'

'OK,' he said. 'OK. So go dance with Maxine, Artyom. Dance with her.'

★ ★ ★

It was getting late. I opened my phone and found another message from Sid, and called my machine and found two more, the last one left around eleven, more stuff about the dead guy near the docks, Maxine was waiting for me.

'Dance with her,' Tolya said, this time in Russian.

So Maxine and I walked out to the middle of the floor and the piano player called out to ask us what we wanted him to play and I said to Maxie, you choose, and she called over to the piano player and asked for 'I Love You Just the Way You Are'.

The trio began to play. Max was a really good dancer and had taught me some steps, and we began to dance, and I concentrated hard.

'Am I singing?' I said in Maxine's ear.

'Yes,' she whispered, smiling into my face, and I smiled and kissed her all over, eyes, mouth, ears, everywhere, and for a while I almost forgot everything else.

6

I have something to tell you, Sid McKay said softly, haltingly, on the phone the Monday morning after my wedding. I need to tell you this, I need you to know just in case. I need to see you. I lied before. I lied when I saw you yesterday morning. I did call it in, it was me. I called the cops.

I told Sid to talk to the detective on the case, and he said, it isn't simple, Artie, please.

Go, Maxine said sleepily. We had gone to sleep around four, and she barely opened her eyes when the phone rang. Go, you won't feel good unless you go, she said, and turned over, still smiling, and went back to sleep.

'I knew him,' Sid said as soon as I got to him at his place in Red Hook.

'Who was he?' I said. 'In case of what? You said 'in case' on the phone. In case of what?'

'Please sit down.'

I leaned against the desk near the window that overlooked the water.

'I thought you said you were getting out of here yesterday?' I said.

He didn't answer me.

'Sid, please, talk to me. I can't keep coming back. I'm working this week and then I'm going on vacation. Honeymoon. I want to give you some phone numbers. Two. Two people. Here, look, one's a good cop, you'll like him, he has a

PhD in English. And you can trust him.' I dug in my jeans for a scrap of paper and held it out. 'The other one, you use for emergencies. Big time stuff. OK? Sid? You hear me?' I wasn't sure if he was paying attention. He seemed to drift away.

Sid took the scrap of paper, put it on the desk without looking at it, and said, 'Thank you.' He sat down in a low armchair and gestured to another one next to it. 'How was the wedding? I'm sorry I couldn't make it. I sent you something,' he added. 'I put it in the mail.'

'Who was he?'

'I'm sorry?' Sid raised his hand to smooth his hair, looked at it, then put it back on the arm of his chair. 'Thank you for coming, Artie. Would you like me to turn the air on? I usually keep just the windows open at night, but it's getting warm,' he said formally, as if I'd come for a business meeting.

'You called me. You said you knew who the dead guy was. You said you called the cops. I came. I need you to talk to me.'

'Yes,' Sid said. 'I'll get us something to drink,' he added and got up heavily and went to the little kitchen. 'Juice?'

The floor creaked as Sid moved across boards laid down a hundred years earlier.

I was tired. I was sorry for Sid, but I was running out of patience. I walked across the room to the table where there were pictures in neat rows, pictures of Sid, pictures of friends and relatives, and of Sid with famous people. He had been important, a player, a guy who knew

80

people, and now he had retreated to this warehouse on the edge of the world.

'Juice, Art? Coffee? Beer?'

'Coffee's fine,' I called back, still looking at the photographs.

I picked one up. In it Sid stood alongside a young man, black haired, wearing a red silk Chinese jacket and grinning into the camera. It was Ricky Tae. Rick looking very young.

Rick had talked about Sid the night before at my wedding. Is Sid coming? You introduced us. Sid was twice his age, Dawn Tae said.

I put the photograph back, turned around and went back to where Sid was waiting, a mug of coffee for me, tea for himself.

I didn't mention the picture of Rick.

I took the coffee, drank a little, sat on the edge of the desk and said, 'When you called me this morning, you said that you knew who the dead man was. You want to talk about that? I can't keep asking.'

He looked out of the window.

'If you want to talk, Sid, talk. Or I can call the guy who's already running this case, or you can use the phone number I gave you when you're ready, or I'll just leave it alone, but make up your mind. I owe you. I know that. I don't want to drop you in any shit, but please, give me a break.'

'I'm sorry.' He picked up his own mug, and removed the teabag.

'Did you know who he was before he was murdered? The homeless guy, the guy you said asked you for money? You recognized him?'

'I suspected. You knew that.'

'Yes. Is this still a case of some Russian hood killing him in your place, or is that idea up for grabs, too. Does he have a name? Did he?'

Sid sipped his tea. 'Could be.'

'Could be? You're telling me the facts are somehow relative, or that they change depending on the way you see them?'

'Often,' he said. 'I saw you looking at my picture of Ricky Tae. You introduced us, you know.' He smiled. 'You brought him along to a party all those years ago, it was you who introduced us.'

'I went to a lot of parties.'

'You don't remember,' Sid said.

'You have his picture because we were all at a party together once?' I put down the mug and got up.

'Something like that.'

It was like wading through a swamp, but I knew Sid would shut up if I pushed him too hard, shut up or trip in the tangle of his own memories and drown.

I said, gently as I could, 'Do you want to tell me anything else about it, the dead guy, the reason you knew him, who he was?'

'I'll tell you about the dead man. I owe you that. I called you. Maybe I'm just getting old, thinking about my own death. Perhaps I made a mistake,' he said. 'Maybe I should get some sleep.'

'I don't think you make mistakes like that, you know.' I got up. 'I don't think you need sleep and I don't think you're senile. OK? Sid?'

'Give me a cigarette, would you?' he hesitated and the room was heavy with his indecision, and I tossed him the pack.

I saw his hand was trembling and he was watching me, making a judgment, sizing me up, waiting until he had the smoke lit and the nicotine in his system.

He sat down again, then leaned forward, his elbows on his knees, face in his hands. He was going to talk.

I'd seen it before. People hesitated. They waited. They called you and called you again. They filled up time with useless talk, trying to get a fix on you, trying to decide what to say, what they could say, processing information. Sometimes they waited so long, you thought you'd go crazy or fall asleep. I had worked cases where I kept asking for cups of coffee just to keep the witnesses moving, just to keep myself from nodding off, keep my eyes open.

I was tense. Sweating. It was hot. From the river came the mournful hoot of a tug. Voices somewhere close by. People out all night coming home. A woman laughed, raucous, shrill. Then it was silent.

I waited.

★　★　★

'OK.'

Five minutes had passed when neither of us spoke, and then: 'OK.'

It was all he said at first but it broke the silence, and Sid's face, a strange dull ashy color, came to life a little. He got up, sat down, got up again, went into the kitchen, came back with a glass of beer, then sat again. He leaned forward, elbows on his knees, a cigarette in one hand, the glass in the other.

'You're wondering if I slept with Ricky Tae, aren't you?'

I smoked.

'It doesn't matter any more,' he said. 'That doesn't have anything to do with this. That's another story. There's always another story, Artie.' He reached over to his desk and picked up a Russian doll, elaborately painted with swirls of color and gold and silver paint; Sid started pulling it apart, removing the dolls inside, lining them up.

'Always more stories inside each other, like these Russian dollies,' Sid said. 'Did you have matrioshka like this when you were a child? Or is it just a cliché notion of Russia, the dolls, the hidden stories? Perhaps it's just that,' he said, half to himself.

I crushed out my cigarette and lit another one. I had never had wooden dolls and this, being here, waiting for Sid, gave me the creeps; it was like being in Russia itself where people told you stories instead of the truth or even the facts because they had lost the habit or couldn't tell the difference or, most of all, because they liked stories better.

I kept my voice even. 'Then tell me this story,' I said.

'The first McKay, Tobias, he was called, came to the US around the time of the Revolution. He was a free black man, he was a painter, he learned his trade in London in the 1770s and somehow he got here down through Halifax, I think, Nova Scotia, I mean, and worked in Boston and bought a newspaper in Massachusetts, then migrated down here to New York. We always worked in the newspaper business, on my father's side, but my father also made money. He liked money,' Sid said. 'I mean he liked being wealthy and he liked the actual feel of coin, do you understand?' Sid picked up his glass, examined the beer in it, then set it down again. 'He used to give me silver dollars for my birthday. He was a born businessman, and he knew that his being very light skinned made it possible. He could pass, you see. He could do business where other black men could not.'

Sid got up and went to the table and ran his hand down the line of photographs and picked them up, one at a time, inspecting the pictures of his family, then turned back to me.

'In my family color was everything. It was what mattered, you understand,' Sid said. 'There's a point to this, Artie. There is. I promise you. I loved coming out here to the docks when I was a kid. It was out of bounds. We lived in a big brownstone in Bed Stuy Gardens where there were whole streets of rich Negro families, and all this, the waterfront, was forbidden. My dad who owned newspapers also owned warehouses here near the docks. He passed. He did business here as a white man. You'd be surprised how many people got on by passing,' Sid said and paused.

'Go on.'

'He did business with Italian mobsters and Jewish gangsters and the Democratic machine, and the city of New York, which were the same thing, and then he went home to our house and was a proud Negro man. He said that of himself. His own language. Once, when I was little, he brought me to the waterfront, but people looked at him funny, what was he doing with a little black kid and after that it was forbidden. I wasn't allowed. But when I could I took my bike and came here alone. I need some water,' he said. 'You?'

'Sid?'

The beer finished, Sid went to the kitchen, got a glass of water, returned, sat down and drank it thirstily.

'Artie, there was a Soviet freighter that ran aground not far from here and it changed everything for me. It must have been late February 1953, just before Stalin died, a few weeks, not more, it came into the channel, the Ambrose Light wasn't working right, or the pilot who went on board and was supposed to guide the ship into the harbor was dead drunk, or the buoys, they were called Red Nuns, got screwed up and it was foggy as hell, but the ship ran aground.

'Do you remember? No, of course not, you weren't born, but then Stalin died, and there must have been terrible confusion, nobody knew what to do or who was in charge. It was quite a famous story. *Red Dawn*, the ship was called. Stuck on the coast of America. Stranded in an alien world while the Soviet Union rocked on its axis. It reminds me of Sergei Krikalyov. Do you remember? The Soviet cosmonaut who was up in space in 1991 when the USSR collapsed. He left his country and while he was away it disappeared and he went on stranded in space. It was like that in 1953.

'There wasn't any money to send the ship back, the USSR was in chaos. It was the height of the Red Scare. McCarthy times. People petrified of Communists. I knew kids who thought they had horns, Artie. There was a TV show on Friday nights. *I Led Three Lives*, it was called. The story of Richard Carlson, a brave American agent who went among the Commies, and I said to my dad, but they were smiling, Daddy, could they be Commies if they smiled? Wouldn't they have slanted eyes? I knew Catholic children who were made to pray for the souls of the little Commie children. People were terrified. Terrorized. And then this ship.' Sid got up restlessly, then sat down, crossed and uncrossed his legs.

'I remember people came out to stare at it,' he said. 'Normally they would have sent the ship back, but the papers weren't in order; this was the depth of the Cold War: the ship was quarantined. We could see sailors on deck staring back at us. I was mesmerized. I was fifteen years old. It went on for weeks. I heard someone took a boat out and sent up some food. Sometimes you could hear them singing on the ship. There were all kinds of rumors. Rumors about sailors jumping ship.

'It was only three or four hundred yards, easy to swim. Hard to remember, but there were no computers, of course, no cellphones, nothing. Eventually, the ship was sent home, but people said some of the Russian sailors were hiding around Red Hood. No one knew how many, rumors went wild, two, eight, ten of them. People wanted to help them; maybe they thought they could save a few guys from the Communist terror.

'I remember a kind of luncheonette where I would hang out and listen. I must have been a strange little Negro boy, tall, skinny and curious, and then someone pointed out two guys sitting in a booth in the back. Russians. They really had escaped. They loved the food, BLTs, grilled cheese sandwiches and fries.'

'Come on, Sid,' I said. 'Who was he? The dead guy?'

'Let me finish. I made friends with one sailor, he was only sixteen, and not much older than I was, and he said his name was Meler. Strange names they had. He said it stood for Marx Engels Lenin Electrification Revolution, poor old Meler, we laughed at his name. Everyone brought him food, he was a runty guy, almost stunted. He would have been very young during the War, probably never had enough to eat as a kid, he was so small. Everyone fed him, I remembered that. The ship was gone. Meler and the other guy disappeared, went to ground in Brooklyn. I spent years looking for him, or Meler. I was obsessed. I had to know what happened.'

'You found him?'

'Excuse me,' Sid said and got up and, limping more heavily now, went towards the bathroom.

★ ★ ★

'I first came to Red Hook because of it,' Sid said. 'Because of Meler. I thought he might have settled around here. I was going to write a book, will write it, it connects me with everything in my life. It became the whole point of my life, the language, the Russian thing, the romance of it. It was the reason I became a reporter, the reason I went to live in the former USSR for a while. All of it. I suppose it was the reason I was interested in you,' he said, and half smiled at me.

I said, 'Who was the man?'

'The sailor?'

'The dead man.'

'I saw the sailor a few times. Meler. You couldn't miss him. He was still a runt. Filled out, though. Stocky. Those dark blue eyes that were too big for the face and popped out at you, you couldn't miss them. Once I thought I saw him in one of the bars around here, and someone said they thought he had moved out to Brighton Beach. I thought I spotted him in the 1970s, I think, out in Brighton Beach. In a Russian video store.'

'You're sure?'

'No.'

'You looked for him after that?'

'For a while, but time passed, and I was in a different place, and I stopped looking. I suppose

89

I let him down. Maybe I let him down, but I
stopped looking.'

'Let's talk about the dead man. The man in
the inlet. The man whose death you called in
after you found the body. Isn't that it? You found
the body? You knew his name?'

'Earl,' Sid said. 'He was my cousin, or my half
brother. I was never sure, not at first.'

★ ★ ★

Sid made more coffee, but he kept talking now,
you couldn't stop him. I smoked and listened.

'When I was a child I was never sure who he
was; he might have been the illegitimate child of
an uncle, I thought. He found me somehow at
school one day and said we were related, and I
could see it, of course, even then. He lived out
near Coney Island. 'Nigger Town', they called it.
Under the boardwalk. People set up shacks and
lived there, they lived there full time, I mean,
they slept, washed, they cooked, they hung out
laundry on lines, whole communities of poor
black people,' Sid said. 'No one mentioned it, of
course, not in my house. People kept secrets in
that generation. Children were never told. No
one discussed it if there was anything that
seemed shameful, cancer, anything unconven-
tional. C, they said, if someone had cancer. They
whispered it like a curse. Shh, C. We had three
suicides in one generation and no one mentioned
it. Maybe I became a reporter because it was
supposed to be a job that was about the facts,
maybe even the truth, you know? In the

beginning that's what I thought. These days people just make it up, they manipulate it, you know? It's why I quit, why I left.' He was rambling again.

'So your cousin?'

'No.'

'What was he?'

'He was my half brother,' Sid said. 'I only found out many years later that when she was a girl, my mother had an affair with one of my dad's workers, a poor boy who delivered groceries. She was only sixteen. They wouldn't let her marry him. The child was put up for adoption, and no one ever said anything. Somehow Earl did find out and he found me, but he didn't speak about it. He made friends with me. It was with Earl that I spent my time hanging around Red Hook and the docks with the Russians who ate grilled cheese sandwiches.' Sid smiled.

'Earl was my idol. He was tough and funny and he wasn't afraid of anything, but he didn't have anything to lose, I guess. He would pick me up after school, and I gave him my bike and told my parents I lost it. I got a new one, a blue Schwinn, and we'd ride over to Red Hook, Earl and I, and sit and watch the ships and the longshoremen and the way they unloaded the huge freighters with cargo in the huge nets. We made friends with the Russian sailors, especially Meler. Then he disappeared and after that, Earl stopped showing up and I lost track of him. Maybe my parents found out. I don't know. I never asked. I couldn't tell my parents I'd been riding my bike to Red Hook, that I'd given my bike to Earl, they'd have killed me. I was frightened that somehow they'd punish him. You have no idea how rigid this society was where I grew up, there were rules for everything. There were pictures of Earl in our house, and once when I asked a cousin who was my age, she played dumb. Or was dumb. Mary Eleanor, she was a tiny girl with a freckled face and bobbed hair and patent leather pumps. She knew. I could see it on her mean face that she'd heard all about Earl, but she wouldn't tell. Our house was full of secrets. Secrets were only good for one thing, you know?' Sid hoisted himself out of his chair.

'What thing?'

'For betrayal.'

'Go on.'

'A few weeks ago, the first time I saw the homeless man, nothing registered. He was disfigured, his face was covered in sores, he was sick and drunk, he looked like a very old man and he was in rags. He stank. I saw him a few times after that, at a distance, and I always walked the other way. I asked around one or two of my neighbors, and they said he was harmless. He like to drink. Maybe he did some drugs if he could get them. He was harmless, but he scared me. He used to come after me asking for change, trying to get my attention, he'd just trot down the street following me, and I'd get away as fast as I could. The other day, Saturday, I saw him. I should have helped him.'

'I see.'

'You understand, don't you?'

'I think so.'

'It was Earl. It was him. That's why he looked at me so hard and why I felt that I was looking in a mirror. It's more than fifty years ago, Artie, but I knew. I betrayed him when we were kids by not telling anyone about him or helping him and I did it again, I betrayed him again. Yesterday morning, I went out early for coffee and I saw the body and I called 911 because I had a feeling it was him, and then later I got a look before they zipped up the body bag. Now it's over. Let someone know, Art, will you? Please. Make sure he gets buried right. I'll pay the bills. I'm sorry if I seemed to be calling in a favor from you, but I didn't know who the hell else to call.'

'How do you think he died?'

'I guess it was an accident,' Sid said. 'An accident that I let happen. I left him alone Saturday night, I didn't give him money, I didn't call anyone, I just walked away and then the next morning, he was dead, maybe booze, maybe drugs, maybe he slipped, or someone pushed him, but he was just a bum, a tramp, a homeless guy who got beat up and drowned,' he added.

'I thought you said someone got to him instead of you, some Russian thug. You changed your mind?'

'I was probably wrong about that,' Sid said 'Maybe I hoped it might give some meaning to the death, that it was intentional, but I was wrong. It wasn't anything, it didn't mean anything, just grief. I'll probably get out of town for a while now, go out to Long Island. I meant to go yesterday. I'll go today, I think. I think I will. I feel there's not much time left for me. I meant to go.'

'Why?'

Sid shook my hand, and I saw on his face a look of unbearable sadness.

'So long, Artie,' he said.

* * *

I went over to the place on Van Brunt Street where I'd dropped Sid the morning before and went in and sat at the counter and ordered some eggs and fries and toast. The guy behind the counter poured me some coffee and put a plate of food in front of me, and I ate it. I was hungry.

He was a good-looking kid, tight T-shirt, sleeves rolled up over big biceps, veins popping, a pack of cigarettes in one of the cuffs of the T like a guy from a fifties movie. He wore black jeans and blue sneakers.

I said, 'You know a guy named Sidney McKay?'

'Sure. I see Sid around a lot. He's a regular. Everyone around here likes him, he's like old-fashioned, you know, real courteous.' The kid had a southern accent.

'He ever meet anyone here?'

'What kind of anyone? You mean was he cruising people or what? Only one sticks out that I remember: a fat Russian. Like a man mountain, you know, maybe six-six, they came in together and sat over in the corner, and drank a lot of Martinis, and the Russian drank Scotch, too, and they were like this real odd couple, but

94

they were obviously like really into each other. You think they were an item?'

I thought about Tolya, and laughed. 'Friends,' I said.

'What about you?' he said, not really interested, just making conversation as he poured more coffee.

'I'm just a cop,' I said, and left, got in my car and cut across Red Hook, heading for the city.

★ ★ ★

On the way, I thought about Sid, about why he stayed out here. For a century, people had moved inland, away from the working docks, if they could, if they were aspirant or had money. When shipping moved out of Brooklyn, the docks were abandoned.

People were coming back; all over the city, people were buying into the waterfront, the last big land grab. The Hudson was clean; people sailed on the river; people swam around Manhattan; foreigners took wedding pictures at the old Fulton Ferry landing under the Williamsburg Bridge, squads of Chinese or Japanese in their big dresses and tuxedos with white limos and champagne, posing, giggling, the river behind them, the Statue of Liberty for scenery.

You could see Red Hook was changing: fancy little signs that hung out front of warehouses proclaimed that artists and film people had moved in. Political banners hung from a few windows, though the old row houses on the side

95

streets mostly sprouted American flags.

A lot of the area was still pretty derelict, the rotting warehouses, waste ground surrounded by chain-link fencing, compounds for towed cars, empty shipping containers rusting into the ground, broken docks.

I'd stopped in at one of the bars over the years on my way back across Brooklyn from Brighton Beach when I was working cases out there. It was cheap to drink here and you could imagine the place as it had been. Red Hook looked ancient, suspended in time, the way it probably looked a hundred, a hundred and fifty years ago, except then it had been jammed with people working the docks.

Red Hook had been cut off from the rest of the city when the Brooklyn-Queens Expressway was shoved through it years ago; the underside of the BQE as I drove through it was desolate and full of garbage; the beams looked rusty.

I drove up on to the elevated Expressway. I could see the river now. I thought about it when it was a streaming traffic lane packed with barges, tugs, freighters, steamships. Red Hook's inlets and canals were full of abandoned boats, a paddle wheel steamer, the skeleton of a burned out Staten Island Ferry. There was still some shipping, some working dry docks in the main part of the Gowanus Canal, the huge inland waterway that cut into Red Hook.

Looking down at the tangle of streets below me, I could see the warehouses, docks, narrow streets, packed in tight against the water; most of the streets were empty.

I thought about Sid and his cousin, and Sid's obsession with Red Hook and his own past; he had come here to escape, he had said. He didn't like it when Earl showed up on his private turf, not the Earl who had become a homeless bum, a guy who stank.

I knew there was still plenty Sid didn't tell me. I didn't know why he said there wasn't much time for him to get away. There was nothing I could do now to help him.

7

'I'm sorry,' I said, kissing Max when I met her over near West Street. 'Honest to God, I'm really sorry. I had a couple of things to take care of, I'll tell you about it later.'

'Do you want to talk about it?'

'I don't know. No. Not now.'

'OK,' she said.

She had on cut-off jeans and a red shirt that left her arms and shoulders bare, and yellow flip-flops.

'That was some party last night, God, honey, it was something, my mom and her friends and my cousins will be on the phone for a month,' she said. 'They think I married a very connected guy. I mean Tolya and his shoes and the Paris thing, I mean, call me Cinderella. I'm on vacation. And we're going to the shore. And then when we get down there, we can leave the kids with my mom and we can go and eat a lot of lobster and fool around, and I wanted to surprise you, there's this really great bed and breakfast, so I booked us in for a couple of nights, just us.'

'Great.'

I'd come to meet Maxine straight from Brooklyn where Sid was going slowly crazy because his half brother had died trapped under a dock. Now I was in the city, a married guy, looking to buy an apartment with my wife.

It made me content that the regular stuff never

98

stopped, not even for death. We had talked about it, me and Max, because she saw a lot of dead people in her job, too, and she got it. I didn't have to explain.

You could be on some case so horrible that it made you puke, that made you drink too much, and gave you ulcers and kept you up all night. The next day, if you were lucky, you could lose yourself in stuff, good stuff — hanging out with friends, servicing your car, worrying about money, looking for an apartment, ordering breakfast from a waitress who knew that you liked your bagel really well toasted, returning calls, playing pick-up ball over near Sixth Avenue, eating a bucket of popcorn at the movies, or a pizza at Totonno's with Maxine.

I looked at her. She fished a pack of the mentholated smokes she loved out of her purse, then hesitated.

'You quit last week,' I said.

'Yeah,' she said. 'Maybe I should really quit and then we could get pregnant.'

'You want that?' I was surprised. 'Do you? You never said anything.'

'What about you? Artie?'

'Do you?'

'You tell me.' She sounded impatient. 'I asked first. Get off the fence.'

I didn't answer. She put the cigarettes back in her purse and we walked up the river towards the building where Maxine wanted to live. I had my arm around her, and I could feel her bare soft shoulders warm from the sun.

She leaned against me, but she was already in

some other place, smiling to herself, already imagining herself in the apartment. I tried to want it for her.

'Did you like the judge yesterday?' I said.

'Truth?' she said.

'Truth.'

'I kind of liked him but I didn't want to say exactly because I knew Sonny Lippert fixed it up for us, and I would have had to laugh if I said anything because the judge reminded me of, who's that actor? The one that sounds like God? James Earl Jones? The big booming voice, you know, and making us proclaim our vows very seriously and I could see the girls were cracking up. You think it's OK to laugh at your own wedding?'

'Essential, yeah, I think you have to, though how would I know?'

'I'm still hungover,' she said. 'I never saw so much champagne in my life.'

'Me, too.'

'He's really something, your friend Tolya, you know, he also gave the girls presents, outfits, stuff for the beach, new bathing suits and sandals and all kinds of things, it was like we all left the party with goody bags. Santa Claus in crocodile loafers.'

I laughed. 'He likes you.'

'As much as Lily?' she said softly, then added, 'Forget I said that.' We crossed West Street and walked another block, and Max got a piece of paper from her jeans pocket, looked at it, took my cigarette from me and smoked some of it.

'Which building?' I said.

100

'Next block.'

I had priced-out renovating my loft for the four of us, Maxine and the girls and me, and it would cost a fortune to do anything nice. The wiring wasn't great, there was only one bathroom. Maxie's place was too small. We had thought about a house in Brooklyn, and most weeks, on Saturday mornings we looked; for months we looked and eventually we found something in Bushwick that we could afford; it was still a grim area but Max said it was on its way up. We were getting ready to call the realtor and make an offer when Maxine had looked at me across her kitchen table where we were drinking wine and said, 'You don't want to leave Manhattan, do you? I mean you really don't want it. It's going to kill you if you have to leave the city. Isn't it? Tell me, level with me, honey.'

'I can do it. I told you I even once thought about living in Red Hook.'

'Yeah, but you didn't, right? You can't, Artie, honey. It took you too long to get to New York, and you'll hate it, and then I'll hate it. Let's try something else.'

'What about you?'

'Why the hell do you think I went out with you? It was my chance to live in the city, right? My mother always said, you're the type of girl that will never make it out of Brooklyn, Maxine, and this is my one chance to prove she was wrong. Once in my life I want to be a New York City girl for real. I do. In Manhattan, not some borough. I mean it.'

Maxie rarely mentioned her mother except in

101

a practical context, babysitting, that kind of thing; she didn't really talk about her otherwise. Her father was dead. She never mentioned him at all.

Maxine was right: after twenty-five years, I didn't want to leave.

A block from the river, she stopped in front of an apartment building with a shiny pink granite façade that looked like plastic.

'Is this it?' I said.

'Yeah.'

'Let's go in.'

In the lobby of the building the realtor was waiting for us; she was middle-aged, in good shape, wearing a beige pants suit; her hair was bright blonde and smooth, and her name was Sally; she was very enthusiastic.

We followed Sally into the elevator and out again and along a hallway that had beige carpeting and striped beige wallpaper that matched Sally's suit. I trailed behind her and Maxine through the empty rooms of three, four, five apartments, all of them with low ceilings and narrow windows. I tried at least to love the little balconies where, if you hung over the railing, you could glimpse the river.

In the fifth place we saw, I slid open the doors to the balcony and went outside, while behind me the two women talked about what Sally called amenities, doormen, a party room, a gym.

Out over the harbor, the sun was high and hot. Along the river was a park and there was a bike path where a few people were out riding. A woman jogged. Another pushed a baby in a stroller. A class of elderly Chinese ladies practiced some elegant T'ai Chi exercises that looked like dancing; a couple of Chinese guys who could have been their husbands leaned against the railing and dropped fishing lines into the river and smoked.

Sid was still on my mind. He was out of town. He had gone to Long Island. He told me he was going.

It nagged at me. He had lied and maybe he was still lying, but it wasn't my case, and there was no reason to think that Sid was threatened except by his own demons, his own history.

I lit a cigarette, and leaned on the railing and looked at the building opposite me. On one of the balconies was a woman in a bikini. She was standing up, and she slowly removed her top, picked up a plastic bottle of suntan oil and began rubbing it into her bare breasts. She was looking down now at her small round breasts, working on the oil. She didn't see me watching at first; it felt like a peepshow; I couldn't look away.

Then, suddenly, she looked straight at me, grinned, and rubbed in more oil, climbed on to a green and white plastic lounger and lay back, her hands reaching down beside her for a glass with something in it — apple juice, iced tea — that she drank in slow motion. She put it back, put on her sunglasses and picked up a paperback.

I walked to the other end of the balcony. We were a couple of blocks from Ground Zero and high enough up you could see the pit. The sky was clear blue the way it had been that day. Three years. Coming up for three years next week. We had moved people out by water that day; from every side of the city, we moved them on boats.

I had helped move people to Jersey from the marina a couple of blocks from where I stood now. I went on some of the boats. Debris fell on us, even as we moved out into the water.

I remembered one trip, people huddled together, me trying to stay calm when a leg fell on the deck of the boat. The leg just missed a couple who were huddled together crying and covered thick with dust, the dust caked on them because they'd poured water over themselves. The leg hit the deck and a man who had lost his shoes and was standing in dusty socks by the boat's railing started laughing. He laughed and laughed and couldn't stop and I had to get him to a hospital in Jersey.

Maybe Sid McKay went a little crazy like the rest of us. Maybe he went crazy and never came back.

* * *

'What do you think?' Maxine came out behind me and put her arms around my waist.

I nodded towards the pit. We had talked about it plenty. It didn't bother her the idea of us living here even though Mark, her first husband, had died in the Trade Center; if anything, she said, she felt closer to him.

'I love it here,' she said. 'I love it that it's in the city and I can walk to work and there are great schools and grass and good security. I think it's

104

beautiful, to tell you the truth, Artie, honey. I loved it on September 10, I think it's important to keep on loving it, or else what's the point of anything if we just change how we feel because of the fucking bastards who did that to us? I could live here for the rest of my life,' she said and we went inside and down the elevator to the lobby along with the realtor in beige.

Maxine took the woman's card, and then the two of us, Max and me, walked silently along the river, past the Irish potato famine museum with grass and potatoes growing on its roof, and then the Jewish museum. We came out near Clinton Castle, the old gray stone fort at the bottom of the island. We looked at the war memorials in Battery Park.

I bought us both some coffee from a wagon and a raisin bagel with butter for Max. We sat on a bench facing the boats that went to the Statue of Liberty.

Acrobats worked the crowd. Four black guys, all of them made out of pure muscle, flipped over each other, made human pyramids, did headstands; music blasted from a boombox; tourists gaped at them. Maxine got up and put a dollar in the hat.

Sitting down again, she said, 'Sonny Lippert lives around here, doesn't he?'

I nodded.

Max added, 'That was incredible, Sonny giving you the Jackie Robinson baseball.'

'It was for both of us.'

She shook her head. 'It was for you. It was his way of making peace between you. You're like an old married couple, you two.'

'What?'

'It's your conspiracy, yours and Lippert's. You carp, you're suspicious, you hate each other, you think he's a piece of shit, but you love him, and he's the same way. Artie, honey, what's eating you? You're distracted as hell.'

I put my arm around her and kissed her. No one had ever paid so much attention to me.

'You're a very smart cookie, aren't you, and I love you,' I said.

'Still? You think that even now we're married? You think I should call myself Maxine Crabbe-Cohen, you think it has like some kind of ring?'

'Do you love the apartment?'

'The last one, yeah I do. It was too expensive, but I loved it, and I was thinking if it was OK with you, I could use some of the 9/11 money I got, which was for Mark, and this would be for the kids, partly, which would be for Mark. I loved it so much.' She got her cigarettes out of her purse and lit up.

'We could manage,' I said, though my stomach turned over.

If she wanted it, if it was what Maxie wanted, maybe I could rent out my loft. Maybe I didn't have to sell. I could rent to some rich assholes. I could get someone in and then in a few years maybe I could take my place back somehow.

I glanced towards Battery Park City with the neat green spaces, the gardens, and the security guards. There was something ghostly about it. It existed apart from the city. It sat on landfill.

Maybe the landfill had come from a suburb somewhere and the place itself had taken on the character of the borrowed earth, suburban, sterile, unmessy.

I kept my mouth shut and listened to Maxine talk and I thought about living by the river.

On a piece of paper, Maxine was doing figures, the down payment, mortgages, loans, and in her imagination, I knew, we were already moving in. I wanted so bad to want it; instead I felt trapped.

My phone rang. It was a message from Sid, one of the messages from the day before that I had forgotten to erase. But I was done with it. I had done what I could for Sid. I tried to get rid of the image of him at the loft in Red Hook. I tried to forget how scared he had seemed, scared and old and somehow facing the end of his life. I had called the local detectives. I had left a message for Clara Fuentes, the cop in the red jacket. I held Maxie's hand and tried to think about us, and moving, and going away on Thursday. It was Monday. Thursday I'd be out of town with Max at the beach.

'What is it?' Maxine said.

'Nothing.'

'It was who you went to see this morning, right? And yesterday. Honey?'

I nodded. 'A guy I know named Sid McKay.'

'Who helped you out on a case in a big way, something like that? I remember you mentioning him. I remember. You liked him. I wanted to meet him but it never happened. You owed him, Artie, didn't you? You care about this guy?'

'Yeah.'

'Then go already,' she said. 'Go do what you have to do. Go.'

'I already did that,' I said.

Maxine was caught up in her plans.

'I'm going over to Century 21 to try to squeeze my fat ass into a bathing suit,' she said.

'Don't fish.' Maxine had a great figure, she was tall and thin and rangy.

She picked up her bag. 'You need anything?'

'Like what?'

She said, 'I don't know. Socks. Underpants.'

'Is this how it works?'

'What?'

'Marriage.'

She kissed me. 'Go away.'

'I'll see you tonight.'

She hesitated.

'What is it?'

'Artie, honey, listen, the girls are restless, and it's hot, would you mind if I just took them out to my mom's today? We were going tomorrow anyhow, they'll probably make you go up to Madison Square to see that the sniffer dogs are behaving right before the politicians get into town, and I'd like to get the kids settled at the shore. Is that OK? I know you can't get away before Thursday night, like we agreed, and I'm OK with it, but I'd like to get them out of the city.'

'Go,' I got up and leaned down to kiss her.

'Artie?'

'What?'

'It's OK, you know. I know you think about

her sometimes. I don't expect it to go away completely. You remember stuff. We all remember.'

'Who?'

'Lily Hanes,' she said. 'I know that.' Max hesitated. 'Did you see her? Do you see her?'

'When?'

'Ever. I know she's back in the city.'

'How do you know?'

'I saw her on the street.'

'Where?'

'Chinatown. I was walking to your place, and I saw her. She didn't see me. I met her with you years ago when we, you and me, we were just friends and you were together with her. Remember?'

'No.'

'I did. I saw her. Across the street. A month ago maybe.'

'Well I don't see her and I didn't see her and don't be silly. OK?'

'OK.'

I kissed her again and started off, waving my hand. Looking over my shoulder, I saw her walk away.

I turned again to look for Maxie but she had disappeared around the corner. Later she told me she had called after me to ask how I felt about the apartment again, but that I didn't hear her, or at least I didn't turn around.

I was still thinking about Sid, and Earl, about Sid's repetition of lies and half-truths so that every time I talked to him, it all seemed more and more impenetrable. I couldn't shut it off, though, not Sid or Earl or their history.

I went to pick up my car. I'd left it a couple of blocks away, and when I got to the lot I felt someone watching me, someone behind me, making me sweat. I turned around. There was nobody, just the rows of cars and the deserted street.

8

You could smell the blood. It was hot, and you could smell it, fresh meat and blood as soon as you got to the Meat Packing District. I went looking for Tolya Sverdloff after I left Maxine because I'd left my jacket at his place the night before, and to thank him and pick up some gifts, and because of what the bartender in Red Hook had said. Sid McKay drank Martinis with a big Russian who drank Scotch and sounded a lot like Tolya Sverdloff. Give my regards to Tolya Sverdloff, Sid had said. But so what?

Sid knew a lot of people, but it was New York. You met people all the time, you met people who knew your friends, you ran into people you couldn't remember who knew everything about you. People you hadn't seen for years showed up after disasters. They heard you'd worked a bad case, they came back into your life to see if you were alive, or wanted to get drunk or keep each other company or get laid. So what if Sid and Tolya knew each other?

'Fucking watch out, asshole,' a guy in a truck yelled when I almost ran a light crossing Ninth Avenue, and I resisted saying 'fuck you' back because I wanted to keep my good mood, and this stuff could escalate fast and you could explode and do something you would regret.

★ ★ ★

Tolya was talking to a guy in a blood-stained coat and a hairnet who was smoking and eating a meatball sandwich. The two of them were leaning against the wall of the warehouse opposite Tolya's building off Gansevoort Street, watching a couple of kids move some beef carcasses off a truck on to the loading dock and then inside.

These days most of the meat business had moved up to Hunt's Point in the Bronx. Real estate and art and hair salons where a cut cost six hundred bucks had replaced them. The meat that still came in here on the west side mostly came butchered and shrink-wrapped and boxed before it was shipped out across the city, but a couple of places still got the meat in whole and you could smell it for days. It stayed in your nostrils. Even at night around the Meat Packing District I could smell it as if it was in the walls, mixed in with the cement.

Wearing a yellow linen shirt like a tent hanging over his blue pants, Tolya saw me getting out of my car. He shook hands with the meat guy, and started in my direction. I thought about the party and the watch and suddenly I was glad as hell to see him. I kissed him three times Russian style, and said, 'I left my jacket at your place.'

'I was calling you,' he said, waving his phone in my direction.

Tolya walked over to a canary-yellow Cadillac Escalade and leaned against it.

'You like it?' he said.

'What happened to the Hummer?'

'Vulgar,' he said. 'I wait for my Maybach to be

112

delivered now. Best car made.'

'You mean she doesn't like the Hummer? Your lady. The severe one. She thinks the Hummer is vulgar?'

'We compromise,' he said. 'She prefers small environmentally fine little design car for small people, I tell her this is impossible, I can't fit in this kind of car, she says I won't go in that thing. So I put my beautiful Hummer in a garage.' He looked at his Escalade. 'OK, so I am still polluting environment, so kill me.' Tolya smiled but his huge face was tight and the eyes flickered away from mine as if he was looking for something or someone over my shoulder.

Tolya was anxious. I didn't want to ask him about Sid, not yet.

'Artyom, do you have a little time for me?' Tolya said in Russian. 'You have some time?' He was hesitant, unsure, unlike himself.

'Sure. Yeah, of course. I'm on call, but I don't have to go any place unless they call me. What the hell is it?' I said. 'What's the matter?'

He shrugged.

'Tell me.'

'Come on,' he said, and he took hold of my arm in his hamsized hand and we walked towards the river.

'Look up, Artemy,' he said. 'Look above you.'

'What is it?'

'The High Line,' Tolya said, exuberant now as if he'd suddenly seen a gorgeous woman. 'I want this. Is very beautiful up there. I want to show you.' He flashed his old smile, and began walking.

We went, Tolya first, under the elevated tracks, moving in the faint broken glare from the light that filtered through the overhead tracks and the shifting patterns from cars on the Westside Highway.

The underside of the derelict train tracks was littered with condoms, beer cans, used needles, smashed-up signs from anti-Bush protests, a pink high-heeled shoe, a straw hat with a red, white and blue band that proclaimed 'I Love Bush'.

Tolya was possessed, insistent, and I followed him. We walked a few blocks, and then he stopped abruptly and fumbled for a key in his pocket.

'What?' I said and my voice boomed out in the deserted space under the tracks.

'Come,' he said and found the entrance to an abandoned warehouse.

We went in. The place was stacked with empty boxes, and the high windows were encrusted with dirt.

I followed Tolya up a couple of flights of stairs to a back door that he unlocked. He walked out on to a loading dock that led straight on to the elevated railway line.

'Is illegal,' he said when we were both outside. 'Is trespassing to come here, but I come anyway.'

Tolya seemed to move lightly across the tracks, though the place was overgrown with weeds and grass, knitted together so it caught at your ankles. I stumbled, got my balance. I stood up. I looked out west.

We were only a couple of blocks from the

river, but the buildings and the old shipping terminals separated us from the water.

'What the fuck is this place?' I said.

'The High Line,' he said in Russian. 'It was built in the late 1920s, used to run to the tip of Manhattan when Manhattan was still a big port. Carried the goods down to the water. At the other end it connected with the trains, the old Empire Line. In 1980, it was abandoned, just like that. Look, look at the Deco detail on these railings, look, Artyom.' Tolya was ecstatic. He put his arms out wide. 'After a while, after the ships stopped coming to Manhattan, the warehouses die, the High Line dies, nobody does anything,' he said. 'Now everyone wants. Like Red Hook,' he added. 'Like every piece of the city. People are fighting over industrial bones of New York, Artyom. Rotting docks and grain docks and container ports and rusty warehouses and cast-iron buildings and meat packing plants and places that made car parts, and printing presses. Brooklyn, Manhattan, Bronx. Up here on the High Line some people want to put galleries for art, others want to tear it down to use the land. Everyone thought the city was dead three years ago and now they grab at it, people betray each other for tiny little pieces. I came to New York, I thought it was the modern city, but it is old and beautiful.' Tolya closed his eyes, then opened them. 'Old, beautiful, crazy. Who knows. I want this so much, but it is owned by the railroads, it is private property, but I want it. Look at how seeds blow in and take hold and all this green grows, like a jungle in the sky. To have a piece of this would make you a king of New York, right, Artemy?' he asked, and then burst out laughing. 'I don't get, of course, but I can dream.'

Something about Tolya made me feel he wanted me to know he was connected to this place. I didn't understand why, but I knew he needed me to know. Maybe it made him feel he already owned it.

'Let's go,' I said and looked down. The grass grew thick under my feet, and the old tracks were supported by iron struts that were spaced far apart. There was jagged wire and broken glass.

We started back. Tolya tripped and I caught him. He was breathing hard. He had always been big, but he seemed tired, out of breath, sick.

'Sometimes, Artyom, I come up here at night, like a thief, like a spy,' Tolya said.

It was something Sid McKay had said of himself as a child. A child spy, he had called himself.

★ ★ ★

When we were back on the street Tolya said, 'So will you take a ride with me, Artyom? You're not working? You have time for me?'

I looked at my beeper. There was nothing. 'Sure.'

'Thank you.'

'What is all this 'thank you' bullshit, Tol?'

For the second time that day, he was strangely tentative as we walked back to his car. Again I had the sense that something wasn't right.

'Your Valentina is lovely,' I said. 'She's a terrific girl.'

'Yes, but is self-conscious,' he said. 'I offer her plastic surgery for the finger, but she says no, this belongs to her past, this horrible thing they do to her, cut off her finger, bastards who kidnap her when she was a little girl in Moscow. Who does this shit, Artyom? But she says it is part of my story, Daddy. Part of my own narrative. What does this mean?' He turned to look at me, face drowning in sadness. 'This is American, that you must have a story?'

'Yeah. Beginning, middle, end. Like a sit-com.'

We got to his car and he added, 'Suddenly Valentina is grown up, and we are in Miami where she is living with her mother, and she says, Dad I want to join up with you, work in your business in New York, I want to leave Miami, other girls are doing this, and I say, I don't care what are other girls doing, I say, go to college, but she wants experience, she wants more, more experience, more life, she says, what kind of life? She is nineteen. This is life, to be model and work in real estate?'

'Give her a chance,' I said. 'Some kids grow up fast.'

'So you'll take a ride with me? You're OK for that?'

'They'll beep me if they want me. I'm OK. Where do you want to ride, Tolya?'

'To Brooklyn,' he said.

'Big place Brooklyn,' I said, figuring he wanted to go out to Brighton Beach where he kept an apartment, maybe get some food, maybe buy the

Russian papers. I figured it for a trip out to Brighton Beach.

'Yes,' he said, and I didn't know if he was avoiding the question but all he said was, 'I'll go upstairs and get your jacket,' then walked a couple of steps to his building and lumbered through the door.

★ ★ ★

I didn't know if I was surprised when Tolya pulled off the BQE, cut under the Gowanus, parked near a chain-link fence on the Red Hook waterfront, got out and gestured for me to follow him.

Silently we crossed some tufts of dry scabby grass and I almost tripped over a Snapple bottle. There was a Snapple factory nearby. Made from the best stuff on earth, the logo on the bottles said. Best stuff, I thought. Sure.

A security guard who was smoking and leaning against the fence put up his hand, but Tolya went over and talked to him, the guy shrugged, straightened up, threw away his butt and looked respectful. Then he held open the gate and we went through. More weeds covered an expanse of ground where there were cars rusting, and we went out to the edge of a decayed dock.

Tolya sat on an overturned crate and motioned for me to sit beside him on a second box. Beyond us, spread out, spectacular against the hot sky, was the river and the city. The sun lit up the water so it glittered.

I kept my mouth shut about Sid, but I wondered if it was accidental, Tolya bringing me here the day after Sid called, the day after the guy died in the inlet. I figured I'd wait and see if he mentioned it. Maybe it was coincidence, maybe that was all. I didn't like myself much for not telling him. Tolya stretched out his arms again as he had on the High Line earlier.

'Pot of gold,' he said.

'Yeah.'

'Imagine, Artyom, imagine to be here on edge of the world, Statue of Liberty in front, New York City there, ten minutes, and all this,' he said. 'Imagine new buildings, imagine marinas and boats, imagine a brand new city.' Tolya's eyes were half shut as he squinted into the hard light. Again came the sound of his breathing hard, trying to catch a breath.

'You sound like shit,' I said.

He didn't answer.

'Are you listening to me?

He said, 'One day I am coming from Brighton Beach to the city and I stop and I think this is beautiful, and I buy a few little buildings here,' he said. 'Most already sold. There is guy, big guy, same like me, and I ask him, can I buy some from you, but he says, what fun is it if you sell your buildings, and I understand, so I buy what I can and I look for more. Land. Like always. Every century.'

'Sure,' I said. 'Fine. So what's stopping you?'

He shifted his weight on the box. 'Information,' he said. 'Who has rights, who owns what, who in city makes promises.'

Sometimes I wondered how the hell he made all the money, tons of money, money mountains, that he used to buy the buildings, more and more every year. He bought buildings like I ate pie. He said it was just good business and tried to get me in on stuff. I couldn't. I didn't have the dough and I never would. I didn't want to think about what kind of deals he did, either. I didn't ask about money. It was part of the deal. We were friends. We had shared more than a pood of salt as the Russkis said, and that was it. I had pushed him on his business stuff once and it almost killed our friendship. He did what he did, I thought; as far as I knew, what he did was legal, more or less. Anyway it was only financial stuff. Not insider trading, either. It was only real estate, stuff everyone did, one way or another.

'Something else is eating you. Tolya? Are we talking some fucking Russian thing?'

He hoisted himself to his feet. 'Artyom, sweetheart, everything is a fucking Russian thing for us, you and me,' he said.

'Everything. You want that we deny this, but it never goes away. Never. I wish it would go.'

It was the first time I'd heard him talk that way. Usually it was me. I put my hand on his arm, and said, 'What?'

'I have become American citizen. US. Wave the fucking flag,' he said.

'When?' I didn't smile, I swear to God, I just listened and didn't say anything.

'Last month. I applied over a year ago, it takes fucking four hundred days until I finally got the passport.'

'I would have made a party for you.'

'Yeah, and to eat? Red, white and blue American cheese sandwiches?'

'You passed your citizenship test?'

'I can tell you names of all presidents of US, OK?'

'Congratulations,' I said. 'But I mean, so how come? You always told me you don't like America that much.'

He shrugged. 'I do it for my girls, OK? I do, but I am not happy. It makes me feel unreal. I do not feel American. New York's different. It's OK. Also, I have my little apartment out by Brighton Beach. I can hide out. Feel Russian.' He snorted ironically.

'The girls are citizens already,' I said.

'Listen, I did this, I like having passports. One is good. Two is better. Three excellent.'

Tolya put his hand on my shoulder to steady himself.

'Let's go drink something,' he said. 'Let's drink.'

He walked back towards the street and the SUV and I went with him. He looked tired.

'There are guys I used to know who are looking over my shoulder, Artyom,' he said. 'Every time I put money down on a piece of real estate, I discover these guys are trying to steal it from me. Russian guys. Guys with guns. In Moscow, you want to be in trouble, get in the way of guys buying real estate. You understand? And they buy everywhere, not just Russia, everywhere.'

'Who are they?'

'You don't know who because they have agents, I mean big players, oligarch type, I don't say names aloud; not even to myself do I whisper names, OK, you know who, you know, they don't get hands dirty anymore, they stay very quiet. These I never scared of but they have younger guys, agents they call them, who work for them who do anything. Give me one of your cigarettes, please, Artyom, I have no cigars.'

I handed him the pack; he didn't light up.

'They don't care, these people who do actual jobs,' he said. 'They are like nihilists of nineteenth century, you know? Nothing matters at all with them, they can live, die, no difference, this makes them very good at making money because it doesn't matter, they buy and sell anything, uranium, opium, plutonium, art, illegals for work, girls for sex, children for sex, oil, cars, body parts, auto parts, real estate, armies, weapons, anything anywhere. Make money. Feed bosses. Oligarchs have so much money, Artyom, they are kings, they own whole countries, and their children are like princesses. Nothing can touch them.'

I looked at his face. I wondered if Tolya's fear connected to Sid or the dead man, Earl. Paranoia grabbed my gut then let go. There wasn't any connection. How could there be?

'And you want this,' I said. 'This kind of money, the power?'

'Yes,' he said, then started walking quickly to his car. 'Come on.'

We got into his Escalade and Tolya reached into the pocket of his yellow shirt, took out a small brown envelope and gave it to me.

'I want you to know everything in case something happens, so you'll make sure they're all right, the girls, and my ex-wife, and you, Artyom. I've made you my executor, though not a lot is written in my will.' He laughed. 'I am a US citizen but not necessarily a complete supporter of the US tax code. Never mind.'

I opened the envelope. There was a key for a safety deposit box.

'This is a bank key for my safety deposit box,' he said. 'I will tell you which bank where. If anything happens, you go there first. You don't help do anything else. You don't call cops, you don't do anything, you go to box before they seal it and you take what's inside.'

'What are you talking about?'

'It's just a safety deposit box key, OK? It's not the secret to the universe, it's not the da Vinci fucking codes, Artemy, just a key to a box with paper, so you go and take what is in it and you give everything to Valentina who is oldest of my children in her soul, and smartest, OK?'

'Why not give her the key?'

'Safer with you. I never felt vulnerable before, but now I feel, OK? So you'll do this.' It wasn't a question.

I nodded and put the envelope in my pocket. 'Are you sick?' I said. 'Tell me.'

'No,' he said, but I didn't believe him. He added, 'You promise? No matter what? No matter who is officially asking questions?'

'Yes.'

'When I was hurt in the winter before the last,

when I am lying in the hospital and cannot talk, I think: I have to do this. I have to give the key to Artemy. I have to ask him.'

He had been hurt bad with a knife on the Billy Farone case when I was on it. He went looking for the creeps involved, and they hurt him, they stuck a big fishing knife with a serrated edge deep inside him, and I found him lying in lousy Coney Island Hospital.

'Why now?' I said.

He shrugged his enormous shoulders and said, shifting between English and Russian as if he couldn't find a comfortable resting place even with his languages, 'I tell about it one day. Now I need for you to take this key. I need for you to promise to be OK with the girls. And ex-wife who is an idiot.' He laughed. 'The ex-Mrs Sverdloff is very nice lady, but she is now retired to very relaxing life of South Florida in Boca Raton,' he said. 'Can you think about this, my wife in Boca Raaaaton? Once, in Moscow, she was a professor of ancient Chinese poetry. She was rock and roll girlfriend also, chick who could recite Chinese poetry and lyrics of Beatles songs. Beautiful, sexy, very rebellious. Now she dates her plastic surgeon, he wears yachting caps, and blue blazers with gold buttons with little anchors on them. The sun has broiled her brain to a very small crisp. Little tiny potato chip of a brain, you know? I'm depressing myself,' he said. 'I need for you to trust me.'

He leaned forward and peered out of the car window. 'I like it here so much,' he said and looked up. 'Look at seagulls, look. Come on. I'm

124

thirsty,' he added. 'It will be OK. I'll make my deals, and after I finish with Brooklyn, I swear to God, I will sell everything. Then I'll retire. Travel. Become humanitarian. OK?'

He started the car and drove slowly until he got to a narrow street where there was a bar. He pulled up in front of it.

You could imagine longshoremen drinking here, and girls looking to turn tricks who stood outside swinging their purses. You could imagine Mohawk tribesmen, who had a bar of their own nearby, Indian steel workers down from Canada to build the Verrazano Bridge. I had seen the pictures of the Mohawk up high on steel beams seemingly suspended from the sky.

On the cobbled backstreet the marine light from the water gave the buildings the colors of an old Dutch picture. The bricks glowed. The light made the place lovely in spite of the broken pavement and seedy storefronts.

Tolya opened the car door. 'Red Hook will be my last big buy, and then I retire,' he said, and looked at me. 'I'm tired.'

Suddenly I thought: he is leaving. He's running. 'Travel where?'

'Eventually Italy, France, Vietnam, Cuba. Maybe I settle in Havana. I will find a nice woman and go travel and eat,' he said.

'Is there someone?'

He smiled shyly. 'Maybe.' He looked at me, and switched to his usual lingo, half English, half Russian. 'Is not severe architect with ugly red mouth, and is not hooker with gigantic tits. Is real nice woman.'

'I thought you bought the building for the architect.'

'She doesn't love me. I buy buildings for her, it doesn't matter.'

'Do I know her? The nice woman?'

He shook his head.

'Russian?'

'Yes,' he said. 'Like coming home.'

'You're really leaving.'

'Soon,' he said.

9

A decrepit air conditioner rattled in the window of the bar where pieces of metallic green tinsel left over from St Patrick's Day blew in the cold air. A few old guys, sipping their brews slowly to make them last, watched racing on some kind of cable channel on a TV hung out on an arm over the bar like a set in a hospital. A bartender leaned over the bar and stared at a copy of the *Post*.

We climbed up on a couple of stools. The sweat dried on Tolya's face.

'What else?' I said. 'You didn't bring me here to show me some real estate. You could have given me the key in the city.'

'No.'

'What?'

I ordered Scotch for both of us.

'Give me another one of those things you smoke.' I passed him the cigarettes and he simultaneously reached across the bar and plucked two bags of nuts off a cardboard stand with one hand, tore them open and swallowed the contents in one gulp.

The bartender set up some glasses and poured Scotch in them.

'Make them triples,' I said. 'Why are we here, Tolya?'

He shifted uncomfortably on the barstool, too big for it, sitting uneasily while he knocked back his drink. He looked in his glass. 'I need more.'

I got hold of the bartender and told him to give us a bottle and I dug some bills out of my pocket. I picked up the bottle and the glasses and made my way, Tolya following me, to the back where it smelled of stale beer and the air was fetid, but where we could sit alone at a table.

We made a silent toast, and drank. I waited for him to tell me what was bugging him, but he was restless. He said the bartender was eavesdropping, though the bartender barely looked at us. Tolya couldn't sit still.

★ ★ ★

In the street, the woman exploded at Tolya, screaming in English and Russian, hanging on to him, trying to claw at his head and his eyes. She was small, about five-one and she wore a sleeveless cotton blouse and blue shorts and red sneakers, and she hung on him like a cat. She had seemed to come out of nowhere, appearing as we left the bar, running at him, trying to gouge his eyes out.

Like a huge animal disturbed, Tolya shook himself but the woman had her fingers in his eyes. I grabbed at her. He was talking Russian to her softly, seductive, beautiful Russian, words that sounded like trapped smoke, trying to calm her down. She went on howling, shrieking, yelling; I couldn't make out what she was saying at first; she sounded drunk.

Finally, I pulled her away from him. She was heavy, deadweight. I held her, but she kept

128

talking, accusing Tolya of evicting her from her building in Brighton Beach. She lost her house, she said; you took my house, you bulldozed my house, you try to kill me, she screamed. She had recognized him on the street because he was her enemy. I held her wrists tight and yanked her off him.

'Let her go,' Tolya said.

'What?'

'Just let her go.'

I let go of her hands. The woman ran down the street and turned the corner. Tolya rubbed his eyes. His big head seemed to sag into his neck.

'She was drunk,' he said.

'You knew her?'

'I don't want to talk about it,' he said. 'Do you understand me?'

'Sure.'

'I want to eat.'

'Where?'

'Farone's,' he said.

I checked my beeper. Maxine was on her way to the shore with the girls. Everything was quiet in the city. 'Fine,' I said to Tolya. 'Let's go.'

'So, Artemy, you want to talk about Sid McKay now? You want to talk about this with me at all?'

I was silent.

'You knew that I knew Sid McKay, didn't you? You think I didn't know about his trouble, that I didn't hear about the dead guy out by his place in Red Hook?'

Al Sharpton was at Farone's. As soon as one of Johnny Farone's captains showed us into the main room of the restaurant, I spotted the Reverend Al at the big table in the center of the room where he was surrounded by a large group, three other black men, two black women and one white. Sharpton was clearly the center of attention.

Sharpton saw us at the same time and he started in our direction, reaching his hand out for Tolya. They met halfway.

Other diners looked up as the two big men greeted each other, hugging, grinning. Tolya introduced me; Sharpton had a mellifluous voice, soft and seductive. He had been a street singer before he became a preacher and a politician.

In a three-piece pinstriped suit, his sleek hair to his collar, Sharpton shook my hand with the politicians' two-handed shake; his hands were soft and manicured. Then he turned back to Tolya and I noticed it was Sharpton who paid equal court. All the time I was thinking about Sid, that Tolya knew Sid, that he knew I knew, and I had kept that knowledge from him.

'I didn't know you were pals with Sharpton,' I said to Tolya when we were seated at a table near the window.

'I make friends with these politicians,' he said. 'So you asked me why I wanted America passport? I met Comrade Putin. Did I tell you, Artyom? I met him at a reception in Moscow.'

I was interested. 'Go on,' I said.

'He was the coldest son of a bitch I ever met, ever, including several killers I know,' Tolya said in Russian. 'I mean ice cold. You see Putin, he wears a nice suit, he makes nice joke, he eats barbecue with Bush in Texas, but all you can think about is how he was as a KGB guy, on the opposite side of the interrogation table, a big white light on you. He doesn't drink. He does karate. He's clamping down on the press, a TV station here, a newspaper there, he's replacing some elections with his own appointed apparatchiks. He talks War on Terror. People trust him for this. It's the good old days back in the USSR, Artyom, and they love him and now America loves him, too. You know what law they're proposing in Russia, in Parliament? Law barring foreigners who do not respect Russia.'

Around us in the room was the buzz of people eating, talking, drinking.

'What else?' I said.

'Putin puts rich guys he doesn't like in jail, you're with him, or against him, he says. Twenty years since Gorbachev arrived, next March it is twenty years, and now we have Putin. Back to old ways,' he said, then stopped short.

Johnny Farone was at our table, proffering a bottle of vintage wine like it was the baby Jesus, and recommending spaghetti with caviar.

'Like they make it at the Four Seasons in Manhattan,' Johnny said. 'I did a lot of new stuff here, new dishes, décor.' He nodded his head at the room. 'You could have my lobster after. I do it a little spicy.'

Johnny beamed as if his fat face would split, too much flesh for the skin that looked too tight and shiny to contain it. His dark brown linen suit pulled even around the shoulders, and he looked uncomfortable, but he hugged me and patted my back like American men did, and said congratulations and what a great wedding party it had been.

'On me,' Johnny handed the bottle to the wine guy. 'The wine's on me.'

It was Monday night but Farone's was packed. A large round table was crowded with Republicans out sightseeing, I guessed. They had American flags in their lapels; all of them wore Bush buttons; one had a cowboy hat on his head.

Johnny Farone had started out catering to rich Russians. Then he got a reputation, and a 26 in Zagat, as he liked telling you. Right now I wished he'd hurry up and beat it so I could talk to Tolya. But Johnny lingered, flattered that Tolya was sniffing the wine appreciatively.

Johnny, when I first met him, had a crappy auto parks shop in Brighton Beach. He was one of the few Italians who got close to the Russians — he even learned a few words — and eventually he opened a restaurant. It overlooked the water in Sheepshead Bay, which was next door to Brighton Beach on the Brooklyn Coast. He married my half sister, Genia, and I saw her across the room, chatting to people at a table nearby. She looked up and lifted her hand and then came over to greet us.

She wore a salmon-colored sheath, Prada, she told me, and gold snakeskin sandals by Gucci,

132

and her red hair had been styled, she said, by Sally Hershberger. Genia pointed out all of her possessions and the provenance of each, as if each one provided ballast, as if they held her together. After her son Billy committed murder and was sent away, it was all she had left.

Johnny stayed beside her, clinging to Genia like a heavy anchor, weighing her down. They had stayed together, maybe because Gen was so grateful to Johnny for marrying her and making her an American, or because of Billy. They had both adored Billy, their only child who, when he killed a man, had also destroyed them. He had killed out of curiosity, nothing more, but they pretended it was self-defense; they bought into the self-defense line that made the papers call Billy a boy-hero.

Once in a while, Genia called me and talked, speaking Russian, weeping. I had been to Florida twice to see Billy. He seemed like a normal kid; the façade was perfect; they even talked about letting him out. It terrified me, the day when Billy would get out. He said, I want to live with you, Artie. When I get out, I want to be with you. I want to be like you, he had said. 'I'll be a detective,' he said.

It was Sid who had fixed it, who fed the press the stuff so that Billy was let off easy and sent to a special school instead of jail — they charged them that young as adults now in murder cases — which would have killed him. Because of Sid, no one labeled Billy the monster that he was. Sid had never asked for anything back until now.

Johnny waddled off towards the front door

and Genia kissed me and retreated to her friends.

I said to Tolya, 'I'm sorry.'

'What about?'

'I should have mentioned about Sid.'

'I want to eat first,' he said.

Tolya believed in food as a way of coping with trouble, a restorative, a form of medication, redemption. Without decent food, you couldn't think, he said.

The sound of voices rose around us; the sound of opera that Johnny played over the sound system soared. The politicians ate; the couples celebrating anniversaries drank Cristal; a trio of women giggled, seated on a green leather banquette under an oil painting; Johnny liked pictures of flowers and dead game birds.

The three women were in their thirties, all in sleeveless satin summer dresses, black, blue, pink, with low necks. They sat together in a row so a waiter could snap their picture. They had big hair, brown, copper, platinum, and pink lips. The middle one with the big copper hair was celebrating her birthday and a waiter brought a cake and then more waiters appeared and sang to her. The women clinked champagne glasses. Johnny brought a ball of pink cotton candy the size of a basketball, studded with candied violets. The trio laughed, high forced tinny giggles. It reminded me of the Diane Arbus photographs Lily had loved. Arbus gave me the creeps.

'I stole the idea from the Four Seasons, too,' Johnny said, passing our table. 'The cotton candy thing.'

'Artyom?'

Tolya reclaimed my attention. The spaghetti had arrived. A waiter in a dark green jacket, with 'Farones' embroidered on it in gold letters, hovered over our plates holding a large blue can of caviar. He scooped up the golden oscietra with a soup spoon and piled it on top of the pasta.

'More,' Tolya said.

I said, 'Enough.'

Tolya beckoned with his hand and the waiter spooned the fish eggs on until the surface of the pasta was covered with caviar. I stabbed mine with a fork and spoon and stuffed some into my mouth.

Tolya drank the Barolo.

'Good, right?' he said.

I was edgy. He ate. I ate and cracked a few old Russian jokes, and we made a few cynical remarks to each other, *sotto voce*, about the Russian couple a few tables away, the man in a gray silk suit that cost ten grand, the woman with a diamond on her middle finger as big as a walnut.

Finally, I said, 'Listen, I went to see Sid, right? I didn't think he wanted it talked about that he called me. I went. I thought he was feeling crazy, and I didn't think it mattered that much. It was nothing. OK?'

'You didn't want to share that with me? You didn't want to tell me? You didn't trust me? You're turning into your father's son, Artemy Maximovich. You don't trust even your friends when there's a case, you wait to see if they offer you information first.'

My father had been a KGB guy all his life. Even after they fired him, even after my parents left Moscow, it was who he was. He had been good at it, he was subtle, he could ask the right questions. Sometimes I wondered if, sitting across the table in an interrogation, people felt fear. I had adored my father, but I hated what he did and it took me years to admit it.

'It's not my case,' I said again. 'It was a homeless guy, a drunk, a junkie who died. How do you know Sid?'

Tolya pushed his plate away and picked up his wine again. 'I knew Sid from way back. Not well. Then a year ago, more, less, I ran into him at a bar in Red Hook. He recognized me, and we talked.'

'What about?'

'You. He knew you. I knew you. I remembered he had helped you with Billy Farone. He was a lovely man, he spoke wonderful Russian, he could recite Pushkin. He had been a good journalist and he was in mourning for his profession. I thought he was lonely.'

'Was?'

'Did I say was?'

'Yeah.'

'I don't know.' Tolya examined his wine. 'I had fallen in love with Red Hook. I tell him, Sid, I want to buy here. He says, I will help you, I know this place, I know the people, the history. I keep notes. I have information. It was an obsession for him, Red Hook. He helps me.'

I said, 'Was Sid in trouble?'

136

'What kind of trouble?'

'When he called me, he said someone was stalking him, he mentioned Russian thugs, he talked all kinds of paranoid stuff, then he says someone is following him, and a guy turns up dead in an inlet near his place. I think it was Sid who found the body.' I picked up my own glass.

I didn't tell Tolya that the dead guy was Sid's half brother; it wasn't his business.

'People get crazy about real estate, about the waterfront, you remember the murder in SoHo when there was a building everyone wanted there?' Tolya said. 'On Greene Street? You remember? Crazier than doing business in Moscow in craziest times, right? When there's a lot of money, people kill.'

'For what? For the real estate?'

'For the information.'

'What did Sid know?'

'Sid knew everything. He knew but he didn't act. He liked knowing. He had files. He kept meticulous notes, he knew everything about Red Hook, every building, its history, its financing. He knew it all.'

'And he told you.'

'Some.'

'You wanted his files?'

Tolya avoided my question and looked at his spaghetti. 'Where is he?'

I said, 'Long Island. He has a place.'

'Good. I have his number. I call. Make sure he's OK. Yes?'

I nodded and tried not to let him see it worried me, his calling Sid, his getting involved.

137

'Is that why you took me to Red Hook earlier? Because of Sid?' I said.

'I wanted to show you was all. Go on vacation, Artyom, go meet Maxine. Maybe I go on vacation, too, end of week. Maybe Florida, yeah, probably for sure, Friday, I will go to Florida, check up on this and that, and then maybe I'll travel,' he said. 'You know that Sid is paranoid, he was a man with nothing left to do except gnaw on the past. It will be all right. You believe me?'

★ ★ ★

In the parking lot, Tolya gave me the keys to his Escalade.

'You think you are too many sheets in wind for driving?' he said.

'No. I'm a cop, aren't I?' I knew I'd had too much wine, but I figured I was OK. 'How will you get home?'

'One of my guys will come,' he said, then added, 'You're wondering if I saw her?'

'Yeah.'

'I saw Lily. She's back in New York for good this time, I think. Beth's in London until school starts. Lily's here alone. She's here to protest the Republicans. She says she'll do what it takes to keep George Bush out, she's willing to go to jail, she says. She's such an innocent,' he said. 'She thinks it makes a difference.'

I said, 'What else?' I was sweating.

'She asked me if you wanted to see her at all.'

I lit a cigarette.

138

'Do you miss her so much?' Tolya said.

'Stop,' I said. 'No. I don't. Leave it.'

'Take care, Artemy. Don't end up one of those sad men who can't stay with one woman, like my father,' he said. 'Like me.'

He hugged me. 'You want to know how I made all my money? Remind me, one day I tell you.'

'How?' I said.

'I stole it,' he said, burst out laughing and turned towards the front door of Farone's place.

'Where are you going?'

He laughed. 'I am going inside to party with politicians, Democrats, Republicans, who gives a shit?' He raised his hands, palms up. 'You know something, Artemy, this election will tear everyone apart. Friends will stop speaking. I make contributions on both sides,' he said.

'What for? What do you need with the politicians?' I said.

'To be safe.'

'You're an American. You're safe. You can vote who you want.'

He looked at me. 'Don't be naïve,' he said.

139

10

It was after one in the morning when I got out, opened the door of Tolya's SUV in front of my building, reached inside for my jacket, and glanced up and down the block where a few people were still out on the street: a man walking his dog; a couple drifting up from some restaurant in Chinatown. I was moving slow. I had driven slow back from Brooklyn, trying not to crash the car.

'Artie?'

The voice was familiar, low and husky, and part of me wanted to jump back in the car and hit the gas and beat it. Instead, I closed the door and locked it.

It was Lily. Lily coming across the street, calling out my name, then standing near me, pushing her thick red hair back from her face, and looking at me. Her hair was shorter than I remembered.

'Hi,' I said, because I couldn't think of anything else to say.

'Hi,' she said, and leaned forward to kiss me.

I didn't move.

'What are you doing here?' I said.

She crossed her arms over her chest, then adjusted the bag on her shoulder. She was tanned and wore white cotton pants and a sleeveless black shirt.

'I was passing, I was in the neighborhood,' she

said. 'I was out drinking. Just out.'

'I see.'

'I was around the corner, I was at that little bar we used to go to, you remember, in Chinatown, the place no one knew about, where they sometimes had big bowls of prawn crackers, you remember? I go there sometimes, and I thought I'd see if you were at home. On my way, I mean.'

'It's late.'

'I wanted to see you,' she said. 'Just to talk.'

'I'm really kind of busy.'

'It's one in the morning,' she said. 'How busy can you be?'

'I'm going away in a few days.'

'I see.'

'Honeymoon,' I said. 'My honeymoon. I just got married.'

'Right.' She sucked on her lower lip. 'I thought you might call me. After that time we talked. You remember? When I came back the spring before last, you were sitting in the coffee shop with Tolya and we talked on the phone and I said I was back in New York for a few weeks. You didn't call. I'm back for good now.'

'Is there something you need, Lily?'

'Can we sit down some place?'

'It's really late,' I said, not moving, standing with my back to the door of my building.

She looked up. 'We could just go up to your house, and sit for a minute,' Lily said. 'I won't behave improperly,' she added, smiling. 'I've missed you, I wasn't just passing by. I go to the bar in Chinatown because I think I might run into you, and I walk home this way because I might see you. I'm too chicken to invite you and your girlfriend, your wife, I mean, over to dinner. I can't really get my mind around it, that you're married. I'm sorry. But I thought I'd just say it, since I've never been any good at smuggled messages, right?'

'Right,' I said and moved towards my front door.

'So you're not going to invite me for a drink or anything? I guess Maxine wouldn't be thrilled.' Lily smiled.

'She's at the shore. New Jersey, down by Avalon,' I said. 'So I have to go.'

Lily put her hand out. 'Can't we even be friends? I know I wasn't so great, but you're OK now, and I was so crazy after 9/11. Never mind. You're right,' she said and touched the back of my hand lightly, then turned to go. As she walked into the light from the street lamp, I saw that she looked tired. She turned back.

'So you're going away,' she said. 'Tonight?'

'In a few days.'

'Can I have a cigarette, please?' she asked. 'Right. Your honeymoon, you said. Of course. I really am sorry to bother you, are you OK?'

I said, 'I'm fine.' I crossed my arms.

'I'm glad.'

The space between us became almost solid with tension. I waited.

She pulled something out of her pocket. It was a set of keys. 'I came to give you these,' she said. 'I forgot I still had them.'

'Thanks.' I took them and felt her hand

142

against mine, and figured if I didn't go, I'd be lost. I was a jerk, I thought. I had always been a jerk about women.

She said, 'So did you change the locks?'

'I don't know. Yes. But not because of you. It doesn't matter. Look, I have to go upstairs.'

'You don't want to see me at all, do you?' she said.

'I have a life.'

'That's pretty brutal,' she said. 'That's hard.'

'I know it is. But you left,' I said. 'You went away, you got married, you took Beth with you, so I couldn't see her, either, you just went and I didn't know what to do without you, I didn't even know how to get along, it was like someone stepped on my oxygen and it took me a long time. I can't afford you now.'

'I had to escape.'

'From me?'

'From everything. New York, America, I began to hate this place, I couldn't help it, the flag waving, the patriotism, the whole thing.'

'And I was a cop and I was waving a lot of flags.'

Lily looked at me. She leaned against the wall of the building and then slowly slid down towards the pavement, half crouched on her haunches, half propped against the stone. I squatted next to her.

'I'm tired,' she said. 'What was I saying? Yeah, you went to a lot of funerals. You had friends who were cops and firemen and you all put flags up and sang 'God Bless America' and went to ball games and sat up with the widows and it was

143

stuff I couldn't deal with, a lot of it, I mean everybody was praying and talking about God and religion, I couldn't. It wasn't who I was. And you came home one night and you said, fuck civil liberties.'

'That wasn't about you. Jesus, Lily, you really think everything is the way you see it, you think you're so tolerant but you don't fucking listen to other people, or how complicated and confused and fucked up we all are. You just pitch your fucking ideological little tent and you sit in it, and you're so fucking sure of everything, you're so righteous.'

'You're finished? Is that it?'

'It wasn't about you.'

'But it was,' she said. 'It was my city, too. And it was like it became the point of it, the grieving, you and your friends were like the widow who's so involved with her grief there's no room for anything or anyone else, and even that's about the ritual. I couldn't even say what I felt. It never ended.'

'So you left for that? For politics? You gave us up for politics? You and me? For fucking politics?' I was dumbfounded.

Where I grew up, politics kept you from being in love; it got in the way of everything good in the Soviet Union; it was perverted and corrupt and shitty. I didn't get it. I couldn't explain it to her, either, and I saw her now, angry, her face red, her body crouched beside me, tense. I wanted to hold her. I could have grabbed her on the street I wanted her so bad, and I knew she felt the same.

144

'I thought it was because I worked too much, because I didn't have enough time for you,' I said.

'That's so banal. You think I'm that lame? That I didn't want you to do your work?'

'But you could never really take on board that I was a cop, could you? Your politics always got in your way.'

'Well, I learned, OK? I was a fool. I married a nice British guy with good liberal politics, who spent a lot of time talking anti-American stuff and he was good with Beth. He had a little boy from his first marriage.'

'And he had lots of money,' I said, but the anger had gone, and the tension.

'It wasn't for that.'

My phone rang, and I grabbed it. It was Maxine. She had arrived at her mother's at the shore earlier and tried calling. It was her second call. I stood up and half turned away from Lily and leaned against my front door. I talked to Maxine about the trip and when I would be there, and how the kids were, and how they dug clams themselves for clam sauce. I told Max I loved her. Behind me, I knew, Lily was listening.

I turned around. Lily was standing facing me.

'Why do you talk like that?' she said.

'Like what?'

She said, 'Like not yourself. The way you say I love you, it's like there's someone listening, you're so solicitous and serious, and you sound, I don't know, brittle. Like a married man.'

'I am married.'

'Don't be so pompous, sweetheart,' she said.

'There was someone listening.'

'Yes. Me.'

'You mean I sound like I'm lying.'

'That, too,' she said.

I didn't answer.

Lily hoisted her bag on her shoulder. She said, 'Take care of Tolya, will you? I don't know what he's doing but he's way out on a limb, so watch out for him, OK?'

'You knew that?'

'Some. He tells me some,' she said.

'OK.'

'So I'll be at the bar in Chinatown tomorrow night, OK, if you feel like it, I'll be there. I go by most nights. Unless you want me to come upstairs now? No, I guess not. I know I fucked up with us. With you. I've missed you a lot.'

Lily walked the few steps towards me, leaned over and kissed me very lightly on the mouth.

'I shouldn't have done that. So see you, sometime,' she said, and turned to walk away.

* ★ ★

Upstairs in my loft, I stood near the window smoking and watched her walk slowly down the dark street. Lily looked thin and seemed to get smaller. I thought again what an idiot I'd always been about women. I knew men who said their best friends were women, but I usually wanted to sleep with them, Lily most of all; if I said we could be friends, and we saw each other, I would want her. Thinking about her felt like a betrayal of Maxine, of Maxine and me.

146

I'd known Lily almost all the time I'd lived in this loft, the only place I had ever owned, a place where I'd scraped the floors myself and fixed the bookshelves, and sat out on the fire escape and watched ball games on TV. I had drunk with the neighbors and slept with plenty of women. Lily and Beth, the little girl I helped her adopt, had spent weekends with me here.

Then, out of nowhere, it came to me that I had met Sid McKay because of Lily.

It was a party she had taken me to. Ten years ago. About ten. It was on Crosby Street, when it was a dark alleyway off Broadway, a few blocks away from my place. Derelicts still bedded down at night there and you slipped in rotting vegetables that fell off produce trucks. I had worked a case around Crosby Street once.

The party was on the top floor in a huge loft with enormous red and yellow canvases on the wall. It was jammed with people. There was the excited buzz of a good New York party, talk, women, music, booze, drugs. Live music, a band, three, four musicians, I thought. Ricky Tae had been there. Of course, I thought. Rick had known Sid first. Or I had invited Ricky along. Couldn't remember. We had all known Sid somehow. Sid still kept Rick's photo. Had they been friends? Lovers? I started for the phone, and I remembered Rick was out of town, on business. Did he invite me to that party on Crosby Street? Did Lily? Was Tolya there, too?

It wasn't a party. It was a wedding. Somebody's wedding celebration, somebody I knew, or Lily knew, or Rick. I remembered.

147

Late that night, a good-looking black guy at the party waves at Lily and then strolls across the room towards us, and she introduces him. It's Sid, handsome, courteous, asking her to dance.

They go out into the middle of the floor and people watch as Sid waltzes her around the room, very expert, very graceful. The band changes to 'You're The Top', and they keep dancing. Lily always said, 'I can't dance, Artie. I have two left feet, you know. Or you think it's because I can never let the man lead?'

That night Sid leads her around the loft and they're good and I can't take my eyes off her.

★ ★ ★

I sat up for a while more. My reflection in the window showed me hunched, uncertain. I reached for the phone, put it down. Tolya said Sid had information that people wanted, and that people would kill for it. I didn't believe it much, but I figured Sid was in more trouble than I'd thought. I picked up the phone again, and then changed my mind for the second time. I went to bed. It could wait until morning.

Part Two

11

There was the noise of a rat scurrying along the stone walls that were thick as a fortress, cool and humid under my hand, a smell like iodine embedded in them, as I made my way up to Sid's place the next morning. The outside door had been left unlocked and inside I heard the rat, heard water running, music playing. Somewhere someone dropped a shoe on an old wooden floor.

I wanted this over. I was going up to confront Sid; I didn't call, I just went. He had said he was leaving town. He had said he was heading out to Long Island, but when I'd called his place in Sag Harbor, a woman answered and said Sid had not arrived. She had come in to clean, she said, and there was no sign of him at all. Sid didn't answer his home phone; he didn't answer any of his phones.

Maxine was waiting for me at the shore, and I wanted to get down to Avalon, hang out with her and the kids, lie in the sun on the beach, swim, forget Lily, forget the city for a while. It was Tuesday morning. I had a few days more on call, and then I would be gone. Thursday night I'd be on the road. I didn't have much time. I had to be there.

I didn't like it that Sid had not showed up on Long Island. Where was he?

If Sid was involved in any way, if he had

covered something up, maybe I could help fix things the way he had helped me when I needed him so bad. I thought about Sid and how he reached out to you without talking about it.

Sweating now, climbing the stairs in the old warehouse, I focused on this. I made myself concentrate. Do this, confront Sid, I thought, and get the hell out of the city.

★ ★ ★

I banged on Sid's door and when no one answered, I pushed at it hard; it was unlocked, and I lost my balance and stumbled forwards. I stuck my head inside, called out. 'Sid?'

There was no answer.

Dread pushed down on me. For a split second I felt as if a heavy wooden press was coming down on me and I couldn't stop it.

From the floor below came music; from outside, the water lapped around the edges of the brick building, and the rotting wooden docks. I reached inside the door and switched on a light, then, feeling for my gun, went in.

'Sid?'

I was pretty sure the place was empty but I went in slowly. Out of the high windows at the end of the loft, pale sun lit up the water.

I took out a cigarette then put it away. I didn't want to mess with any smell Sid might have left, anything that would tell me if he had been here or when he'd left, if he was alone, or with someone else.

On the desk was an ashtray but it was empty

and had been wiped clean. A blanket was folded neatly on the couch where he sometimes spent the night. I picked it up, a rough Hudson Bay blanket, cream with a wide red and black stripe, and sniffed it. It smelled of new wool, but nothing else, nothing human, no smell of smoke or sweat or sex, only wool and a faint reek of cleaning fluid as if it had been bagged in plastic; it was a different blanket from the one I'd seen the day before. I thought it was different, but I wasn't sure.

Did it mean anything? I didn't know. Maybe Sid never slept on the couch. Maybe he sat up all night like he said. The loft was his office, his publishing company. Maybe he went to his apartment in Brooklyn Heights but I had stopped by on my way, and it was shut up tight and an old lady in the basement apartment said she hadn't seen him in weeks.

Suddenly, my beeper vibrated. I grabbed it, called the number. There was a message to go up to Madison Square Garden and the Republican Convention that day; somebody needed a cop who could talk Russian. I scribbled down the name of the contact on the back of a piece of paper I had in my jeans and shoved it back in a pocket and went to look around Sid's place.

Above the bookshelves that ran the length of the brick wall were the old prints of Brooklyn, some from the nineteenth century, some newer, some hung neatly, others propped on the top shelf. There was a framed faded photograph of a Russian ship and I took it down and went over to the window where the light was good. I probably

153

needed glasses, but I didn't want to admit it.

I held the picture up to the light. I could just make out the name of the freighter in Russian: *Red Dawn*. The ship that had run aground off Red Hook.

Stuck in the corner of the frame was a small black and white snapshot, the edges already turning brownish yellow from age, the paper brittle. In the picture was a boy with a Russian sailor's cap, looking straight at the camera, wary, worried. He was probably fifteen or sixteen, but so small he looked like a kid; after the war, everyone in Russia was small; a whole generation of children had grown up, starving.

I turned the picture over. June '53; they must have put the dates on snapshots in those days, I thought. 1953. The year my parents got married. Stalin dead. My own father, only a little older than the boy in the pictures, had been in the navy before he was in the KGB. He had loved the sea and he had taken me fishing, though mostly to a river outside of Moscow. We went on weekends and fished together standing in the river, or sitting on the bank we ate sandwiches and ice cream and talked and he tried to show me how to read the water. I was lousy at it.

I shook the framed picture and a second snapshot fell out from between the picture and the glass. I picked it up from the floor. The same Russian sailor was in it, and next to him was a skinny black teenager holding on to an old-fashioned Schwinn bike. Behind them was the faint outline of the Statue of Liberty. In the black kid's face you could just see the ghost of

Sid McKay. Not the ghost, I thought, the precursor, the boy who would become Sid. There was no one else, no sign of Earl, Sid's half brother. Maybe Earl had taken the picture. I put the two snapshots in my pocket. I needed a cigarette.

For a minute, I sat on the edge of the desk chair, rocking back and forth, listening to the wheels squeak, looking at the boats on the water, barges, sailboats. Over by Jersey cranes picked at the sky like giraffes. It was addictive, the view, the sense of space, the way you were surrounded by water. It lulled you.

A police boat cruised up to the edge of the basin and sputtered away, maybe routine, maybe checking for problems. The port was vulnerable; the word had come down early in the summer that the ports were easy targets for attack.

Then I saw that the red light was flashing on the answering machine on the desk. I hit the play button. A petal with brown edges fell off a rose that was in a glass jar and dropped on to a pile of about thirty manila folders stacked on the desk, and while I listened to the messages, I opened the top folder. It contained newspaper clippings.

Sid's phone messages included a reminder of an appointment with his orthopedic surgeon because of his ankle, someone from the *New York Times* about lunch, a real estate guy who wanted to buy Sid's apartment in Brooklyn Heights, a woman asking him to a dinner party on St Luke's Place. Nothing. I kept looking at the folders.

Information, Tolya had said. Sid had information, but all I saw were news clippings and some scribbled notes about Red Hook's history.

'Call me back,' said a voice on the answering machine that I recognized. 'Call me back, man. Call me!' No name, just a number.

I knew the voice. My stomach turned over. I listened to it again, and called the number, and it was busy. I picked up the files on the desk and put them in a plastic bag I found in a desk drawer.

Again I looked around. Nothing seemed out of place. It looked as if Sid had simply walked out, leaving the door unlocked. Maybe he had gone out to get cigarettes. Or someone had called and he had gone to meet them and forgotten to lock up. There were keys hanging on a hook by the door, and I took them. I wasn't sure why, but I took them.

I stole Sid's keys, his files, closed the door and left it unlocked in case he came back.

I needed nicotine. I lit up as soon as I got outside Sid's, then went downstairs and tried to find the loft where the music had come from. I banged on the door, it opened, a young guy, maybe twenty-five, looked out. Behind him was a huge mass of metal. There was some New Age music on a stereo; it sounded like dripping forests.

'Hi,' he said.

'Yeah, hi. Listen, sorry to bother you.'

'It's OK, man.'

'You know Sid McKay?'

'Sure. Yeah, sure I love Sid. He's the only other

guy around here who's up early like me, sometimes in the winter it's pitch black and I'm still awake trying to like make fucking sense of this sculpture shit I do, and there's Sid, going out for a walk on the pier, or to get coffee. He always bangs on my window and asks if I want something and sometimes I go out and walk with him.'

'You saw him this morning?'

'Every morning. Sure.'

'What time?'

He laughed. 'Don't know. But early. Maybe five. Six. I saw him out of the window. I knocked on the glass, he tapped back like always. Sure. Something wrong?'

'You saw him come back?'

'No. I waited, too, he said he'd bring coffee, and I wanted to talk, but I didn't see him, so I went to bed. Maybe I should have called. You think he's OK? You a friend of his?'

'Thanks,' I said, my phone still in my hand, redialing the number on Sid's machine, already heading for my car when I noticed a pair of guys in a kayak floating towards me.

I stuck the bag with Sid's files in the trunk of my car and walked out on the pier towards the little boat.

★ ★ ★

The two men, middle-aged, both in T-shirts and shorts, worked hard keeping upright. They paddled seriously, intense, benign expressions on their faces, heading towards the inlet where the

157

homeless guy, Earl, had been found. One of them turned his face towards the sun.

Suddenly, from around the corner of the warehouse, a three-wheeled vehicle appeared and stopped short. A security guard, a fat nimble guy with an angry red face the color of pastrami, leaped out and ran to the edge of the water where he leaned over and put his meaty face as close as he could to the guys in the kayak.

'Get out,' he screamed at them. 'Get out of here. Private property,' he shouted, pointing to a battered sign that hung on some chain-link fencing.

The men in the kayak looked at him and each other and then at me. I was a few feet away. I went over to the fat guard and took out my badge and shoved it in his face.

'I don't remember anyone owning the river,' I said. 'I don't remember this being private property.'

'It's fucking private property now,' the guard said.

'Whose property? Who hired you?'

'I don't know,' he said. 'Some company. Listen, I get eight bucks an hour to make sure no one ties up any boats around here, so that's what I do.'

'What company?'

Reaching in his pocket, he backed off, found a card, tossed it at me. 'These people,' he said, and scrambled back into his toy car and buzzed off.

'Hey, thank you,' said one of the men in the kayak. 'Thanks.'

I said, 'That kind of thing happen a lot?'

He said, 'All the time now. People are fighting over property out here like crazy. They want to put in a cruise ship terminal. They want to put up parking lots. You get a decent developer who wants to make it nice, plant some trees, someone else comes and tries to screw with it. You get them fighting. You get other people squeezed. You get people who figure they own the place because they been here, even if they didn't do anything to fix it up, and others who figure they own it because they arrived the day before yesterday. New York. We're killing each other for a place to live,' he added.

I said, 'You know Sidney McKay?'

The second man looked up. 'Sure,' he said. 'Everyone knows Sid. He comes and goes, but we see him once in a while at the bar over on Van Brunt. On the water once in a while. He had a nice little boat. Nifty little sailboat,' he added. 'Swedish, I think.'

'It had a name?'

'Who?'

'The boat?'

'Can't remember,' the other guy said, and waved and they paddled away and I went back to my car.

By the time I got through to the number on Sid's machine, I was already on my way back to the city. The number belonged to Sonny Lippert and I had given it to Sid in case of emergency.

12

I wasn't back in Manhattan and inside Sonny Lippert's apartment thirty seconds before he told me Sid had been beat up and was in a coma, next door to dead. No chance, Sonny said, and I turned and made back for the door.

It was my fault. I should have acted. Sid was scared; Sid knew someone was after him. He told me whoever was after him went for Earl by mistake and now they had gone after Sid.

'There's nothing you can do, man,' Sonny said. 'He's in the hospital. He's hooked up to every fucking life support. His family is there. There are people on this. Sit down. You knew Sidney McKay, from a long time ago, you told him he could get me at home, right, man? It was you gave him my number.'

I said, 'What are the chances he'll come out of it?'

'No chance. One in ten million. One in a hundred million,' Sonny said.

'How did it happen?'

Sonny was on the balcony of his apartment, sitting on a green canvas chair, drinking tomato juice. He had moved here after his divorce, and it was a depressing place, the leather and tweed bachelor furniture that looked rented, the desolate little balcony where he sat and read and thought about his childhood in Brooklyn.

He held the glass of red juice and examined it

160

with distaste as if it were blood; he was coughing like he would spit out his lungs. Emphysema, the doctor told him. Bad heart. Bad lungs. The machinery rusting, he had said. Like the docks out by Red Hook. Like the sugar refinery that had burned and twisted and rusted.

'You called him? You knew?' I stood over him.

'Sit down. Yeah, I called him. He called me, he left me a message yesterday, but I didn't call back until this morning. I was too late. And how the hell did you get my message off his machine, by the way? You were at his place? You're on this case? What? Sit the fuck down, man, there's nothing you can do for him.'

'He's not going to make it?'

'I told you: no.'

'How did you hear?'

'Someone from the hospital called me. Someone found my number on Sid. Piece of paper in his pocket.'

'How did it happen?' I leaned into Sonny's face, my skin drenched with sweat. Sid had been attacked. He was in a coma. He was dying. I was involved. 'What hospital?'

'Give me a cigarette,' Sonny said and I tossed him the pack.

'Sid said he didn't have much time. He said to me, please come. Please hurry. Then he said he was going out of town. He was a lot more scared than I took it, he knew he was in trouble. I just figured some of it for his getting old,' I said.

Sonny snorted. 'Yeah, well, aren't we all, man.' Barefoot, in khaki shorts and a white polo shirt, Sonny was so thin he looked almost like a boy, except for his face; his face was an old man's now.

'You better lay it out for me, Artie, man,' Sonny added and I sat down on a yellow canvas chair next to him.

'Look, Sid called me Saturday night about some homeless guy he said was stalking him. Calls again the next morning,' I said. 'The guy's dead in Red Hook, trapped under a dock practically next door to where Sid has an office. I went Sunday morning. He had some crazy fucking story about how someone was after him and they killed the homeless guy by mistake, then he changed his mind. I went again yesterday. I owed Sid, I gave him your number in case he needed anything. He was scared, and I gave it to him. I was going to be working the convention and going away to meet Maxine at the shore and I wanted Sid to have someone to call.'

'You didn't want to share that with me, that you gave McKay my home number?'

'I'm sorry. It was stupid.'

The apology worked. It was what Sonny needed from me, and seeing him like that, seeing him small in his chair, I didn't mind. Also I needed his help with Sid. For years I had hated it, the way Sonny told people he had invented me, that he got me my first good job, that he used me because I could speak languages and wear a nice suit, that I was his creature. I had hated it but Maxine made me see it didn't mean squat, that it was just talk. Now I felt sorry for him. I sat down and tried not to look at my watch again.

I said, 'Listen, the baseball, it was great. Place of honor in my house, Sonny. I mean, honest to God. You didn't talk to Sid at all, is that what you're saying?'

'I never talked to him. He called me. I called him back, but it was too late. They found his body out near the docks, over by the Gowanus Canal where there are still some shipyards working, you know where I mean?'

'Yeah.'

'Someone tossed him in the water near a wrecked boat, a burned-out boat nobody used for years. An old ferry boat, I think. Staten Island Ferry.'

'Go on.'

'So they pushed him in, and somehow his clothes got caught on a rusty anchor, something like that, I don't know from boats, but it caught him, and he hung from below the water level. You get it?'

'Jesus.'

'Yeah.'

'They found my number on him when they got him in the hospital,' Sonny said. 'You have anything on the first murder, the guy who was stalking McKay?'

'How do you know it was a murder?'

'You think I didn't check, man? You think I'm that useless? It looks like a murder, and I'm betting you know that, too, so how was McKay connected?'

'He found the guy.'

Sonny said, 'Sid's in the hospital, Methodist,

over by Cobble Hill. They brought him in worse than dead. Someone beat him over the head with some kind of metal bar, rusted, a piece out of some machine by the docks. Someone picked up a metal plank and hit him and there were metal splinters sticking out of his skull. Then they dragged him on to that boat.'

'Christ,' I said, remembering Sid told me someone beat Earl over the head with a wood plank before he went into the water. It was as if they were using pieces of the old docks to murder people who got in the way, but in way of what?

I stood up.

'Wait.'

'What for? I have to go to work and then I'm going out to see Sid.'

'You can't help him.'

'Then help me.'

'Sit down,' Sonny said.

My skin was crawling. Someone had attacked Sid the same way they attacked his half brother, Earl; they beat him and then they pushed him off a rotting dock in Red Hook. I needed Sonny's help, so I sat on the edge of the canvas chair and tried to listen. He was wandering the way he did these days, drifting back to his childhood.

'When I was a kid they used to train up the Murder Inc. guys out there by Red Hook, you know, it was their training camp, man, they ran the place, all of them, but this is fifty fucking years ago, when the Jewish mob ran it, and Italians, too, the longshoremen were tough as nails and their union was corrupt as fuck, we're

164

talking the old days. You ever see *On the Waterfront*, man? It was just like that, it really fucking was, and us kids we were never allowed out there, never, but we were like interested in the gangster thing, I mean, you were a Jewish kid in Brooklyn, it was baseball players and gangsters even if your mother said so be a doctor, you know?

'I went out there once, a year back, nothing there except some lousy housing projects and a few yuppies making art or something, you know, and a lot of developers with itchy fingers, right?' Sonny picked up his juice. 'I wouldn't go near the place, who the fuck wants to live in a dump like that? So I was surprised when some cop called me about my number being on Sid and I can't remember now if I told him Sid had left me a message. I'm not remembering too good these days, and I thought I called Sid back. Too late. I was vague, man, and you know the worst fucking, thing, Art, man, I know it. I'm losing it and I know. I can read. I can read fine, Melville still makes sense to me, Tolstoy, Conrad, all the big bastards I always loved, but I can't make sense of anything around me. You think I'm crazy? I want a drink. I wish I called him in time.'

No one got back to Sid in time, I thought.

Sonny stared at me, and for a minute I wondered if he knew who I was, and then he smiled the old calculating sardonic smile, and said, 'So, Artie, man, if Sid McKay was one of your pals, how come I didn't see him at your wedding?'

165

I needed Sonny's input because, however crazy he was getting, he knew his way around the city's network of law enforcement, especially in Brooklyn which was always a foreign country no matter how many cases I worked there.

'I think we're all crazy these days, Sonny.' I said, as gently as I could and looked at my watch.

'You're in a hurry? You're working the Garden? Republican Convention in New York City. They're really milking it, man, all of it. War on Terror, load of horseshit, you know, the way they're doing it. I mean why didn't they just hold the fucking convention at Ground Zero? Drink one with me.'

I nodded.

Sonny went inside and came back out on the balcony with a couple of glasses in one hand and a bottle in the other. He looked at the Johnnie Walker, and said, 'I used to love a Scotch called King's Ransom, can't get it anymore.'

He poured the Scotch. On the path down near the river, a few people were jogging. Sailboats were out on the smooth water, puffed up with humid wind. I could see the building where Maxine wanted us to live.

'You like it over here?' I said to Sonny.

'It's OK. Why?'

'Maxine wants to move here.'

'We could be neighbors,' Sonny said, sipping his drink. 'Be nice to her, man. Maxine is a good girl.'

'You been to the doctor lately, Sonny?'

Sonny shrugged and looked over the railing of

his balcony at the people on the path by the river.

'You know how many people in this city are on drugs, legal, illegal, or all boozed up?' he asked. 'The developers say New York is back, man, let's build some more skyscrapers, let's build a Westside stadium, let's make it great. Weird isn't it how all the yups want to live down here, look at them, jogging and biking and bouncing up and down there on that path by the river, and keeping real fit, look at them go, Artie, all those girls with their tits bouncing up and down, and the financial guys coining it, half the city's terrified of losing out on a good apartment downtown and the other half is terrified of getting hit again, and coughing their fucking lungs out. Asbestos, all the other shit that came out of the Trade Center, makes you think about what we get every fucking day, our buildings killing us. Freon, neon, asbestos, you know how many neon lights got crunched up when the planes hit, how much crap we're ingesting, stuff I never heard of, asbestos, who-the-fuck-knowstos?' He laughed. 'But the real estate prices just keep going uppity up, man.' He gazed out at the boats. 'New York Waterways, who run the boats to and from Jersey, the Staten Island Ferry people, you hear they're going bust? Everyone's so high on the waterfront. I hear they're fucking going bust, man, and no one mentions it.'

He had always been angry, but it was worse now that he was semi-retired; before, Sonny's ambition drove him, it made him cunning and

167

kept him alive. He had too much time now. He got up again, went into the living room, put on a CD, an old Art Blakey album.

Back in his chair, eyes glazed, he jiggled his feet, beating out a rhythm on the arms of his chair. I was impatient. I started to get up.

'Sit down and fucking listen,' he said.

He loved jazz, which was the good side of Sonny; he had always loved the style; he had cast himself years before as a kind of 50s hipster, and once, when we'd been out late on a job and got drunk afterwards, we went to some club where Max Roach was playing. Roach was the coolest man alive, one of the last of the bebop greats. Sonny just looked at him, in thrall and then I heard him whisper: 'Smoking'. I had tried to forget about it. Finger popping daddy-O, right Sonny? Right, he had said that night, that's me, man.

'I'll make you a deal, Artie, man,' Sonny said now. 'I'll help you out here, if you tell me what you really know about the bum who got killed on Sunday, the one who scared Sid McKay.'

'OK. The dead guy was probably Sid McKay's half brother, maybe named Earl.'

'No shit.'

'Yeah. There was a connection that went way back in their past. I think Earl was following him around, hassling him. I think maybe Sid didn't want Earl to surface and fuck up his life. OK? Sonny? Like I said, he told me maybe it was Russian thugs who wanted information from him, from Sid, and whacked Earl by mistake. But he didn't believe it and I don't believe it.'

168

'Sid's never going to tell us now, is he?' Sonny was pouring another drink, tipping the bottle into his glass, losing himself. 'Poor bastard. How did he look, this Earl?'

'I only got a glimpse of him in the water. He was dead is all.'

'You know who the first dead people I ever saw were?' Sonny said.

'Let's talk about Sid,' I said, feeling nuts.

'The Rosenbergs,' Sonny said. 'Ethel and Julius Rosenberg, you know who that was, Artie, man? You're old enough? Yeah, you know, you're a Russki, they were probably idols over there, right? You probably knew all about them, even in your history books. Every kid in Brooklyn who had parents, what did they say, we were Progressive.' He laughed. 'Progressive, shit, that was the polite term they cooked up in '48 when people were already scared of the House Un-American Activities, Progressive, fuck it, every fucking decent asshole had been in the Communist Party, and most of them still were, and now it's 1953, and now the kids figured, they're going to fry my mommy and daddy, right? Because they fried Ethel and Julius in the electric chair up at the Sing Sing New York, June 19, 1953, because they said they were spies. They brought them to the funeral home in Brooklyn, it was Brownsville.' Sonny reached for his bottle again and I thought about Sid and the ship in Red Hook that came aground in 1953, same year as the Rosenbergs.

Stalin dead in 1953. The Rosenbergs. Sid meeting the Russian sailors. In my pocket were the snapshots of Sid and the Russian sailor.

'Listen to me, Art, man, so they fry them, and every kid in Brooklyn with any balls wanted to look at Ethel and Julius. So my friend, Herman Pearlstein, we called him Pearly, his father is a typesetter and a member of the Communist Party, and he said, let's go look at them martyrs for solidarity. Me, I wanted to see dead bodies. We snuck in. I'm practically shitting in my pants, I was so scared. I thought being electrocuted they'd look like fucking grilled meat. We got in this long line, it was like people weeping and wailing and some just thinking it was entertainment and some, probably some Irish Catholic fucking bastards, thinking good, more dead fucking Commie kikes, and a couple of Negroes who were on our side, very nicely dressed, the men were union guys, the ladies wore hats and carried handbags even though they did washing to make a few bucks, but they dressed nice, and we got in line and then we looked in the coffins. The coffins were open, which we never saw, they didn't put Jews in open coffins, so it was like weird, and there they were two middle-aged people laid out on white satin, and they looked like my aunts and uncles, you know, just a couple of middle-aged Jewish people dressed up in good clothes like for Passover or something, they didn't look grilled or anything. Just dead. I thought: this is what dead looks like, big fucking deal, so we left, me and Pearly. Sit down, Art.'

I was feeling pretty desperate. Sonny could go on for a long time, and I said, 'Help me out over Sid, Sonny. Who would want to hurt him? Is there anything going on around Red Hook? Something I'm missing?'

Sonny shrugged. 'He was your friend. You gave him my number. I wasn't in on this. You could have called me yourself,' he said.

'What about Red Hook?' I said. 'Sid was pretty obsessed with the place.'

'I heard you, I might be crazy but I'm not deaf. Maybe it could be about Red Hook, man. Apparently, according to stuff I've been hearing, and take it with a pound of salt, they are fighting over that one square mile of New York City like it's the last piece of meat on the plate.' He sipped his drink and retreated, his eyes glazing over. 'Or maybe not. Maybe it was racist shit with McKay. Maybe gay shit. I don't know.'

'What are they fighting for?'

'Who the fuck knows? Land. Ego. Waterfront. A safe haven for creeps. It always was. Bring in illegal cargo, booze, drugs, whatever. Or just real estate. Nowhere left to live in New York, everybody wanting. Why don't you ask your friend, Sverdloff? I hear he's been buying buildings like monopoly pieces. I hear he's not dish of the day back home in Moscow either where they're seriously killing each other at the intersection of mafia and real estate. Name of the game this year, real estate. A lot of dead people in Russia involved.'

It was what Tolya had said. Sonny had never liked Tolya.

'You knew that about Sid, that he was gay?'

'Everyone knew,' he said. 'He was pretty famous for a while. The *Times*. CBS. PBS. Who

171

can remember? Everyone was famous for a while. I broke a case with him, did you know, I gave it to him when he was at the *Times*, he kept calling me up to do cases with him, he thought I was fucking God.' Sonny snorted. 'He was good. He did me some favors. He helped me dig up some shit on nukes coming into the city through Brooklyn, you remember, around the time you broke the Red Mercury story and before the TV people came after us wanting to make a movie out of it, you remember?' He laughed. 'We thought we were going to be rolling in it, you and me. Movie deals. Movie stars. Who was going to play me, man? Pacino, I think we said Pacino could play me, and who was going to play you? Some good-looking bastard, right, I can't remember who.'

'You're thinking nukes in Red Hook?'

'Sure I could like Red Hook for illegal nukes, put the stuff in some canisters bring it in on some Lebanese freighter. But how the fuck do I know anything, Artie? Maybe it was random, maybe it was sex or drugs or race. I make one call, they hate me in Brooklyn now. They don't know shit there anymore, I tried too many cases, and after I worked the child abuse stuff year before last, they didn't want to know. But I got a few favors left, maybe.'

'Thanks.'

Suddenly as if emerging from some kind of fog, Sonny seemed to sharpen up. He put his drink on the little plastic table beside him. He got up and rubbed his eyes, and picked up his phone off the floor and went inside where I heard him talking.

I looked across the river. It was hot out and I was sweating and Sonny, in the living room, talked into the phone softly so I couldn't hear him.

★ ★ ★

When Sonny came back, I said, 'So?'

'So I'll do what I can do.' He reached down for a book that lay on the stained concrete on the little balcony and picked it up and held it out. 'You ever read this?' he asked, and showed me his copy of *Moby Dick*. 'Everything's here,' he said.

'I have to go, Sonny. If you can help me on the McKay thing, or his half brother, give me a call, OK, just call me. I have to go uptown. Then I'll go to the hospital. Just do this for me. OK? Do it. Sid was a good guy and he's as good as dead, so fucking do something, or else I'm going to give everyone on the case your home number.' I let off steam in his direction for no real reason and for once, he took it. He just absorbed it, or maybe he was already too drunk to care.

'Sure,' he said, picked up the bottle, went inside and switched on the television where politicians were screaming at each other.

13

I went to the hospital in Brooklyn first. No visitors, they said. No one. I couldn't get near Sid. I was late for work, I left my car at home, took the subway and came up near Madison Square Garden. Slabs of cement like the Berlin Wall had been lowered into place. There were gates in the cement walls. Metal detectors stood every few feet.

Along the sidewalks city cops stood holding machine guns. Squads of traffic cops leaned on bikes and mopeds, there were FBI agents on foot, some in blue jackets with logos on the back, others in the bad suits they always wore; secret service guys, big men like movie extras with short hair, milled around and talked into their lapels as limos pulled up and disgorged delegates.

From a few blocks away, where the protestors were penned up, I could hear the chanting, or thought I could, and I wondered if Lily was there. I thought about going over but she was probably busy with people who hated cops. The orders were out: get them locked up, as many as possible. I tried to stop myself thinking about her.

'Hard to tell if it's to keep the Republicans in or everyone else out,' I heard someone say. 'Fuck politics,' said someone else.

News crews in pairs and trios wandered

around looking for people to interview, and banks of broadcast trucks lined the streets. I got out my phone and called the guy who'd called me, looking for someone who could speak Russian. A minute later he pulled up in an unmarked car, a maroon Crown Vic; he got out, shook my hand.

'Thanks for coming,' he said, and walked me half a block, where a Russian woman about fifty was sweating in to her Bush T-shirt, and leaning against an NYPD car. She was fat and her belly hung out from her T-shirt. In the back seat was a kid, maybe eleven; he looked scared. A cop sat next to him.

'What happened?' I said to the woman in Russian and she looked up and told me she had seen the kid on the street acting suspicious. The kid had a backpack that looked funny. It had a bulge, she said, so she started yelling out that he had a bomb, he had a bomb. A cop was in the crowd. He hauled the kid in. Turned out the kid was carrying a soccer ball.

I calmed the woman down and she told me she was in town for the convention from Moscow. She was part of a group of Russian politicians. They were here to observe democracy in action, she said.

It had happened before. It was June when I was crossing Times Square real early in the morning, hardly anyone on the streets. Just by the Marriot Marquis Hotel, I see him, a kid, thirteen maybe. Hot day, and the kid bundled up big in a puffy silver winter jacket. For a split second, I think he's crazy, a crazy young kid who wears winter clothes in the summer. I'm almost passing him when I see a wire hanging out of his pants, the way you sometimes see a fringe hanging out on those Hassidic boys on 47th Street.

A cop in uniform is coming across the street and somehow we stop the kid and we get hold of Bomb Disposal. And he is wired up good; the kid is all wrapped up with a vest loaded with explosives that would have gone off, would have gone boom right in Times Square.

★　★　★

Stuff happened. We didn't talk about it. We didn't talk about the suicide bombers, the one that almost made it on to a plane, the one that almost got into a Yankees game at the Stadium, or the 6 train at the 59th Street stop, underneath Bloomingdales. We didn't talk about it. I knew because once in a while I got calls from people in the department desperate for information. They figured that, having lived in Israel, I knew about this kind of thing. I hadn't lived in Israel for twenty-five years. I went every year for a week to see my mother if I could, but that was it. But they called me like I knew about suicide bombers and the kind of detonators you could hide under your clothes. That's how desperate they were: they were asking me.

★　★　★

The rest of Tuesday and Tuesday night and then all Wednesday into Thursday, I worked the convention. All the time, I was calling Sonny and the hospital in Brooklyn, trying to get a fix on Sid who was still in a coma. No news. I tried to get away, but everyone in law enforcement in the city was in midtown, everyone doing double, triple shifts. I got a couple hours sleep and then I went back. I was exhausted.

I couldn't leave and it made me nuts because I was doing dumb stuff, checking delegates' badges, making sure news people stayed in their pens. I did a couple of hours at one of the checkpoints, watching people come and go in limos, and I thought I saw Dick Cheney, his face pasty and angry, a white cold face like a KGB man, but he probably came by helicopter, and I only imagined it. Helicopters buzzed the hot sky; there were snipers on rooftops. New York midtown looked like a war zone.

Most surreal of all was that I was assigned to a delegation of politicians from Moscow, including the fat woman who saw the kid she thought had a bomb in his backpack. They were special guests of the Republicans. Bush always referred to Putin as his friend, 'Vladimir.'

I escorted four of them, three guys and the fat woman, all wearing cheesy cowboy hats with Bush-Cheney bands on them, to Virgil's on West 44th Street. They ate ribs and fried chicken and told me how great it was now there were strong leaders like Putin and Bush. They invited me to go to Rasputin out near Brighton Beach to party later on. I looked at them, barbecue sauce smeared on their faces, guzzling beer. I listened to their crude accents. Small potatoes, I thought;

they would never be players in a country ruled by Putin who didn't drink.

Then, early Thursday, the story of the school siege in Russia began filtering through: rumors about kids held hostage; rumors about children murdered, of parents forced to choose which kid to take out of the school with them; rumors of slaughter. I saw my Russians on a street corner that day, huddled together, weeping.

I caught some of the convention on monitors outside the main hall and I thought how much the politicians sounded like men I grew up watching on TV, same rhetoric, same bullshit: strong government was what mattered; anyone who didn't was an enemy of the state. 'Enemy of the state.' I heard some asshole use the expression, and it made me feel physically sick. Stalin's favorite label.

I was never political. I voted some of the time; sometimes I didn't vote. Depended who was up. I liked Clinton OK, but, and I never told anyone, I mostly liked him because I felt a lot in common with a guy who like me, if he was honest, if I was honest, wanted to sleep with practically every good-looking woman he saw.

All I ever really wanted was to be a New York City cop, and maybe for the Yankees to be good again like they were in the 90s, and the Red Sox to lose big.

Growing up, first Moscow, then Israel, I had choked on politics. By the time I got to New York, I figured I could live my whole life without it.

By Thursday, when I got off work early thanks

to a friend who helped me out, I was desperate to get out of the city and I got a cab and called Maxine and said I'd set off in a couple of hours. She said they were having a great time, and they missed me, and I told her about the Russians eating ribs at Virgil's and made her laugh. I didn't mention that I'd seen Lily on the street.

'I'll see you really soon,' I said.

'You'll come, though, won't you? The girls would be disappointed if you didn't come.'

'Sure, I'm coming,' I said, wondering why she was suddenly anxious.

'Is there a lot of security?' she said.

'Like a fucking war zone,' I said. 'Only up around the Garden, though, around midtown.'

'Protestors?'

'Yeah. I think they're going to lock up as many as they can.'

'Well, maybe they should just be glad they live in America, you know?' Maxine said. 'Where are you?'

'On my way home,' I said, as we sped down Seventh Avenue.

★ ★ ★

It was ghostly in downtown Manhattan; it was like a neutron bomb had dropped: the buildings were standing, but there were hardly any people, even on this balmy summer night. The cab cut east on Spring Street. The restaurants were empty. The terrace at Aquagrill, usually packed in nice weather, was almost deserted. The Tasti-D-Lite store had shut up early.

179

I couldn't remember so much silence in the last few years, not since 9/11. A million people had left town. I heard some were scared of attacks. Some were scared of the security, or the protestors, or traffic, but all week I'd felt it like a light layer over the city: fear; quiet; anxiety. What I always loved about New York was the noise.

I loved the street noise, the way people felt free to yak or yell or sing, speak, mouth off, even lean on the fucking car horns. When I was a kid in Moscow there was almost no noise, hardly any cars, hardly any laughter or music in the streets, everyone afraid. My uncle who had lived in Prague told me that the thing he adored about the Prague Spring was the noise. The Soviet tanks rolled in, Prague went silent.

I got home, got the bag with Sid's files out of the car, got my mail, went up, dumped everything on my desk, ripped off my clothes, went to the fridge and got a cold beer.

While I drank it, I glanced through Sid's stuff, and all I could see was a bunch of newspaper clippings and some notes on the old ship he told me about. I didn't have time for more. I couldn't see anything, and I wasn't going to ruin my vacation, or Maxine's, reading the files. I put Sid's folders away in my desk drawer, locked it, put on a T-shirt and jeans, picked up the bag I had already packed for the beach and went out. I was going to the shore. I was going to meet Maxine and Millie and Maria. One stop, I thought; I'd make one more stop and then I'd go. I had promised. I'll be there by midnight. I'll be there. Love you, Maxine had said. See you soon.

On my way, I drove through Chinatown. Across the street from the bar where I used to go with Lily, I stopped. Crouched down in the front seat, looking out, I felt like a creep.

Through the window of the bar, I saw her. She was sitting on a barstool, her back to me, her hand around a wine glass. For a couple of minutes I watched her. I wanted so bad to go in and talk to her, but I pulled out of the space, and stepped on the gas hard.

★ ★ ★

As soon as I got out of the hospital elevator in Brooklyn, I heard the sound of rubber soles on linoleum, the way you always did in hospitals. Someone trundled an IV down the hall; two male aides shoved a patient on a gurney; there was the hot sour metallic smell of hospital food; somewhere a patient cried out. At the end of the floor I found the room I was looking for. The door was ajar.

In the middle of the private room was a bed and on it lay Sid, or his shell, his body, the outer casing that had been Sid, because the rest of him was gone. His face was blank, shut up. I felt bad. I felt like I wanted to cry for him, and for me, too, for fucking up.

'He's never coming back,' a male nurse named Luis whispered to me as I entered the room.

'Why don't they pull the plug?' I said.

'They did,' he said. 'Nothing happened. They

gave permission. He didn't die. It's like he's hanging on for something.' He gestured to the group around the bed. 'They've been there since yesterday some time.'

Four people were on chairs around the bed where Sid lay. An elderly woman in a linen suit with a straw hat sat in a Naugahyde armchair, her back not touching the chair; next to her, a wine glass in his left hand, was a middle-aged man in Bermuda shorts and a polo shirt with polo players on the pocket, as if interrupted in the middle of a game; there was a woman who appeared to be his wife, wearing a plaid skirt and sleeveless pink blouse, and a girl in her teens in jeans.

On a table in the corner someone had set out a large coffee urn and a platter with pastries, and I could see the slick sugary shiny surface of the Danish, and the blue of the berries in the muffins; there were bottles of wine, a row of glasses.

Luis, the nurse, backed out of the room. I followed him and asked about Sid.

'After we pulled the plug, and it was the son who gave the OK, nothing happened, and they had to sit and wait,' he said. 'I heard one of the women call someone on her cell and say, 'Bring some wine over.' A little while later, a young kid, maybe nineteen, twenty, arrives with a bag, and unloads bottles of wine, puts it out, puts out glasses, starts pouring. People have been coming to visit, and in-between the family argue about some bullshit and they all sit and drink and he just lies there.'

'Where's the son?'

'I saw him go out a while back, maybe for a smoke,' he said.

'Thanks,' I said.

I stood against the door and for a while no one looked up, and I listened to the low buzz of family talk that came from around Sid's bedside.

Finally, the teenage girl got up from her chair. 'Who are you?' she said.

'I was his friend. You?'

'My great uncle, but we were close.'

'I'm sorry,' I said and we moved into the corridor.

'I wish they'd just let him go.'

'I thought they did.'

'Yeah, but he wouldn't die. He won't die.'

'It's tough.'

'Not for them,' she said, gesturing at the group inside the room. 'They love it, the bedside thing, the ritual, they do it all the time, makes them feel saintly,' she said. 'I can't stand it. I don't know why I'm here except for Sid.'

'You called him Sid?'

'Sure. We were friends.'

'You saw a lot of him?'

She shook her head, started to cry. 'I wish,' she said softly. 'They wouldn't let me. They didn't want me around him. They thought he was weird, that he was different, that he didn't behave the way the family wanted him to behave. I liked it. I liked him. I have to go back now.'

'Weird how?'

She turned around. 'You know, gay. And the

183

Russian thing. He was obsessed. He was crazy for Russians.'

'Can I talk to you later?'

'Sure,' she said. 'I'm not going anyplace.'

★ ★ ★

I didn't talk to her, though, not then or later. I went over to the nurse's station. Luis, the nurse I'd seen in Sid's room, was at a desk, working on the computer. A tiny Jamaican woman was standing at the desk, packing her bag, getting ready to leave, shift finished.

'You a cop or something?' she asked me.

'Something.'

'I would appreciate less attitude,' she said, hostile. 'Cops been, of course, cops, family, everybody on my case,' she said, speaking rapidly. 'I was off duty fifteen minutes ago and I stayed on trying to help and you all just get in my face.'

I needed information. 'I apologize,' I said.

'You don't like the way I run things I can get an administrator,' she said. 'I can get them to send you hospital policy. Printed. I just can't talk about patients, even if you are a cop. Not to mention I didn't see your badge.'

I got out my wallet to show her my badge. Stuffed in the pocket beside it was the card the security guard who stopped the kayakers gave me. Orwell Properties, it said. An address in Red Hook.

I could easily have stuffed the card back in with the rest of the junk in my wallet. You could look at something five times and not see it for what it was. Every detective knew that most of what you found out was half accidental: something clicked, or it didn't, or you made the connection or you overlooked it. I wasn't any better than a lot of cops. The card would have stayed in my wallet, forgotten, except for the Jamaican nurse wanting to see my badge. She was starting for the door when Luis looked up and said to me, 'What about the Russian?'

'None of his business,' the short nurse said, and then she picked up her bag and left, tiny but imperious even in the way she walked.

'What Russian?' I said.

Stethoscope hanging from his neck, Luis leaned on the counter between us, arms folded near a potted plant in a pot with pink tinfoil and a ribbon on it. He took a chocolate from an open box and said the guy who had been in to visit Sid was a big Russian. Huge.

I said, 'He had a name?' Cold sweat broke out on my back.

'No, but Russian, I think for sure, yeah, and really big. He wanted to know everything that happened. He shook hands with all of us. He tipped everyone. He was crying after he saw the way Mr McKay was. Why? You know him? You don't look so hot, man. Sit down for a second. You want me to take your blood pressure?'

The business card that had been in my wallet was in my hand now. For the first time since I'd gone to see Sid Sunday, I was really scared.

Panicky. Maxine was waiting for me. It was getting late. I was late. Sid was as good as dead. The card in my wallet read Orwell Properties; it belonged to Tolya Sverdloff.

14

My shoe caught in the crack of a piece of broken sidewalk, and I stumbled and broke the fall with my hands. It hurt like hell. I felt like an idiot, but there was no one to see me here on this shabby side street in Red Hook.

On the narrow street were two houses with high stoops out front, the walls covered with cheap masonry siding. They looked shut up. So did the row of four stores, corrugated metal shutters smeared with graffiti, pulled down tight; a squat evangelical church with a flat roof, was silent; a couple of burned-out cars rusted in an empty lot. At the far end of the street, I could make out where the water began, but it was getting dark, and the light from the single street light pooled in one place so everything else was hidden in shadows.

Give my regards to Tolya Sverdloff, Sid had said. Sid has files, Tolya told me; he has information. A big Russian had been into the hospital; he tipped everyone. The security guard in Red Hook was paid to keep people away from the waterfront by Tolya's company. Orwell Properties.

Tolya had dozens of little companies, he once told me, and reeled off the names; I only remembered Orwell because he thought it was his best joke, naming a company for George Orwell. Tolya carried a tattered orange and white

Penguin edition of *Nineteen Eighty-Four* with him everywhere, the same edition he bought, black market, in his school toilet in Moscow when he was a teenager. I always told him *Brave New World* was a better book, a hell of a lot more prescient, but he didn't care. Orwell had been his god for too long.

When I called Tolya, there was no answer. I kept going, my hands raw and hurting like hell from the pavement where I tripped.

Florida, Tolya had said. I'll probably go to Florida. End of the week. Friday, he had said; it was Thursday night.

I found Orwell Properties two streets over, but it was locked up, a metal gate pulled over the front door. I glanced around, thought about breaking in, tried to shove aside the gate. I didn't have anything to work with. All I had in the trunk of my car were a few wedding presents and some stuff for the beach.

I should get moving, I thought. Make it down to Jersey in three hours, four maybe, depending on traffic. Every few minutes, I kept saying it to myself. I should go. I looked at my watch. Instead, I drove over to the water and pulled up near Sid's building. There was a cop in uniform outside. The place would be sealed. I'd have to work a dozen angles to get into Sid's place, and there wasn't much I could do for him now.

Right now, I needed Tolya Sverdloff telling me I was crazy, that he wasn't involved in some way with the attack on Sid, that he didn't need information that bad.

I opened the door and got out of the car and

went out on the little pier. It was a clear evening, sun dropping into the water that was like a stream of silver. I sat on a bench.

'Lily?'

I had the feeling that she was there suddenly, next to me, on the bench, her red hair ruffled in the slight humid breeze off the river, smoking alongside me, chatting about the day, the world, us; we had always talked all the time; if we were apart, we called each other four, five, six times a day. We could never talk enough. We could never get enough of each other, or maybe that had been me. That night out on the cement pier, out in the river, I had the most intense sense of her being beside me. I woke up. I had dozed for maybe half an hour.

I was so whacked I was hallucinating. I was hungry. I hadn't eaten since Virgil's with the Russians the night before, and I got my car and went to find some food and coffee.

I still couldn't reach Tolya; the car radio was reporting a hurricane, second big one in a few weeks, beating up the south coast; the airports in Florida were beginning to shut down. The forecast for the next day was worse. Maybe Tolya was already caught in it. Maybe he was stranded on some highway down there.

★ ★ ★

A small woman plugged into a Discman she carried in one hand jiggled up and down to her music in front of a grocery store on Van Brunt Street. I recognized her. She was the woman who had attacked Tolya outside the bar in Red Hook, the woman who had climbed on him like a cat and tried to gouge his eyes out.

She wasn't bad-looking, and she seemed sober this time, not drunk or high. She wore cut-off pink sweat pants, and a turquoise T-shirt with a picture of Jimi Hendrix on the front. She was twenty-five, maybe thirty, short, thick, sexy in an athletic way like a gymnast. Her black hair was tied up in a ponytail. She ran inside the store. I pulled up and waited.

A few people were on the street, going into the pub and towards a restaurant with some tables on the sidewalk. Two black women waited at the bus stop. There was no subway on this isolated peninsula.

My eyelids sank over my eyes while I waited outside the store. Worried the woman would get away, I finally got out of the car and went into the store where I stood, partly hidden behind the beer and soda. She was examining boxes of cookies. I watched her while she read the labels carefully.

Eventually, she picked a bunch of bananas out of a bin and gathered up some potatoes from another one, asked for a pack of cigarettes from the guy at the counter, exchanged gossip with him in Spanish, stopped to light one of her smokes and carried her groceries back out to the street.

For half a block I followed her on foot until we were clear of the shop and then I called out in Russian. She turned around. I could see she knew who I was. She tossed her smoke away and ground it out with her foot.

Close up, she was a pretty girl. I took out my own cigarettes and offered them to her, but she shook her head so I lit one for myself. I spoke in Russian to her, my father's Russian, formal, polite, respectful. I always imagined it was the way he had interrogated people, at least in the beginning. I asked what her name was.

'Rita,' she said.

'Just Rita?'

'Is not enough?'

'Can we talk?'

'Yes,' she said and I was pretty surprised she was so forthcoming, so ready to talk, especially since I knew she recognized me as the guy who had been with Tolya when she attacked him.

'Come home with me,' she said, and I gestured to my car, and we both got in, and she directed me a couple of blocks away to the housing projects.

★ ★ ★

The projects were at the front of Red Hook, away from the docks and closer to the highway. Surrounded by scruffy grass, some of the buildings were thirty, forty years old.

Rita looked at the pink plastic watch on her wrist. 'I have to cook,' she said in English and I didn't understand what she meant, but she indicated a parking spot and we stopped, and I followed her out of the car and into the dank hallway of a building and up to the top floor.

I could have been in Moscow. The damp stink

of the long hall, green paint on the walls, the cooking smells coming from other apartments, the sound of people fighting, it was a long time since I'd been in a building like this. I wanted out.

Somewhere dogs were barking. They sounded like they were tied up, barking, whining, howling.

'I think they still fight dogs around here, you know? Cockfights, but also dogs. For money,' Rita said, stopped in front of a door, and unlocked it.

* * *

It was a small apartment. She said she shared it with a Mexican friend. In the living room was a couch, an armchair, and a table that was covered with a green and yellow flowered tablecloth. On the wall, on a shelf with a candle in a red glass jar, was a shrine to some Catholic saint. Next to it was a little Russian Orthodox icon and beside it a photograph of Stalin cut out of an old newspaper and framed behind glass. A bedroom was visible through an open door. A second door led to a kitchen where I followed Rita.

'Tamales,' she said, setting down her bag of groceries on a table that had one leg shorter than the others and was propped up with a few sticks of wood. 'We cook for soccer games. Is big deal here, weekends, holidays, everyone playing football in park. Also, I make pelmeni.' Rita smiled, and put on some latex gloves and picked up the top of a large pot full of glass jars. She checked there was water in the pot then turned on the stove to boil the jars.

'Jars for borscht. I make real good borscht. One day I am queen of borscht.'

'What?'

She took off the gloves with a snap and put them on the counter near the stove, and leaned against the window.

'So over by old warehouses, little businesses all over Red Hook, you know, people doing this, that, blowing glass, making pies, designing stuff, kites, one lady makes so beautiful kites, so I start business, too, pelmeni, borscht, my friend Cecilia says, OK, you help me make tamales, I help with borscht, we gonna sell fancy restaurants, food stores. We gonna be big. Fancy.' She giggled. 'We already give down payment on warehouse space by Snapple plant.'

I said, 'There's a lot of Russians around here now?'

'There's Russians everywhere,' she said. 'I'm born in Brighton Beach, I go back to Russia until I'm twenty years, then come back. I find place in Brighton, then I lose, move to Flatbush and I lose, and I have no place to go, story of poor Russians, we move, we get fucked, so I meet Cecilia and she says I can share. She is alone like me. So I make tamales,' she said in Russian now and glanced up at the shrine. 'Where you from?'

'Manhattan,' I said.

'I mean in Russia.'

'Moscow.'

'You speak nice,' she said, 'I speak shitty both

193

languages, I lost both, English, Russian, moving around. You want something? Tea? Soup? Please.'

I said I'd eat some of her borscht — I was starving — and she heated some up, put it in a bowl and carried it into the living room where we sat at the table. I ate. I asked about the icon on the living room wall.

'Yours?' I said.

'My friend she makes shrine to some saints, so I make icon. Everyone praying a lot around here, Americans like praying, so I pray also.'

'To Stalin?'

'I get from my father,' she said. 'So I keep. You think Stalin was so bad? Plenty Russians in Brooklyn loving Stalin.' She looked at my bowl. 'Good?'

'Great,' I said.

'So you are surprised I invite you to my place? You think I just ask like that? You think I don't remember that you are friends with fat Russian guy?' She smiled. 'So is your friend, this fat Sverdloff bastard?'

'Yes,' I said.

'Which is why you are following me?'

'I wasn't following you. I saw you on the street.'

She snorted.

I said, 'Why did you attack him?'

'Are you cop?'

'Yes.'

'Is OK,' she said. 'I am not scared of police like other Russians. I didn't do nothing. You want to know why I attack him? If I tell you, maybe you keep him away from me, OK?'

'OK.'

Rita got up and went to a black wood cabinet with a glass front, squatted down in front of it, and extracted a bottle of vodka. She pulled off the foil around the neck and opened it, then produced a couple of glasses and held the bottle out towards me.

'Yes?'

'Sure.'

She poured the booze into the glasses, then sat on the couch. I went and sat next to her. Rita said, 'I am very, very drunk that day, OK, so I feel bad after, but Sverdloff making trouble around here. Always here, always talking, always wanting to know, Red Hook this, Red Hook that, where can he buy property, what goes on. I meet him at soccer game, I see him at a bar, he makes nice, you know, also he buys my food, then he says I will invest in business. He promises but nothing happens.'

I drank my vodka.

'Not so many people speak Russian around here,' Rita said. 'So first I help him. He pays me something, and I help him, I tell him what I hear, what I know, who has bids on spaces, how much, then I find out he wants to buy everything. He don't give no shit about people here, he wants to buy and make houses for rich people.'

'He does this stuff himself?'

'No. He has people. He has people, you know? He don't do small shit. Is like movie business, you know? He is Mr Nice Guy, helps everyone, gives money for everything, kids, schools, charity, artistic stuff. Not him. He does not get hands dirty. I moved enough,' Rita said. 'You understand? I don't want to move no more. I keep this apartment.'

'Yeah, but I'm not sure he's interested in this apartment.'

She finished her drink and poured some more. 'So is your friend?' she said. 'Friend from long time?'

'What else?' I said. 'I could give you some money for your business. If you want. I could make an investment.'

I took out my wallet and looked inside. I'd been to the bank. I had vacation money. I took a fifty and put it under the empty borscht bowl.

'I mean I like borscht.'

'Your mom made?'

'Sure,' I said and thought of my mother who never cooked if she didn't have to, who hated Russian food and dreamed only of a life in Paris that she would never have, who cut out pictures of France from magazines she bought on the black market when she had a little extra money.

From her stash of photographs, she pieced together a life of Parisian pleasure, of museums, and bookshops, and cafes and delicious food and wine. She never made it to France, but after we were kicked out of Moscow, when we went to Israel, a few times, on birthdays, my father took her to a French restaurant. She ate paté and French bread and they drank wine. She saved the menus.

For a few seconds, I wasn't sure if Rita would take the money or throw me out, but she was a smart cookie. She did her primitive shtick, and I listened and smiled and we drank more vodka and cracked jokes in Russian and I complimented her on her soup again.

She pulled her legs up under her and sat cross-legged next to me, leaning forward. She gave off heat. I was wearing a T-shirt, it was warm in the apartment, no air con, and Rita reached over and touched the bare skin on my arm.

'OK,' she said. 'If you want, you can invest in my company, so I tell you this friend of you is big creep and sometimes I see him with black man, they walk and talk a lot by docks and sometimes they are arguing.'

'Which black man?'

'Mr Sid McKay.'

'You know him?'

'Everyone here knows,' she said. 'Small place.'

'You liked him?'

'Sure,' she said.

'What else?' I said, but the front door flew open, and a tall skinny Hispanic woman burst in, followed by a pair of teenage girls, arms laden with shopping bags that sprouted ears of corn.

The two girls spread a plastic garbage bag on the floor, and began husking the corn; the corn silk piled up like shorn hair.

Rita got up. I suddenly wondered if she had spotted me first on the street, if she just wanted some money. She wrote down her phone number on a piece of paper and gave it to me.

At the door I said, 'Did you know that Sid McKay was attacked?'

'Yes,' she said. 'Everybody knows. He is dead?'
'Not yet.'

Not yet. Not yet, it went through my head, it kept time with the sound of my steps in the hallway outside Rita's door. I ran, the sound echoed in my head. I left the building; it was dark. Teenage boys loitered close by. Somewhere there was the sound of gunfire, or maybe just a car backfiring.

Hurry, I thought to myself, but where to? I should have been on the road to Maxine hours ago, but I had to know about Tolya. When I got through to someone at his condo in Florida, the woman said she had no idea where the hell he was, no idea, and it sounded like a lie. Everything sounded like a lie. I ran for my car.

15

'He's dead,' Sonny said on the phone when I answered it from my car. 'He's dead, man. They unplugged Sid, you knew that, and finally he went. He's dead. Someone beat him with the metal plank, and left him, and it took him days to die. You figure he didn't know? You figure he didn't feel anything once he went in the coma? Who the fuck knows? Maybe he was lying there and he knew it all. So here's a wackola thing, man, he had metal in his brain and he had wood splinters deep in his hands, go figure.' Sonny sounded sober. 'Go have your honeymoon. I'm with this now.'

I felt lousy when I heard. I already knew Sid was finished, but you could hope. This was final. I felt lousy. I should have paid attention when Sid told me someone was looking for him and killed his half brother Earl by mistake, but who would mistake Earl, a homeless drunk in rags, for Sid? It still didn't compute.

I said to Sonny, 'Where are you?'

'I'm at the hospital, where do you think? You said fucking help the guy, so I'm helping.'

'I'm on my way.'

'Don't. There's nothing you can do.'

'What kind of wood?'

It was the thing that had been lodged in the back of my mind, and now I had to yank it out and look at it. Did Sid kill Earl? It occurred to me now that this was how Sid knew about the wood plank, about Earl maybe being hit over the head before he went into the water. It was Sid who had called in the case. Would he do it if he really was the killer? Because he suddenly felt guilty? Because no one would suspect him anyhow? Because I wouldn't? Did Sid read me so well?

'Artie, you there, man?' Sonny was still on the phone.

'What kind of wood, Sonny?'

'What?'

'The splinters in Sid's fingers.'

'Fuck knows,' he said. 'You having some thoughts about this?'

'It doesn't matter,' I said.

If it was Sid who killed Earl, what the hell difference did it make now? Earl was dead. Sid was dead. If I kept my mouth shut, the waters would close over it all. If it got out, it was all anyone would remember about Sid McKay, that he killed a homeless guy who was probably his half brother. I'd make sure Earl got a decent burial, like I had promised, and let it go. I'd let it go. Sonny was waiting on the other end of the phone.

'Artie, man, you there?'

I told him I'd call him later and hung up, then left Maxine a message that I was on my way. I didn't head right out for Jersey, though. I had another stop.

★ ★ ★

200

Behind the gate of Tolya Sverdloff's apartment building in Brighton Beach was a doorman wearing a Cossack-style getup. His cranberry red shirt with puffy sleeves was buttoned on the shoulder and his pants were stuffed into knee-high boots. He was talking Russian into a cellphone.

Behind me along Brighton Beach Avenue under the elevated train tracks, the street was crowded with people shopping. The shops had Russian signs in the windows: books, underwear, minks, smoked fish, fancy imported china; everything was still Russian here. You could tell by the signs: the sign in one window read FISH in English and FRESH FISH in Russian. The old days, Soviet times, fish was almost always frozen, and the shopkeepers who ever got anything fresh always underlined the word. Fresh fish was real status.

Sid was dead and I couldn't get hold of Tolya, and I needed him to tell me that he wasn't involved.

Tell me, I thought. Tell me you didn't kill Sid because you needed information about some fucked up real estate scheme. Tell me the girl Rita with the borscht business is just another crackpot Russian, and you didn't betray everything for more cash. Tell me you didn't send one of your guys to hurt Sid.

Tolya had guys for everything, drive him around, help out friends, and god knew what else. I had used his guys plenty; I had taken the help. I never asked what else they did for him beside driving his cars around and doing errands

201

for his friends. This time I had to ask.

In front of the building was the ocean and the long boardwalk that ran alongside it. Strings of colored lights were coming on at the cafes and restaurants that were clustered along the boardwalk. The sound of Russian pop music blasted out of speakers at every cafe. People drifted in for dinner.

Tolya's building itself had a fake Art Deco façade with shutters trimmed in mint green and cranberry. I banged on the gate a second time, and the Cossack with the cellphone looked at me. I held up a twenty-dollar bill. He opened the gate and I said I was Sverdloff's brother and implied I had keys for the apartment. He took the money, waited while I passed him twenty more, and then let me through.

In the elevator I got stuck at the back of a pack of Russian women, all babes, great figures, big hair, their arms piled full of shopping bags and boxes, one with a huge black plastic dress bag over her shoulder, something red and furry sticking out of the bottom. They were talking Russian loud. Peasant Russian, my mother would have said. She was a snob once. Now in the fog that Alzheimer's had wrapped around her, she didn't speak any language, not Russian or Hebrew or the French she had loved. I had to get to Israel to see her soon; it was over a year since I'd been and maybe I'd take Maxine, though for months after I saw my mother, I was always trapped by melancholy.

★　★　★

Outside Tolya's apartment, I listened for a minute. I rang the bell. Then I knocked. I rang again and listened again, and looked up and down the corridor which had dark red carpeting and flocked green and gold wallpaper.

Originally he had bought the place for his mother for her visits to America. During her last couple of years, she wanted to stay in Brighton Beach. 'With my people,' she said over and over, but by then Lara Sverdlova was pretty much nuts.

After his mother died, Tolya kept the place. He told me he sometimes came out here to hide. Or to feel Russian. Or both.

'Who thinks I am ever living in this place in Brighton Beach, right Artyom? Who ever imagines even that I have such a place in my possession? When I am hungry, I go for an overnight,' he had said once when we were sitting out on the boardwalk eating tongue and smoked sturgeon and roast lamb, him drinking the Kvass that he loved.

When I was sure the apartment was empty, I picked the lock.

All the time I was thinking: Was Tolya involved with Sid's death? Then I was thinking, maybe Tolya was dead, then thinking: don't be dead, man. For a second, I felt he was dead, then I rejected the idea and figured he was alive.

My skin crawled with anxiety. I wanted to call Maxine and tell her, wanted to ask her what I should do if Tolya was involved. She had a good moral compass, she didn't suffer from confusion about right and wrong; she was a Catholic girl who knew; she just knew. I didn't call.

★ ★ ★

The living room had a couple of huge black leather couches and tons of computer stuff. A flatscreen TV covered most of one wall.

In the bedroom the bed was still covered with the pink silk spread that Tolya's mother had used; the dresser held her perfume bottles; a Russian book on astrology was on the nightstand next to pictures of her husband, and of Tolya and his children. A votive candle, unlit, stood in a glass holder. I picked it up. It was cold.

Furry brown slippers with bears' heads that had belonged to Lara Sverdlova were on the floor. In a small bookcase were old Soviet magazines she liked to read, magazines with pictures of herself as the young, beautiful actress she had been, so unlike the crazy old woman I remembered who had terrorized people around Brighton Beach. She yelled at people. She told them they were fat or ugly. She just let fly whenever she wanted. Tolya had been sweet, though, and patient.

I remembered how he had carried her out of Farone's restaurant one night when she went berserk; she made his life hell, but he picked her up and carried her gently to the car.

When Sverdlova had died earlier in the summer in her dacha outside Moscow, Tolya went to bury her in the cemetery in Peredelkino near her husband and within sight of Boris Pasternak's grave. She had always claimed that she had been up for the part of Ophelia in a production of Pasternak's translation of *Hamlet* and that she had had an affair with the writer. I never knew how many stories she made up. I thought of Sid and his wooden dolls.

In the living room, I looked at the answering machine, but there were no messages. I hoped like hell that Tolya would show up. I had left him messages to meet me. I leaned on the window sill and looked out at the beach and the dark ocean, with tiny lights from a ship on the horizon.

For an hour I waited, but no one came. It was getting late. It was a long drive to New Jersey. I had to get to Tolya first, but it was getting late. Where was he?

★ ★ ★

On the boardwalk, I went into some of the cafes where Tolya ate, but no one had seen him. Tourists strolled by, inspecting the menus posted outside the restaurants.

'It's so Russian here,' I heard a woman giggle.

'Brighton Beach is theme park now, little Russian theme park, like you could have practically Mickey Mouski, you know,' Tolya had said to me.

Old men sat on all the benches along the boardwalk and watched the ocean. Some wore overcoats even in the summer. All of them smoked, and talked about Russia. They came every night, even in the winter, even when there was snow on the ground and ice in their beards, and they spoke only Russian. In their minds they were here on a temporary basis, even after

205

twenty, thirty, forty years. They yearned for a place where they believed there was some kind of order, a way of life they understood. There wasn't any. The best it got was the strict arrangement of seating on the boardwalk benches, a kind of acknowledged ritual. They looked at the water and thought about going home. But where would they go? The country they had known had disappeared. The Soviet Union was long gone. On those benches, they always seemed shipwrecked.

I recognized one of them, a fat angry old man in a striped shirt like a sailor's and I asked him if he had seen Tolya. He knew who I was; he turned away, suspicious; I was a cop; I was an outsider.

On Brighton Beach Avenue, I checked a few of the nightclubs but they were jammed and I couldn't spot Tolya in any of them. In one I sat at the bar and watched a girl with breasts big as footballs wrap herself around a pole on a platform above me. I drank a glass of wine. When the girl finished, I gestured to her, she leaned down, tits in my face, I put some money in her thong. She hadn't seen Tolya, though she knew him.

Eventually I drove the mile or so over to Sheepshead Bay and Farone's. The place was full, the crowd loud and hungry. I saw Johnny.

'I need to talk to you.'

'It's Thursday night, Artie. I'm overbooked.'

I grabbed his sleeve. 'I need to talk.'

'Come upstairs to my office,' he said and I followed him up a flight of stairs. There was a private dining room on one side, the door open. Through it I saw a group of women. Genia was there, and she looked up and saw me, waved, then came out and kissed me.

'Hello, Artemy. Please come and meet my friends,' she said formally in Russian.

I peered into the private room where a dozen women, well dressed, sat at the table, heads low, talking softly like women in mourning. In spite of the designer clothes and hair, they looked like Russian women at a wake.

Genia touched her own short hair self-consciously, and straightened her black cashmere sweater.

'They're abducting children, maybe killing them,' she said. 'In Russia now, then where? In Beslan first. Here next? Here, Artyom? It will happen.'

I kissed her.

'We get news ahead of local TV. We are getting phone calls from Russia. We try to raise money for the families,' she said, gesturing to the group of women in the room. 'We try.'

People were scared, she said. They left Russia for America and the American empire cracked up, airplanes attacked buildings, and now in Russia people were dying in Moscow theaters, in schools. It was like a perpetual earthquake, like a tsunami.

No place safe, Genia said to me and told me she heard people say, 'If only we had Stalin. All the time I hear this, strong is good, Stalin was great, Putin is good. I'm frightened, Artemy,' she added and returned to her friends.

I went into Johnny's office with him and he opened a bottle of wine, sat behind his huge mahogany desk and gestured to a black leather chair.

'You're looking for Sverdloff, Art? That it?' he said.

'How'd you know?'

'He said you'd be by.'

'When?'

'He came in earlier, said he needed a fix of my soft shells, I fixed him some nice crabs, some nice pasta, I got him a good bottle of the Barolo he likes up from the cellar, you know, and he said, if Artie comes by, tell him I got his message. I'll find him.'

I got up to go.

'I have to go down and see Billy next week, you want to send him something from you?' Johnny looked at me and I saw his eyes were wet. He was a weepy guy to begin with; since his boy killed a man, he cried all the time.

'What time?'

'What time what?'

'Sverdloff was here, what time?'

Farone looked at his watch. 'Shit, man, I don't know, earlier. I got so much fucking business, you believe that? I must be famous, right?'

'Did he say where he was going?'

Johnny shook his head. 'I was busy. Listen, Art, did you tell me everything you found out about Billy? You never did, I know that. You kept it a secret from everyone. Tell me now.'

'Don't, Johnny. Please. I can't do this now.' I felt trapped. I had to get out; Genia's misery and

208

Johnny's sorrow drenched me; it was like napalm; I felt I couldn't move.

Johnny said, 'It was that Sid McKay guy, wasn't it? He fixed it with the press so people wouldn't say my Billy was a killer. I met him. He was a sweet nice man.'

I got up, and Johnny tried to hug me but he was too fat.

'Sid McKay is dead. If you see Tolya Sverdloff you tell him I need him. Just do it,' I said and hurried out.

Running out of the office and down the stairs, I heard Johnny behind me, panting, breathless, still talking even as I got to the door of the restaurant.

'That fucking hurricane is coming in like a bastard, you hear the news?' Johnny said. 'Taking out everything in the Bahamas, right up the coast, they say it's going to rain cats and fucking dogs, gonna kill Labor Day weekend. Gonna kill the party-boat business out here.' He pointed towards Sheepshead Bay beyond the glass windows of his restaurant. 'Airports all shut down in Florida,' he said. 'What a summer. You think this global warming shit means anything? Genia says we have to vote for Bush because he's strong on terrorism, and he's friends with Putin who is also strong. I don't know anything anymore, Artie. Have a drink with me.'

'I can't.'

'Wait. Please.'

I didn't wait. I pushed open the heavy front door of the restaurant, bumped into the doorman and ran for my car.

Tolya had been at Farone's, but not at the apartment. He didn't answer my calls. I drove like a maniac across Brooklyn, heading back to Red Hook and Sid's where I figured I'd talk my way in. I had a feeling I'd find Tolya there. I had a feeling there was still stuff in Sid's place that mattered. It was late. I tried to reach Maxine and couldn't get her cellphone.

Crazy now because it was late, because it was two in the morning and I couldn't reach Maxine, I was half a mile away from Sid's when I stopped for a green light and a car rear-ended me. I heard the metal, the crackle of a broken tail-light. The prick who hit me drove away and left me under the Gowanus Parkway, my car all screwed up.

16

My car wouldn't start. I called a tow truck and gave them the address and then I walked. It was desolate, deserted. My ribs hurt. Something in my neck didn't feel right. The battery on my cellphone was down, but I kept it in my hands. I felt like I could hear the sound of my bones.

I managed to get to the grassy patch near the pier, close to the place where I fell asleep and dreamed about Lily. I wanted to look at Sid's building from the end of the pier. Sid could have seen Earl out here, and Earl could have seen Sid's window. He could have watched Sid come and go.

A light fog drifted in from the water, but I kept going out on the cement pier where people fished in good weather. The Statue of Liberty was just a faint shape, the city spread out over my shoulder, lights veiled through the mist. I could hear the sounds of boats, but I couldn't tell where they were.

Tolya's phone was busy when I tried it again or else the circuit was jammed, and I walked out farther, but there was no signal at all. Out of breath, I sat down on the bench for a minute. Tolya had been my friend for almost ten years and I had to know if he killed Sid, had slammed him with a metal slab that destroyed his brain so it took him days to die.

211

Out of the fog, the shapes emerged. Two men. It seemed that there were two of them, and I had them figured for junkies as I started back, but I was uneasy. Maybe they were the creeps who had crashed my car. I peered at them. I shifted my jacket so I could get to my gun, and began to walk faster, working out how to get around them. They filled up my sight line. They were big.

A few feet further and I could hear them. They were speaking Russian, crude peasant Russian. I hoped they were just drunks. I couldn't see their faces. Their backs were to me.

Squat, heavy men, they were crouched down, their backs round, their arms huge and long, in the dark they seemed to move like something not really human. I was desperate to get away, but they blocked my exit. I waited for them to come for me. There was no way I could get around them and it would be easy for them to grab me, push me into the water where my head would hit the rocks and split open.

The decision to shoot was something I had to make fast, I had a second to do it as the two men came towards me, menacing, sinister, these lumps of humans, these animals crouched low like runners setting up for a sprint. My ribs hurt like hell, my shoulder burned, pain spit through my head.

One of the men, his face visible but the features blurry, seemed to jump at me, huge, his arms out, a knife in one fist, the blade glinting. I could see it, and I held my gun steady. I heard it go off, but someone already had me from behind, grabbing me, clutching at me, holding me in a hammerlock so I couldn't move, couldn't turn either way. He was holding me around my chest; the pain in my ribs exploded.

What the hell was I doing out here in Red Hook, in this fucking miserable place? I didn't care how many yuppies moved in and called themselves fucking artists or about the water or the light or the real estate.

My lungs seemed to shut down. I struggled for air the way I did once when I went 13,000 feet up a mountain out west and couldn't get any oxygen in me. People said you thought about things that mattered, you thought about your life, your death, about people you loved; it was bullshit; all I thought about was trying to breath, get some oxygen.

Gasping, I only saw one of the bears, and he looked up and then collapsed, blood streaming on to the ground. Blood covered my hands and arms. Warm blood all over me.

'Let the fuck go,' I tried to say, but the man behind me held on and I was helpless.

The only image I could hold on to while I was trying to breathe, the only thing that shimmered in front of my eyes and I didn't know if I was dead or asleep or unconscious, was my father's face, the handsome smooth face with the blue eyes. Then his face changed into mine. The next face I saw was Lily's.

It was surreal. The pain was bad, there was more blood on my arm; I thought about letting go.

17

I had killed him.

It was getting light. I could see better. I saw him. Face down, the man on the pier was bleeding bad. The blood soaked into the concrete walkway.

Somewhere in the distance I could hear the wail of a siren but I couldn't tell if it was coming closer or going away. Head down, I breathed as deep as I could, and then I tried to lift the bear of a man off the ground. He was huge and heavy and I couldn't lift him. I stuck my hand into his neck. I couldn't find a pulse. He wasn't breathing. He was dead. I fumbled in my pocket for my phone. It was gone. So was my gun.

'Stop it. He's not dead,' a voice said and then someone pulled me off the man.

I was shaking and I could hardly stand up. Tolya, who had pulled me off the man, held on to me and kept his arm around my shoulder.

'Come on,' he said softly in Russian.

'I lost my phone.'

'I have your phone. I have your gun. He's not dead, Artyom,' he said. 'It's a leg wound. I called 911. The ambulance will come. I think we should go.'

'There were two of them.'

'The other one got away,' Tolya said.

'Who the hell were they?'

'I don't know.'

I looked at him. He was wearing a light blue jacket that he took off and put around me, then he looked up as if he was listening for something. The sound of a siren came closer.

Again he said, 'Let's go.'

'We have to wait until someone comes. I can't leave like this.'

'We'll wait in the car. We'll wait until we see them come. The cops, OK? We'll do it right,' Tolya said.

'I have to wait here. I have to wait here and then I have to get my car back to the city.'

'You can't drive like this.'

'I'm OK.'

He was half dragging me towards his SUV. My arm was bleeding.

'Where were you? I called you.'

Tolya kept moving, kept me moving. 'I'm going to take you to a doctor,' he said, and reached in the back of the car and pulled out a beach towel. 'Here.'

I wrapped my arm up in the towel. 'I'll be OK.'

'I was in East Hampton with Valentina,' Tolya said. 'Why?'

I said, 'I shot him.'

'You didn't shoot him,' Tolya said. 'I did.'

'What?'

'He was coming after you, both of them, two creeps, and one got scared when he saw me, and he ran, but the other one keeps coming, like he's on something, like he's some kind of robot, and he has a knife.'

'You walk around with a weapon?'

'When I think I have to,' he said. 'I keep it in the car, OK? I have license, if you want. You want to discuss this, or you want to just get out of here? Please come with me. I don't want a conversation with cops, OK? He'll be OK. He was a hood, a creep, a nothing. I recognized him from Brighton, OK? He was a guy people hire for shit work. Nobody. He'll be sorry he's alive when they find out who he is.'

'You knew this guy?'

'I told you, I saw him a few times around Brighton Beach. He's nothing,' said Tolya. 'Come on.'

I hung on to him.

He opened the door of the SUV, and helped me into the passenger seat. He got in, slammed the door, turned on the ignition and drove slowly away from the pier and the water until we got to a quiet side street where he stopped, kept the engine running, waited. An ambulance appeared, lights flashing. It turned off towards the river and the pier.

'They'll take care of it,' Tolya said. 'We can go.'

I was still trying to get my breath.

'You almost fucking strangled me.'

'You passed out,' he said.

'Yeah?'

'The guy had you by the neck and you couldn't breathe. I had to grab you away from him, I had to.'

I glanced at him sideways. His face was large and very white in the flat light. I didn't know what to believe.

'You think it was me? Why would I try to

strangle you, Artyom?' He looked puzzled, and he drove slowly. 'You're pretty out of it, yes? You passed out.'

Before I said anything, I stopped myself. When I finally spoke, I made my tone of voice soft. I didn't want to confront him. It wouldn't get me anything and I didn't feel so hot anyhow.

'You have anything to smoke?' I said.

He held out his gold cigar case, and I opened it and took one. Tolya lit it for me.

'You got my messages?' I said. 'You just happened to be in Red Hook to rescue me,' I said and smiled. 'I mean, like always, right?'

'Like always. Sure I was looking for you,' he said. 'Artyom, come on, please, you can do interrogation later. You left me messages and as soon as I could leave Valentina and I figured out you were in the city, not with Maxine at the seashore, I went to find you. Remember? I went back to my place in Brighton Beach, and the doorman, the idiot in the Cossack shirt who would let Osama into my building if he gave him twenty bucks, told me you were there, and then I met someone at a strip joint who saw you, a girl, you remember, one of the girls who used to be in that Anna Karenina routine, remember?'

'Who?'

'A girl who knew who you were from the old days. I tried every place I could think of in Brooklyn. I asked around. Johnny Farone said you'd been in talking about Red Hook. You're not that hard to find. You drive that fucked up old red Cadillac. I'll get one of my guys to get it fixed and haul it back to the city for you.'

Behind the building where he had his office, Tolya parked in an empty lot, then hustled me through the back door. A small sign read: Orwell Properties.

The dim space had two windows on the street with bars across them, and a door with the gate pulled down. Two desks held computers, and one wall was lined with filing cabinets, most of them padlocked.

I went into the bathroom, threw the remains of Tolya's cigar into the toilet, took my shirt off and washed off my arm, found some Band-Aids and stuck them on. The cut didn't look bad. I put my shirt back on.

A large closet was inside the bathroom. The door was half open and inside were shelves that were filled with bags and boxes from Bergdorf Goodman, Armani, Prada, sets of luggage and a bag of golf clubs. From a rail hung a trio of fur coats.

'It's like Aladdin's fucking cave back there, you think you need Shopper's Anonymous or something?' I said to Tolya when I got back to the office. I was trying for a joke. He didn't smile.

He said in Russian, 'I buy Valentina and her sister a few things, you know, make them smile, so what? Sit down.'

Tolya made coffee in an electric pot that stood on a shelf behind his desk. From the same shelf, he took a bottle of Scotch and a couple of glasses, poured some and handed it to me. He asked me again if I wanted a doctor. I said I was fine. I wanted to get back to the city, and then out to New Jersey. He told me to stay still for half an hour, make sure I didn't have a concussion, some bullshit. He found a bottle of aspirin in a drawer, and a plastic tube of pills.

'Take,' he said.

'What is it?'

'Antibiotic,' he said. 'Take two.'

I took the pills. The Scotch and coffee helped. Tolya didn't speak. Again I looked around the office, taking in the locked cabinets.

'Listen, Artemy, you want to look around? You want to come back when I'm not here? Something is on your mind. Here, take the keys if you want.' He took a platinum ring from his pants and threw it across to me. I tried to separate the key from the key ring which had a big diamond in it.

'Keep it,' he said. 'You can always pawn it when I'm dead,' he added, and laughed, but it was bitter. 'You're so interested in my business all of a sudden? All these years, I say, come into business, come and I make you some money and you don't want, so you don't want. Now you're interested.'

'I'm sorry,' I said. 'I feel like shit. I don't mean anything.'

He knew I was lying. Flipping through the pile of mail on his desk, Tolya looked up regularly at the window, and seemed to be listening for the sound of sirens. He ignored me, then he took a crumpled pack of Lucky Strikes out of his desk and passed them to me. I tried to light one. My hands shook.

'Just ask me,' he said. 'Just ask me whatever it is.'

'You knew Sid McKay was dead?'

'Yes,' he said.

'When did you know?'

'Earlier.'

'You didn't want to talk to me about this, or call me? Nothing?'

'What for?' he said. 'He's dead. Is very sad.'

'Tuesday morning very early Sid walked out of his place and left the door open for someone or he forgot to close it because he suddenly went to meet someone.'

Tolya's face closed up. 'Yes? And?'

'Nothing. Forget it. I'm sorry.' I tried smiling.

'No,' he said. 'Don't do that. You want to know where I was when Sid was attacked, is that right?'

'You want to tell me?'

'I don't want,' he said. 'I don't want because you should trust me.' The antagonism in his voice rose. 'Maybe you also want to know what I was doing near Sid's last night. Maybe you want to go there with me so you can play policeman and watch me to see if I look guilty.'

'Don't,' I said. 'Stop.'

He picked up his drink and tossed it back, then took a cigar from his case.

'OK, I know you got hurt, so we stop this stupid talk. So, you saw Lily,' he said. It wasn't a question.

'Yes,' I said.

'Do you remember how we all went to the same party? On Crosby Street?'

'Sure. Why?'

'Since you're so interested in my friendship with Sid McKay, that's where I met him the first time. I liked him so much,' Tolya said.

The anger had gone, but Tolya's face stayed weirdly immobile. Gripping a coffee mug, his knuckles were white through the skin. For a big man, he had large but slender, beautiful hands; maybe he got them from his father who had been not only a famous actor but a jazz pianist who played in private houses when jazz was more or less outlawed in Russia. Another time. Another story.

Tolya said, 'I'm not your enemy.'

I didn't know what to say.

'Did you find it?' he said.

'Find what?'

'What you were looking for at Sid's? Weren't you on your way to Sid's tonight?'

'There was nothing to find out. I'm not working Sid's case. I tried to help him, I fucked up. End of story.'

'So you were out on the pier for what reason? I had to pull the creeps off you there because you like the view?'

'Who were they?' I said.

'They were trying to get to me through you.'

I reached for the Scotch. He pulled it away.

'It will make you sick if you drink more.'

Getting up, Tolya went into the bathroom and came back with a blanket and put it around me.

'I'll take you home,' he said.

221

I nodded, got up, and then sat down again, hard this time.

'Give me a few minutes,' I said.

'I liked Sid,' Tolya said. 'I told you, we spoke Russian, we ate once in a while, we talked about news, it was his obsession, the death of the news, the truth, the way he understood it. He tells people he quit his job, but they threw him out. Threw him away. He made a fuss. He looked for people who faked stories, and he tried to see they got punished for it and people got sick of him. Who needs this? Sid knows I understand this. Americans are so easy to propagandize because they don't expect it, they think of themselves as free. I understand. Propaganda, Artyom, Putin cracks down. Same here now. TV people fall in line, yes, sir, Premier Bush. So we talk. We talk, and Sid tells me he has files he wants me to have. You found this stuff?'

'Go on.'

'I was helping him,' Tolya said. 'He was writing a book about a Russian ship that ran aground off Red Hook, a long time ago, in the 1950s. I got him some information. I could get material for him. He was looking for a Russian who came over on that boat, some sailor he got to know. He thought the man was still alive. He said he'd heard he was alive. I would like to have someone finish this book for him. I would like to do this for Sid. So I want his files.'

'I hear you.'

'You don't believe me.'

'I have Sid's files,' I said.

Tolya sat up. 'Yes?'

I said, 'So the file you want is about a Russian ship from the 50s, that's the one you want, right? Nothing else?'

'Sure,' he said but I could see it wasn't what he expected. 'You want to sit here some more?'

While Tolya talked, he looked at a picture on the wall and I followed his gaze. It was a photograph of himself aged about twenty. He was skinny. He wore black leather pants and a ponytail and he held a Fender Stratocaster in his arms like a love object.

'Back in the USSR,' he said, but not smiling. 'The 1980s. They said rock and roll was musical AIDS and they banned me from playing, and I spent a little time in not such a nice place.'

I knew he had been in jail briefly; his parents' connections got him out. I let him talk.

'Sometimes you ask me how I make money. You asked once. You don't ask now, but you want to know.'

'Sure.'

'I told you but you think it was a joke,' he said. 'I stole it.'

18

'Who did you steal from?' I said to Tolya, who had poured himself another half glass of Scotch and was sitting behind the desk in his office, legs stretched out in front of him, his red snakeskin loafers kicked aside.

He snorted, half laughing, half bitter. 'I'll tell you, if you want.'

'Go on.'

'You remember the dacha? My parent's house in the country? You remember it?'

I nodded. I remembered the house with a big porch, the wild garden that led to a river, the pack of dogs running around, Tolya's father singing American show tunes, his mother hurrying in and out of the house with trays of food. I remembered the trestle table under the trees laid with platters of food: tongue and horseradish, rice pilaf and pork roast, caviar. Candles flickered everywhere in glass jars, and there were fireflies, and a view of the woods, the silver beech trees, the sound of people picking mushrooms. It was the first time I went back to Russia, the fall I almost married his cousin. That night she had worn a red shawl.

'Stop remembering,' Tolya said. 'It was not like that. What you saw was façade, was stage set, was just theater.'

★ ★ ★

It strikes Tolya one day at his parents' dacha that nothing means shit except money. Out of the blue sky it comes to him. Gorbachev is out, Yeltsin is in, kids in Moscow say they desire most to be hookers or croupiers because this is how you get a few rubles in your jeans. In the new glassy modern hotels in Moscow he has seen them, he has seen eager wannabe businessmen lick salt off their fingers as they eat bowls of free peanuts at the Aerostar Hotel bar, and wait for foreigners to buy them drinks. He's been to the food markets with stalls overflowing with fruit, flowers, meat, butter, everything available now, for money. If you have money, you can have every delicacy. Other people wait in line at the back door of the National Hotel kitchen, trying to buy a two-day-old cake.

The gangs are dividing up the businesses: Azeris, the drugs, Georgians, the casinos. The rumor mills turn out stories of godfathers and crime bosses, and money-making schemes. You go out with some foreign capitalists for burgers at Trenmos, and you talk and you make a deal. American TV shows are on everywhere, and everyone sees what money buys in the real world.

So he's leaning over the railing of the porch of the country house, smoking a stinky Indian cigarette, which is all he can afford, listening to his father playing the piano and drinking whatever brandy he has left. His parents' state pension will probably last them about a week. They gave most of their money to some crook who promised a thousand percent return and left the country.

Tolya has never thought about money in his life. There was always enough of what you needed, his mother a famous actress, his father an actor and musician, his friendship and knowing Moscow kids who could get around rules. There was always money to buy an illicit rock and roll record, *Records on Ribs*, something scratched out on a piece of plastic, an old x-ray plate; he had heard all the good music, one way or another.

He and his friends used to watch with real pity and maybe a little contempt the redneck guys who went to Afghanistan to fight. They stayed home and went to university and played music in somebody's bedroom and hoarded pictures of the Beatles someone got from a western newspaper and tried to figure out which one was John.

Tolya eventually got a job as a DJ on a radio station out of Moscow broadcasting in Chinese to the Chinese about Russian rock. No one knows what the hell he's saying so he says what he likes. He gets a reputation for smuggling out news, jokes, rock and roll information, a few seditious jokes.

Now he looks across the lawn that's ragged and uncut at the last survivor of his father's dogs, a hairy mutt lying in the wintry sun. What he also sees is that the house is falling apart. Two of the wooden shutters have come loose; they hang down from the window ledge. The house needs a paint job; the surface is scarred and patched. His mother now makes cherry jam all day. Tolya is thirty years old, he has a wife, two daughters and nothing to show for himself except he can speak five languages, at least one of them useless if you count his Ukrainian. He still lives with his parents in the Moscow apartment. And he is dying of talk.

Everyone talks. Tolya's parents, their friends, his friends, all day, all night long, they talk, socialism, democracy, theater; they talk in the kitchen over dinner, they talk in bars, they sit up all night talking and getting drunk at the Writer's House and the Film House. For seventy years no one was allowed to talk; now everyone talks, yak yak yak, talk the country to death. That afternoon in the country listening to the cicadas like little men in the bushes winding their watches — this is something he read by an English writer — he thinks he might die from the talking.

'I quit,' he says half to himself, half out loud, and throws away the butt of his shitty cigarette. He does it. He quits his job as a DJ. He looks for how to make money. He goes out into Moscow and undertakes to educate himself in capitalism.

People are grabbing what they can. One family rents its dacha to foreigners. 'We put in lavender color bidet,' they say. 'This is big selling point with foreigners.' Another guy sets up a cooperative toilet in Red Square where you can take a comfy shit for fifty kopeks. Someone sells vintage propaganda posters to a Swede who is a collector. People play rock gigs and charge. This is not for Tolya; he is not interested in hustling hard currency or fur hats or pimping or smuggling fake caviar.

'What the hell do I know about business?' he thinks.

In Moscow, he starts going to the coffee shop at the Radisson Hotel. He listens in to conversations. His English is good, and he makes friends with some guys, usually Canadian at first, and later Germans, and he listens and he thinks: this is easy. The thing he realizes is that nobody really knows who owns anything; gas, oil, electricity, land, real estate, who the hell knows? The State owned everything, but the State has disappeared up its own ass.

A friend whose family is leaving for Australia calls him. They live in a nice apartment, very central, a couple of blocks from Gorki Street. Tverskaya. It's now the main drag that goes right from the airport to Red Square. It is a good location. People say to him good locations are important. Good, he thinks. This is good, and he says, OK, I'll buy it.

Tolya borrows from friends. He promises big returns. He puts together a little deal. Most of his friends don't exactly know what the hell he's talking about but he's the smartest guy anyone knows, so they lend him money. He buys. He sells. He trades up. He returns money with interest.

'I am a capitalist,' he thinks suddenly one afternoon, strolling around the Arbat, heading for the Irish Pub that has opened where you can drink Guinness. 'I love capitalism. I love business.'

It is, he thinks secretly because he can't tell any of his friends yet, as much fun as rock and roll. It is new rock and roll. It makes people hot. Business. Money.

To him, money is for pleasure, for buying things, for giving his parents presents of books and brandy and getting their house fixed, for having fun. It's a game, a prank, a send-up of the whole system he grew up with where he couldn't read the books he liked or play the music he loved, except in secret. Tolya's revenge.

He's made for it, but he needs bigger lenders, and now he's meeting plenty of westerners, journalists who introduce him to businessmen. He plays the part, Russian but efficient, Russian but understanding West, Russian who loves and plays rock and roll. He starts going out to good restaurants where he tells his stories about his life as a rebel rock star. He moves into a nice apartment. He buys nice furniture. He invites new western friends over and they drink vodka and eat caviar and he plays them old Soviet rock records, and his wife talks to them about Chinese poetry; his girls, his twins, Valentina and Masha, appear in matching pajamas and say hello.

Tolya starts to travel. It's like a door to Wonderland opening. It's thrilling, it's like sex all the time, but better. He goes everywhere, Hong Kong, Cuba, America, France, Italy, South Africa. He eats. He drinks. He feels free. One day he realizes that Tolya, the businessman, has grown into himself.

★　★　★

Behind his desk at the office in Red Hook, Tolya stopped talking abruptly, reached up for the picture of himself as a young man in leather pants with a guitar and threw it hard in the garbage can; the glass frame shattered.

'I don't remember this young guy anymore,' he said.

'What happened in Moscow?' I said.

'I did something stupid,' he said. 'I made a deal with people who were not so nice, and I cheated them, not even from greed but because I didn't like them, so for a kind of fun. I laundered some money; I did a lot of fast talking. I sold real estate for more than I said. I kept the extra. I bragged to friends in Moscow. Some creeps kidnapped Valentina and cut off her finger, and no one ever found them because everyone was taking bribes. I thought: I'll stop now.'

'You didn't stop.'

'No. I think to myself: I'll make a little more money. A few more deals. A few more,' he said. 'I kept going. I start buying in New York. After 9/11, when the market goes down, I buy I think, first I make money out of wreckage of Communism, now I buy what nobody wants in New York. Out of wreckage, something new, I tell myself. I lie to myself. I give away money to victims to make myself feel good, I give a lot, but I feel like shit. Sometimes I don't know who I buy from, I do it by third-party deals.'

The hair stood up on my neck.

'You found out that some of the deals were with the same people who hurt Val in Moscow?'

'Yes,' he said. 'I did that. I can't stop. This is

what I know. Who I am.' He turned his back to me, and for a minute I thought he was crying, but he turned around, and said, calmly, 'You don't look so good, Artyom. I'll take you home.'

I wasn't feeling so hot, the bruise on my forehead was swelling up, the cut on my arm was bleeding, but I said, 'What do you need more money for?'

'To feel safe,' he said.

★　★　★

Back in the city at my place, I got the files I'd stolen from Sid out of my desk drawer, gave them to Tolya and went to take a shower. I only gave him the stuff I'd already looked at.

In the shower, I turned the water up as hot as I could stand it. I was shaking. I figured I had some kind of fever. The cut on my arm was bleeding, and I watched the red trickle into the water and down on to the shower floor.

Turning off the water, I got out, wrapped myself in a towel, got some jeans from the bedroom, put them on and went into the living room.

Tolya was at my desk, back to me, hunched over, a cigar in his hand, looking down at the files. Turning to me, his face was blank with disbelief.

'It's bullshit,' he said. 'All paranoid crazy bullshit. McKay just lied to me. Nothing is new in here, all stuff about how news business is fucked up, old history, and stories from his childhood. Bullshit,' he said and tossed the files away from him hard so the papers scattered across the desk and on to the floor.

'I thought that's what you wanted?'

'Fuck you, Artyom, I want to buy some real estate, I want to make deals, I want names and phone numbers of people who own, of people in city who matter, you understand, and who owns them, OK? Sid says he has all this. Or maybe you found other stuff you don't want to share?'

I sat down on a chair. My arm was bleeding, and I looked at it, and said, 'I'll call you later.'

'Sure.' His voice was cold.

The idea formed in my head out of the blue: he wanted Red Hook like an object. Something about it obsessed him; he was willing to do anything to get it. It was what Sid had been trying to tell me one way or another: Tolya had come up against people who wouldn't give him what he wanted and it had made him crazy.

'I'm going home,' he said. 'You can meet me later, if you want.' He took a gold pen that was fat as a cigar out of his pocket along with a little notebook, scribbled some phone numbers, tore out the page, and threw it on my desk.

'You need me, here are some addresses. I'll be around, Artie, you don't need to follow me like a dog, you don't need to hang on me like I'm a criminal.'

He walked out and left his cigar burning in the ashtray on my desk.

★ ★ ★

After I took some more aspirin, I got a fresh towel from the bathroom, put it around my arm and called Maxine.

'I waited for you,' she said. 'We waited all night.'

'Shit. I'm so sorry. I really am. I did try. I called you.'

'My cell doesn't always work out here. You know that. You could have called my mother's phone.'

'I'll get out there as soon as I can, I just have a few things, honey, I got into this thing, I think Tolya Sverdloff is in trouble.'

I didn't want to tell her I got beat up; I didn't want to use it as an excuse.

Quietly, she said, 'I couldn't reach you. You said you'd be here last night after the convention, I knew you left early, so we waited for dinner. I tried to call, and your phone wasn't on, and the girls woke up and they were like, where's Artie? I lost it. I yelled at them. I meant it for you. Then it got really late and I got scared.'

'Max, I'm a jerk, tell me how the girls are. What did they do all week? Did you get up to Six Flags? Did they go swimming?'

'We didn't know anything. About you.'

'I'm sorry.'

'Right.'

In Maxine's slow responses I could hear that she didn't completely believe me. She had a slow temper; she almost never lost it; she kept stuff to herself.

'What's the weather like?'

233

'It's OK. The hurricane's coming,' she said.

'How bad? You think you should stay?'

'I don't want to talk about the weather.'

'One more day and I'll be with you. I promise.'

'So you're not coming today either?'

'I'm trying.'

There was a long pause. Ten, fifteen seconds, I couldn't tell how long, when she didn't say anything at all.

'You know what, Artie?' Maxine finally said.

'What?'

'Don't try. Don't come. I can't stand waiting to find out if you're coming, last night, this morning, now you're saying you have one more thing, one more day, so you know what? Just leave us be and we'll finish our vacation.'

'I'll be there. I swear to God.'

'Don't. I mean it, Artie, it's not fair to the girls, they just ask, when's he coming, and then we hang around. You have something to deal with in the city, do it. Please just don't come. We'll be home at the end of the week. We'll pick up again then. I mean it. Please don't come now.'

'I miss you.'

'We'll do something else sometime. We can go to Paris or whatever. We'll go back to our life, I hope, you and me. Right now, I need you not to be here,' she said.

I tried to say something but Maxine was gone, only the click and the dead line and I tried to get her back and couldn't.

★ ★ ★

For a while I tried to read some of the material in Sid's folders. The towel around my arm turned pink. I couldn't stop the bleeding for ten minutes, and I thought about going over to St Vincent's to the Emergency Room. I couldn't stand the idea of it, dragging myself over, sitting around for hours next to the banged-up junkies and the women with their babies and kids who had asthma and old men whose hearts were fucked up. I sat on the edge of the bathtub, a cigarette on the sink, and bandaged my arm as best I could. I called Maxine again. She was out, her mother said.

I found a couple of Percodan in a plastic bottle in the medicine cabinet, took them both and fell asleep. When I woke up it was already dark and my sheet was stained with blood.

19

She was there. Lily was sitting at the bar, her hand around a drink. She'd told me she was there most nights and I went because I could talk to her about Tolya. Lily had known Sid McKay, too.

Maybe I was just looking for excuses to see her, but I made them to myself and late, when it was almost midnight, I found myself in the bar. I was a little fucked up from the painkillers.

As soon as I saw her, I started to back out. I stood in the doorway of the bar, paralyzed. Her back was to me. She had on a thin white cotton shirt, damp from sweat that had only partly dried in the cold air in the bar.

As if she knew I was looking at her, she turned around and said, 'What's the matter?'

'Nothing.' I walked towards her.

'You look lousy,' she said. 'You have a bump on your head.'

'Some jerk in Brooklyn hit my car,' I said.

'But you're OK?'

'I should probably go.'

'You just got here. Come on, let's sit for a minute.' Lily got off the barstool and went to the table by the window. I sat down opposite her.

The place was empty except for two guys at the far end of the bar and a couple who emerged from the gloomy back room and hurried out into the street.

'You were looking for me,' Lily said. It wasn't a question.

I didn't answer.

'My car's somewhere out in Brooklyn,' I said. 'I have to go get it. I got smacked into by some jerk. Some end, it would have been.'

She laughed.

'Did they arrest you?' I said.

'Yeah,' she said. 'Assholes. They locked up whatever protestors they could get hold of and dumped us over by the river in some horrible place for like two days with practically nothing to drink or eat. It was a shitty experience, to tell you the truth,' she added. 'But now I can talk about it for months. Bore people to death. Sometimes I bore myself to death. I'm sick of fucking politics, Artie.'

'You?'

'Yeah.'

'You want wine?'

She nodded.

At the bar, I ordered us some drinks. The Chinese kid who was on duty poured white wine into two glasses, took my money and went back to his book. Picking it up off the bar, he jiggled his head to the music on the sound system, some techno thing. Fine with me, I thought. I didn't want to listen to music I had loved listening to with Lily, the stuff the regular bartender had always played. I went back to the table.

Lily said, 'This is nice.'

'I don't think I can be here with you,' I said.

'We could talk about the election,' she said. 'That would cool us down.'

Fumbling for cigarettes, I said, without thinking, 'Don't let me sleep with you. Promise me.'

She laughed. 'That's the nicest proposition I've ever had. I'll try,' she said.

'Lily, I'm scared.'

'What of?'

'Everything.'

'Is that why you came looking for me?'

I said, 'Yeah. I'm worried about Tolya.'

'Tell me what you're scared of.'

'You knew Sid McKay, right?'

'Sure. Once. A little. Not for years, though. Why? He was a nice man. I liked him. He was good to young reporters. He was a good guy.'

'How well did you know him?'

'I told you, a bit, I knew him a bit. With you, remember? We met him together, and we saw him once in a while.'

'Where?'

'Around. I don't know. Maybe Raoul's, other restaurants, maybe with Ricky. We knew everyone, didn't we, I mean, we were good that way, you and me. Why are you asking me about Sid McKay, Artie? This is me. You came here to talk to me. You can't just ask me things out of the blue and expect me not to want to know why.'

'No.'

'So what is it?'

'He's dead.'

'My God. I'm sorry. What of? What did he die of? He wasn't that old.'

'He was murdered. Someone beat him over

the head with a piece of metal and shoved him into the river, I don't know for sure.'

'I'm really sorry. I liked him,' she said.

'Everybody liked Sid, as far as I can make out.'

'You think that's weird? Why can't people just have liked him? Maybe he was just a nice guy.'

'What else?'

'Obsessive about work. He thought if you didn't have three perfect sources you could confirm, you shouldn't report a story at all, he was living in cloud cuckoo land and it made people angry,' she said. 'I remember he was brave, though. I met him once in the Soviet Union in the old days, and he would do anything it took to get the story right. But people don't kill you for that stuff.' She looked at me. 'How the hell did Sid McKay end up murdered?' She finished her wine. 'I almost forgot that you live in a world where people get murdered.'

'You could never stand that about me, could you?'

'You bet.' Her tone turned acid. 'I want another drink.' She got up and went to the bar where the bartender filled her glass; she paid for her drink herself.

'I guess in your world it's different, all the dead people are someplace else,' I said when Lily sat down. 'You can worry about them long distance, in front of the TV. You could never just say you hated my job. You hated what I did.'

'How come you're baiting me?'

'You started.'

'Don't be a jerk, Artie, I didn't hate what you did.'

'You fucking wanted me to go to law school.'

'I thought you were smart. You think that's patronizing? OK, I didn't like the guns. OK?'

'How's Beth?'

'She misses you.'

'Don't do that to me.'

'You asked, didn't you? Grow up,' she said, 'Just get over it. I left you. I'm sorry. You're telling me you never fucked around when we were together, you were Simon-pure? I did something I had to do, I left, you want to talk about it, talk. But don't be such a baby. Don't be so fucking suburban, Artie.'

She was suddenly in a rage and I remembered how it could happen. She never lied; she never said anything she didn't mean; there were no smuggled messages with her, and for me, coming from a country where everything was smuggled, it had been astonishing.

I said, 'Well, why don't you tell me how you really feel?'

'I just did.'

At the end of the bar, the two guys looked in our direction, then back at their drinks. The kid behind the bar was asleep on his math book.

Lily was still mad and I could feel the heat, and I wanted to touch her so bad, I had to literally sit on my hands, and she knew it. She was angry and her eyes were bright, her hair a strange red in the dull light.

Pale, shirt smudged with dirt, her skirt wrinkled, Lily looked wrecked. She looked older and thinner and vulnerable, and I had never seen her like that, never thought of her as vulnerable.

240

Reaching up to fix her hair, she stretched and then scraped her hair back. She leaned over the table and reached for my cigarettes. I didn't know if she did it on purpose but her breasts were visible.

'You know the problem with you, Artie, you wanted it all ways, you always did, you wanted to be the good guy at work, and you wanted the moral high ground when possible, and when you couldn't quite have it, you'd settle for at least being nice to people, and charming, charm was always your thing. People liked you. Sonny Lippert used to say it was why he hired you, you could charm suspects into telling you things, isn't that right? You know what? I'm pretty drunk, I've been here for hours, thinking about you, and what I'd really like now is to get down under the table here, and, never mind, you're married, you don't do dirty things anymore, isn't that right? Artie?'

The shifting traffic just outside the window made shadows on Lily's face. She spoke too fast, was too angry. It didn't matter; I couldn't get enough of her. I thought: I have to get away.

We sat like that and I didn't know how much time passed, and then Lily said, 'I just missed you,' and all the heat went out of it. She put out her hand to touch mine.

'Come on, we'll try to get a cab and I'll drop you at your place, if that's what you want,' she said.

'What about you?'

'I just wanted to sleep with you,' she said, and turned her head to look out the window.

'Do you see Tolya much?'

'When I can,' she said. 'I see him because Beth is crazy about him, and because if I'm honest, I can talk about you with him.' She picked up her bag and rummaged in it, and when she looked up she was blushing. 'I like talking about you. I'm like a teenage girl that way. Also, he takes me out to eat at great places. Politics at my level doesn't pay so hot, you know?'

'I thought you married money. But I'm guessing you wouldn't take anything when you left him, right?'

'Yeah, well, I had my old apartment here, I sublet, I got it back and Tolya gives Beth whatever she wants, so what do I need?'

'Tolya scares me, Lily. He has this vision of himself as a Russian oligarch, he wants to buy more and bigger, no matter what. You think he'd do anything to get what he wanted?'

'Tolya? It's mostly an act. You're talking like a cop.'

'I am a cop,' I said. 'Do you remember a party we went to where you danced with Sid somewhere in SoHo? Crosby Street?'

'Yeah, of course I do. You always had a lousy memory. We were already together, you and me, just at the beginning. Crosby Street. Jack Santiago was getting married, I think it was his first, maybe the second, she was an artist, and the place was packed, and I brought you and you brought Tolya, and McKay was Santiago's boss at the *Times*, or was once. We all knew that. Good band and vodka, gallons of it. I used to go out with Jack, did you know that?'

'Yeah.'

'Before you, OK? It was before we met.'

'Wasn't he a little young for you?'

I never knew how old Lily was but she was past fifty. She wasn't coy about anything except her age. I never knew why because I never cared how old she was.

'Fuck you,' she said, smiling. 'He was really smart. He was a real hotshot, and then I think he went sour. He got so puffed up with his own legend, and there was poor Sid half in love with him, half wanting to make him into the world's greatest reporter, and then realizing Jack had his own agenda. But Jack would have betrayed anyone.'

'Including Sid?'

'Why not?'

'Santiago and Sid were an item?'

'Not lovers. Sid was his mentor. But I remember that wedding all the time. I think about it. I think about those times, downtown was still fun, and a little scary, lots of crack and crime, and people hung on to each other, people were still dying a lot of AIDS, there were memorial services all the time, and everyone was doing a lot of drugs, and fucking a lot, and crying a lot, and you could still see the chicken man out on West Broadway, you remember, he had this huge rack he pushed around, and it was hung with furry yellow toy chickens and you'd see it coming down Broadway and people would stay at Raoul's, drinking half the night, and other stuff. Is that right? Am I mixed up? Maybe that was the '80s. Did we know each other already? I feel like we always knew each other. I think it was then.' She smiled. 'I've had way too much. I got here early. I've been drinking wine for a while.'

'What other stuff, darling?'

'I met you.'

I reached for her hand, but she pulled it away.

'I don't want to talk about it anymore,' she said. 'Everything is falling apart. I want to go home, let's go home, Artie, or let me go get a cab if you don't want to be with me.' Lily stopped suddenly and without warning burst into tears.

For a minute, maybe two, Lily who never cried, wept; tears poured down her face. I held her hand and waited until she stopped sobbing.

'What made you cry like that?'

'I feel like I have to tell you something Tolya said to me.'

'What did he say?'

'He said that Sid had something he wanted badly, and he didn't know how to get it,' she said. 'He said it was bothering him like crazy and it made him pissed off, he said to me, I am pissed off, Lily, I want this thing and McKay knows and he doesn't help me.' She looked at me. 'I don't want to know any more about that. Don't tell me. Let's just go home now, or let me go home.'

We didn't go, not then. We sat for a while longer — I couldn't tell how long — and drank a lot. Finally, Lily got up from the table, looked at me and scraped her hair back from her face again and started for the door slowly, and I wondered if that was it, that I would never see her again. I knew that she wanted me to come with her and I thought that if I went with her I was the world's biggest bastard and if I didn't I was a fool. So I just sat, and watched her.

★ ★ ★

I got to Lily halfway down the block.

'Where should we go,' I said. 'Where do you want to go?'

'Let's walk.'

'What for?'

'You made me promise I wouldn't take you home,' she said. 'Let's just take a walk.'

'Where?'

'The fish market, like we used to. It won't be there much longer,' she said, and she took my arm, and we started over towards the river.

During the week, before dawn, men in rubber boots waded through melting ice as they unloaded fish from the trucks parked near the stalls where bright lights were strung up on metal hooks. It was Saturday and there was no one out, just the faint stink of fish in the dark morning.

Lily looked around. 'This time next year, the market will all be gone to Hunt's Point in the Bronx,' she said. 'I'll miss it. You want an early breakfast?'

'Breakfast sounds good,' I said. 'Sure.'

We were quiet now. There was nothing left to say. We found a diner that was open and we sat in a booth and she fiddled the salt and pepper shakers and we ate bacon and eggs and drank coffee. When we were done, Lily looked at her watch, and got up. She bent down and kissed me on the cheek.

'I'm going home, Artie. I'm going to try to be a good person, OK? I'm going to try, so I'm going, and then you go and get your stuff and go meet Maxine, your wife, I have to make myself say that, and maybe we can be friends some time. Look, I'm just going,' she said, and turned and went out of the diner and out into the street and jogged away. This time I didn't try to follow her.

For a while, until it was light, I sat and then I walked over to the edge of the river. I lit a cigarette. I felt that someone was watching me. I'd felt it before during the week, the sense of a shadow, someone's shadow falling on me. I wondered if it could be the creep from Brooklyn who got away, or just my tumbling towards chaos. I moved away from the edge of the pier.

The ground was slippery from some garbage, remains from the fish market, something a tourist had tossed on the ground. I threw away my cigarette, and started to walk. I walked faster, still feeling someone following me.

When I got back to my block, I saw my car was parked out front of my building. I figured that one of Tolya's guys got it repaired, then delivered it. From the coffee shop across the street, Mike Rizzi waved me over.

'This came for you yesterday,' he said holding up a large flat package as I went in and sat at the counter. 'I forgot. You want some pie, Artie? I got really nice lemon meringue.' I shook my head but he gave me a slice anyhow. 'On me,' Mike said.

Inside the padded envelope was a note from Sid. Congratulations on your marriage, it said. The envelope also contained a photograph of Stan Getz by Herman Leonard. My favorite musician, favorite photographer. I looked at the postmark on the package. Sid had sent it the Saturday he started calling me.

'Great party,' Mike said. 'Terrific. What's the matter? You look like you saw a ghost. Good pie, right?' Mike invested heavily in the fact that he served the best pie of any coffee shop in New York.

He watched while I dug into it. It was good, sweet and tart and wet, the meringue sugary and firm. Even in my lousy mood I couldn't resist and while Mike watched me, I ate the hefty slab of pie, drank two cups of black coffee and, since there was no one else in the place, leaned on the counter and held up a pack of cigarettes.

'Sure,' Mike said. 'Smoke if you want.'

'There's something on your mind, Mike?'

'I heard they're going to hit the stock exchange and other financial stuff next week, third anniversary of the Twin Towers, fucking terrorists, that's what they're saying, you believe it?'

'I don't believe anything. I sure as shit don't believe any politician, not this summer, Mikey, what about you? You buy it? You think it's real, or it's the election coming and us falling for fear like we were two years old?'

He reached up and turned on the TV that sat

on a shelf over the cereal boxes. 'All I know is I was supposed to take the truck out to Jersey and that getting through the tunnel's a nightmare and there are guys with AKs walking around near the bridges again like the winter before last, nothing's any better, and I feel like, you know, tired of it, Art. I feel like I want a permanent vacation.'

'Yeah, I know.' Out of a corner of my eye I was watching the TV. Stories of dead children were coming out of Russia. The picture changed to Bush.

Mike looked up and said, 'He's OK. He's like a regular guy.'

'You're kidding me.'

'I like Bush. I got a right.'

'But that's stupid, man.'

I had never seen Mike Rizzi get mad in all the years I had lived on the block. His face was red.

'I don't think I'm stupid,' he said. 'And I don't think it's any of your business who I vote for, OK? I'm not stupid, you know, I listen to the news, I watch Fox, I watch CNN, I like Bush. He makes me feel he gets it about ordinary people, like me. He makes me feel safer.'

'I'm sorry,' I said.

'Who for?'

I started to apologize, but he just kept his back to me and waved his hands to acknowledge what I said or maybe tell me to get lost, then threw some bacon on the griddle. The fat spattered. Mike turned around.

'It's OK,' he said.

I didn't want to put my foot in it, so I left.

Outside I almost tripped over a black guy lying on the ground. He was naked except for a filthy undershirt and a ragged towel over his dick. That was it. Nothing else. Just lying there. I bent down and took his pulse. He was barely alive. I saw a lot of guys like him now, a lot of bad drugs coming back into the city, no housing, no nothing except politicians saluting the flag and talking tough.

Everyone was tired, everyone drinking too much. I remembered suddenly that Mike Rizzi had a boy in the Air Reserves who had been posted to Iraq.

The black guy on the sidewalk didn't move. I went back into Mike's and asked him to call 911 and I waited until the medics came and loaded the guy up into an ambulance. While they were loading him, the filthy towel fell off and left him naked, except for the undershirt and one dirty sneaker.

20

I recognized Sid's son as soon as I saw him through the open door of Sid's loft in Red Hook. I went in, introduced myself as a friend of Sid's. I'd been hoping I could get another look; I still had the key I stole, but the door was open.

'Alex McKay,' he said briefly, then introduced the woman who sat near him on the edge of a chair as Miss McKay.

She was Sid's sister. I had seen her at the hospital. Holding a box of photographs, she sat straight, her back not touching the chair. Her hair was gray, cut short, she wore pearl earrings and a black linen dress and though she was older, she was a dead ringer for Sid.

Alex returned to the shelf where he had been examining his father's books.

'What's your interest?' he said.

'I was a friend of Sid's,' I said again and didn't mention I was a detective.

He looked like his father. He had a light smooth face that was expressionless and looked as if it had been poured that morning. He looked young for his age — I knew he was about forty — it was what I noticed first about him. He wore an expensive blue summer shirt and black jeans. He was taller than Sid and he had broad shoulders and big arms. Sid had married briefly and Alex was the product of that marriage.

Obviously rattled by his father's death, he

moved around the loft fretfully but I didn't see any sadness.

'What kind of friend is that?' he asked, faintly sarcastic. 'I bet he had a lot of those friends.'

'Alex,' his aunt said, 'enough.'

As casually as I could, I said to Miss McKay, 'Tell me about Earl. Sid told me that he had a half brother named Earl and they were friends when he was a boy. You must have known him. Sid said they were very close when they were teenagers.'

She remained expressionless. 'I've never heard of such a thing,' she said. 'I don't know of anyone named Earl. Not in our family. No, no one that I can imagine.' She looked down at the box she held. 'There were so many pictures of Sid. I don't even know who most of the people are.' She held one up and looked at it. 'I wish I knew.'

When I asked for her phone number, she reached into her handbag and gave me an engraved card with her name, address and phone number.

'You're a cop,' Alex said to me, putting down the book he held. 'Aren't you?'

'We've already seen the police,' the aunt said. 'We've told them everything. It was an accident. Right, darling?' She turned to Alex. 'We agreed that, didn't we? I know we talked about suicide, but I think it was an accident.' She said it as if she could prescribe the means of Sid's death.

'I need some air and a smoke,' Alex said to me. 'You want to walk?'

We went outside and walked along the pier out

over the water. In the gusts of wind that came off the river, a few boats bobbed around.

Alex took a thin ropey little joint out of his pocket and lit it. I had assumed he meant cigarettes when he said he needed a smoke. He seemed unconcerned that I was a cop. He didn't pass the joint to me either.

He was tight as a drum, the skin was stretched taut over the bones. Alex was a tense man.

Finally I said, 'When's the last time you saw him?'

'A year. Around a year ago,' he said.

'But talked to him, I mean.'

'I don't know. Months.'

'He told me you sent him an iPod,' I said, remembering how Sid told me he was listening to it on the deck of the Mexican restaurant the day before my wedding. 'You didn't talk to him but you sent him a gift?'

'Say that I was a dutiful son.'

'Why didn't you see him? How come?'

'I didn't like him,' he said quietly.

'That must have been rough.'

'Who for?'

'You want to tell me where you were over the last week or so?'

'I think I already told about ten people, but if you want to know, I'm OK with it,' Alex said. 'I was working in Borneo. I'm a DP.'

'What?'

'Director of Photography,' he said. 'A cameraman. I make ethnographic documentaries for people like *National Geographic*, I probably thought somehow in a Freudian moment that it would put them right out of joint, the family, me doing stuff about tribes, you know, black people with lip plates, the kind my family figure for cannibals. Maybe I hoped it would drive them nuts or something, and then I won a few prizes so they all talked about it for a while, and I was a kind of family star for a month, and then it was just what I did. I heard about my father and I had to get about six damn planes to get here.'

He was cool. Most people, a cop asks them where they were during the time someone they know was murdered, they get disconcerted. Alex looked at his watch.

At the end of the pier, we leaned against the low wall. I fumbled for my cigarettes in my pocket. It gave me a couple of seconds to look at Alex.

'He named you for Pushkin?' I asked.

'What?'

'Never mind.'

Arms crossed, Alex stood still, waiting. He had an eerie ability to stand almost motionless; maybe it was his profession; maybe he was always waiting for the right light, the right shot. Even his face was still, but he watched you very carefully. His eyes were two different colors, one blue, the other hazel.

'So, how was it?'

He said, 'Who for?'

'For you? For him? The not getting along,' I said. 'The not speaking, finding him like this after so much time.'

'I gave it all up years ago,' Alex said. 'I just quit caring or worrying about what he thought of

253

me, you know?' He looked out at the boats on the water. 'It's windy,' he said and shaded his eyes from the sun.

'That bad?'

'That nothing,' he said. 'My father was there for everyone, he was a guy who loved the whole world, but he was too busy, too self-obsessed to care much about me. Everyone loved Sid, he would bring his young reporters to the house, he would stay up late reading their copy, he was always there for them, boys, girls, the ones he slept with, the ones he didn't sleep with. And he had these ideas of justice and truth that he couldn't break with, so if anyone strayed, you were fucked. I mean, tell a lie, he froze you out even if you were a kid. I'm talking any lie, like, you ate the Almond Joy candy bar, and you said you didn't and he found out, you got the deep freeze for days. He did it with everyone. So I went away to boarding school when I was sixteen. Up in Vermont,' he added.

'What about your mother?'

He shrugged. 'What's the difference?' he said. 'She died when I was in college. She drank. Quietly. I didn't even know, I thought she was always drinking glasses of water, and sitting by herself, and it was gin. She kept it in tonic bottles in the fridge. So I went back to live with him for a while, I think I kept waiting for the redemptive moment, you know, for the good stuff to click in, the way it's supposed to. Never mind.'

'Any idea who killed him?'

We started back to Sid's. Alex threw away the

remains of his joint.

'I don't know,' he said.

'You'll be around?'

'I'll be around for a few days. Few as possible. Fucking New York.'

'Yeah?'

Alex said, 'Me, I love LA. I love it where I am, it's suburban and plastic and clean and the cars are fast, we have a house with a pool, the girls are pretty and people are superficial, that's what he felt, anyway, it's everything my daddy hated. I hated New York before. I hate it worse now, people, noise, everyone scared, pretending they're not scared, I feel like the whole thing could sink into the harbor and it would be no bad thing, you know? My father sold the beautiful house he grew up in, and bought an apartment in Brooklyn Heights he never used, then he sets up at this rundown warehouse.' He gestured to the building. 'What's he want with Red Hook? To me it's a dump. Apparently he was obsessed with it.'

'There was a story about an old Soviet ship that ran aground here in the early 1950s,' I said. 'Sid said he met some of the sailors. He said one of them never went home. He tried to find him. He wanted to write a book.'

'It sounds like one of his stories.'

'You think he made it up?'

'He didn't make things up, he was a hawk for truth. Trouble was it was his truth that mattered,' Alex said. 'So you're what? You said you were a cop.'

'Yeah, but it's not my case,' I said. 'I'm just

someone your dad helped out once.'

He laughed bitterly. 'Didn't he always.'

'How long will you be here?'

'You already asked. Until I can arrange a funeral. I have to worry about the family.'

'You talk a lot about the family, I mean, what is it?'

'I was an only child. Far as I'm concerned my father and mother probably fucked once and they got me.' He stretched his arms over his head, then let them hang loose, then cracked his knuckles, stretched again. 'I get tight,' he said. 'It's the job.'

'You keep talking about the family.'

'They're all very social and they do things a certain way, God help me, you don't know what I'm talking about, do you? You ever hear of the Boule Club, or the Link? Jack and Jill? The élite of African-American society?' He snorted with derision. 'You should have seen the debutante balls, even when I was a teenager, all those black kids turned out in ball gowns and white tie and tails, fraternities, sororities. I ran like hell. California was my salvation. The sunshine, the movie business, be who you want to be. Everyone from somewhere else.'

For the first time, Alex cracked a smile. He bent over and touched his toes, straightened up, and said, 'As long as you're good, or pretty or sharp, you can reinvent yourself in LA. You can make up your own fucking myth. Why the hell am I telling you this?'

For the first time I liked him. Like me, he'd fled somewhere else.

256

'Get away from what you grew up on,' I said. 'The system, the rituals, the crap.'

'You said it,' Alex said and asked me for one of my cigarettes.

'Go on.'

'Did my father ever talk to you about color, I mean actual color, the whole thing about passing or not? My grandfather passed for white in order to do certain deals, but it was also about status, for a sense of who you were. They didn't quite want white babies, they wanted very light-skinned babies, and they paid a whole fucking lot of attention when every kid was born, especially the older ladies who came to look at them.' Alex stopped. 'Do you understand?'

'I'm not sure. Sid talked about it a little, but go on.'

'They inspected the skin and felt the texture of the hair. People thought about skin color, you knew it from the time you were little. The women talked about it in private, the way people in some families talked about disease. Silently. Quietly. Even the texture of the hair. One old lady would say about a little girl, 'She'll have trouble with that nappy hair.' Nappy hair, they'd say. 'She'll have to stretch it if she can.'' Alex paused. 'Everyone in my father's family was light skinned, except him. My father came out darker. Not black, but darker than some of the others who were very light and freckled, that generation of babies, they came tumbling out some even with blond hair. So they actually laughed at him when he was little. It made me like him better except when I found out he played the game, too, and when I started dating, I could see every girl I brought around he was looking at her color. He married a white girl, of course; except it turned out he didn't like girls. Fucked up or what?'

'Did he ever talk about his half brother, Earl?'

I noticed for the first time that there were men repairing the dock, maybe making sure no sign remained of Earl's murder. I had tried to get a copy of a police photograph of Earl, see what he looked like, didn't have much luck. For Sid's sake, I'd keep trying. I didn't figure the family kept his picture, and I wasn't surprised when Alex McKay snorted in response to my question. Weird to think if Sid had been telling the truth, and Earl looked like him, then Alex looked like Earl, too.

'You heard my aunt. No kids named Earl in the McKay household,' he said. 'Listen, I have to get on the phone. I want it over and out of my life. You think he was murdered? You think it was some boy he picked up? It would sure as hell freak them out.'

'What would?'

'That it was a sex crime. Dead from a heart attack, my father would have been a McKay. Even suicide they could handle. They could say, well, Sid was a writer, you know? He was sensitive. Murder is much too sleazy. We don't have murders in our family, Alex, darling, they all said to me. That's what they'd like,' he said. 'Who do you think killed him?'

'I think he was murdered because he had information that people wanted, or didn't want

258

him to have, or didn't want him spreading around.'

'Information was all that mattered to him,' Alex said. 'Or truth. Whatever. He was obsessed. In the last few years with so much news being manipulated and politicized it made him a little crazy. He kept notes on everyone who screwed with the news. He sent e-mails about it. He made people crazy. He was fired from his job. He became an old man suddenly. Sad. Everything was about justice for him and this was injustice. He believed in justice for the world, but real people, that was something else. He had a young reporter once, guy worked for him, he could do no wrong, then he fucked up, it was over. The guy begged him. Jack said, please, come on, Sid, I remember, I heard them once. It was principle. He told me as a point of pride. You know what my middle name is? Justice. Yeah.' He laughed, bitter.

'What was his name?'

'Who?'

'This reporter? This Jack?'

'Santiago,' he said. 'Why?'

'They made it up? He forgave Santiago?'

'Who knows. Probably. If Santiago begged. Why do you care?'

'But they were close?'

'Yeah, they were real close. He figured Jack could be the good son.' Alex hesitated. 'You know what, maybe he was. Maybe he was the good son. I spent years hating him and then I met him once, and he was OK. I have to go.'

I handed him a card with my number.

He said, 'Yeah, yeah I'll call if and when.'

'I'll let you know if we get anything.'

'Sure,' he said. 'Thanks. It won't make any damn difference, but thank you.'

'Where are you staying?'

'My aunt's,' he said.

'You ever hear from Jack Santiago about Sid's death, since they were so close?'

'How would he know? We'll put the obituary in the *Times* tomorrow or the next day. We kept it quiet. Work the system. Try to get it recorded as an accident, accidental death by drowning, or some kind of genteel suicide, a man who couldn't cope. Whatever. There's no reason to contact Santiago, or for me to hear from him. Why would I?' Alex hesitated.

'Something else?'

'Yeah.'

'What?'

He looked down at his feet, then up at me. 'I'm suddenly so fucking sad I didn't see him, you know?' Alex said. 'I'm sorry for it, for him, and me. He wasn't bad. I miss him.'

★ ★ ★

At the inlet, the workers were sawing off pieces of the rotten dock now. The noise was jarring. It was Saturday and quiet.

Jack Santiago had been close to Sid. Jack said he had moved to Brooklyn, told me at my wedding. I was betting he lived close to Sid. I called information, but he was unlisted. I put in a call to someone who could help.

I started walking, waiting for a call back, maybe half looking for Santiago. In a studio space on the ground floor of an old warehouse, through a door propped open with a brick, I saw a piece of beautiful blue glass on a stand. I went in and watched a man blowing more pieces. An open furnace glowed orange. He seemed to spin air on the end of a long metal rod and then he blew it and made another fantastic shape out of glass, gold this time. I bought the blue bowl for Maxine and went and put it in my car.

★ ★ ★

The park was a few blocks away on the other side of Red Hook, near the Expressway and the housing project where Rita lived. It was filled with people watching a soccer match. Little kids were out on the pitch; big-league players warmed up on the sidelines.

Latin music came from competing boomboxes. People sat on fold-up chairs and on blankets on the grass.

On the sidewalk at the edge of the park were makeshift stalls where women set out food for sale. You could smell the meat grilling a block away. You could smell the onions and cilantro. A barbecue was loaded with yellow ears of corn roasting. There were stalls heavy with platters of tacos, tamales, fried plantains stuffed with cream, sausages and yellow rice and ribeyes and fried chicken. Everyone spoke Spanish.

Oil spit from a hot griddle where a woman was making patties out of dough, shredded pork and mozzarella. I bought one of the pupusas off her. She said she was from Salvador, but she spoke good English and I asked if she knew Rita, the Russian girl who made tamales. She shook her head. I bought a can of Coke.

At another stand, a guy was bagging chunks of papaya, pineapple, watermelon, mango. The heap of bagged fruit grew. A little girl bought some watermelon and went away, picking pieces of the pink fruit out of the plastic bag with a plastic fork, the juice running down her chin. In a yellow shirt and satin soccer shorts, a boy of about nine marched up to a stand where bottles of colored syrup stood and bought an electric green snow cone. He went away, licking the mound of ice.

Finishing my Coke, I sat on a bench and watched, looking for Rita. I was a few blocks from the warehouses on the Red Hook waterfront, but I could have been in a different city and I was betting there was plenty of tension between the two communities; I wondered if Sid somehow got caught between them. I called about Jack Santiago's address again. There was no listing.

A little girl in a frilly pink skirt and a Minnie Mouse T-shirt putting out bowls on one stall waved at me with a yellow fork. I was wasting time. I didn't see Rita, I didn't see Jack. I didn't know how he was connected to Sid, but I wanted to talk to him. I threw away my paper plate.

21

Jack Santiago was plenty high by the time I found him propping up against the bar at a fancy new restaurant over in the Meat Packing District.

'Where's Val?' I said.

'In the restaurant,' he said. 'Have a drink with me first.'

Valentina had told me that she liked the bars in the Meat District. When I called her in East Hampton a girl told me she'd gone back to the city. I had changed into a good shirt and clean pants and I was hoping I'd find her and Jack with her.

It was early Saturday evening, but already people were pushing their way into the restaurants and bars around Ninth Avenue, the tourists gaping, New Yorkers preening.

Until recently, the neighborhood had been owned at night by hookers, transvestites, assorted derelicts and a few artists. I'd never seen a neighborhood transformed so fast: a couple of blocks of warehouses, some of them pretty crummy, had become the hottest real estate in the city. At night you could feel the area coming into full heat.

At the door of the restaurant where I found Jack, a crowd had formed. A guy from the suburbs all in suede was explaining to the maitre d' why he deserved a good table and who he knew.

The area around the bar was gridlocked with single people drinking and wading through the sexual anxiety. Next to me were a couple of women who looked like refugees from *Sex and the City*. They clung to their drinks. One had a blood orange mojito. The other was drinking Lillet with an orange slice.

'No sex in this city,' the Mojito who was standing beside Jack said to me woefully. 'I had a date. I got him on J Date, on line, and he brought me here and just got up and left, and fucking left me with the check.'

I bought her a drink.

'So what about the suitcase nukes, Artie?' Jack said.

'Boom,' I said.

'People like you, you'll be making jokes when the city blows up and there's a hundred thousand dead. You'll still be joking. You read my series about portable nukes, you read it? The stuff is everywhere.'

Jack talked into my ear and drank bourbon. I let him talk because I knew he was drunk enough and probably vain enough to let something slip. I wanted to hear how he felt about Sid but I didn't want it tainted by questions from me he thought he had to answer.

So for a few minutes I listened to Jack talk about suitcase nukes. I got bored. He changed the subject. He was leaving town, headed for Beslan, he said. He was going to cover the massacre in southern Russia, kids murdered at the school, children slaughtered on a basketball court. He lit up. Big Story. Right?

'Yeah, Jack, right. Where is she?'

'Big table in the back with her friends. So. Beslan. My kind of story,' he said. 'I like to get to the real places. Off road, I always called it that, people thought I was an asshole.' He ordered another drink. 'I am an asshole,' he added. 'You think I don't know that? Have another drink, Artie.'

As soon as you figured Jack for a man whose self-regard was as impenetrable as cement, the minute you got pissed off at that soul patch he wore on his chin, he said something that won you back.

He regaled everyone at the bar in hearing distance with stories of terrible places he'd covered and crappy hotels he had stayed in — Communist guest houses with holes in the wall, and rusty stains on the floor, or hotels where hookers appeared in your room uninvited along with the cockroaches. People at the bar laughed. All reporters liked to brag about the lousy conditions they had endured, but Jack was funny.

One thing about Jack, people always said, was that he laughed at himself. He never took anything, either. Not like the other journalists, the big timers, the ones who wrote the Pulitzer Prize-winning books and showed up at international conferences in Davos and Aspen and pretended they were there to observe and enjoyed the goodies, the hotels, champagne, adulation; he never took, not that way. Wars, massacres, terrorism, he had been there, and he knew the flip side, too, he knew the New York

265

scene because he had once been married to an editor at *Vogue*, or maybe another fashion magazine. I couldn't remember all of it, but he reminded me, tossing back bourbon, talking about himself like he was plenty wired.

'So you moved, Jack, right? You used to live downtown some place but you told me you moved.'

'Yeah,' he said. 'I had a place in SoHo, but it's so over, and I got out and made some dough and went to Williamsburg, but now I got a sweet little deal in Red Hook, very cool, a piece of an 1880s warehouse, nice views. Not right on the water, but close by. Red Hook is where you want to be, you know? Val doesn't like it but she's only been once, and I'm OK staying in the city with her. Nice.'

Come on, I thought, tell me about Sid. I didn't want to ask, not yet. I wanted him to tell me.

'Anyone you want me to say hello to in Russia, Art, any good contacts for me?' Jack said, then looked past me and suddenly stopped talking.

Tolya Sverdloff had arrived. Jack addressed him in Russian, using his patronymic, which sounded ridiculous in the middle of this mob in the Meat District in New York.

'Where's Valentina?' Tolya said in English.

'Eating dinner. With her friends,' Jack said.

'I want to see her.'

Tolya had had plenty to drink by the time he arrived. He had eaten at Pastis down the block, where he normally ate, he said, as if Santiago didn't know how to choose the right restaurant.

He shook my hand. He was friendly enough, but cool.

As he started for Valentina's table, the restaurant's two owners appeared from a back room, and embraced Tolya who towered over everyone. He introduced me to them.

Jack, left out, was restless now.

'Let's go find Val,' he said.

'I'll follow you,' Tolya said. 'Tell her I'm here.' He put his hand on my arm. 'Stay with me, please.'

I was impatient. I wanted to talk to Jack. Jack had a place in Red Hook because it was cool, he said, but I didn't believe him.

He picked his way through the crowd to a table where I could just see Valentina.

'You think she's in love with him?' I said.

I already knew that Tolya wanted to rip the guy's head off.

'Is a prick,' he said in English.

'You only think he's a prick because he's dating Val.'

Tolya leaned over me, talking Russian now, very low, very intense, sober.

'He is forty, twice her age, and he is a fantasist,' Tolya said. 'I've met his kind before, he wants information from me, he likes stories about nuclear smuggling, he likes mob stories, he likes to talk about hoods, he believes in conspiracy theories, he asks about my background. Tell me about your past, he says, and tries talking Russian. He uses my patronymic to show respect. What the fuck business is it of his, my past? He claims he's half Russian, and I think, who gives a shit. He sucks up to me, you understand? He considers himself a great journalist, he talks about this, he says to me there are nuclear materials coming into the US, he is obsessed with this, with nukes coming into all the ports, people bringing them in suitcases, it is a big story, he says, and it starts in Russia, and I think: so fucking what? I'm a real estate guy. I don't like him and I don't want him near my Valushka.'

'So he's Russian,' I said. 'So he's paranoid. So what else is new?'

'He's not a real Russian. Cuban father. Russian mother. Maybe she was Russian, partly Russian. Who invited him to the wedding party?'

'Not me,' I said. 'I hardly know the guy. Maybe Valentina invited him.'

'Santiago has some kind of agenda, like I said. He cooks it all up, he makes stories out of smoke and mirrors, then he asks you questions and if you don't answer, he refers to this story he made as if it was real. He likes putting people on the spot,' Tolya said. 'He's one of those guys who would kill you for a story. You see the way he swaggers, you say this, swagger?'

'Yeah.'

'Your English is still better than mine.'

'Thank you,' I said. 'Val likes him a lot?'

'She's nuts for him, and I hear him telling stories, very funny, very entertaining, how he knows people, how he gets her into the movies, he knows Tom Cruise, he knows everyone. Bullshit.' He put his hand on my shoulder. 'Val is a nice girl, right?'

'She's wonderful,' I said. 'Let's go find her.'

★ ★ ★

In the restaurant, waitresses in some kind of Asian outfit clattered around on backless slippers, explaining the food to people who sat on low chairs, squealing over the noodles and spring rolls.

Val was at a big table surrounded by her friends. As soon as she saw us, she jumped up and threw her arms around Tolya, and then kissed me on both cheeks.

'Daddy! Artie! Come meet everyone.'

'Where's Jack?' I said.

'He ran into an old friend.' She gestured to another table where I saw him sitting with a guy in a black T-shirt. At the same table, I thought I saw my dentist, Dr Pelton Crane, and I couldn't believe it. Drinking up my money.

Val added, 'He'll be back. Sit down with us.' She made me sit next to her. Tolya took the chair beside me.

Music boomed, voices rose, ice clinked on glasses, china clattered; I looked around. The four guys at our table were in their late twenties, older than the girls, and they owned restaurants and clubs and Ferraris from what I could make out. Two of them were Russian. One of the others was an actor whose name I recognized faintly and when he got up to shake my hand, I thought he was still sitting down. He was handsome, blond and very short.

269

All of them Russian and rich, the girls were dressed up to the teeth in fancy outfits that probably cost thousands. One wore a neon blue strapless dress; the others were in miniskirts up to their crotches, and tiny glittery tops that showed off their sleek bellies and perfect tits. They were nineteen, twenty, Val's age; they had perfect skin, hair, legs, arms.

Waitresses brought trays of Asian food on little plates and a stream of cocktails in fancy colors and Val and her friends ate and drank, like a herd of hungry, thirsty, beautiful young animals at the trough.

The girls spoke unaccented English. They had been born in America, though a couple said they still had grandparents in Moscow.

Half focused on Jack at the next table, I only caught snatches of conversation. Val's friends were in college, but business was what they loved; one worked for her parents. Big money was involved. She mentioned to Val that her summer rental in East Hampton cost a hundred grand, but she was planning to buy the house anyhow.

At the end of the table next to me in a low armchair with a leather seat, Tolya looked uncomfortable. He was drinking hard, straight Scotch, keeping up a running commentary in my ear: the girl in blue was the daughter of Krushkov; the one next to her was a Lepinsky and next to her was Klimov's niece. Look, Tolya said, the blond boy's daddy is in oil in the Far East, or was it oil pipelines? I had trouble hearing him. I had trouble concentrating as Tolya recited the roll call of oligarchs and real estate barons, of men who stole and put the gold they stole in Swiss banks, and those who simply helped themselves to aluminum, diamonds and nukes as the Soviet Union fell apart.

The children, the sons and daughters who were Valentina's friends, had been born in America and were growing up here in Manhattan or Miami. The girls went into business or to law school and some did modeling and one pined for an acting career.

'Look,' Tolya whispered. 'The girl in the pink skirt with the ten-carat heart-shaped pink diamonds in her ears, her father can buy Real Madrid, the soccer team, and owns most of Vladivostok, and sixteen Picassos, sixteen, Artyom, big ones, and the little one there, you see, with the glorious tits hanging out of the white T-shirt that cost five hundred bucks, you see her, her pop has oil flowing in his veins and a chain of hotels in Dubai, uranium, diamonds, rain forests in South America that he cuts down secretly so nobody ever knows. Her uncle has real estate in China. These people are players, Artyom,' Tolya said. 'These people own real things. Entire cities. Land.'

In Tolya's voice I heard the kind of desire I'd never heard from him, not even when he was talking about women. He wanted it all. He believed. He was as devoted to money as any Party hack to his ideology. Maybe I hadn't really listened to him before. I looked for a waiter; I needed a fresh drink.

Around the table, Val and her friends were unaware of Tolya or me. Laughing, drinking, gurgling into their cocktails like babies with fancy bottles, they ate and drank. Maybe they were popping pills, too, or snorting coke. Maybe they were just high on themselves.

Two of the girls were discussing with a boy — he couldn't have been more than twenty-five or -six, but he apparently owned a string of bars — if they should buy a bus to go campaigning door to door for John Kerry in Ohio; everyone was doing it, there were rumors that Britney and Beyoncé were going. All those poor Republicans in swing states only needed a little encouragement to switch, it was agreed.

I thought about these girls in outfits that cost ten grand going out to the boondocks, going from one split level to another, houses with a basketball hoop out front, asking people to vote for John Kerry, a man who paid two hundred bucks for a tie and bought two hundred ties at a time and went windsurfing for fun.

'Let's give a party,' one of the boys said. 'Let's invite some Republicans downtown for a party. Let's show them New York,' he added and everyone laughed. I hated their contempt.

'Too too late,' the girl in pink said. 'The convention is over over over. I went to some of their parties, they were dull dull dull.'

Val turned to me, reaching for my hand. I couldn't help looking at the missing finger. She smiled, and I saw that her eyes were the blue of marbles but that one was flecked with gold or brown depending how she moved or how the light fell on her.

You couldn't stop looking at her. Val wore a

plain white T-shirt, very tight, and a thin white cotton mini and white sneakers without laces on her tan feet. She was really something. A dirty thought flickered through my head, and I exiled it, and kissed her on the cheek.

'Uncle Artie,' she said sardonically.

'What do you want to eat, darling?' Tolya said to Val in Russian, and she replied in her bland Florida English.

'I ate already, daddy,' she said. 'I ate tons and tons and tons of food, I ate spareribs and spring rolls and satay, honest.' She smiled. 'He feeds me like I'm in training for the ladies, heavyweight class for the next Olympics.'

'She's a good kid,' Tolya said. 'I love this, the way she never takes anything for granted, like every nice meal is her first, you know? I love this.'

They grinned at each other. I said, to make conversation, as she settled back into her chair, 'How's your sister?'

'Very serious. Masha's the good twin, I guess. It's like she wanted to go to college, she wanted to go to Yale and then medical school, and she will, she'll do it, and she'll be a doctor and heal the sick and have three perfect kids and win a Nobel Prize, and that's OK. She's good. I'll be the dissolute but fabulous aunt, like my grandma, Lara.'

'She's in college already? Masha, I mean.'

'You're kidding me. In college? She's starting her junior year. She skipped two years of high school.'

'You didn't want it?'

'It was boring. I went last year, I lasted a semester, I already spoke four languages, daddy made us learn, and I read a lot, and I thought: I just want to work. I want to be in the world. It drives him crazy.'

'We compromised,' Tolya said. 'She promised me she'd take courses at NYU if she could be in the city, so I said OK, if you do it. So I gave her one of my businesses to run. A little business. I got her a little apartment.'

'Close to yours, Daddy,' she said. 'Across the street. But I like that, and anyway I mostly stay with you,' she said and kissed him.

But Tolya was restless. He got up, and said, 'I'm going out to smoke,' and pulled himself out of the low chair and made his way across the crowded room. A few minutes later I saw him through the window, lighting up a cigar on the street. I started getting up. Val put out her hand and said, 'Stay a minute, OK?'

'Sure.'

Val pulled her chair closer to mine so that we were separated from the rest of the group. She leaned close to me, and said, 'Do you think I'm beautiful, Artie? I mean, tell the truth. Brutal, total, absolute, no bullshit truth.'

'Why?'

She let out a tiny giggle. 'Oh, Artie, I'm sorry. I'm not hitting on you, I'm not looking for you to tell me I'm gorgeous because I'm coming on to you. Although, I think you're pretty cool, I do. I think you're a cute guy. I could go for you.'

I kept my mouth shut and felt like a fool.

'Tell me. Go on.'

'Yes,' I said. 'Very. Very beautiful. One in a million. I mean that. I'm not saying it because you're like family, you asked me, and I'm telling you. Yes. Don't you know it?'

She looked up. 'It depends. Sometimes it makes me uncomfortable. You want to jump me, right? I mean it's OK, guys do, and if you weren't my dad's friend and married to the completely fabulous Maxine I'd be flattered. I always had a crush on you, to tell the truth, from afar mostly, as they say. Even when I was little, I thought you were cute.'

I was feeling stuff I couldn't admit even to myself, and I fumbled with my drink and then with some chopsticks. I tried to get noodles off a plate and dropped them. Val picked up a napkin. I grabbed it from her, and rubbed at the stain on my shirt.

'I'm sorry,' Val said. 'I was flirting. But I see it in men, and I think, OK, that's pretty neat, they want me, and they think I don't notice, the nice ones, the ones who are too old for me or married or whatever, or even once with a shrink, that they hold entire conversations with me looking in my eyes like some kind of weird mesmerist, great word, right? Like they're afraid to glance at my mouth or legs or tits or anything else, so they just stare in my eyes.'

'I can imagine.'

'Thanks.' Val sipped at her pink cocktail. 'I'm not being like self-obsessed or anything,' she said. 'I can see it, you know, but I don't feel it. I know it's true, I mean people ask me to pose for pictures and stuff, so I'd have to be a halfwit not to know and people turn around in the street, I know that, and I play to it, I mean you don't go around being six feet tall and dye your hair platinum and get a crew cut and wear little teeny skirts with your ass hanging out without knowing you look pretty good, unless you're an idiot, right?'

'You're a wise woman. How come you're asking?'

'I don't know. Artie?'

'Yes, sweetheart?'

'Do you feel completely American?'

I nodded.

'Sometimes, I don't know, I don't. Did you know I went to see Genia on my way back to the city? Your half sister, right? I met her at your wedding.'

I was surprised. 'How come you went?'

'She's raising money for the kids in Beslan. I liked her, I liked being with the Russian women who are her friends. I liked listening to them talk Russian, I even liked that they wanted to cook for me.' She swallowed the rest of her pink drink. 'Maybe I'm growing a soul.'

'Genia cooked?'

Val said, 'You never know, right?' She touched my cheek. 'Thanks, Artie.'

'What for?' I said, but her attention was diverted.

Jack was standing by the table and I was jealous as Val half rose from her chair when she saw him.

'Hi.' Val lit up like a bulb.

'Hi, babe, I'm sorry. I had to talk to that guy,'

said Jack who kissed her and then sat in her chair, pulling her on to his lap, playing with her hair and neck.

He whispered something to Val and she got up and moved over to sit next to one of her girlfriends. He waved at a waiter he obviously knew — everyone knew Jack — and asked for bourbon. He didn't ask for a brand. I liked that.

From where I sat I could still just see Tolya on the street. I was restless. I was shaken by Val; for a second, I had wanted her. Come on, Jack, tell me about Sid, I thought. Tell me!

'So, Jack, what's going on with you?'

'So, Beslan, like I said. You have contacts? You have anyone there?' He didn't give up when he wanted something.

'I don't know anyone in Beslan,' I said. 'I told you. Why would I?'

'I wish I could get Val's old man to help me.'

I couldn't wait much longer to hear from Jack about Sid. I'd have to ask him. I didn't have time. The obituary would be in the paper by morning, the funeral would be held, Sid would go into the ground; it would be over.

Jack was holding court now, talking about the massacre at the Russian school. Suddenly the table grew quiet. One of the girls who had not seen the news began to cry. Her mother was in Russia, she said, and she got up, clutching her cellphone. For a few minutes the table was suspended in the silence, then the noise started again.

'Let's go home,' Val said abruptly to Jack. 'I want to go now. I don't feel like being here now.

I'll meet you outside,' she added, got up and went towards the bathroom.

Jack took a wad of crumpled bills from his pocket.

One of the guys at the table — he owned clubs, he'd said — pulled out a black American Express card.

'I'll do it,' Jack said. To me, he added, 'I want to make a good impression on Sverdloff. I'm crazy about this girl. It's not just my usual bullshit stuff with women. I mean I really love her.'

'She's nineteen.'

'People are different,' Jack said earnestly. 'She's different. She's an old soul. I can't help it. I tried, but I can't. Do you think Sverdloff will have me offed or something because of it?' he said, smiling. 'Do you think he'll kill me, Art?'

22

We were outside the restaurant, Tolya still smoking a cigar, Jack and Val together, me a couple of steps away from them. I looked at my watch. I couldn't wait anymore. I turned to Jack.

I said, 'Were you a friend of Sid McKay's?'

'Sure,' he said. 'More than a friend. He was my boss once, he was like a father. He got crazy the last few years, paranoid. He kept these files, everyone knew, he thought everyone was manipulating information, that the media was corrupted, that it was all propaganda, that we were all making up stories. He was getting old. I was betting he had plaque on the brain. Sid kept files and everyone wanted them, and there was nothing in them. Why? How come you want to know?'

'I heard that he fired you. I heard you screwed up.'

He laughed. 'That was years ago. Another time.'

'Where were you all last week, Jack? Since my wedding?'

'With Val at her place in East Hampton. We just got back to the city.'

'So you didn't hear?'

'Hear what?'

I didn't make it nice. 'Sidney McKay is dead,' I said.

Jack was standing near the wall of the

restaurant and suddenly, as soon as I told him about Sid, he slid to his knees. Val saw him and reached over and put her arms around him, and sat down on to the pavement beside him. People passing stared. She ignored them, and kept her arms around Jack who was crying. I couldn't tell if his tears were for real or if Jack was a great actor. Maybe it was both.

'My God,' he said.

I crouched down next to Jack, 'You were close?' I said. 'You and Sid?'

'Sure we were close. Of course. Shit. He helped me.'

'What with?'

'Everything. Work when I was starting out. Everything. Even helped me buy my place in Red Hook. Oh, Christ, and I didn't call him back last week. He called me, I didn't get back.'

'Why's that?'

'I was tired of his obsessions about the news, that kind of thing, the accusations, he would fucking go on and on. But who killed him? Which son of a bitch decided he had to get poor old Sid McKay?'

'What accusations? He accused you of something?'

'Do you know who killed him?' Jack said.

'I thought it might be you.'

He struggled to his feet, helped by Val. Pushing her aside, Jack went for me. He was shorter than me, but he was in good shape, and he came at me so fast I fell off my feet and was on the sidewalk when Val grabbed at his sleeve.

'Stop it,' she said. 'Stop.'

Half dragging him to the curb, she waved at a cab and pushed Jack into it. Tolya ran. Tried to keep her from leaving. The cab driver slammed on the gas and the car disappeared up Ninth Avenue.

Doubled over, Tolya was panting. He held on to the street lamp. When he stood up, I could see he looked bad, trying to catch his breath, his whole body heaving. He scared the hell out of me. He'd had trouble breathing in Red Hook. He was sick and he was keeping it from me.

'What's wrong with you?'

'Where did they go?' He looked around, his eyes darting.

'I don't know. Let's go up to your place. I'll call a doctor. You look like shit,' I said.

'You let her go with him?' he said and reached in his pants pocket for his phone.

'I'll take you home,' I said.

'Forget it.' He was dialing his phone frantically. 'I want her back. I want Valentina with me.'

I took hold of Tolya's arm; his skin was clammy. I didn't want him dying on me and he looked half dead, his face sallow and shriveled, the skin slack. Walking to his car, he stumbled.

'Stop being so fucking solicitous, OK?' he said. 'I'm OK. Just leave me the fuck alone, will you? You want to help, then help out. Give me the rest of Sid McKay's files. Right now I'm going to find my child.'

I got to Tolya's SUV ahead of him, and stood in front of the door.

'You're not going anywhere.'

'Get out of my way,' he said, but he leaned against the side of the car, half slumped like an elderly prizefighter, his expression somehow defeated.

'I'll drive you.'

'No.'

'Just tell me what's going on. I'm not the fucking enemy.'

'You have the rest of the files, right? You stole them, so share with me. You don't trust me, isn't that right? Isn't it, Artemy Maximovich?'

He used my patronymic, he addressed me formally in Russian, and the tone was sarcastic, a kind of taunt.

'What do you need them for?'

'I want them because Sid was obsessed with the corruption of information, with lying and cheating.'

'So?'

'Sid knew that Santiago was involved. He knew. Santiago who asks me how I made my money, who calls my friends to ask about my past. Please, let me get into my car.' He pushed me aside.

The door to the SUV open, Tolya hoisted himself up. It was like climbing a mountain for him.

I said, 'You want to go after Santiago, is that what you're saying?'

'Yes.'

'Because of Val. Or other reasons?'

'Sure.'

'Why can't I come with you?'

'Give me McKay's stuff.'

282

'I'm a cop, man. I can't just give you stuff,' I said. 'You want me to pick him up because of Val is all. Isn't it? You want me to lay it on him because he knows about you and because he's with your daughter. I'm sorry about it. But I can't.'

'It's not because you're a cop,' he said. 'It's because you think I killed Sid. You accuse Jack Santiago, but you don't believe it. You just believe it was me.'

For a second I was distracted by my phone ringing with a message from Sonny Lippert's office. In the time it took me to answer, Tolya slammed the car door.

★ ★ ★

Rhonda Fisher, Sonny Lippert's secretary, was in the outer office, even though it was Saturday night.

At her computer, Rhonda was half watching a Yankees game in extra innings on a portable TV that sat on top of a filing cabinet next to a plant with yellow flowers, and when she saw me, she raised her palms, despairing a little, the way she usually did.

She had worked for Sonny for twenty years, and was probably in love with him. I kissed her and we talked about the Yankees for a minute, her regretting, like always, that there were no men like Paul O'Neill anymore, asking me to try to keep Sonny from drinking, and knowing it was all impossible. I had to get to Tolya before he crashed his car, but I didn't know where the hell he was. I had to get home and look at Sid's files, but Sonny had been leaving messages.

I went in. Sonny looked up at me, and took a bottle from his desk drawer. 'Nightcap,' he said and poured Scotch into two glasses that were already on the desk. He had been expecting me. 'They want me out of here,' he said and gestured at the office. 'I'm not leaving.'

'That's why you called me? You left messages. It's late. What?'

'Yeah, sit down. You want the bad news or the other bad news?' he said.

I took the glass. 'Go on.'

'I have to tell you something, man. I don't want to but I have to.'

'What is it? Jesus, Sonny, what?'

'It's about you.'

'What do you mean?'

'I got a call from a guy. Someone who knows I know you.'

'What guy?'

'It doesn't matter what guy. A guy I had asked about Sid McKay for you. Call him my Deep Throat,' he said and snorted. 'He said, you're talking Detective Artie Cohen, aren't you, and I said, yeah and I'm about to ask him about the McKay case, and he says out of nowhere, listen I know Cohen's a pal of yours, so I want to tell you that someone got his license number off one of the Al Qaeda intercepts.'

'Excuse me?'

'Yeah, I know this sounds like fucking Tom Clancy stuff, but it's what they do, you know the reports coming in about attacks on Citicorp earlier in the summer, whatever, they get real detailed stuff from somewhere, they got sleepers everywhere, man, they got measurements of every skyscraper in New York City, they got the architectural plans, they got the locations of vents and air conditioning, they probably know the names of the president of every fucking co-op board that's fighting about who puts a plant on the roof garden, and they probably got people on the co-op boards, and among other shit, they got the badge numbers of officers on the beat and licenses of cops and license plates from guys on cases. You have no idea. They write it down, they send it back to whatever shit-hole in Pakistan or Saudi they work out of, and once in a while, we capture some stuff and there it is. Your license plate. Your badge. You don't have to be some fucking whiz kid.'

'Fuck.'

'Yeah, fuck is right,' Sonny said.

'So what am I supposed to do?'

'Nothing. I'm just telling you. You know how the Feds get, they get a shred of information they turn it into something to get media play because otherwise they would never get anything positive, and the politicians climb on board, I'm just telling you, I mentioned your name, this is what comes back, so anyone stops by your place, you call me, or if you get stopped at an airport, or your car breaks down and you get hassled. Something like that. OK?'

'Thanks.'

'OK, I'm just saying.'

'OK,' I said but I was nervous. A while back

the Feds had been in my place looking through my stuff because someone told them I could speak a little Arabic.

'You think it's related to Sid McKay?' I said.

Sonny said, 'I doubt it. But it will make people look at you. Some people. Some people in the department. You have to talk to me about this thing with Sid McKay. I heard the family is saying it was some kind of accident. What kind of accident? He hit himself over the head? You know anything about this?'

I drank the Scotch and asked him for another, and then I told him everything I knew, except for a few details about Tolya Sverdloff.

I said I was thinking that maybe Jack Santiago could work as a suspect for Sid's murder. I floated it at Sonny. I floated it like a little Chinese trick paper flower and the more I sent it out, the more it made waves and blossomed; I waited to see if it would open up real nice.

They had been close, Sid and Jack, I said. Somehow Jack betrayed him. Maybe Jack knew something about Sid's half brother, Earl. There were files, too, I said. Sid kept notes.

Sonny looked at me pityingly. 'Art, man, everyone knew. Sid passed files around like boxes of fucking chocolate cherries. He was nuts, what can I say? He showed up on TV shows, he was like this liberal pundit they hauled in when they wanted one. Then his paper canned him and he went nuts. His stories never amounted to much,' Sonny said, 'I been talking to a lot of people since you dropped by on me at home, man, and it woke me up. You got to give me more on

Santiago than that Sid McKay didn't think he was doing his job. I get called by people all the time, editors, whoever, see if there's criminal activity on any of those cases of reporters faking stuff. You want to eat at Rao's with me tomorrow night? I have my table. Or Peter Luger's if you want?'

Listening to him talk about Sid and the news business, I replied by saying how much I really liked Jack for Sid's killer. I drank with Sonny for an hour, and I sat opposite him at his desk and made a case.

I told Sonny things I wasn't sure about. I threw stuff out at him like the fact that Jack lived in Red Hook, stuff that didn't mean anything by itself. Told him about the way Jack had come to the wedding, the way he made a play for Valentina Sverdloff. I built a scenario. I made connections, I introduced characters, I erected a plot and pieced it together and embroidered it and gave it conviction.

Cops did it all the time. Sometimes it meant they figured out, looking at the neat arrangement of the parts, who the killer really was; sometimes they got it wrong; they did it because they needed a collar, or were sick to death of a case and yearned for a conclusion. Sometimes, by the end of the story, they convinced themselves. I was convinced.

'What's the matter, man, you cold or something? You want Rhonda to turn down the air?' Sonny was glazed from the booze.

There was gooseflesh on my arms. I kept talking. Sonny drank some more. Inside I felt something shift. My arm still hurt from the cut.

Jack Santiago was on his way to Beslan in Russia to write about the kids who were killed by a bunch of terrorists, I told Sonny, I said, how come Jack got assigned over there so fast? Wasn't it convenient? Stop him from leaving the country, Sonny, I said, and he said, stop him how? Just get in his way, I said; call someone in Immigration, or Homeland Security.

Stop him, I said. I leaned over the desk and cranked it up, how Jack killed Sid. Stop him, I said.

Sonny got more and more remote, but, as I made my story good and tight, I could see him buy it. He was a reader, he understood narrative in his gut. By the time I left, I knew I had made him believe in the Santiago scenario, that Jack killed Sid McKay, because that was what I wanted to believe.

23

When Sid McKay's obituary finally appeared Sunday in the *Times*, it had been scrubbed clean. I picked up the early edition after I left Sonny's office around midnight Saturday, and I read it on the street outside the newsstand.

The obituary did not give the precise cause of death. It suggested a medical condition, and an accident. The rest of it described his education, his family, his professional achievements, his awards. He was survived by his son Alexander Justice McKay, and two grandchildren, it said. Alex McKay had never mentioned his own children. The obituary referred to other family members. There was no real news in it, only the list of accomplishments and a picture taken maybe ten years earlier, Sid smiling slightly, in a suit and tie.

I knew the McKay family had moved in fast and taken control before any real news stories emerged. Lucky for them that Sid died during a week when barely any news south of Madison Square got reported.

* * *

'Artie? Let me in. It's me, Rick.'

It was Sunday early, and I realized I had fallen asleep, the phone in my hand after I came home with the newspaper and tried to get through to

Maxine. When I heard the banging on my door, I made out that it was Rick's voice and I ran and opened it and found him, dressed only in some cut-off jeans, his face pale with tension. In one hand was a copy of the *Times*.

'Come on in. I didn't know you were back.'

He stumbled into my place. I hadn't seen him since my wedding almost a week earlier. I knew he'd been away, probably Singapore, where he did business. He was white and under his eyes were hollows big and stained like teabags.

'I'll get some coffee,' I said. 'What is it, Rick?'

'It's Sid.' He held up the newspaper, then went into the kitchen, picked up the espresso pot and shook it to see if it was full, then poured himself a cup, stood by the stove and drank it in two gulps.

'I'm really sorry,' I said. 'I've been working this case unofficially as best I can.'

'You've been working it and you didn't tell me?'

'You weren't here. I didn't know you and Sid were that close.'

'We were close.'

'You want to talk?'

He looked at the folders I had laid out across the kitchen counter and on the floor. I gathered them up and took them to my desk.

'What's all that?'

'Just work stuff.'

'I didn't help him, Artie. Sid called me, and I didn't help him,' he said.

'Go on.' I poured myself what was left of the coffee, and put on some more.

'Nothing, he called me and said he was worried, and I didn't go. I couldn't get in it again. I knew him a long time ago.'

'You and him?'

Rick nodded.

'Yeah, but he didn't want anyone to know. He wasn't really out back then. He said he was too old for me. I took him to see my parents once, my father looked at him like he was a baby killer, it was bad enough he had a fag for a kid, but bringing an old man over, and an old black man. And his family. My God, you never saw anything like it, it was like they were living out some fantasy life, I met an aunt once, I think she imagined I was Sid's houseboy, you know, did the cooking. It was bizarre, you know, like an alternate universe?' Rick stared into the coffee cup. 'After that Sid retreated. We split up. Around 9/11, we met up, you know how everyone was getting together, and we had a fling, but it was a 9/11 thing, you know. We stayed in touch, I don't know, we'd talk once a month and have dinner.'

'I'm really sorry.'

'Just make sure you find the bastard who did it, make sure for me,' Rick said. 'I have to go.'

I said, 'Call me if you want.'

'Sure,' he said, and again I thought how sad I was that we had drifted apart.

He went to the door, opened it, then turned around.

Ricky said, 'I really loved him a lot, you know.'

★ ★ ★

I moved fast now. I needed a real fix on Jack. I needed it soon. He could disappear into Russia for months if he wanted. Had he left the night before, after he and Val took off in the cab? When did the last flight go?

I started calling the airlines. I hit a dead end with Lot, the Polish airlines, and then it occurred to me that Jack could have hitched a lift with a friend who had a plane. He was that kind of guy. I called around facilities for private planes. The only person I knew who flew private was Tolya. I once asked him about it, and he had looked at me pityingly and said, 'You don't think I fly commercial, do you?' But Tolya wasn't giving any rides to Jack.

I threw a few things in a bag, and packed up all the files. I didn't want anyone seeing them, not Tolya or Rick or anyone else coming into my place, especially not some Fed who knew Al Qaeda had my license on a satellite intercept.

Sonny said that Sid's files were bullshit, but what else did I have left? I wanted one last shot at them. Maybe I'd been lazy or stupid. Anyhow, to move on Jack, I needed a reason and I knew I had to get through the files, one piece of paper at a time, get it figured out. I took the bag and got my car to drive out to Maxine's place in Brooklyn where no one would think of looking for me. Also, I missed her. On the way, I stopped in Red Hook.

★ ★ ★

Jack's apartment was in a white building that had once been a cement factory. It looked like a crumbling pile of stale white bread. It was a few blocks away from Sid's, an easy drive, an easy walk. Jack was on his way to Russia by now. I still didn't know what route he took. I was sure he was gone, but I took a chance.

I buzzed his apartment. No one answered. I hung around the building downstairs until a good-looking woman showed up, carrying a carton of coffee. She wore sweat pants and a red halter top, she was around fifty, I figured. Great figure. There was something that looked like glue in her dark long hair.

'Yeah, yeah, sure I know Jack,' she said and leaned against the front door and said she'd talked to him the night before.

'Did he have a girl with him?'

'No,' she said. 'No girl.'

He left with a suitcase the night before, she said. Late. She couldn't remember what time. He rang her bell, like he always did when he was leaving town because he knew she was up all hours, and anyhow he didn't care who he woke up. He told her he was going to Russia. He asked her to take up his mail. He told her he was going to do the real story about Beslan, about the school and the dead kids over there, on and on, she said, the way Jack always did, blah blah blah, making sure you knew what a big deal he was.

'Like always?'

'Yeah,' she said. 'Like always.'

'You're sure?'

'Jack doesn't do not sure,' she said. 'He was

fucking always sure. He was sure about everything,' she added. 'Sexy, though. Great fuck, you know? Fucked everything that moved, but he was nice about it.'

'Yeah?'

'Yeah, what's the saying? He'd even fuck a Venetian blind, someone wrote that. That was how Jack was. I'd know.'

'You see a lot of him.'

'Whatever,' she said. 'He comes and goes.'

I thanked her, and started for my car. I turned back and said, 'You go out for coffee early a lot?'

'Yeah, all the time. You get crazy working by yourself, you know what I mean?'

'Where do you go around here?'

'There's a couple stores open early, convenience store over on Van Brunt makes the best brew. Everyone gets coffee there,' she said.

'Jack, too?'

'Sure. Why not?'

'Last week, you saw him there last week?'

'Last week when? It was a long week,' she said. 'A lot of days. I saw him Tuesday for sure. I know I saw him then because I was out all night Monday, and I stopped for cigarettes on my way home real early. He was with another guy. Black guy. Elegant.'

'You knew the other guy.'

'I saw him around a few times, I saw him having dinner at 360, like that. He was some kind of writer. Sixty, sixty-five, I'm guessing. Why?'

I thought: the morning Sid went out and left his door unlocked he was with Jack. He met Jack

294

and never came back.

I said, 'You like it here, you like living here?'

'It's OK,' she said. 'Some homeless bastard got shoved off the pier last week, I could have done without that, but I mean we're just a couple of condos away from turning into SoHo, you got a lot of nice little businesses, artists, and now we got two good restaurants, and they're fixing the waterfront over by Beard Warehouses, parks and stuff for kids, and hey, we'll have a marina any minute and architects and design stores, and then Bloomingdales will come to Brooklyn, and what the fuck, we'll be made. Right?' She grinned. 'I actually love it here,' she added. 'It's still pretty wild.'

She asked if I wanted a cup of coffee, and I said I was in a hurry, so we talked a little more, standing in her doorway, and to be polite I asked what her business was because I could see a large loft space behind her. Kites, she said. I make silk kites. She reached up to her dark long hair and pulled at the glue that was stuck in it.

'Three, four, five hundred bucks a pop,' she said, giggling. 'I once got a grand. For a kite,' she added.

I said what were you before? Before what, she said. I said before you made the kites.

'Married,' she said.

'What?'

'I was married. I lived in Westchester, in the suburbs. Now I make kites in Red Hook.'

Part Three

24

SUITCASE NUKE WASHES UP OFF RED HOOK read the headline. Suitcase nukes. Dirty bombs. Jack Santiago's big subject. Did you read my series? he had asked in the bar the night before.

Jack was gone. I didn't know how he traveled, the night before, this morning, but he was in Moscow and maybe already traveling south in Russia and the only way I could convince anyone to get him back was if I found out how he killed Sid, and why. Why, they'd say. What for? What made him kill Sid?

I was at Maxine's place in Brooklyn, out by Bay Ridge, reading through Sid's files, looking for evidence that Jack killed him. One at a time, I laid the folders out across the kitchen table and on some chairs. I picked over each piece of paper. Some pieces were stuck together from damp or age; I separated them and left them out to dry.

By the time I'd been at it for an hour, the kitchen table, dining room table and living room floor were covered with paper. My instinct was to keep moving, head for the airport, find out which plane Jack took, get someone to call someone, drive around. I had looked at the files before, but I knew I hadn't been careful enough. I had to know. So I kept going, stomach churning.

Hurry, I thought. Hurry up. Maybe he was still in Moscow. Sonny promised he'd get the word out. In Moscow, you could get your hands on him. Stop him at the airport. If he went south, it would be much harder.

Someone knocked on the door, and I reached for my gun. It was only Maxine's neighbor who thought we were all away. I said I was working, leaving later, I said, and smiled, grinning, pretending I was picking up stuff for the beach, I said. The woman probably thought I was crazy.

The living room of Maxine's apartment was small and neat, with two windows that looked out over the river. I'd spent hundreds of nights here, sitting on the couch that was covered with a red bedspread, eating pizza, kidding around. She had given me the keys and said, 'This is ours, OK? Our place. Both of us.'

I felt like an interloper now. I had screwed up. Maxine didn't want me out at the beach. I didn't know if she even wanted me at all, and all I could do was focus on the piles of paper that Sid had left.

I picked out the file labeled 'Suitcase Nukes', the words written by hand on a green tab.

The piece with the headline was from a Russian rag I recognized, one of the papers that picked up stuff from the *New York Post*, some of the British tabs, and Russian news services. It was printed in Brooklyn. People poured over it for gossip, news, and astrological forecasts. I'd seen it on the stands out in Brighton Beach.

I looked at the date. It was a couple of months old. I turned it over, saw it was attached by a paper clip to a more recent piece printed off the

Internet with Jack's byline. He had his own website.

In the girls' bedroom, I switched on their computer. I was lousy at this stuff, but I could at least get as far as Jack's web page where I read up some more. Same stuff as on paper. A suitcase nuke at one of the derelict docks in Red Hook. Nobody hurt. I knew it had happened more than once in the city. Mostly city officials kept this stuff quiet, if they could.

I kept reading, smoking, scanning the stuff about radiologicals, most of it gossip from Internet sites that recycled what passed for news, and some blogs that didn't tell me anything I didn't know. Denials, assertions, fear mongering, the kind of stuff TV sometimes picked up to fill the space between news cycles.

I switched off the computer, went back into the living room and put on *People Time*, the somber album Stan Getz made when he was only months from dying and could barely play. But he did play, exquisite music. It was one of the albums I'd given Maxine that she didn't really like but that she listened to attentively, trying to get it. If she worked hard enough, listened carefully enough, she felt she would understand. I could see her, on the couch, her legs under her, nibbling a piece of pizza, like a schoolkid, listening as if for an exam, trying to work out what it meant. I had wanted to say, just let it happen. But that wasn't the point. It was enough that she tried.

Restless, I read more newspaper pieces, more about nuclear smuggling, some pseudo-science, government reports, statistics, conjecture and endless articles by Jack. He was bluffing half the time.

I wandered into Maxine's bedroom, opening drawers I shouldn't have opened. In the top drawer of her bureau was a tape for learning Russian and a notebook covered with her attempts at making Cyrillic letters. I felt like getting the hell out, getting to her. She was trying to learn Russian; she never told me. Her big loopy handwriting, the effort to make the Russian letters, touched me more than anything she had ever done.

What else didn't I know? We had been living together for a year and a half, more or less, and I had known her for much longer. I found a photograph of her father, an unsmiling man in a fireman's uniform, then put it away. There were no pictures of her mother.

I went back to the files and looked at a diagram for a suitcase nuke. Crap, most of it.

I knew what people thought, though. Max and me, we'd discussed it because they talked about it at her job. We had laughed about the suitcase nukes. People imagined a miniature silver nuclear missile like a toy with a little warhead at the top, secreted in an old-fashioned brown leather suitcase that had latches and locks and leather handles, a suitcase out of a Hitchcock movie with brightly-colored stickers that read: Ritz Hotel, Paris, or the Orient Express, Istanbul, or National Hotel, Moscow. They imagined that you opened the suitcase, and presto, the little missile popped out of the suitcase and a miniature fire ball rose over 34th Street or Times Square or Wall Street; a baby mushroom cloud fell over Manhattan like something in a Terminator movie, and there was a terrible wind that swept everything with it. I knew it was what people thought; it's pretty much what I thought until I did a couple of cases.

Suitcase nukes. The radioactive stuff, the enriched uranium, plutonium, cesium, beryllium, usually came from some poor slob who hadn't been paid for months and carried it out of a nuke plant in Russia in a saucepan. People were hungry in the Russian hinterlands; old people didn't have heat; scientists didn't get paid so they did what they had to. The big players took it from there.

American ports were as leaky as it got and you could get anything in. Usually the radioactive shit got through tucked in with antiques from Indonesia or tablecloths from Ukraine. I'd seen one of the canisters; it had held cesium. It was lead and painted yellow, the paint chipped. It looked like a cheap coffee thermos, but it was heavy. The hardware, labeled as tool and die machines, could be shipped through Germany, and then south, Iraq, Iran, Syria.

You didn't need a fancy nuclear bomb, either; everyone knew. You got enough of the radiologicals, and added some crappy parts — a detonator, a piece of an alarm clock — put it with conventional explosives and took it on a ship or on board a plane or even a subway. Hit the Trade Center with that, you had a nuclear missile almost as terrifying as anything buried in the ground out in Wyoming. Fucking boom, as a friend of mine once said.

A hundred thousand people would be streaming up Broadway, the unlucky ones, their faces falling off, their skin peeling off, dying as they walked, and then thousands more, and no one at St Vincent's with any idea what to do.

Jack had described it all; I could read his lust for the subject. It wasn't that no one else had reported it. It was that Jack was obsessed. He sketched out fictional scenarios that would scare the socks off your fucking feet. There were clippings of his pieces from Long Island newspapers and local Brooklyn giveaway sheets, stuff reprinted in foreign papers and magazines.

He had covered the territory for years, he had consulted with medics, engineers and weapons specialists, he had even calculated the numbers of deaths; behind the cool calculations and figures and language, you could see that he was hot for the subject and he had been everywhere, traveling on any story he could get that took him to Russia, Iran, China, anywhere he thought he could detail sources of radioactive material; he described the mules who humped the stuff out of the Middle East and through Central Europe, some of them girls who worked as prostitutes and did it unknowingly, just carried canisters of the stuff in their bags. Some got cancer. A few had died of radioactive poisoning.

Probably it came down to that: Jack sat in front of his computer in the building in Red Hook that looked like crumbling bread and outlined the end of the world.

Weapons of Mass Destruction. Jack was in with it before it had a name. He got himself into conferences and spoke at universities.

For hours I read through the stuff that Sid had hoarded in his folders, moving through it, trying to make sense, restless, panicky that I'd never get to the end.

I spread the files around again, and picked my way over them, and kept looking for something that would show me what Sid knew about Jack that made Jack kill him.

★   ★   ★

By now, a sea of paper was scattered on Maxine's floor. A snowstorm. I was getting nuts from it. A blizzard. Shut up, I thought. Read. Hurry.

I tried to picture Sid carefully cutting out pieces from newspapers, printing out stuff from the Internet, filing it, attaching paper clips, writing labels. There had not been a TV in his loft. Didn't like the noise, he said. Sid liked his news recycled on his own time.

After about my fourth cup of coffee, my head cleared up and I realized I felt like I was reading a bad novel. Something didn't click, didn't fit, didn't hang together, the jigsaw puzzle was missing a piece of the sky.

At the window, I looked out at the green lawn that sloped down to Shore Drive and the Belt Parkway. Cars buzzed past, and beyond them there were a few boats on the water. The

Verrazano Bridge stretched elegant, a thin whip of metal across the Narrows to Staten Island, and I thought of how Maxine loved to stand at the window when the sun went down over it.

The 'Guinea Gangplank', she told me her uncle used to call the bridge, when *guinea* was a common slur for Italians, and people thought the mafia pushed their victims off the bridge.

The water was smooth, but the hurricane that had flattened Florida was coming up the East Coast; it was the worst hurricane season in a hundred years. I began worrying about Maxine down on that little Jersey peninsula, the scraps of beach that a storm could flood. She'd only laugh at me.

'It's New Jersey, Artie, honey. Nothing ever happens here.'

Anyhow, she didn't want me there.

'I don't want you to, Artie. I just don't, not right now,' she had said when I called the night before. Maxine sounded sad and I knew we had lost something.

★ ★ ★

What was I looking for those hours locked up in Maxine's apartment?

I kept reading. I always resisted paperwork. I didn't like the smell of old paper from the time I was a kid in Moscow and my mother leaned on me to use libraries. Love libraries, Artyom, she would say; there will always be something worth reading and she would give me some money to bribe the librarian who would slip you forbidden books for a price. I once got caught. I was thirteen, fourteen, can't remember, but I remembered that I was working on some subject I didn't like, some Marxist-Leninist crap — hard to believe there was such a time — and I was looking through a copy of a Philip Roth novel and I got caught. My father had to come and get me from school.

It was getting late and I was already jumpy but I made more coffee, waited until it boiled, turned off the music, drank the coffee and found some stale Entenmann's donuts in the fridge. I ate two and got powdered sugar on my shirt.

In the kitchen, I sat on a stool, upright near the window where it was bright so the light would keep me awake.

The last three folders were on the Formica counter in front of me. I opened one. The pages from a yellow legal pad were covered in Sid's tiny handwriting, beautiful writing done with a fountain pen, as if he had studied calligraphy.

I couldn't remember having seen these pages. Had I given them to Tolya? Did he put them back? There was a single sheet of the yellow paper, brittle with age, which contained lists of Russian vocabulary. I thought about Maxine's attempts to learn Russian for me.

There were notes about Sid's life as a young boy, the meeting with the Russian sailors, his search for the one sailor, Meler, who became his friend.

A couple of pages of notes were stuck to the back of the vocabulary list with some kind of glue. Sid had hidden it, not sure he wanted anyone to find it at all.

★ ★ ★

The handwritten notes in Russian were all about Jack as if Sid had written them in code. The notes dated back to Jack's first job working for Sid, followed by more notes he kept over the years. Year after year, he kept an eye on everything that Jack did. He read his articles and columns, he saw him on TV. He took notes on his performances. It gave me the creeps, Sid watching Jack like that.

They must have talked on the phone, too, because there were notes on conversations, and references to tapes from recordings of the calls and receipts from meals they ate together. If you believed Sid's notes, Jack had become increasingly delusional, paranoid, nuts, or just plain bad.

I shuttled back to the folder with Jack's newspaper pieces: the articles about the Russian mob in Brighton Beach were full of the mystique of the new mafia, that kind of garbage, and while I picked out a couple of the stories to read, I spotted something that made me spill my coffee.

One of the articles was about a case I had worked almost ten years earlier, the first case I did in Brighton Beach, the one that took me back to Moscow. It was a nuclear smuggling case, real small potatoes, but one of the first. I had never seen the piece before.

There were names in it, mine, Tolya

Sverdloff's. It was the case where I first met Tolya. I wondered how the hell Jack had identified us. I looked at the date. How did he know I worked that case so soon after it was over? Later, maybe he could have looked it up, but back then no one knew.

Maybe his affair with Valentina Sverdloff wasn't accidental. Maybe what he wanted was to get to her father. Maybe he came to my wedding to get close to me.

I got up. Deciphering Sid's Russian was hard work, and I was beginning to sweat, not just from the effort, but from fear.

According to Sid, Jack didn't just fake his datelines, he corrupted his own source material, so that after a while, even if people went back and looked at the stuff he had based his reports on, it seemed valid. You could do that with computer sites, go back generations so that even people who checked could be fooled, and who checked these days?

Jack didn't care about facts; what he cared about was an idea of himself, a mythology, a narrative. Jack wasn't interested in facts any more than the politicians were. He didn't care if there was a canister of radioactive shit floating off Red Hook. He was interested in making the legend. Jack was only interested in making the next big urban legend: Nukes in New York.

I flipped the page in my hand, then turned it over, then checked back through a couple more pages of Sid's notes. According to Sid, Jack was taking money from the government. Some federal agencies were giving him tax dollars to shill for the government, to push its line on certain issues, especially nuclear smuggling.

According to Jack, he took the money and he retailed propaganda as news about nukes. The news about smuggled nuclear weapons, the possibility of a dirty bomb, these made terrific propaganda weapons in the government's arsenal of fear. Sid used the phrase: Arsenal of Fear. Melodramatic, maybe, but he believed it. For a price, Sid wrote, Jack was retailing fear for the government.

★ ★ ★

I started gathering up folders, putting things in order when something struck me: why did Sid keep it to himself? Did he feel he couldn't admit he had been wrong about Jack in the first place, about his golden boy, the good son, the guy he hired, mentored, helped? He had even helped Jack buy into Red Hook. To keep him close? To watch him better?

Did Sid feel he had to check and check again? Had it only been the Jayson Blair mess at the *New York Times*, the kid who faked his stories, that made Sid pay more attention? He had been gathering material for years, though, adding to it, working on it, rewriting it, getting the evidence.

The more I read, the more I could see that Sid was almost as obsessed by Jack as he was by the facts; they were locked in it together: Sid building up the folders year after year, no longer sure what was true and what was fiction. The two of them, speaking, not speaking, Sid with his folders, Jack working on obscure websites. I had met them both at the same time, at Jack's wedding on Crosby Street all those years ago.

He knew. I suddenly understood that Jack knew that Sid was watching him, keeping track, making notes. Somehow he knew. It was a game they were both in. Sid appointed Jack to be the good son, and Jack exploited it and then let him know he knew.

Year after year, Jack invented not just his work but himself; he made himself up. Only Sid knew all of it, all the lies and inventions. If he let it out, there would be nothing left of Jack. He would disappear into his own lies. Sid was dead; Jack had needed him dead.

★   ★   ★

I had to get to Jack Santiago somehow. He had gone to Russia, but maybe he was still in the air, maybe he wasn't at the airport yet, or at the airport; for the second or third time, I thought: you could stop someone at an airport. Sonny could get someone. Tolya could find one of his guys.

I got up in a hurry and dropped all the files on to Maxine's kitchen floor.

The paper scattered everywhere, and the warm breeze coming in off the river picked up a single sheet that drifted out of the window.

25

The sun was almost gone by the time I got on the FDR Drive where the traffic was moving OK. It was getting dark earlier, fall coming. I was back in Manhattan, heading uptown on the highway, driving too fast.

The water was on my right, the Pepsi Cola sign winked red at me from Queens. Overhead, when I passed 59th Street, the little suburban tram shunted people to Roosevelt Island. All the years I'd been in New York I had never been to Roosevelt Island.

The city was spread out across the islands, not just Manhattan or Staten Island, or Roosevelt or Randall's in the East River, but specks of empty land which meant you could land illegal material or people or drugs in a thousand places.

I was tired and I tried to keep focused on the files, on the nukes Jack said had been coming into the ports, on whether he made it all up, working my phone, still trying to get through to the airlines, to Moscow, I was distracted by the water turning dark, the lights coming on.

Tolya had the clout, he could track down Jack Santiago if he was in Moscow, but Tolya, tight-lipped on the phone, just gave me an address in the Bronx and hung up. Hurry, I thought.

My window was open; the humid air closed in on me, I stepped on the gas, moving between trucks and cabs and cars, everyone leaning on the horn because I was driving like a drunk. I wasn't drunk, but I was tired, and I was going too fast, passing too close. I put on the radio, tried to keep awake, listened to the news.

Up to my left now were the fancy buildings on Sutton Place like cliff dwellings hung out over the East River. I had done a case in one of those buildings. It had been full of rich people and I wondered if they still felt safe, or if they sat up nights now, locked up and scared.

I put on some loud Brazilian music to keep me awake. Took it off. I was nervous. I put on a Stan Kenton big band album, hit stop, turned on the radio again so the jagged loop of instant news battered my brain. Hurricanes. Destruction everywhere down south.

Finally, I turned into the mind-numbing tangle of roads that led to the Triboro Bridge and the Bronx, and then on to Bruckner Boulevard. Overhead, the traffic on the Bruckner Expressway roared by.

The streets were deserted, there were broken sidewalks, one-story buildings shuttered with metal gates, businesses gone bust, factories shut down, gas stations closed.

There wasn't much crime up here anymore, not the way there had been when this was *Bonfire of the Vanities* territory and guys I knew who had to work it were scared. Fort Apache, they called it. Someone I knew who had a business down one of these crumbling streets in those days told me that he drove a Jeep so he could run down anyone who got in his way. The

South Bronx? Move fast, ask later, he said.

'I got a Jeep, I got a gun permit,' he said. He wasn't even a cop.

You didn't get trouble up here anymore unless you went looking for it. People were even eyeing the South Bronx for real estate.

Hunt's Point, where the food markets were, sat on the edge of the water. Two hundred years earlier, five or six rich families kept summer estates here. I took a dead-end road and found myself staring at a chain-link fence and an old pier and the water beyond it. From the south end of the Bronx, you could look down along the East River to Manhattan.

Behind me a truck was honking and somewhere from a car radio I heard the ballgame. Getting my bearings, I realized I wasn't far from the Stadium. It would have been nice to drop everything and head over and catch the game, watch Mariano close for the Yanks, sit there with Maxine and drink a few beers. I hoped to God I hadn't fucked up that life completely. Tomorrow, I thought. I'll get to her by tomorrow. It will be OK, if I do that. I'll spend the holiday with her. It was Labor Day, the last holiday of the summer.

I made a deal with myself: if I got there for Labor Day, Maxine would forgive me.

I took another wrong turn, doubled back, stepping on the gas, desperate to get to Tolya Sverdloff. Up one avenue was a huge produce market, the endless rows of warehouses where fruit and vegetables were shipped out across the city.

In the distance I could see the new fish market. Fulton Street's market would disappear; the fish would be delivered here. I was looking for meat.

Hunt's Point was the biggest food depot in the world. Everything came in, and then moved out again and even on Sunday night there was activity, as eighteen-wheelers thundered off the highway and through the security check and into the market.

My badge got me through security. I drove to a parking lot. On the other side, a row of trucks was attached to huge accordion-like tubes hanging from an overhead rail. It was some kind of clean air deal, someone told me; it was bullshit, he had said. No one used it, it was just a useless sop to some environmental group. There had been other deals up here, rumors of price fixing. It was clean now, more or less, but all the business was done in cash.

The market was like a city: there was a bank, a couple of coffee shops, stores. Some of the purveyors sold to small stores, but most were big wholesalers. A long building with loading docks out front was divided up into separate businesses — lamb, pork, beef. A couple of trucks were backed up to the docks, men unloading goods, a lot of it in boxes, some animal carcasses. Soon it would all be here and nothing left downtown in the Meat Packing District except restaurants serving blood orange mojitos.

The whole place was dense with sound: a few trucks had their engines running; a generator whined somewhere; air conditioning units rattled; planes flew low into LaGuardia; guys on the loading docks yelled out to truck drivers; radios blared the ballgame. It was how the Brooklyn shipyards must have sounded once.

I drove around looking for the address Tolya had given me, getting screwed up in the endless rows of warehouses, worried now.

Hurry. My heart skipped a beat, slipped down, seemed to go wrong. I had to get this thing finished tonight. I wanted it over. Get Jack picked up wherever he was. Get him back to the city. Get it done.

Finally, I saw a guy directing a truck as it backed into a loading dock and I leaned out. He gave me directions.

★ ★ ★

A sign out front proclaimed that the wholesaler specialized in the world's best lamb. The letters 'RK' were on a sign, the company name, I guessed. Next door was a chicken operation. It was a warm, humid evening and I got a strong whiff of the stink of chicken.

I kept going into the RK receiving office where a guy at a computer terminal made a call and then got up and escorted me through the warehouse.

It was huge, two stories high, and almost empty. Most of the boxes had been moved out across the city; more would come in before dawn. A man bundled up in a one-piece quilted jumpsuit passed and waved his hand. It was

316

freezing in the cavernous dark space. It felt like hell.

'In there,' said the guy who brought me to the office.

I opened the door.

Two men, their backs to me, were at the desk, and I could see a bottle of vodka on it. One of them was Tolya. He heard the door open. So did the other guy. Ronnie Kruschenko, he said, and got up to shake my hand. He had a patch over one eye, like a pirate, or else a man who had had a cataract operation. He congratulated me and I remembered he had been at my wedding.

On the desk was a large blue can of caviar and a plate with bread. The desk itself was eight feet long and made out of fancy inlaid wood. The walls were covered in gold wallpaper and there were framed pictures of Ronnie with various dignitaries. On a shelf that ran the length of the room was a collection of china sheep.

Lamb was Kruschenko's thing, and I guessed the sheep were some kind of icon for him. There were a lot of them. Rows of them on glass shelves. Pictures of Ronnie with various prize animals and famous chefs. I noticed the carpet had a flock of sheep woven in it.

Kruschenko offered to show me around. He was a voluble, genial guy and he let me know he began as a butcher at the market, like a lot of Russians, and had worked his way up to buying the place. He asked if I needed anything, lamb, beef, he could put me on to some prime retailers, or give me a whole side, since I was a friend of Tolya's. Anything he said. These days, he added, the market catered to everyone, goats for Caribbean customers, halal butchering for Muslims.

'We can do live slaughter,' he said. 'You smelled the chickens, right?'

He gestured at the vodka, and I shook my head. There was a knock on the door. Kruschenko yelled, 'Yeah? Come in.'

In a butcher's coat, a man walked into the office, went over to Kruschenko, whispered in his ear. Kruschenko didn't introduce him. The man looked at me warily, and said, 'Who's he?'

Kruschenko told him to relax and walked him out of the office.

'I'm sorry,' he said, returning. 'People get nervous about outsiders. Please, forgive me.'

'Sure,' I said. 'We have to go anyway.'

'Give me a minute, Artyom,' Tolya said.

'No,' I said. 'I need you.'

He lowered his voice. 'Give me a minute. Please.'

While they finished talking, I waited at the other side of the room, impatient, staring at an oil painting of lambs. When I turned around, I saw Kruschenko take an envelope out of his desk and hand it to Tolya. It looked like money.

I said, 'Let's go.'

★ ★ ★

'What the fuck was that?' I said to Tolya when we were in the parking lot. 'I had to come all the way up here to find you because you needed meat?'

318

'I need cash,' he said. 'I told you on the phone. It's why I couldn't talk. I told you I had to do this. What's your problem, Artyom? I do even a little deal, you follow me?'

'What do you need so much cash for now?'

'I need,' he said and took a cigar out of his case and lit one, and stood in the dark smoking furiously. He peered at me. 'What?'

'You went after Jack and Val last night, right?' I said. 'I saw you drive off. I was worried. You looked terrible. You didn't get to them?'

'What could I do?' he said. 'I didn't feel so good. Listen, I crashed my car. I lost them.'

'You didn't call me? Where's Val?'

'What?'

'Jack knew all about you before he started dating Valentina, he knew about me. I'm talking years ago, I mean ancient history. Come on.' I started towards my car. 'Let's get back to the city. We can talk on the way. Where is she?'

'I'm calling,' he said, walking with me, then running, short of breath, smoking.

'I found stuff in one of the files I took from Sid's place, articles Jack wrote where he identified you and me as working that Red Mercury case back in Brighton Beach, years back, you remember, the year we first met Jack, at that party, his wedding at his place on Crosby Street. We were all there, I remembered, you, me, Lily, Sid. I think Jack's dating Val because he's interested in you. Your past. Your history, your access, your money. You were right,' I said. 'And he's still obsessed with nukes. He thinks they're coming in through Brooklyn. Hoods in

319

Brighton Beach. Ships in Red Hook. He wants to get at the Russians through you. Through Valentina.'

Tolya stopped dead in the middle of the street and sank into himself like a frog, his head sinking between his shoulders. He stared at me. 'Where is he?'

'I think he went to Russia. I thought you knew. Where is she?'

'My God.'

'What is it?' I said, watching him tremble. 'What?'

He seemed to shake himself and he ran now, towards his car. It was a new black Escalade.

'Valentina!' he bellowed.

I said, 'Where is she?'

'She calls me, she says, Daddy, I want to go to Moscow. Mom's going, and I'll go with her. She lies to me. Artyom. She's going with that asshole.'

I grabbed his sleeve, and he stopped and looked at his watch, a new fat Rolex, platinum, with numerals that glowed green in the dark surrounded by a thick ring of diamonds.

I said, 'Can you stop her?'

He opened his phone and made three calls in succession, calling the airport, the airline, someone in Moscow. He said to everyone he called, 'Call me back.'

'I think Jack was involved with Sid's death,' I said.

'My God,' Tolya said. He yanked open the door of his car. 'My God.'

Before he could get in his SUV, I said, 'Get in

320

my car. You can't drive the way you are. Just get the fuck in.'

Silent, trying to get some breath back, he obeyed, and I must have done a hundred down the drive. I almost killed us. In front of Tolya's place on the west side, I slammed on the brakes. He ran.

★ ★ ★

A few minutes later he was back. From the doorway of his building, he waved at me and tried to smile. I thought the effort might kill him.

I got out of the car and put my hand out.

'No, is OK. Is good. She didn't leave,' he said. 'She is with her girlfriends in East Hampton. She leaves me message. She leaves little note, not on phone, on my bed, she leaves note with bunch of flowers, and box of chocolates on my pillow. Dear Daddy, I am in East Hampton. Is OK. So I call, is OK. I hear her voice. I'm going to see her,' he said. 'I have to see her.'

'That's good. She's OK. I need you here.'

He looked exhausted. 'I'll get a helicopter. I'll be back in a few hours. I need to see Valentina. Make sure. OK? She said Santiago went to Russia, he went, I'll make calls, there are people I can reach out to, when he lands, while he's at the airport. Wherever he is. Your friend Sonny Lippert, I never liked him, but get him to make some calls, OK? Calls to Immigration. He'll do it?'

'Yes,' I said. 'You want the rest of Sid's files?

321

You want to read the stuff on Jack, the other things?'

'Later,' he said, looking at his watch. 'I have someone coming to pick me up to take me to heliport now. I can't wait. You think I give a shit about real estate right now?'

'But you still want them?'

'Sure. Why not? I'll get them from you some time,' he said, and I knew he was grateful about Val, but still angry I didn't give him what he had asked for. It wasn't the way friendship worked with him.

'I can take you to the heliport,' I said.

'I have someone.'

26

'I'm addicted,' Sonny Lippert said when I found him on the viewing platform at Ground Zero. 'I'm more addicted to this than to the booze, you know?'

I'd been to his apartment building and when the doorman said he was out, I gave him ten bucks to tell me that he knew that Sonny sometimes went over to West Street late at night, that he mentioned he sometimes went to look at the pit.

'I can't stay away.' He leaned against the fence that separated him from the hole in the ground.

'Come on,' I said. 'You can't do this anymore. Let's go back to your place. I need your help, Sonny. I need you to help me. I'm pretty sure that Jack Santiago killed Sid McKay, I read the files, there was serious stuff.'

'You stole the files?' Sonny looked amused. 'You actually broke into McKay's place and stole from him? I thought you were joking about his files. I told you everyone talked about them, but no one ever saw them, people figured it was just part of McKay's crazinesses. Did you tell me you stole? You're the Watergate One, all by yourself, man.'

'I thought you were going to call Immigration, try to stop Santiago,' I said, impatient now.

'You asked, I didn't say. You made me a story the other night at my office, man, you think I didn't notice you were spinning it? You think I didn't know? You thought I was too drunk?'

I kept my mouth shut.

'You got to give me a lot more if you want me to use up a big 'ask' with Immigration. We been down this road, Artie, man. So McKay thought Santiago was a fake, and he felt betrayed, so what? Everybody makes up stories these days, one way or another. You manipulate a photograph, you can do that with digital shit, you know, you crank up the prose; you don't have to file from places you've never been. You can do it much much easier.'

I tried to get Sonny to start walking.

'Jack was out with Sid on Tuesday morning when Sid didn't go home, when they found him beaten up. They went for coffee, and there's other stuff, reams of shit that Sid kept about Jack. He was going to turn him in. Jack was taking money to shill for the government on nuke smuggling. He faked everything. I read it. It was like he made himself up.'

He turned back to the pit. He leaned against the chain-link fence that was covered with something green, real grass, fake grass to keep people from peering into the hole in the ground. You were allowed to look but only from the official viewing platform. Also, city officials were worried that cars would suddenly stop so people could look. Or was it to keep people from being upset?

Through a little hole in the fence, on the other side of the huge, empty, silent space, I could see Century 21.

'You think they'll ever build anything down there?' Sonny said. 'You think they'll build, or they'll just keep fighting about what to build and why they should build it or not build it? Fucking New York.'

'Jack has a bug up his ass about suitcase nukes. You believe it all?'

Sonny looked up from his peephole and shrugged. 'For sure there's been radiologicals that have come into the country,' he said. 'A small group of Port Authority people ran some trials, they ran in depleted material, they got stuff right through one of the ports in a fancy teak chest. If you can believe it, Homeland fucking Security said, well, if it was the real thing, it would have been stopped, yeah, like sure, and then we had reports the real thing made it through. We fucking know that, but so what? We stopped some. What we stopped we stopped. We don't talk about it. We don't tell the public. They don't want to know. The public has a right to know, they say, but they don't want to know. I heard there was something recently.'

'In Red Hook?' I wasn't surprised.

'Close by. By the garbage incinerator on the way to Coney Island. You know where I mean?'

'A suitcase thing?'

'Yeah.'

'Anyone hurt?'

'No, nothing went off,' Sonny grunted. 'We found it in a shed. Someone must have brought it in for sale, got scared, dumped it. A few ounces of Yellowcake, nothing much. Weapons of Mass Destruction, man, like what was that? A

325

myth? A phrase? Just a sign of things to come. More fear value than anything else, man, that's what, more value for someone like Jack Santiago, or the politicians.' Suddenly, he began coughing.

'You think Jack just wanted his story?' I said.

'Yeah, probably, could be.'

'The wacko thing, Sonny, is that the way I read it, Sid's stuff sounds almost as paranoid as Jack's, he couldn't stop collecting stuff, he couldn't turn him in, he was just sitting there spying on him, stashing these newspaper pieces and Internet pieces and notes he was making, and he couldn't let go. Tons of paper, folders, envelopes, stuff scribbled on old notebooks.'

'Like Dickens,' Sonny said. 'Jarndyce v Jarndyce.'

'What the fuck are you talking about. Please, Sonny, please make the calls. Get Jack.'

'Maybe McKay didn't want to hurt the guy, you ever think of that? Maybe they were close. Maybe he couldn't stand it, couldn't turn him in, couldn't stop thinking about it.'

'Anything else at all on Sid?'

'Like I said, there won't be any news,' he said.

'What?' I took out my cigarettes.

'Give me one of those.' Sonny reached for a cigarette.

'You saw his obituary?'

'Yeah, they really worked the system, the family McKay. They closed ranks, it will go down as an accident. I tried, man, and McKay's family says it was an accident, or maybe a suicide, suicide by default, he was depressed, he had taken a sleeping pill, he wandered too close to the water, he fell accidentally on purpose, and then he let it go. It's easy. You suck up the water. Maybe like you said, he killed poor old Earl, and who cares about that, because he was a drunk and a junkie.'

'I want Jack back from Moscow. Get him,' I said, panic setting in. 'Before he leaves Moscow. Before he leaves the airport. I been trying and all I get is different versions from different airlines. I have Sverdloff on it. Jack left his place Saturday night. I got people said he went via Paris. Someone else said Polish Airlines or Aeroflot.'

Sonny turned back to the pit and started walking and I followed alongside until we got to the viewing platform. No one else was out. It was late, and we stood together and he looked down.

'I miss it, man,' he said. 'I miss it. It seemed simple, you know. We were all on the same side then, or so we believed. Three fucking years next week, is it next week? Yeah, this week.' He looked at his watch. 'They'll play all the songs, 'God Bless America', and the families will still hurt and the politicians will make speeches and the dirty little secret is we're not over it, but now it's tearing us up. I miss the way it was.' He turned his head and started coughing, and for a minute I thought he was going to cough up his lungs.

'Go back to Red Hook,' Sonny added, 'go back one more time if you want and see if you can find anything at all on Jack Santiago that will nail him, some little thing we missed that will help us make a case before they just plant Sid and it's all over. Funeral's Tuesday. Do it before that crazy family of his just plants him in the ground.'

He set off towards his building. The sky was a smudgy gray. I took a step in his direction, but he was coughing and walking, and he just put up a hand, to say no, leave me.

I followed him. He was coughing so bad he could hardly walk. I stayed with him in case his legs gave out. We got to his building and went upstairs.

'It's OK, man, I'm fine,' Sonny said.

He opened the door. The apartment was dark and he fumbled with the light switch, but when he flicked it on, I saw that something was different from a few days earlier when I'd sat with him out on the balcony while he drank tomato juice. It took me a second to orient myself. The studio apartment had had bare walls, as if Sonny hadn't intended staying long. Now the walls were covered with a jumble of photographs, some framed, some stuck up with tape.

Sonny followed my gaze as I looked at the wall to the left of the front door. The photographs reached almost to the ceiling. There were photographs of the Twin Towers, of the planes smashing into them, of the fireballs rising up, of people running covered in thick white ash, firefighters, cops, an abandoned bagel cart, workers emerging from the pit with orange fires burning as if from hell, a tea set covered in dust like something from Pompeii, a hundred more photographs. Sonny had created a shrine.

'I'm addicted to it,' he had said; now he just

stood and looked at his wall.

'You know what I hated, Sonny, you know what made me really pissed off almost the most?'

'Yeah, what's that, man?' He moved away from the wall and shoved some newspapers off a table and extracted a half-empty bottle of Scotch.

I said, 'I hated it when people used it, politicians, you know. I hated it when people took stuff for souvenirs from the pit.'

'Yeah.'

I hesitated.

'What?'

'I hated it when reporters lied their way down there, like dressing up as firemen, you know, I fucking hated that, all of us busting our asses, and them lying and putting on firemen gear, which was like sacred stuff.'

He looked at me. 'You're telling me Jack Santiago did that?'

'Yeah,' I said. 'Yeah, I seem to remember he was one of them. I remember that.' I was feeding Sonny. I was fueling him up.

'You want Santiago real bad, right?'

'Yes.'

'I'll do what I can, Artie. I'll call Moscow. I have someone over there I know. After that, fuck knows, he could be anywhere; he could disappear into the middle of nowhere if he wanted. You're sure. It's probably my last big 'ask', Artie, man, they want me out, they want to retire my ass, and if this goes bad, that'll be it. If you say, I'll push the buttons. If you really need it, if you're fucking positive that he killed Sid McKay, I'll get him, I'll reach out for you, but

329

tell me you're sure.'

I nodded.

'I always thought Jack Santiago was an ambitious cock-sucker, anyhow. Take care of yourself, Artie, man. Be careful. You don't want any idiots picking you up because your name got on some list, OK.'

'Sure, Sonny. Thanks.'

'What the fuck difference does any of it make, you know? I wish it was all over.' He looked at his wall. 'Enough,' he said. 'Enough.'

27

After I wasted hours at the airport, still trying to find out what airline Jack had used, after I got the run around from a lot of suspicious people wanting to know who the hell I was and peering at my badge as if it might be a toy or a fake, I finally got to Red Hook. I went to Sid's to try to break in.

I wanted to get another look. I planned to replace the files before the family figured out I'd helped myself to them. The sun already up, the water alight, surface shimmering, boats bobbing on it, it looked exactly like the little paradise where Sid escaped the real world.

His loft was sealed, the locks changed. I didn't know who did it, local cops, city, the family. The key I'd stolen was no good. The new lock was too hard to pick. What else could I do? Shoot off the locks? Trespass? I had no warrant. I didn't have anything. The funeral was the next day. Tomorrow Sid would disappear into the ground.

I was sweating some now. I went out, found a security guard and tried to give him some money but he backed off, frightened. I realized he was the same guy who had screamed at the men in the kayak and he recognized me.

I went out on the pier, but there was only a small boy with a limp fishing line who looked up expectantly, smiling, obviously glad for company. The kid said hi and waved for me to come over and look at his fishing gear. I just waved back and walked away.

On the other side of the old loft building from the pier was the inlet. The repairs to the dock where Earl died were finished. It was a week since Earl, if he had been Earl because even now there was no firm ID, had been trapped in this tiny stream of water, head and arms under the pier, legs adrift.

The sound of the buzz saw echoed in my brain. I remembered the noise as they took off his arms to free him from the rotting pier; I remembered the stink.

I drove to the other side of the Gowanus Canal and the burned-out ferryboat where Sid's body had been found. It was still a crime scene but I had my badge. I didn't know what I expected but I needed to see it.

Black, charred, it was the skeleton of a boat, still tied to the dock. Standing near the edge of the water, staring down, was a woman. She looked up. It was the detective I'd met the first day I was in Red Hook, the morning I watched them pull Earl out of the water, the morning of the day I got married. Clara. Clara something. Fuentes.

'Hey, Artie, right? Hey. How are you?' She was wearing jeans and a red shirt, and a pair of Nikes. I offered her a cigarette, she held up her pack of nicotine gum.

I said, 'You're on this one, too?'

'No. I just came by to take a look. My day off,' she laughed. 'I've got a whole week. A whole week,' she said again, chewing.

'What do you think happened here?' I said, pointing at the wrecked boat and the yellow tape.

'What do I know? Everyone says he drowned here, you know? That he just fell and drowned, that's what they say, or maybe he jumped. They say it was suicide or an accident, accidental death by drowning, but I think it stinks of a cover up. What do I know?'

'What do you know?' I smiled.

'Me, personally? I think someone dragged him here. Someone who had a hard time doing it. There were marks.' She waved at the rough stretch of raw dirt between the street and the edge of the docks. 'I think someone dragged him who had trouble dragging him, you know, like they had to drag and shove him a little at a time. I didn't figure that out myself, I heard someone say.'

'Who said it?'

'I heard a couple of detectives talk about it, and then one of them said about the dragging and the other one said, forget it. It was an accident, or suicide, that's what it's supposed to be, he said, and it was like they just decided to forget the other idea, or somebody told them to forget it.'

'What else?'

'That's it. Just that maybe he didn't die here, maybe he was dragged, so if he killed himself, how come he was dragged here, you know? I don't know. Maybe it's just better to say it was an accident. I have to go. Get the fuck away. Up to New Hampshire,' she added.

'Thanks,' I said. 'Have a nice time.'

'Glad the fucking politicians are gone.' She looked at her watch, then took the gum out of her mouth and lobbed it in the water. 'You want to give me one of those coffin nails before you go?'

'Sure,' I tossed her the pack.

She took one and handed it back. 'Good luck,' she said. 'You have my phone number, right?'

I tried to remember how tall Jack Santiago was. He was about five-nine. I wondered if that passed as small.

★ ★ ★

On my way to see Rita, the woman who made borscht and tamales, I passed three young guys. Outside her building, wearing soccer shorts and shirts, they eyed me suspiciously. I didn't know if they recognized me as a cop, but they didn't smile much, just looked at me and then looked away and went back to their conversation, huddled together, their long young bodies bent over in some private ritual.

I was at the front door of Rita's building when I heard the guys talking, a mixture of English and Spanish, soft, but staccato, and something occurred to me. I turned around, and walked the few steps back.

They looked up, not hostile, but surprised that I would somehow have the balls to interrupt. The tallest — he was probably nineteen, tops — said, 'Yeah, man? You need something?' He was real

334

polite, only an edge of sarcasm, or maybe irony. Hard to read.

I said, 'I been looking around for a guy named Jack Santiago. You ever meet this guy? He's a reporter. He lives over the other end of Red Hook. Smart guy. Pretty famous. Black hair. Wiry. About forty. Five-eight, five-nine.'

The surprising thing was that the three of them started laughing. They laughed for real and they also cranked up the laughter so it became an act, and they chortled and giggled and held on to each other, until one of them produced a red bandanna and wiped his eyes, and then another of them pulled out a pack of Camels and passed it around and included me. I took one, lit up.

I said, 'It's funny? Santiago's funny?'

'You want to buy us a beer, man?'

'Sure,' I said. 'Where?'

He pointed at a convenience store, and I pulled a fifty out of my wallet and handed it to him, and he nodded, so I knew it was OK money. He went across the street to a store and came back with a paper bag with four coffees, and passed them around.

'Too early for beer, right?' he said, but he didn't offer me any change.

'Never too early,' I said.

'Santiago's a jerk,' he said. 'He was always coming around, talking that lousy Spanish, he wasn't really a Latino boy, he said his mama was Cuban, but he was a liar, you could see it, and he was, like, suitcase nukes this, and suitcase nukes that, and everyone here knows that was last year,

335

that one time they found something on a ship and the guys came in from the what do you call it, hazardous something, guys in big white moon suits with hoods?'

'Hazmat,' I said. 'The guys in moon suits.'

'Yeah, right.'

'They came over to the Gowanus Canal where there's still a couple ships coming in, and those big box stores, and they found something, or they said they did, who the fuck knows anything now, and they carried it away, and everyone talked about it for like a day, it was one time, and we heard they didn't find nothing much, but the guy, Santiago, he was on it like crazy. He was like so fucking excited by the whole thing, he was like OK, we're all in danger, man, you gotta leave this place, and we gotta get the government to turn up the heat on these bastards, and we're like, fuck that shit, man, and he's like it's still so dangerous, boo hoo, they're gonna send in those airplanes again and crash them and this time they're gonna be full of flying suitcases with nukes in them. He pissed everyone off, you know? Flying fucking suitcases.' He laughed. They all laughed. 'They didn't find nothing, turned out someone was testing the waters, so to speak, seeing if it was leaky by the Gowanus, you know, for terrorists and stuff, you know, man?'

The first guy said, 'I told them Santiago made it all up.'

'I can imagine.'

'You can imagine. I like that.'

'Yeah?' I said. 'Good. I'm glad.'

He gestured around. 'This is a crazy place,

man,' he said. 'You got us in the projects out front here, and over back on the water, you got rich people trying to get in, you got people who want to keep it like it is, which is like shit, you know, they call themselves urban pioneers, you got developers, and some people who actually care about the place, you got the whole fucking package, like they call it a microcosm, so to speak, fuck microcosm, right, and then you got the people like Santiago that's just sniffing around.'

'There's a lot of stuff going on out here?' I said.

'You never could dream, man, how much. You never could fucking dream. Or maybe nothing. Maybe just a football match. Soccer to you.' He grinned. 'So thanks for the beers, we got a game. You come see us kick some ass today, we got a match against some boys from Senegal. They're like fucking genius. Come see, man, OK?'

I said thanks, and I left them still laughing about Santiago, and smoking Camels, and I went into Rita's building and buzzed her, but there was no answer. I stuck a message under her door with a note to call me.

I was sure that Rita knew more than she'd told me, about Red Hook; maybe she knew something about Jack that I could take to Sonny. On my way out I asked the guys on the corner if they knew a Russian woman who made tamales and they said, sure, they saw her head over to the park.

28

'There is an old man,' Rita said. 'I don't know his name.'

On the slats of wood that formed a trestle table, she had laid out platters of steaming tamales and paper plates, and condiments and plastic cups. In the park, kids were playing soccer. People were arriving. The last holiday of the summer.

'No borscht?' I said.

She glanced out at the playing field.

'Not unless Russians are playing. What do you need?'

I looked at my watch. 'Help me,' I said suddenly, and took her wrist.

'OK,' she said. 'Sure. For free,' she added, thinking my hesitation had been about money.

'How come?'

She shrugged. 'I like Mr Sid McKay is all. I like him a lot. I think maybe this old man threatens him. Maybe not so old, this Russian.'

'Why didn't you tell me?'

'I didn't say because I was scared, I told you I was not scared, but I was.' Looking down at the tamales on the table, she paused, and it was as if she had seen an opportunity. 'So I change my mind, OK? I change. I can be wrong.'

'What kind of Russian?'

'What kind of Russian is there?'

'Tell me.'

She smiled. 'Russian that been here a long time and doesn't talk so good English. Russian that hangs around a lot just looking around. Russian that sometimes I see with Mr McKay. Russian once I saw around Brighton Beach then here in Red Hook, which is how come I'm noticing this Russian. He comes always here for food, not Russian food, I think how come he wants this stuff?' She put a couple of tamales on a plate and handed it to me.

I took the plate and said, 'Go on.'

'I ask him his name, he don't talk to me. Don't want to talk. Just watching. This kind of Russian.'

'What does he look like?'

'Short.'

'What else?'

'He looks short. Very short. Little man,' Rita said, 'Hello? You with me?'

I said, 'This little short Russian, what else?'

'Once I seen him with Mr McKay and one other black guy that was some kind of bum, all three together, over by Coffey Street.'

'You were there?'

Rita switched to Russian and kept her voice low. 'I am looking at space for Borscht Works, you like this name? I'm thinking, maybe Borscht Works, or something snappy, Borscht Belt, but what the hell does belt have to do with it, and I'm talking to people, and walking around, and there's not so many Russians around here, but I'm hearing people speaking so I listen, and who doesn't say nothing and looks like a bum, I look and it's Mr McKay, and the other black one and the short Russian.'

Earl, I thought; the bum had been Earl.

'How did you know he was Russian, the short guy?'

'I told you, didn't I? I saw him around Brighton Beach. Then here.'

'What else?'

'That's all.'

'You heard them?'

'Only that they were talking Russian.'

'What about?'

'I don't know.'

'I think you know,' I said, put down the plate with the uneaten food and took her wrist.

I noticed that Rita didn't mention Tolya Sverdloff this time. All she was interested in was the short Russian. Looking nervous now, she pulled away from me and waved at a friend, gesturing for her to come over as if for protection. I let go.

The other woman who was wearing jeans and a yellow shirt jogged to Rita's side, and smiling, started to chatter about food.

In Russian, I said something to Rita by way of an apology. She didn't look up. Two families with a trail of kids in tow arrived in front of her stall wanting food and she huddled with them.

I started to walk away, went back and said to her, still in Russian, 'The short guy, the little Russian man, what color were his eyes, did you notice, did you see his eyes?'

'Sure,' she said, serving up food, keeping her distance from me. 'You couldn't miss this.'

'How come?'

'Real blue. This color people in Russia say naval blue, sea blue.'

'Where did you see him?'

She said, 'Near the place where they throw the old cars. Columbia Street.'

I was already on my way when my phone rang; Lily was at the other end.

★   ★   ★

Hurry up, she said. Please! Get to the city. Hurry, Lily said again, get here now, I can't talk, just come. I need you here, Artie. She was babbling, panicky. I heard her voice, I didn't want to go, didn't want to see her, I would drown in it if I saw her again, I wouldn't be able to leave her. She sounded bad. The line broke. I closed my phone. Opened it.

I'm on my way, I said. What is it? What?

He's dead.

Who? Tolya? Tolya's dead? He's dead. I'm coming, Lily. I'm coming.

The line broke again. Somewhere I could hear a steel band playing. The punchy merry music made me crazy. It was the Caribbean Day Parade in Brooklyn. I slammed my car window shut.

★   ★   ★

Dead, she had said, and my stomach turned over and I opened the window again to get some air. I couldn't get her back on the phone for ten

341

minutes, all the way into the tunnel and into the city, back past the hole in the ground and Battery Park City where Sonny lived with his shrine made out of photographs, and where I knew now I could never live with Maxine — I would live with her, but not here — and I thought I was going to pass out or vomit. It was Monday. I had promised myself to be with her Monday, but I wasn't going to make it.

The light turned red, and I thought I was stepping on the brake. I hit the gas instead and the car jolted forward. I ran a couple of red lights, and heard a siren behind me. A blue and white had picked up on my speed, and was chasing me. I felt trapped. Tolya was dead and a cop was on me for speeding.

I pulled over. The cop pulled up alongside me, and I showed him my badge and I was trying to explain, and he thought I was crazy. Then the phone finally rang again, I ignored the cop who was now leaning in my window, inspecting my license with obsessive attention. My license number interested him; I was on a list.

The phone rang. Lily was waiting for me. She was at her apartment on 10th Street. Stop up if you need me, she said. I called her.

'Where is he?'

'Who?' Lily said.

'Where's the body? Why are you at home, if he's dead?'

'What are you talking about?'

I said, 'You told me he was dead.'

The cop looking at my license was on his cell, and I didn't know why, but I didn't wait, either. I just went. I drove north, trying to call Lily back.

★ ★ ★

Before I turned off the highway I heard the sirens, saw the flashing lights, stepped on the brakes, pulled up and saw the crowd that had formed near the High Line.

Police cars were parked everywhere, an ambulance was at the curb, the noise of the sirens rose up into the hot afternoon. I left my car near Tolya's building and followed the flashing lights.

A knot of people, tourists out for the holiday, was standing near a row of mounted cops, whispering, giggling, pointing up. 'It's just like *Law and Order*, just like a real episode of the show, like TV. Take a picture.' They were pointing at the High Line overhead.

A teenage boy in a striped shirt pulled a disposable camera out of his pocket. A cop tried to stop him, but he snapped a picture anyhow, and backed off, then turned and ran, grinning. A woman held up a little girl to pat the nose of one of the horses, and the cop sitting on it — they were probably from over at the First Precinct on Hudson Street — leaned down and patted the girl's head. Her mother took a picture.

'I heard he fell over or something,' I heard someone say.

'What?'

'Yeah,' a cop in uniform said to me as I came up to the barrier and leaned over and showed my

343

badge. 'Crazy accident. You see those old iron struts up the side there?' He pointed up at the High Line. 'The poor bastard fell through them or over them, right here, the south end of the High Line. There were rolls of barbed wire on it, and he got stuck, he was like hanging down, probably fucking dead drunk or something, and he dropped over. What in hell was he doing up there? He must have been high as a fucking kite. Or dead drunk. You ever been up there?'

Yes, I thought. I've been up there. I thought: What was Tolya doing up there alone at night? He was too fat to be up there. It was illegal. He had said to me, I go at night, like a thief, like a spy.

The cop said to me, 'We used to do sweeps regular when a lot of homeless made camp up there. Not recently. I hate it. It's slippery, like a jungle. You can kill yourself wandering around on the High Line.'

29

It was Jack, not Tolya. Jack had not gone to Russia. He had lied about it, or maybe he intended to go and someone stopped him, but he was dead. It was his body they had found early that morning, stuck in a fence, under the High Line.

A detective I knew slightly from the Sixth Precinct said, 'You OK, Art?'

Leaning against the wall of a warehouse, I had my head down, trying to get some blood back. I looked up. 'What happened?' I said.

'I saw him before they cut him down from the fence where he landed. You couldn't tell if he was pushed or jumped. He must have snuck through one of the warehouses. That place is way off limits, I mean *way*. Trespassing, if you go up there it's like private property and they're very antsy about it, you get arrested. The people who own it are big time unhappy about that. You know who this guy was? He was a big deal or something?'

I nodded.

Officials were all over the place, cops in uniform, detectives, forensics, people from the Mayor's office. Jack Santiago was a name. I counted three TV crews and six reporters with little notebooks. From around the corner, a young guy trotted over to one of the TV people, holding a stack of newspapers. An early edition of the *Post* was out. I grabbed one and tossed him some money.

On the front was a picture of the High Line, and a smudgy picture of a body — what looked like a body — hanging from a fence underneath it. The picture had been taken from a distance, but you could make out that it was probably Jack. It reminded me of a picture of a lynching in the South, a man hanging from a tree, the body like a sack of beans, just hanging down, lifeless.

A reporter who worked for the paper had been out until late, early this morning, drinking at one of the bars in the Meat District. Around five, he saw a cop arrive at the scene.

The article included an account of Jack's life, a lot about his partying, hints about drugs, women, the usual stuff they printed in the *Post*. There was something about Jack's stunts. I remembered Jack at my wedding, walking on the wall of Tolya's terrace.

Tossing the paper in a garbage can I went across the street to Tolya's building and went in, thinking how weird it was that a guy like Jack ended up dumped like a bag of trash. Jack, with a Pulitzer Prize, three ex-wives, a million other women, with all the access, the private numbers for every restaurant and club, whatever he wanted, could disappear over night. He just fell through the cracks, someone on the street said. He wasn't in Russia at all. He was dead.

* * *

I got to Tolya's elevator at the same time as a family coming home from the beach. The man held the door open while the others — a woman and two girls — piled in the elevator with blankets, pillows, buckets, coolers. They took their time. I fiddled with a cigarette. The woman, who had an ugly skinny body and a face that had been worked on too many times, stared at me. 'OK, we're sorry,' she said in a peevish tone.

I wondered what the hell they were doing in Tolya's building anyway. Maybe he was renting out residential space. Maybe the money was drying up.

I turned and slammed through a door and ran up six flights. Tolya knew his way around the High Line: he had shown it to me, had wanted me to see it, wanted me to know that he knew it, that he could get access to it. I banged on the door, and waited. I hammered on it, then rang the bell.

★　★　★

Wearing white slacks and a thin black shirt, Tolya embraced me formally, Russian style, and then without saying anything turned and went ahead of me into the living room, empty now of the tables and flowers and waiters and noise that had filled it at the party.

A couple of large white couches, some chairs, a huge expanse of glistening pale wood floor, a couple of immense abstracts on the walls, it was quiet. Light came through the wall of windows, but no noise.

347

Valentina was sitting on the couch. She had on one of Tolya's shirts, a yellow shirt I'd seen before, which covered most of her shorts. Dry-eyed, she was very pale and held a liter bottle of water in one hand.

'Her sister is coming from Boston tonight to be with her here,' Tolya said. 'Masha will be here soon.' He stood close to her, one hand on her shoulder.

'No she's not,' Val said. 'I don't want anyone. I'm OK. Masha has school starting. She doesn't need to come, Daddy. She really really doesn't. I called her. I'm fine.'

'She's coming anyway,' he said, and sat down beside her and put his arms around her. For a minute, she was quiet. Then she looked up, her face scrubbed and shining, and said to me, 'How are you, Artie?'

'I'm sorry,' I said to Val. 'About Jack. I'm really sorry.'

'I know.' She turned to Tolya whose eyes were closed, his face shut, expressionless. 'Are you OK, Daddy?' she said gently. 'Can I talk to Artie by myself, please? Would that be OK? I mean, I just need to talk to him a little bit. You don't mind, do you? I mean he's kind of like family, right?'

She was tentative with him, as if he were an old-fashioned patriarch. I had seen Tolya do business with men who looked up to him. I had seen him as a ringmaster, an impresario, at my wedding. I had seen him flirt with women. He had rescued me half a dozen times, efficient, fast on his feet. He knew how to make money. The last week, I had seen him angry and defeated and sick. His daughter, in spite of their easy banter, saw him as requiring respect; with him, she deferred.

'Daddy, would that be OK?' she repeated.

Tolya nodded. He pulled himself to his feet and Val got up too, and he kissed her three times.

'I have to go out for a while. I have some business,' he said in Russian. 'I trust Artyom,' he added, then walked away from her and went into his bedroom.

I sat down on the couch beside Val. 'What is it?' I said, but I could see she didn't want to talk until Tolya had gone. For a few minutes we sat, me and Val, silently, and waited for him.

Tolya reappeared in a dark summer suit, white shirt, plain black tie; even his shoes were black. Picking up keys and a wallet from a chair near the door, he left the apartment and closed the door behind him. A few seconds later he was back. He gestured to me, again formally, a man I barely recognized as the freewheeling guy I knew who had once been a rock and roll hero. I got up.

In Russian, he said to me quietly, 'You'll stay with her until I get back?'

'Sure,' I said. 'Where are you going?'

'Something I have to do. Yes. For a few hours.' He looked at his watch. 'You promise me, Artemy, you won't leave her alone?'

'Business? On Labor Day? It's a holiday. What about Santiago?' I said, still thinking I could get away to the shore before the holiday ended.

'He's dead. We'll talk about this later.' He went

349

out again and I heard the grunt of the elevator.

Val picked up the water bottle she had set on a low green glass table in front of the couch, and pulled her legs up under her, then seemed to change her mind. 'Artie?'

'Yes, honey.'

She looked towards the kitchen and said, 'I need some caffeine. Will you stay and drink some coffee with me?'

'Sure. Let's go ahead and make some coffee, and maybe you should eat something, too,' I said and we started for the kitchen, walking together, not saying anything.

★ ★ ★

In the vast stainless steel kitchen, Val made coffee in a red espresso machine. She moved slowly, and waited silently until the coffee was ready and then she poured it into green cups with gold rims and served me. She sat down at the table. I sat opposite her.

'I thought you'd be away already. I was even surprised to see you Saturday night,' Val said.

'I had some things to do.'

'But, oh, it was your honeymoon.'

'I know. I'll try to go tonight.'

'I liked Maxine so much. I thought she was wonderful. Is wonderful.'

'Me too. Are you OK?' I said. 'About Jack?'

'Sure,' she said. 'You think that's cold? You didn't like him anyhow, did you? I could see that the other night.'

A faint edge of anxiety inserted itself, I felt my

pulse speed up and I was sweating. Val didn't seem to care about Jack being dead. If she had anything to do with it, I didn't want to know, but she was going to tell me. Don't tell me, I thought. Keep it to yourself.

I said, 'You feel how you feel, you don't have to borrow your feelings from anyone, you know, you can feel something and not show it. It doesn't matter what I felt about Jack,' I said and I thought she knew I was lying.

'It's not that.'

'I don't understand.' I drank down the coffee and got myself another cup.

'It was me,' she said. 'It was my fault. I'm twenty years old, I'll be twenty next week, Artie, and I don't know, it must be genetic, you see.' She put out her hand towards me and I took it. Her skin was soft, unwrinkled, perfect. 'I feel like an ordinary American kid,' Val said. 'I'm the Echo generation, the team player, the desired child, I'm the kid who grew up in a suburb, in Florida, in Miami, with all the stuff, I had music lessons and ballet lessons and soccer and I wanted to be a soccer superstar, you know, like Mia Hamm, and I was editor of the school newspaper and I started a Spanish lit club, not Russian, of course, just to be cool, and I started a garage band, and I was a fucking cheerleader, can you believe it? I was going to be an American. Shit, Artie, I even tried out for some junior Miss America thing, but that was too much even for me. I was only eleven when we came from Moscow.' She held up her hand. 'You know about this.' She nodded at the missing

351

finger. 'You know about it? My dad told you? The kidnapping thing? He blames himself. He thinks he did it.'

'Yes.'

'I went to shrinks. Russian shrinks, you can imagine, American shrinks who had no idea what I was talking about. Dad wanted me to have plastic surgery, but I said no. My sister doesn't get it because she's so guilty that it happened to me and not her. My mother has turned into an American so completely that she supports Jeb Bush, can you imagine? She likes him. She likes the Bush family.' She laughed. 'I'm so sorry to unload on you Artie.'

'It's all right, honey.' She held on to my hand like a lifeline.

'He needs you, Artie.'

'Who?'

'My dad.'

I said, 'Tell me what you mean, genetic.'

'I think that somewhere deep down, no matter how much I pretend to be American, no matter how good I am at it, I'm kind of Russian, kind of complicated in that way, I mean I made myself over. I was still really young so it was easy but it was conscious. I really worked on it, I made sure I didn't have a trace of accent, not a single trace or a phrase, nothing, I wouldn't even play tennis, you know, once those little tennis girls started coming over, all those sad little girls from the Russian provinces turning up in Florida, seven, eight, nine years old, with their parents, or even alone, trying to make it, trying to be the next Anna Kournikova. But I couldn't get rid of some of the ways I thought. When I came up here to New York and I started hanging out with people who were Russian, who were closer to it than me, it was, I don't know.'

I knew. 'It gets to you,' I said.

'Yes. I think I'm more devious than a real American. I think I'm able to like betray people in a way. I don't know. I'd like a cigarette, is that OK?' She pulled her hand out of mine.

I got a pack out of my pocket and opened the kitchen door that led on to the terrace. Outside there was noise from the river, the cop cars below, the crowds. I started to shut the door.

'It's OK,' she said, got up, went out and leaned her long arms on the railing and her head on her hands. I stood next to her. She smoked awkwardly. 'What about you and Lily?' she said. 'Was that hard, I mean, losing her?'

'You knew about us?'

'My dad always talked about it,' she said. 'He talked to me about stuff. My mom is an idiot. I mean she's a nice lady but she's heavily into her plastic surgeon and her TV reality shows and stuff and my sister is a complete geek, which is fine, she's a huge success at Harvard and Daddy will love that, but he can sort of talk to me. I'm the grown up, he says. I'm the old one. He was like, not jealous or envious or anything, not like he wanted Lily at all. He just thought you had something with her he could never have with anyone.'

'What was that?'

Val leaned her head on my shoulder.

353

'Friendship,' she said. 'That you were friends. He'd like that, but he doesn't know how.'

'I thought he had a new girlfriend, a Russian woman?'

She turned to me, a knowing smile on her mouth, and said, 'He dreams about it, but it's make-believe. He meets someone, he meets a Russian writer, very elegant, very warm and cultured, and she likes him, you can see, I saw that with this woman, and then he starts buying things. She thinks, who is this asshole who buys me stuff I would never wear? He's like a child.'

For a few minutes we smoked and she talked. I tried to look at my watch without her noticing.

'I know,' she said. 'You have to go. I just have one other thing I have to tell you, had to, without Daddy around, OK?'

Don't!

Don't tell me!

'Let's go back inside,' I said, and we went into the kitchen and I shut the door.

We sat at the table again. The motor in the huge refrigerator vibrated. Val picked up her coffee cup and drained it.

'I like cold coffee,' she said. 'Weird that I got together with Jack at your wedding. Didn't you know that?' She looked at me. 'Yeah. Anyhow. So. Me and Jack. We met at your wedding.'

All I remembered was the electricity between them, a kind of comic book electricity, as if you could see the jagged line of sparks.

'I thought you invited him,' I said. 'I thought you came with him. You looked like the two of you were already pretty much an item. I didn't know Jack well enough to invite him.'

'It was a big party,' she said. 'Maybe he just showed up. Maybe someone else brought him. I don't remember.'

'You'd never met him?'

'Yeah, I'd seen him around. Clubs, that kind of stuff. I thought he was kind of old for me. He was always hitting on me. It was a game. I liked him, but I wasn't sure I wanted to do anything. He knew a lot of the Russian girls, he said he was half Russian, yeah, like which half, Jack? You couldn't tell what he made up, you know?' she said. 'He was obsessed with being cool and young, which was why he moved to horrible old Red Hook, stuff like that. It doesn't matter, does it? Not anymore. So, like, yeah, so there he was and it was kind of fun in a stupid way having this famous forty-year-old guy who everyone knew was hitting on me, I don't know, maybe I was a little bit drunk, and he was very sexy. I mean, like you would do it right there with him.' She looked at me, and bit her lip and said, 'Oh, God, I'm sorry, I shouldn't be saying this to you.'

'Don't worry.'

'He was in love with me, he said. We went out that night after your wedding and the next couple of nights, and my friends were impressed and I was an idiot, and all of a sudden, he says, let's get married, and I'm like Jack, I'm nineteen, and he says, you're an old soul. He was always going, you're the one. He'd look in your eyes, you know how he had those hot little coal eyes, and he could talk about everything, he'd been everywhere.' Val paused. 'Daddy thought Jack

355

was using me to get to him, get stuff on his, Daddy's, background or the Russian mob, something. It made him a little crazy. Anyway, I tried to blow Jack off, but he wouldn't go away.'

I thought back to the night in the Meat District when I had seen them together. I thought about the tender way Val put her arms around Jack when I told him Sid was dead.

I said, 'You seemed pretty intense with him Saturday night.'

'I get like that, you know. I'm a kid, after all. I want something really bad at first, and then they come on too strong, and I'm out of it. For like five minutes. It didn't last. Call me superficial. I liked him. I just didn't want so much.'

'Why don't we go out and take a walk or something?'

'There's more.'

'I don't need to hear it.'

'I need to tell you.'

'What about?'

'My dad. I think he's way out on a limb,' she said. 'I need you to know because I'm going home, Artie.'

'To Florida?'

'To Russia, I mean. I can't do all this stuff. I mean the Russian princess thing, the nightclubs, the restaurants, the money, the hanging out with girls who live in ten-million-dollar apartments, it was fun, and I tried, and I don't despise it, I just don't want it. I think being with Jack that week taught me that. I didn't like myself. I didn't want to be in one more club or drink one more cocktail or wear one more stupid outfit. So I'm going.' Her voice was calm.

'Where in Russia?'

'We have an apartment in Moscow. I'll go there first. Then, I don't know exactly but I have friends who can help, you won't think this is stupid?'

'No.'

Unbuttoning the top button of her yellow shirt, Val pulled a little gold chain from between her tan breasts. A small cross hung from it. She held it out. 'I think I want to work with kids. The school thing in Beslan. I don't know. Or AIDS kids. Something. Better than this. I don't want to come on all Mother Theresa, but I have to do it. I told you it was genetic. You think I'm going to come on all religious, you think I'm going to end up some kind of Russian religious nutbag?'

'I don't think so.'

She looked at her watch.

'Does Tolya know you're going?' I said.

Val got up and started for the living room and I followed her. We stood near the front door.

'Daddy will just get crazy and say she's going to work with kids, with AIDS, she'll get sick, she'll get offed by terrorists, you know, he's a dad, right?'

'Did you know that you wanted all this before Jack?'

'It's been coming.'

'And Jack?'

'He was fun, like I said.' She shrugged. 'He was great for a week,' she added. 'I have to get ready now. I have to get going.'

'Where to?'

'To the airport. Please don't tell Daddy, Artie. Please let me have this.'

I held out my phone. 'At least call him,' I said. 'At least tell him you're going.'

'He'll stop me. You know that. He'll call some creepy guy to meet me at the airport. I'll be OK. Please. Just wait for me a minute, OK? I have to change. Will you wait for me, Artie?'

Val went into her bedroom. I took the cigarettes back out of my pocket and picked off the remaining cellophane and the crackle of it seemed unnaturally loud.

★ ★ ★

A few minutes later, Val reappeared wearing black jeans, black T-shirt, sneakers and a white denim jacket. She had a bag over her shoulder and a baseball cap on her head and she was dragging a red suitcase on wheels.

'Did you know that Jack wasn't in Russia, that he never went?' I said, asking the thing I had not wanted her to tell me.

She hesitated. 'Yes.'

'When did you know?'

'I knew all the time,' she said softly. 'He asked me not to say that he wanted to take a couple of days off to do some writing before he left, he said he had stuff to tie up. After we left you at the restaurant Saturday night, I dropped him off at his place in Red Hook before I drove out to East Hampton. He said he wasn't going to stay at his place, just wanted to pick stuff up. He was going over to stay at a friend's apartment, some guy who was away, so he wouldn't get interrupted and stuff. So I went to Long Island and I talked to him again from out there a bunch of times. He said, so don't tell anyone I'm still in the city. I just don't want anyone to bug me.'

'But you saw him? He couldn't have been calling you from somewhere else?' I said.

'I called him on a landline so that's how I know, and he was like I miss you, blah blah, kiss kiss, let's meet tomorrow, and we made a date. We talked a lot, and then I said I had to go.'

'When?'

'Late yesterday. I think it was late.'

'You told someone. You told someone that Jack didn't go to Russia, Val?' I took her hand.

'Yeah. I did. I don't know why. Just careless I guess, or because it's genetic, this betrayal thing. I don't know why. He kept asking and asking, so I told.'

'Who kept asking you? You want to tell me who you told?'

Nervously, she picked at her short hair. 'I should probably go now,' she said.

'Who was it?'

She hugged me. 'I told my dad, Artie, OK? Please take care of him,' she said and went out and closed the door behind her.

30

I stayed, waiting for Tolya; for an hour, then two, I waited. I called him. I wandered around the huge apartment that covered the whole top floor of the building.

In his bedroom, I opened the closets and stared at the rows of custom-made suits, dozens of them, over-scale suits made out of cashmere and alpaca and fabrics I had never heard of. He liked showing me. He liked taking me shopping. Brioni, he would sigh, like it was a girl's name.

I looked at the shoes. I opened drawers and found dozens of pairs of cufflinks with diamonds and other stones in them. There were drawers piled with brand new shirts, cotton so thin it felt like silk.

On top of the dresser was the model for a group of buildings with a park around it; there were tiny green plastic trees, and little plastic people, the kind you put in a doll's house. It stood on a wooden stand with a small brass plate that was engraved with the name of some architectural firm. It was like looking at a kid's toy.

Tolya wanted it all so badly; he wanted to be the biggest kid. I was alone in his place, looking in his closets, his drawers, spying on him.

From the window I could see the High Line. I thought about Jack slipping off. Tolya had known that Jack was in the city; Val had told him. He had known even while he was pretending that Jack was gone, going along with me, playing the game, calling people in Russia. He had known. This was the thing I had been scared of almost from the time I had met him ten years ago, that one day I'd have to decide.

I thought about my father and wondered if he had been frightened when he was a young officer and had to arrest people he knew and loved; I wondered if he ever did.

So I waited. I knew he'd come back because he thought Valentina would be here. He had trusted me to stay with her and I let her go. I went out on the terrace and watched the water. I watched and waited and then it occurred to me that Tolya had put on a black suit on a hot summer day. Maybe he wasn't coming back, not even for Val. Maybe he was gone. My heart pounded like crazy. I had to decide fast.

★ ★ ★

'Where's Valentina?' he said when I found him at the office in Red Hook. 'What are you doing here?'

'You went to the funeral home to pay your respects, they told me. Alex McKay told me. I figured there was a chance you'd come here afterwards. It's not far.'

He had taken off his jacket. His white shirt was stained with sweat and he was drinking Scotch from a coffee mug. It was dim inside the room, and the air conditioner rattled in the window.

'Where is she?' he said, getting up.

I told him and I thought he might punch me.

'You let her go? You said you'd stay with her, and you let her go to the airport?' He went for the phone. I knew it was too late. Val would have gone already, but I let him call.

'I have the files you wanted,' I said. 'I have all of Sid's stuff. You can have them. OK? Tolya? You want the files. I have them. They're in my car.'

Tolya stood over me, face pinched with rage. 'You let my girl go and you offer me paper.'

'I didn't let her go. She's a grown up. She did what she had to do. You keep a tight rein, man. Let her be. Let her grow up. She has her own grief.'

He snorted. 'She doesn't mourn for Santiago.'

'How do you know that?'

It was after midnight. I looked around. There was a suitcase near the back door.

'What the hell are you doing here anyhow? You're leaving? You knew you were leaving when you left your place earlier, before you knew Val was going away?'

'I told you last week I am leaving,' he said.

'Where for?'

He held up the Scotch bottle as if to offer me some, started to talk, then stopped, listening for someone or something outside.

'Valentina was sick of him. She told me. Santiago hit on her, he fell for her. He follows her around to get to me. It was me he wanted. She liked to go dancing with him was all she told me.'

'You think all they did was go dancing? Don't

362

be naïve.' I sat down on a broken desk chair. I was tired.

'Whatever,' he said in English. 'This is a very ugly expression, you know. Whatever. You should have stayed with her, Artyom. I ask you, you do what I ask. This is what friends do.'

'I'm sorry.'

'Santiago didn't want her,' Tolya said. 'He wanted me. He used her. Santiago was a bastard. He was a drunk and a junkie, and he hurt her, too. I saw the bruises, right? You saw, didn't you? No? She didn't show you? She was ashamed.'

'She showed you?'

'I walked in on her in her room. I knew. I saw on her arm.'

'It could have been anything,' I said.

'He didn't want her, he wanted me.'

'What did he want with you?'

'You could have stopped all this, you know, you should have gone when Sid called you the first time.' His voice was cool. He poured some more Scotch, then held the bottle out to me again. I refused it.

'Take a drink.'

Tolya poured Scotch into a second mug, and when I drank it, the whisky tasted of stale coffee.

I said, 'We could eat. We could go eat something.' I knew it was idiotic, but I wanted him to talk to me. I wanted to cool things off between us.

He drank.

I said, 'You think I betrayed you.'

'Yes,' he said.

'I'm sorry.'

'What's the matter with you, Artyom? Just ask me what you want.'

'Did you kill Jack Santiago?'

'It was an accident, Jack Santiago.'

'OK.'

'Do you believe me?'

'Yes.'

'Thank you,' Tolya said.

Rummaging in the desk drawer, pulling out envelopes that looked as if they contained cash, Tolya stowed them in his pants' pockets.

The picture of himself that he'd thrown in the garbage can Friday night caught his eye and he picked it up, carefully removed the shattered frame and looked at it, the picture of himself in a rock band in Moscow, the tall skinny boy who offended the officials when he played underground illicit rock in crappy venues. I looked at it.

'I had left Moscow by then,' I said. 'I only remember rumors of underground rock from when I was a kid. I was too timid. We were all scared at my house. I was never brave anyway, you know?' Tolya smiled and reached across the desk and put his ham-sized hand on mine for a second. 'Brave is bullshit, you know? Brave is dead. Brave is cant,' he added, and then looked at the picture of himself again. 'I don't have my history anymore,' he said. 'I've been too long in this country, Artyom.'

He drank steadily, watching the window constantly as if he were afraid.

I said, 'Do you think that Jack killed Sidney McKay?'

'Maybe. Maybe not. One day. Family says McKay's death is an accident. People here are happy if this is accident. Better for real estate. So all is OK, right?'

All Tolya's anger was gone. With his huge face like a supplicant bulldog, for the only time I could remember he invited pity. He slipped into his mix of English and Russian, not to mock me this time but because he seemed almost too tired to remember one or the other.

'So all is OK, sure, my kid going to Russia to be with sick people, Sid McKay who was good guy dead, this man, the other one, his half brother, whatever you say he is, also dead,' Tolya said.

'What about you, Tolya?'

'What about me?'

'What will you do?'

'I don't know.' He looked at his watch. 'It depends on you.'

I said, 'You don't want to be in Red Hook anymore? Buy buildings?'

'No,' he said. 'I dreamed to be here, but no more. It was a fantasy. A fairy tale. I think I would be oligarch. I would have my own piece of New York. I could never own New York. I dreamed it all up, and I don't want anymore. I want to go.'

'Where will you go? You said Russia's dangerous for you,' I said. 'They're locking up rich people, people who don't play the game. You said if you fool with property, the mafia kills you, if the government doesn't put you away.'

'Maybe I go for long vacation somewhere else.

365

Nice place,' he said. 'Maybe I invite Lily and her baby to come and I take care of them.'

'Good,' I said and was jealous. 'Good.'

I picked up the picture of Tolya as a young guy in Moscow.

'Can I have this?'

'Sure,' he said. 'Sure.'

From outside came the noise of a truck pulling up to the building. Nothing moved in Red Hook this time of night, but now there was a truck and it ground slowly up towards the door, and then stopped. We waited.

The gate on the front of the building was down and locked. It would be easy for someone to break a window, though, I thought.

'Where's your car?' I said.

'I left it in the city. I came in a cab,' he said.

I took my car keys out of my pocket. 'I'll take you.' I said. 'My car's in the back lot of the building.'

When it seemed quiet on the street, I looked out. I couldn't see anyone. Slowly, I unlocked the door, and pulled at him.

'Get in the car,' I said, and we ran for it.

★   ★   ★

'Please go to the airport, JFK, please,' Tolya said when we were both in the car, waiting to leave the back lot of his building, lights still off, listening. I put the picture of Tolya in the back seat.

All I could hear was the silence, and the sound of the single truck.

'You'll take me?' Tolya added.

'Yes.'

'I'll be fine,' he whispered.

'Yeah.'

'Thanks,' he said. 'I'm OK.'

'How do you know?'

He smiled. 'I'm hungry,' he said.

'Tolya?'

'Yes, Artyom?'

'How do you know Jack killed Sid.'

'He told me,' he said, reaching for a cigar.

'Don't light it. Not yet.'

I looked out of the car window. It was dark. I couldn't see much and I didn't want to put on my lights, not yet.

'When did he tell you?'

'Last night. Sunday night.' Tolya said. 'He told me last night before he fell over the railing. He fell down and got stuck on the fence. He told me, before he slipped.'

There was a grinding sound from out front of the building. I realized the vehicle that had pulled up to the building and scared us both was only a garbage truck. I turned the key in the ignition.

Finally, I asked Tolya what he was doing with Jack Santiago on the High Line the night when Jack told him he killed Sid McKay, before Jack slipped over the edge.

Tolya looked at me and said simply, 'I invited him up.'

'What for?'

'Let's say I invite him to talk about Valentina, OK? Or maybe just to see the view.'

By the time I pulled away, a faint light was just fingering the sky over Red Hook. Tolya glanced out of his side window at the old brick buildings turning pink in the light, and at the water, and the Statue of Liberty, and then stared straight ahead while I drove him to the airport. He asked me to stop near a hotel. He opened the door.

I said, 'You're going to Russia, aren't you? You're not going to Cuba or Italy, you're fucking going to Moscow. They'll kill you.'

He leaned across to me, kissed me three times, reached in the back seat for his suitcase, got out of the car and walked towards the airport hotel.

31

It was warm and bright out on Tuesday afternoon, and quiet in this part of Brooklyn Heights where the trees were still loaded with leaves. Heavy and green in the late summer, they rustled, a canopy over the wide street of handsome brownstones and the big church, its stained-glass windows alight with color.

Up and down both sides of the road, black limos were parked. The drivers in black suits and caps stood near the cars, some smoking, others leaning against them, dozing in the warm afternoon.

The doors of the church were slightly open and the sound of music poured out, Russian music, a choir singing, then a solo singer, a deep bass voice. And then the sound of people getting up. I couldn't make out the words of the song, but I went to the door and looked in as people rose from the pews; I could see Sid's coffin at the front, white flowers on it.

I went down the steps again, leaned against a thick tree trunk and listened to the soaring sound of the music. I'd left Tolya at the airport hours earlier, and I didn't try to call him or ask around, just went home and got a shower and changed into a suit. I called Maxine. Tried to make up with her. All I had left was Sid's funeral. I had come because I was Sid's friend, or maybe I wanted to see who showed up.

369

I didn't feel right about going in somehow, so I just listened and thought about Sid for a while, and about Earl, the 'John Doe' up in Potter's Field on the island in the East River. I would get him a different place when this was all over and no one would ask what my interest was.

Jack Santiago was dead. He had killed Sid McKay, but McKay's family had already made sure it would go down as some kind of accident. As for Earl, only I would ever know that Sid killed him. No one would remember Sid McKay as a guy who killed a homeless man, his half brother.

No one would mention Earl again unless I raised it: a derelict black guy, his head pinioned under a dock in Red Hook, wasn't much of a story. Everything would be reduced to a crawl along the screen on the local evening news, the kind that runs alongside weather warnings: homeless man found dead under dock in Red Hook; man in accidental death by drowning; man found under the High Line.

Maybe there would be some celebrity stuff about Jack Santiago, some of his women would show up and talk about how brilliant he was, or some writer would say he had been a natural, something like that. But unless I made a fuss, it would all be over. Unless I opened it up, and what was I going to do, play Moses? Part the fucking waters? Everyone in the city wanted a few quiet days; anyway there wasn't much crime in New York. Crime in the city went down for another year. Fear went up. The weather got warmer.

★ ★ ★

Inside the church, people were beginning to rise from the pews. A group of men in dark suits went solemnly up towards Sid's casket.

Outside, I backed away. I stayed leaning against the thick old tree for a while, didn't know how long, scanning the people as they emerged, looking for cars to take them to the cemetery. It was getting late. Late for a funeral. Maybe Sid had requested burial at sunset. Who the hell knew?

I didn't know who I was looking for. Maybe I'd wait for Alex McKay, tell him I was sorry about his father, leave it at that, let it be.

Lighting a cigarette, I half noticed the little man who emerged from the church. He came out alone, ahead of the others. He was a small thick man with a barrel chest, not more than five-two, and he walked half a block, and sat down suddenly on the third step of a brownstone as if he had run out of steam.

My car was at the curb on the other side from the church and I crossed the street and got into it, slid down into the front seat, heart pumping as I watched the man who sat on the brownstone steps.

The rest of the mourners appeared, coming out of the church, standing around on the street in little groups, heads bent forward. Alex McKay was surrounded by people, but I had stopped thinking about him. Gradually, people got into the black limos and cars, headlights on, drove away.

The short man got up, stretched and patted his pockets for cigarettes. I could see him clearly now. He was about sixty-five, the same age as Sid, more or less. He wasn't fat, but thick, dense like the stump of a tree. The heavy double-breasted blue serge suit he wore was tight across his chest, and heavy for a summer's day. His only suit, I thought. He unbuttoned the jacket.

He turned his head, seeming to stare at me, but then I saw he was simply looking in the direction of the church. He was still a handsome man with a high round head and thick white hair slicked down to his scalp. I couldn't see the color of his eyes, but I was betting they were blue, the kind of eyes you saw in the Russian North, up in the Baltic states or around Archangel. Sea eyes, my father had called them. Sea blue. Naval blue.

Reaching into his pants pocket, the man finally found what he was looking for and extracted a crumpled pack of cigarettes. He sat down again on the brownstone steps, lit a cigarette, took a few puffs, put it on the edge of a step, then crossed one foot over his leg and removed a black shoe as if it hurt him. He examined it. He pulled up the tongue and seemed to try to stretch the shoe before he put it back on and tied the laces.

I stayed in the car. The man finished his cigarette, and leaned back against the step for a few seconds, got up and started walking, his jacket hanging open now in the warm breeze.

It was late. The music from the church — my car window was down — was still playing, an organ this time, maybe recorded.

I turned the key, started my car and, doing five miles an hour, I followed the short man. I had to get a lot closer, so I followed him, keeping back.

Clouds moved in. Rain was forecast. The hurricane was coming that night. I looked at my watch. It would be dark soon.

He was still there, in front of me, unaware I was following, walking steadily, not watching the light. The man crossed the street in front of me, ignoring the traffic. I almost ran into the curb. I followed him. He kept moving in the same plodding way, not stopping, not running, but walking like someone used to walking long distances.

From Brooklyn Heights to Cobble Hill, and then across Carroll Gardens where a few old Italian ladies still sat out on the street in the early evening, he walked.

I realized he was heading for Gowanus. The closer we got to the canal, the shabbier the streets were. The man kept going down the empty streets, night closing in, I lost my sense of direction, but I knew when he turned into 5th Street, we were near the water. Then I lost him.

★ ★ ★

I pulled up fast, parked my car, got out and jogged across a deserted playground; the empty swings banged in the gusts of wind; somewhere was a flagpole, the metal bits on the string clicking against the pole. A few spots of rain hit my face when I saw him again. The man was heading out along the pier now. I ran faster.

All I could see was a basin of some kind, a narrow body of water, some looming buildings, a few cranes maybe used for dredging. I had never been here before. I was a mile from Red Hook and I was lost. The man walked easily along the edge of the narrow basin of water until he reached a boat that was tied up to it. I could make out a few other boats. There was no one around.

I called out to him, first in English, then in Russian. He didn't answer. It was as if he wanted me to follow him, wanted to lure me to the boat somehow. By now I knew he had seen me. He never turned around, but I knew he had sensed I was behind him.

I didn't have a gun. I had planned to leave town after the funeral and I didn't take a weapon with me. I looked at the boats bumping against the dock, at the black sky, at the rain that had started. I was alone.

I didn't have a gun, I was a lousy swimmer, the good suit I had put on for the funeral was getting wet, and I didn't know which was worse.

I could have turned and gone away. Just go, I thought, but I couldn't, because of Sid and Earl. And because of Tolya Sverdloff. I didn't know where Tolya was, but when someone looked hard at Santiago's death, his name would come up. Maybe the short Russian could help me; maybe there was something else. I kept moving.

The narrow unpaved road alongside the basin was littered with trash from an overturned garbage can. Thunder boomed. Lightning zipped open the sky and I could see the water for an instant. Even in the protected basin, there were waves. The man jumped on to the boat.

Debris floated on the water near the boat. As far as I could make out, the boat itself wasn't more than twenty feet long, it was painted a dull grayish brown, and an outboard motor hung over the back.

Crouching down, I tried to get a better look. I couldn't see the guy, but I could hear him somewhere, maybe inside the low cabin at the front end. I tried to work out what I could use for a weapon if I needed one. There was an empty beer bottle on the ground and I picked it up and felt like a jerk. It was Corona Lite.

Maybe he was just an old man who had been to a funeral.

It was completely dark. The rain fell hard in slanted sheets. I grabbed hold of a piece of rope tied to a railing, tried to jump into the boat and hoped to God I didn't end up in the water, or trapped under the dock, or dead.

32

There was a light hanging from the dashboard of the boat, and in its beam I saw the short man clearly. He sat on a seat in front of a steering wheel. Next to him was another chair; both seats were bolted to the floor of the boat. There was a dashboard that ran between the two seats, and a windshield behind it, and between the seats was a small louvered door that led to the cabin which was lit from inside.

Overhead, a piece of dirty canvas tied to a couple of poles attached to the sides of the boat made a kind of partial roof over the seats. The boat was rocking. The wind howled. I got into the chair next to the short man.

Unconcerned, he turned to me, and said, 'Yes?' His eyes were dark blue. Big and dark blue, opaque like marbles. His face was heavily lined.

I said, 'You were a friend of Sidney McKay?'

He nodded, and put out his hand. 'Name is Mack,' he said. 'People call me Mack. You? You are?' He had a heavy Russian accent.

'Your other name?'

'Mack is enough.'

I didn't give my name but I shook his hand. He didn't seem to recognize me, so I said, 'I was also a friend of Sid's.'

I knew who he was. I had probably known as soon as I saw him at the church in Brooklyn

Heights. He was the boy in the picture I'd stolen from Sid's apartment. He was the boy from the ship that ran aground off Red Hook in 1953. He was the sailor whose name was Meler. He had the same eyes, same thick nose. The jowls were heavier, the body was thicker, but it was him. He had been Meler. Now he was Mack. It didn't matter. They were the same.

★ ★ ★

As I steadied myself on the seat that was made of fake leather, beer bottle still in my hand, I realized the boat was bobbing around pretty bad. I looked behind me and along the side of the boat was a canvas pocket that held fishing poles, a paddle and what looked like life jackets. I tried to get a look into the cabin through the louvered door. It contained two bunks that filled up the whole space. You couldn't stand up in it, not even if you were as short as Mack. There was only enough room to crawl in and lie down. Mack saw me examining the boat.

'My boat,' he said in English. 'I get her second-hand, five hundred bucks, I make her good.' He punched a couple of buttons on the dashboard. 'I must smoke,' he said; I reached in my pocket and pulled out some cigarettes and offered them to him.

The boat bounced; I dropped my beer bottle over the side.

He took one of my cigarettes, picked up a lighter from the dashboard, lit it, tossed the pack and the lighter back on to it where they slid from side to side slowly as the boat rocked. The windshield in front of us and the canvas overhead kept some of the rain off.

'I saw you come out of Sid McKay's funeral,' I said.

'What?'

I talked louder over the engine and the wind. Mack pulled a pint of vodka from another canvas pocket on his side of the boat and offered it to me.

I drank. It wasn't too bad in the little boat for now. I was OK. I drank a couple of shots to make me numb. I wasn't big on dignity, but I didn't want a suspect watching me puke because I couldn't stand boats.

Mack's face was lighted from the side by the lamp hung from the dashboard, and from below by the light coming up from the cabin. He smiled.

Was he laughing at me? Was he enjoying it? I told him in Russian that I was a policeman. For the first time I could see a faint flicker of fear.

He had grown up under Stalin. My being a cop had registered; it made him scared. We were equal now.

He knocked back some more vodka, and without any warning got up and untied the boat from the dock and pushed off. The motor whined. A gap opened between us and the safety of the dock. I could feel the water underneath us. Rain belting down on the fragile canvas roof overhead made a pounding noise. The sky was thick with cloud, the color of iron.

'Take the boat the fuck back to the dock,' I

said but he ignored me, and the wind snapped my words away.

It was still OK. We were in a small basin. I could see the shape of land. Even when I realized we had moved into the Gowanus Canal itself, it wasn't too bad. Distances were hard to judge, but I could just make out the docks, warehouses, bridges overhead. Solid land. My skin was slick with sweat and my suit was soaked.

I said, 'Where the hell are we going?'

Mack, who was busy doing things with the boat, didn't answer at first. Then he settled back on to his seat, watching me.

'Is OK,' he said.

'You knew Sidney McKay a long time ago, is that right?' I asked in Russian. 'You knew him when your name was Meler.'

He reached again for his vodka, crossed one foot over the other, drank, put the bottle on the dashboard, and took hold of the steering wheel. We were still in the canal. He held the boat steady. We were moving slowly. Mack started talking.

He told me about the ship that ran aground in Red Hook when he was a sailor on it. He was fifteen years old back then, he said. February, 1953. Half the officers drunk. The pilot who came on board was drunk. The ship would have been sent back, but the papers weren't in order.

'It was Cold War,' he said. 'People speaking of spies.'

Men from Immigration came on board, Mack said. The sailors sat on the boat looking at America. When they heard that Stalin was dead, the sailors wept, terrified. They drank raw alcohol. What would life be without Stalin? No one knew a life without Stalin.

'For weeks, they keep us,' he said, remembering how the sailors stared at New York, the harbor, the Statue of Liberty. 'People on shore stared at us.'

Then Mack heard about a couple of sailors who went overboard. It was easy to swim to shore, he had heard; easy to swim to America.

So he went. One night, Mack swam to shore.

People were so nice, he said to me now, softly, in Russian; they were nice. Mack remembered it in tiny details; he remembered the smell of the street when he got off the ship and it smelled like cocoa beans, and cashew nuts, which was not something he had heard of before he got to America.

Or had he? He stared at me with those opaque pop-eyes, and said he wasn't sure because he didn't know if cocoa beans smelled when they were stored in a warehouse or if he had read about it in a book, but he knew cocoa came in through the port.

He had been terrified. He had never been away from home, it was his first time out on a ship, he came from a village near the Baltic. People used carts and horses if they had any to take goods to market. Growing up after the war, he had barely seen any cars.

His first day in Red Hook, he was frightened of the noise, people, cars, huge trucks lumbering down the narrow streets, the ships; a wall of noise was how he remembered it. Then someone said, 'You want a sandwich, kid?'

Once he started, Mack talked endlessly, as if he had to finish his story. I was aware we were moving faster, maybe towards the open water. Maybe it was my imagination. I couldn't measure the distance in the dark. I kept my eyes on Mack. The vodka bottle on the dashboard slid from one side to the other. He grabbed it, and held it between his legs.

'Sidney's death was suicide, right? Everybody says so,' Mack said, leaning towards me. 'He feels very mad about death of this homeless guy, he can't stand it, he feels so terrible because he kills him, right? His half brother named Earl. I knew Earl.'

'How?'

'So he kills himself by accident, this is what everyone in family saying, because is poetic and Sidney is poetic man.' He smiled. 'Like Russian.'

'Like a Russian man, sure, that's right,' I said to keep him talking. 'So when did you see Sid for the last time? You saw him recently?' I said and in my wheedling, in the insistent soft tone of my voice, I could hear my father the KGB man who made people tell him things they didn't want to tell.

'Sure.'

'Sure what? Maybe last week, maybe Tuesday morning?'

'Maybe. Yes, I tell him let's go drink some coffee, I call him and say, I am outside of your place waiting for you, Sid, please come. I wait.'

I didn't answer. He had called Sid. He had asked him to come out. It was that morning,

381

Tuesday, when Sid left and didn't come back, when he left his door open. A call from the Russian, Sid running out to meet him, forgetting to lock his door.

I said, 'You invited him to come out with you, you asked him out for coffee, is that it, you were friends with Sid so you knew if you said come and have coffee and we'll talk about old times, he'd do it?'

Mack held up the cigarettes. I shook my head. He flicked his lighter over and over. It didn't work. He found some matches in his windbreaker, reached into the canvas pocket again and produced a glass jar, unscrewed the lip and tossed the match into it. He set it on the dashboard for an ashtray and watched the ash from his cigarette topple into the bottom.

'Sure.'

'How did you know?'

'He was always looking around for me, always asking people, I didn't want this. I didn't want to be in his book,' he said. 'I don't want people to know my story. I don't want them to send me back.'

'What book,' I said.

He held up his hand. It was small and thick like the rest of him. He talked mostly in Russian. He talked about the ship. He talked about Red Hook in the 1950s, and his forays into the neighborhood, where he hid, who took him in, how he got braver and started walking around Brooklyn. He walked for miles everywhere. Once, he said, he went into Manhattan. It scared him; he never went back.

Want a sandwich, kid, people would say once they got to know him. There was a bar near the docks where they gave him Coca-Cola to drink and sometimes beer, and where he ate his first hamburger.

He became a pet. A lot of people in the community were Catholic, Irish, Italian; they decided to rescue him from Communism, he said; they thought he was retarded. They thought he was simple because he didn't speak English, didn't speak much at all to tell the truth because he kept his mouth shut, feeling it was safer. A couple of the older women fed him and took him to church and had him baptized. When the freighter finally went back to sea, Mack — everyone called him Mack by then — wasn't on it. He had disappeared into Red Hook.

★   ★   ★

The wave hit me from the side. I could make out the waves, ten, fifteen feet tall, black, tight, close up to me, practically on us, the wind roaring, the boat rolling up, and then down, like a plane hitting an air pocket. The water slammed me. The rain hit my face. I was soaked now, my suit heavy as lead. Somehow I got out of the jacket. Then another wave. The piece of canvas overhead began to shred. Strips of canvas hung down from it. The wind blew one of them into my face. I clawed it away.

All I could see at first were Mack's hands as they gripped the wheel. The glass jar on the dashboard slid off and crashed on to the deck of the boat, spilling ash. My mouth tasted like shit. I had smoked most of a pack of cigarettes. Something about the jar bothered me. I tried to focus. We were in open water. We were in the river.

In the distance there were a few faint lights.

'Red Hook,' Mack said, following my gaze.

I wondered if I could make it to shore if I had to swim. The storm roared, the outboard motor made clunking noises; Mack was silent now.

Another wave hit us. Water sloshed over the edge. The rest of the canvas blew away. Salt water filled my mouth.

★　★　★

When Mack started talking again, he yelled out his words over the storm and the engine. He kept the boat steady. We were in Buttermilk Channel, he said, but I had no way of knowing if it was the truth and we were heading towards the city, or moving towards open water, out to the ocean.

Mack told me he had never seen a black person until he met Sid and Earl. They were his own age. They had bicycles. Sid had a bright blue bike, very shiny, with a bell and a light. It had a license plate. Schwinn was its name. It had a flag, too, that read: Brooklyn Dodgers, World Champions, 1953.

He couldn't read it, not at first. He could barely read Russian, much less English, but one of the boys explained what it was. Baseball, they said. We'll teach you. We'll bring our stuff and show you how to play, they said. Bat. This is a bat. This is the ball. This is the glove. They brought things and showed him.

The water was a little calmer now, the waves down to six feet; we were in the channel. We were close to Governor's Island. Mack kept talking and talking, I was desperate to hear him, and scared I was going to go over the edge as the wind came in huge gusts.

He talked about how eventually he melted into the community and people stopped noticing him. Two other sailors from the ship also disappeared and no one ever heard from them. He suspected they left New York on another ship, Canadian maybe; there were a lot of Russians who went up to Canada. It was cold up there. Empty. They could get a job in the oil fields up north, or head for Yellowknife where they could work in the diamond mines. Later he heard that one guy ended up in Nome, Alaska. No one except Russians would work that far north.

Mack stayed in Brooklyn. He went to ball games at Ebbets Field. He found a girlfriend. He worked around the shipyards. For years he stayed in Red Hook; in the 1970s, when the Russians started arriving in big numbers, he drifted out to Brighton Beach and met a woman named Irina and got married and had a daughter, but Irina didn't like America and she took the kid back to the Soviet Union.

What about Sid, I said.

Sid went away, he said. He went to college. Earl stayed. They were friends, Mack and Earl.

They took care of each other, he said.

'You stayed in Brooklyn for fifty years?'

Why not, he said. Many people disappeared. Many people just disappeared into New York City all the time, just got off the boat or the airplane and walked away, no visa, nothing, just melted. He grinned. They are still doing. Is easy, he said. Very easy. Somehow Mack lit up another cigarette. In the light I saw his face; he was unafraid, of the water, the storm, the boat, me.

I said, 'But you met Sid again, didn't you?' I was shivering.

'You want to go inside?' He gestured to the little cabin.

I shook my head.

'You do not like boats?' he said in Russian.

'You met Sid again?'

'Yes,' he said. 'I am in Red Hook two years ago, and there he is Sidney McKay, professor, historian of Red Hook, philosopher, he is everywhere, making his little notes, asking people do you know this or that, do you know Russian who came on ship many years ago. You knew him well?'

'Yes.'

He stared at me, squinting and said suddenly, 'I know who you are. I saw you. I saw you go into Sidney's place, yes?'

I didn't answer.

'I saw you go in Sunday morning, Monday morning also,' he said. 'You don't know about boats, do you? You don't like boats. I can tell you don't like this, you don't like water.'

'What about this book?'

'Sidney is writing a book about ship. *Red Dawn*. Everyone knew. He wants to write history. He wants to tell story. I see him, he asks me questions, I say don't write, please, don't, leave history alone. Nothing comes from history except shit, I tell him.'

'What did he say?'

'He says is all there is, history. I say for you this is writing, for me, is my life, I don't want to be prisoner from history, please. I am not even legal, OK? You are not legal, people send you away. I know this. I leave Russia when they kill you if you break law, I say to Sid. I find Earl, I say, tell him. Tell him. Earl drinks all day, but he listens, is my friend. I say, if this comes out, they send me back. I leave Stalin time, go back Putin time. Same studio, different head, like they say Hollywood. OK?'

Mack made the joke but in his voice I could hear the panic he felt when he thought about going back. He thought of Russia as the same place it had been when he left and Stalin was alive.

'I do anything not to go back,' he said, yelling above the wind.

'Earl went to see Sid? He did it for you?'

'Yes. To make Sid stop. Make him leave me alone. Earl says, go with me, please, and I say, no, every time I see Sid he just asks me questions, what was ship like, what was Russia like, who was on ship, which other sailors, where they from, what you did all these years in Brooklyn, who you met, saw, which gangsters on waterfront, tell me about smells, sights, sounds,

387

name ships you noticed, what kind of cheese in first sandwich you ate on American soil. What kind of cheese? Who gives one shit? He says, God in the details, and I think what does he mean, I don't understand. So I told Earl, go, talk to Sid. Then I go, too. Is too late. Earl was drunk and sick. Sid hits him.'

'What with? With a walking stick? A cane?'

'I don't know. Yes. Maybe. Or Baseball bat. Old bat he has from old days. Bat with Dodgers on it. Championship year. I watch, then I run away.' He was drinking and his eyes filled up with self-pity. 'I run away, and Earl is dead.'

'But you went back,' I said. 'Why are you telling me?'

He looked out over the water and up at the rain. There was water on the floor of the boat, and he waved his hand at it, and said, 'Why not?'

I knew then that he didn't care if he lived or died. I wanted to say, take the fucking boat back to shore, let's just go back; I felt that I'd do anything at all to get off the boat, but what could I do? I was with a man who didn't care.

I shouted, 'Take the boat back.'

'Why?'

'It's raining.'

He laughed. 'Is good answer.'

Holding on to the edge of the boat, I fumbled frantically for something I could threaten him with. 'Take the boat in,' I said again. 'Do it. You don't do it, I'll make sure you go back to Russia. To jail there, you understand?'

In the water in the bottom of the boat, the broken jar sloshed up against my ankle. I

388

reached down and picked it up, half thinking I could use it as a weapon. I was holding the top half. A piece of the label was still stuck on the glass.

The boat rocked furiously, and Mack did something with the steering wheel or whatever the hell you did with boats, and I thought again I was going to vomit. It was comic, me the tough cop, throwing up off a bobbing sailboat a mile from home in the middle of my own city. We came around the tip of Governor's Island. I knew because I could just make out the ferry landing. I looked the other way, looked for the southern tip of Manhattan.

I held the broken jar close to my face, and read the label. Borscht Works. It had contained soup.

'So,' Mack said, face wrinkled with fear.

'You got married?'

'Yes,' he said.

'You had a daughter?'

'Yes, I told you that. Why?'

'Rita is your daughter.'

He didn't answer me.

'Rita is your daughter and she didn't want you around, God knows why, but she didn't, so she told me there's an old man, she told me about you,' I said.

I was my father's son after all.

'So we'll go back to shore now,' I added softly, and got up somehow, trying to keep my balance. The edge of the glass jar cut my hand, and I could feel the blood mix with water. I threw the jar overboard. If I could get my balance, I could grab Mack. But then what?

'I couldn't let Sidney do that to Earl,' Mack said, almost dreamily now. 'I couldn't, and I didn't want to be in his goddamn book. Don't want people to know. I didn't want to listen to all questions from the past. Do you understand?' he got up from his seat, the rain beating on him. 'I killed Sidney.'

I went for him, but he seemed to move backwards. I was falling. A wave socked me smack in the face. I couldn't stay upright. We were in wild water again.

'I don't go back to Russia,' he said. 'Not ever. No.'

Over Mack's head, I looked up, thinking I could make out the shape of the Statue of Liberty. It disappeared. The city emerged from the dark, the lighted walls, the solid buildings, but I couldn't tell if it was real or not, then it all faded away as another wave cut into me.

The single place on earth that I really loved, where I had felt safe, receded farther and farther from me, and I could smell the salt, and thought that we were going in the other direction, to open water, away from New York.

For a second, trying to see through the rain, I took my eyes off Mack. When I looked back he was gone. So fast I barely saw him, he got over the edge of the boat and was in the water.

33

Sonny Lippert didn't say anything much when he met me at the dock near Red Hook where the Coast Guard boat brought me. It was still dark, though it was almost morning and rain was pelting down solid from a pitch-black sky. I heard one of the Coast Guard guys say anyone who went out in this kind of storm was crazy. I thought about Mack. He was a sailor. He must have known it was crazy. Maybe he had done it to get rid of me. Maybe he never planned to come back. After he went over the edge of the boat, I had reached out for him. I grabbed his hand. I felt it, wet, cold; I tried to grab hold of his wrist, but he let go of me. All those years of fear, of hiding in Brooklyn, of wondering when they would send him back, he had let it go.

Sonny offered to take me to the hospital. He offered to take me home. I said I was OK, I just needed my car and dry clothes, and he didn't insist, just let me do what I had to and kept everyone else away.

After one of the Coast Guard guys got my phone number and took some notes, Sonny drove me to my car. In the trunk, I found some clothes I had packed for the beach and a towel. I dried off with the towel that had red sand buckets on it, put what was left of my soaked suit in the back seat, and changed into dry stuff. In the back seat of my car was the picture of Tolya as a young rock and roll guy.

Sonny waited near the car. I had swallowed a lot of water, but I was OK. He watched me get in my car and drive away.

★　★　★

For what was maybe the twentieth time in a week, I made the trip back to the city, listened to my car bang around, knew I needed to turn it in, didn't care, and cut across Canal Street. A Chinese woman was setting out piles of brown lychees on her stall in spite of the rain.

The light turned red as I got to my block. I saw Lily before she saw me.

She was in front of my building, holding an umbrella, looking up. Her bag was slung over her shoulder. She had called that morning and asked when I'd be around. She asked if she could stop by and I didn't say no, so it wasn't as if she was intruding. It was me.

I looked at her. I was far enough away so she couldn't see me, and I just sat like that for a while, didn't know how long. I looked like an idiot. I had a kid's beach towel wrapped around my neck. My head throbbed. My throat was sore as hell from all the salt. I was bleeding some, superficially, but bleeding, and I couldn't stop thinking about the poor bastard who went over the edge of the boat, who let go of my hand. I had yelled, but there was nobody to hear. I couldn't save him. He disappeared with his history.

I wanted so bad to talk to Lily about it all and

she was there, a few yards away. I could almost touch her. I didn't know how long I sat there looking at her.

I thought about all the betrayals, Sid and his half brother, and the short Russian who had swum off a freighter fifty years before. I thought about how close I'd come with Tolya. Everybody afraid. I looked at Lily one more time.

I turned the key, started the car, put on some music, leaned back over my shoulder, backed the car up, cut across town west to the Holland Tunnel, the New Jersey shore and Maxine, and hoped like hell that she'd come home with me.

We do hope that you have enjoyed reading this large print book.

Did you know that all of our titles are available for purchase?

We publish a wide range of high quality large print books including:
Romances, Mysteries, Classics
General Fiction
Non Fiction and Westerns

Special interest titles available in large print are:
The Little Oxford Dictionary
Music Book
Song Book
Hymn Book
Service Book

Also available from us courtesy of Oxford University Press:
Young Readers' Dictionary
(large print edition)
Young Readers' Thesaurus
(large print edition)

For further information or a free brochure, please contact us at:
Ulverscroft Large Print Books Ltd.,
The Green, Bradgate Road, Anstey,
Leicester, LE7 7FU, England.
Tel: (00 44) 0116 236 4325
Fax: (00 44) 0116 234 0205

Other titles published by
The House of Ulverscroft:

DISTURBED EARTH

Reggie Nadelson

Winter 2003: War is looming and New York is paralysed by the worst blizzard in years. Artie Cohen, on the verge of making peace with his life, is called in to investigate a case — a pile of blood-soaked children's clothes has been found on the beach in Brooklyn. Almost against his will, Artie finds himself drawn into a case that involves the death of a child and the unaccountable disappearance of another, all against the background of a city already stricken by fear. In his increasingly obsessive search for the missing child, Artie finds himself in the remote coastal suburbs of Brooklyn, among the Russian community he thought he had left behind — and way out of his depth.

SOMEBODY ELSE

Reggie Nadelson

'You were some dish,' says Betsy Thornhill's boyfriend on seeing an old photograph of her. A casual remark, but Betsy, a fifty-one-year-old American living in London, finds herself conscious of age. She goes in for a 'little work' on her face and comes out looking marvellous, younger by fifteen years. She goes back to New York, where she has not lived for thirty years — to a city devastated by the aftermath of September 11. A few days after she arrives, Betsy is accused of murder. She looks at the police sketch. 'It isn't me,' she says. 'It's someone younger.' 'Look in the mirror,' says the cop. Betsy is trapped by her own face . . .

HOT POPPIES

Reggie Nadelson

A murder in New York's diamond district. A dead Chinese girl with a photograph in her pocket. A plastic bag of irradiated heroin in an empty apartment. A fire in a Chinatown sweatshop. The worst blizzard in New York's history. These events conspire to bring ex-cop Artie Cohen out of retirement and back into the obsessive world of murder and politics that nearly killed him. The terrifying plot uncoils first in New York — in Artie's own back yard — then in Hong Kong, where everything — and everyone — is for sale.

THE STRANGER HOUSE

Reginald Hill

The slow life of the village of Illthwaite changes when two strangers arrive with the intention of digging up bits of the past that the locals would rather keep buried. Sam Flood is a young Australian whose grandmother was dispatched from Illthwaite as a child. Miguel Madero, a drop-out from a Spanish seminary, has come to the Stranger House in pursuit of an ancestor who had set sail with the Great Armada . . . The antipathy between them is instant, but their paths become increasingly entangled with clashes metaphysical, and shocks natural and supernatural, as the tension mounts to an explosive climax.

ASH AND BONE

John Harvey

When the take down of a violent criminal goes badly wrong, leaving two people dead, something doesn't feel right to Detective Sergeant Maddy Birch. Then she starts to believe someone is following her home . . . In Cornwall, retired Detective Inspector Elder discovers that his seventeen-year-old daughter, Katherine, is running wild. Elder feels remorse and guilt, for it was his involvement that led to the abduction and rape that has so unbalanced Katherine's life . . . Maddy and Elder have a connection — a brief, clumsy encounter sixteen years earlier. When the unhappy Elder is once again persuaded out of retirement, a cold case has a devasting present day impact with sinister implications for the crime squad itself. But Elder must battle his own demons before he can uncover the truth.

PLAY TO THE END

Robert Goddard

When actor Toby Flood arrives in Brighton whilst on tour with a Joe Orton play, he is visited by his estranged wife, Jenny, now living with wealthy entrepreneur Roger Colborn. Jenny is worried about a strange man who has taken to hanging around outside her shop in the Lanes. Roger has dismissed her concerns and she hopes instead that Toby will be willing to get to the bottom of the man's behaviour. Next day, Toby confronts the man. Derek Oswin blames Colborn for his father's death from cancer, on account of dangerous practices at the defunct plastics factory run by Roger and his late father. Before he fully understands the risks he is running, Flood finds himself entangled in the mysterious — and dangerous — relationship between the Oswins and the Colborns . . .